Listening Still

Center Point
Large Print

Also by Anne Griffin and available from
Center Point Large Print:

When All Is Said

**This Large Print Book carries the
Seal of Approval of N.A.V.H.**

Listening Still

ANNE GRIFFIN

CENTER POINT LARGE PRINT
THORNDIKE, MAINE

Chapter 1

The minute my father told me he was retiring and handing Masterson Funeral Directors to me, I wanted to run. Run to the edges of this world, to teeter on its sheer cliff tops, to lift my head skyward, to breathe in the air that demanded nothing of me. To let that freedom from expectation reach each extremity, smoothing every crease and frown, unfurling my tightly gripped fists.

I had wanted to run once before but had failed. Obligation, you see. Obligation, Obligation, Obligation. Get the stonemason to carve that word in capitals and in triplicate under my name on my headstone so that everyone understands who Jeanie Masterson really was. What it was that drove her, dampened her, and yes, if I'm honest, delighted her, entangled as I was in a world I both loved and feared, my heart torn between so many who needed me, as I needed them.

'Baltimore,' my father said. They would be retiring to Baltimore. Mum and him, Gráinne and David Masterson, packing their bags and leaving in six months or so. You'd be forgiven for thinking that it was Baltimore in the States he was referring to, sounding so exotic as it does.

But I knew the place he meant, the coastal village that lay not so far away, at the tip of Ireland's sixth stubby toe. Three hundred odd kilometres southwest in Cork, away from Kilcross, this midlands town in which we lived our lives. No need for planes and air miles and passports, they would simply drive to where we'd spent our summers when we—myself and Mikey, their children—were small. Mostly it was just a long weekend but sometimes, when Dad could extract himself from the pressures of the funeral director's, one whole precious week. No sign could be put on our door, you see, to ask politely that people call again when we returned. The dead were not ones for waiting. Although perhaps it could be argued they had all the time in the world. It was Harry, my aunt, our only embalmer back then, who held the fort while we walked the pier and played on sandy beaches and licked our Ninety-Nine's. I loved Baltimore. *We* loved Baltimore, and now it would be their new home, leaving me and Niall, my husband, to finally have the house and business all to ourselves.

'But you've only just turned sixty,' I exclaimed as my parents sat opposite me and Niall, telling us their news. We were in our morning room, one of our two sitting-rooms in the large house we all shared—five bedrooms, six if you included the one Mum had converted into a walk-in wardrobe. She'd wanted to transform another into a sauna, but Dad had put the foot down. 'No one retires that early.'

'I don't know about that, school principals take early retirement,' Dad offered.

'But you're not a principal are you? You're a man with a business without a generous public service pension.'

'Ah, but there's a bit put by and anyway, I have a gifted daughter well capable of keeping us all fed and watered. Not to mention that man beside you, the best embalmer in Ireland.' He winked at Niall, beaming as if he was his prize bull at the Kilcross Agricultural Show.

'Harry might have something to say about that,' I said curtly, before realising how unkind I'd been. 'Sorry, Niall.' I reached my hand to touch my husband's knee. 'I didn't mean it to sound like that.'

'It's OK, I understand.' He smiled and held on to my hand, not allowing its escape just yet. 'We all know Harry is brilliant. Taught me everything I know.'

'And she's going nowhere,' Dad added. 'You couldn't get rid of that sister of mine if you tried. She'll be embalming in her nineties if she has anything to do with it.'

'But you've never mentioned retiring before, Dad.' And neither, in truth, had I ever allowed the thought to enter my head, so dependent had I become on him.

'We know, darling,' Mum interjected, 'but your dad and I just feel we'd like to take advantage of the time we have left. While he can still cast a fishing line and I can finally get to my poetry.'

Mum looked at Dad and they shared a loving smile.

'Poetry, Mum? I thought you'd given that up after that evening class you took, saying it was all just too difficult and what the hell was wrong with good old rhyming couplets.'

'My point is, Jeanie, that running the hairdresser's means I never had the time to give it what it deserved. And besides, the house we used to rent down in Baltimore has come up for sale. If that isn't kismet, I don't know what is.' She smiled to herself, tipping her perfectly manicured nails to the ends of her shoulder-length balayaged hair, delighted with her word choice, as if savouring its taste in her mouth like the melt of chocolate.

'Thought you didn't believe in all that kind of "sixth sense" stuff, Mum.'

'Oh now, Jeanie, not this again. You know well I believe that you and your father can hear the dead. I simply don't appreciate their constant intrusion in our lives. Your father has earned his break.'

'But it's OK to leave me here with them, is that it?'

'But we thought that's what you wanted, Jeanie.'

10

I could see the hurt in her eyes as the ground shifted further beneath her. She clasped a hand to her chest, where it sat as wide as butterfly wings on clover. 'It's all you've ever talked about, listening to them. Hearing what they have to say, sorting out the issues they've brought with them.'

When I was five years old maybe, I wanted to say childishly.

'And what about Mikey?' I asked, distracting her with her favourite subject. 'Where does he come into all of this?'

Mikey, my older brother by two years. When I was little, when trying to explain him to the world, I used to say he was different; until, at thirteen, he was diagnosed as being on the spectrum—though only just, Mum liked to qualify. Those tests had finally handed me the right vocabulary. Mikey was 'high functioning,' 'highly capable,' only not always in the ways we would have liked.

'We've spoken to him and—'

'You spoke to him before you spoke to me, Mum?' Mikey was the one we usually protected from things in this family—leaving him until everything was thought through, and every support we could think of was in place.

'Only in a hypothetical sense.'

'Oh come on, we all know Mikey is not one for hypothetical. It's definites or nothing with him.'

'Well, yes. He was very concerned to know

when the move might be and how he was going to get his journal collection down. We spent some time exploring which removal company might be best. He's such an expert on so many things,' Mum said proudly.

'So he's going with you?'

'Of course he's coming with us. He's hardly staying here. We don't expect that of you, Jeanie. He's our son, we want him with us.' That's how Mum had always wanted it, her son close by.

'But not me?'

Mum seemed shocked at such childishness from her daughter of thirty-two, and who could blame her. But in times of panic, it is truly amazing what the brain will let out of your mouth.

'But you're married, Jeanie. You live here with Niall.' She even pointed to him, in case I'd forgotten I had a husband. 'This is your life, your work. We didn't think . . .' She looked at Dad. 'David, you can jump in here anytime you like.'

Mum crossed her legs in distress at the direction the conversation had taken.

'Your mother's right, Jeanie. This move is obviously about us stepping away but it's also about giving you the chance to run this business as you want, to be at the helm. Now you get to make all the decisions without having to run a single one by me. There's a lot to be said for being your own boss.'

'And what if I don't want that? What if what I

want is exactly what we have now, or maybe it's something totally different? Maybe it's hundreds of miles away like you two will be.' And that, I'd said that.

'Well, we didn't think . . . I mean, is it? Is there something you want that we don't know about?'

All three heads looked back at me—Mum with her mouth open, Dad with his bunched-fabric forehead, and Niall with his brushstroke of worry that I never intended to cause—waiting for my answer. I stopped short of admitting that I'd always wondered what it would be like to lead a completely different life. But if I finally left now to chase that dream *and* Dad retired, well, that would be it for the dead, no one left to hear them. I was the last one you see, the last listener of the dead, the line ended with me.

'Look,' I said, sidestepping everything, 'I'm merely saying that you've come to me with a fait accompli. Like I don't have a choice in all of this.'

'OK, hold on, Jeanie,' Dad said, holding up his hands defensively, 'your mum and me only want you to be happy. We thought our news would be a nice surprise.' He looked around then at the cake he'd bought, with its 'Congratulations' icing. On first seeing it when I'd walked into the room, I'd smiled eagerly. Dad had grinned, telling me I'd have to wait until he told me the news. Now

13

he looked at it as though it was the pet dog we were going to have to put down. 'It's even your favourite—coffee.'

He turned to Niall for help. 'You're happy with all of this, Niall, aren't you?'

'I'm . . .' Niall started cautiously, glancing at me, a man caught between two sides, not knowing what to say. '. . . delighted for you both. You deserve the break. And I can't thank you enough for such an opportunity. I suppose it's just such a big surprise.'

'Did you know about this, too?' The question popped out of my mouth before I could stop it.

'No!' Niall stared at me in disbelief.

'My God, Jeanie, would you give the man a break.' That was Mum.

'What? You think I'm horrible to my husband now, is that it?'

'Jeanie, can we all just calm down.' Dad pushed forward to the edge of his seat and held up his right palm like a traffic guard in an effort to stop any further eruptions. 'Niall, go out and get us a drink there before we have nervous breakdowns. G&Ts for us and whatever might sedate this one here.'

Dad looked at me while Niall left the room, and then bravely came over to sit by my side.

'Is it that you think this is some kind of betrayal, Jeanie, is that it? That we're abandoning you? Because we're not, love. It is so far from that. We're like every other couple out there hitting their twilight years, realising we need to slow down a bit. And it's hard to do that when you live where you work. You and Niall might feel the same way about this place someday too and then, well . . .'

And then well, you'll have to sell up, would've been the end of that sentence if he'd been plucky enough to finish it, because so far their daughter, much to their disappointment, had given them no grandchildren, and unlike them wouldn't be passing the business on to anyone.

'Look, love, we're sorry, OK? We honestly didn't think this would upset you so much. We should have sounded you out first, not come with everything signed, sealed and delivered like that. We get that, don't we, Gráinne?'

'Yes, of course, darling.' Mum stretched out her hand to pat my knee. It was enough to make me feel awful about my behaviour and to offer the tiniest of smiles.

It was then Dad decided the time was right to pull his daughter in for a hug.

'We misjudged it, that's all. Don't be too hard on us, OK? We'll get this sorted. We don't need to be hightailing it out of here that quickly. We can halt our gallop a little and make sure we do this the right way. How does that all sound?'

I tucked myself in against the chest of the man who had always protected me, pointed me in

15

the right direction whenever I lost my way. My fingers tiptoed over the softness of his woollen suit. Always immaculately turned out, Dad never wore anything but the best. The simple truth was that part of me didn't want to be on my own with the dead. It meant something that Dad could hear them too, that we were together in this thing that neither of us had asked for but were born with. Because sometimes it wasn't so easy what the dead asked of us as they lay in their coffins. Even if Dad didn't talk about it as much as I might have liked, it mattered to have someone who understood both the burden and joy of this gift. And yet, I thought, if my father had managed on his own before I came along, surely I could too. Was it too much to ask to let this man retire in peace without the worry of me?

I managed to whimper a tiny OK as Niall walked through the door with a tray of drinks.

'Good man, Niall.'

Dad let me go to retake his seat opposite.

'So Mikey's really OK about going?' I asked, a kind of reluctant calm to me, Niall putting a G&T in my hand. 'Thank you,' I mouthed.

'So it seems.' Dad took his first sip and sighed in appreciation.

'But he hates change.'

'Well, not when it means he gets away from the dead, apparently. Cut out of your mother he is.'

Dad smiled at his wife as Niall sat down beside

me again, taking intermittent sips of his drink while surreptitiously glancing at me. And in my regret at how I had behaved and my desire to make everything right, to soothe his worry, I turned to smile, to hold again the hand that held mine earlier, to squeeze it, to try to make him, as well as myself, believe that everything was going to be just fine.

Chapter 2

The following morning I watched Niall and Mikey chat outside in the yard. I could see them clearly through the kitchen window, husband and brother, on that dry day. No rain, yet. For a month it had felt like no other weather system existed in Kilcross, only those weighty drops falling from a miserable grey cocooning sky, causing water butts to fill to capacity, drainpipes to overflow and grassy green fields to dull to mucky brown. But that April morning there was light and colour, and now Niall's laughter. Returned after his run, he leaned a shoulder against our closed back door, held a hand to his chest trying to catch his breath and laughed at whatever it was Mikey had said. I couldn't quite fathom what it might be. He wasn't known for his wit. My appreciation of Niall's ever-present kindness to Mikey momentarily nudged aside my lingering panic from the previous evening's announcement. I smiled and fought my instinct to find out what it was Mikey had said, instead letting it be, this moment of pure delight when my brother had made someone laugh. This was to be treasured, to be stored away with the rest of my history that told the story of me and why I was still here.

My brother pointed at something inside his

shed—I say shed, it was actually more like an apartment: bedroom, bathroom, sitting-room, kitchenette, PlayStation—every man's wet-dream shed. It was my mother who'd insisted on the term, and we followed suit, as that was easier all round. 'Shed' essentially shielded her from the truth that my brother had moved out. Niall shifted from his lean to look inside too and nod. As Mikey gesticulated more, Niall ramped up his head-bobbing. The laughter had subsided now but still Niall held an encouraging smile. I suspected this was about the new shelving unit to accommodate my brother's bulging military history collection of books and magazines and DVDs. Mikey had been exceptional at two things in school: history and carpentry. Being very handy with the latter meant he would always be able to build enough units to house his obsession with the former. Mikey had been suggesting this expansion for a while now, more to himself than the rest of us. Change came slowly to my brother. He needed to coax and gently push himself toward it before his arms could open wide and finally welcome it in. I wondered if he fully understood what was ahead of him with my parents' retirement.

Niall motioned toward the house, indicating to Mikey his need to get on with the day. Looking over, he saw me and waved. Mikey looked too and smiled. My brother's smiles were as rare as an empty wash basket in our house, but when produced, were wholly authentic. Nothing my brother did seemed capable of being anything but genuine.

I stretched over the sink to shove open the window, my right foot on tiptoe—at five foot two-and-a-half, my ability to scale things was limited.

'You two coming in? I have coffee and toast on.'

'Sounds good to me.' Niall looked at Mikey to see if he might come too.

'Am busy, sis. New shelving.'

I nodded and smiled. 'Well, if you change your mind, you know where we are.'

As Niall made his way into the house, Mikey looked back into his shed and nodded at it, like this was it, time to grasp this change in both hands and make it his own before disappearing inside.

'He seems in good form,' I said, as Niall came through the kitchen door.

'He is, although that shelving has him panicky.'

'You didn't mention anything to him about last night?'

'God no.'

I handed him his coffee. 'How was the run?'

'Great. Ten k this morning. Dublin marathon here I come,' he grinned.

'Aren't you maybe leaping before the jumping there, Niall?' I teased.

'Not sure they're that different, a leap and a jump? Besides, you have to aim high, just like I did with you.' Being tall, six three, he was able to impart his love with a graceful bend and kiss to my forehead. I'd been drawn to tall people my whole life, jealous and enthralled by their ability to see over heads or reach the top shelf or to seem important by virtue of those extra inches rather than lost in the crowd like me.

'How's the town looking out there? Is it waking up?'

'Eight o'clock, it'd want to be. Arthur's on the rounds already. Says he'll be in at the usual time.' For years, Arthur, our postman, had taken his elevenses at our table. 'No calls yet?'

'No. All's quiet for once.'

'Perhaps we're in for a slow day. Maybe they're all hanging on for the sunshine. It's not often the midlands can boast a cloudless sky in April. No one wants to die on a stunner like that.'

I looked out at it, squinting at its dazzling brilliance, appreciating its efforts and wishing to be out there under its blue clarity. If there was anything I could do with today it was peace and quiet. No calls, no deaths, no speaking, no listening. Simply silence. Perhaps even a walk out at Barra Bog.

'How are you doing after the big announcement? Has the shock eased?' Niall looked at me over the rim of his cup as he took the first and only sip of his coffee that day. We hadn't talked further on the matter the previous night; I had been too exhausted when we finally left my parents and went to bed and had asked that we leave it until I was more able. His question now shook my pretence of everything being perfectly fine so that I found myself reaching for the stability of Mum's chair at the top of the table.

'It'll be OK, Jeanie.' Niall sat next to me. His hands, still clammy from his run, reached for mine. 'We can do this, me and you, can't we? We're a great team. We can run this place, no problem.'

I turned away from him to look at the walls of the kitchen, the same pale yellow colour they had been since I was small, repainted every ten years without fail. When my parents left, I could change it if I so wished. I could rip out every press, pull up every tile, knock down walls if it took my fancy. I opened my mouth to give him something but was stopped by the phone and my father taking the call in the hallway.

'Masterson Funeral Directors. David Masterson speaking.'

His greeting came out like a song, full of the hope and joy of the freedom he was about to hold in his hands.

Chapter 3

It was my aunt Harry who first realised I had Dad's gift, she who missed *that* gene, as she often told anyone who'd listen. When I was a toddler, I loved to trail after her in the embalming room, following her every move. Sitting under the one embalming table we had back then while she washed the dead, giggling as I pulled up my legs away from the drips that breached the sides. I should say, to be around the dead, naked or clothed, from birth meant I never realised the outside world might think it horrifying. To me they were as natural as the two wood pigeons who lived in our oak tree in the yard. I liked it when Harry massaged their limbs so that the embalming fluid could reach every nook and cranny. They liked it too. I could hear them sigh. I joined in their laughter when the ticklish ones couldn't hold it in any more.

'Is that funny, Jeanie?' Harry'd ask, finally won over by my giggles to stop what she was doing and play the game I wanted her to play.

'Yeah,' I'd laugh in reply, waiting, knowing full well what was coming next.

'Well, if that's so funny, wait until I get you.' Already she'd begun to tiptoe after me in her white lab coat and red Doc Martens. And I'd run or totter as fast as I could, but not too fast, as the bit I loved was when she caught me and swung me high in the air and sat me in the chair to tickle me. Under the arms was worst, her fingers didn't even need to make contact and I'd be wriggling and loving every second. And then she'd blow on my tummy. And all the while the person would wait patiently, sometimes laughing along, sometimes crying, perhaps thinking of their own little ones that they'd never touch again. Not that at two years old I was that in tune with the whys and wherefores of human emotion. It was simply what they did, laughed or cried or talked. It was my world.

Mum never wanted me to be in the embalming room and would often bring me to her hair salon next door. But I'd howl and say: 'Dat, dat' pointing in the direction of the funeral director's. And she, or one of her apprentices, would carry me back as I screamed all the way, trying to escape their grasp until I was with Dad and Harry and the dead again.

As the story goes, it wasn't until I was able to fully speak that Harry finally clicked that I could hear them like her brother. Harry listened to music as she worked—David Bowie, Patti Smith and Leonard Cohen, although sometimes she said he brought the mood down far too much even for the dead. Once she went through a Clash phase. That, apparently, caused all sorts of problems when the families of clients called in and Dad rushed in from the reception where he liked to meet with them to discuss the arrangements, to tell her to 'turn that blasted racket down.'

'Sorry, Dave,' she called, then smiled to herself. Harry was the only person who called Dad 'Dave.'

'She wants to hear the other one,' I shouted to Harry this one day when she'd nipped into Dad's office before beginning her morning's embalming. I suspect I was about four by then. I was sitting at a little desk Dad had set up for me in the embalming room in the hopes I'd stop running around causing his sister to chase me, and simply colour instead. He'd even bought me new colouring books.

'What you'd really like is ones with dead people in coffins, isn't that right? Then you'd do colouring all day,' he'd said, the blue eyes that I'd inherited flitting down to me as I held his large smooth hand, while he perused the different colouring books in Frayne's Newsagent's and Toy Shop.

'What, my love?' Harry said, coming back in, exaggeratedly cocking her ear as she turned on the Porti-boy, the embalming machine that looked like an enormous white juicer, sitting on the counter pumping fluid into the lady lying on the table.

'She wants the other song,' I shouted.

Harry turned off the noise to be sure she'd heard me right.

'Who wants the other song?'

'The lady.' I pointed with my colouring pencil at the woman with white hair so long that it flowed over the end of the embalming table.

'Did Agnes tell you that?'

Agnes Grace, the first dead person I heard, or the first dead person I admitted to hearing. Can't remember what she'd died of now.

Harry hadn't moved from beside the Porti-boy. She was always good at that, not overdramatising things.

I nodded.

'I see. Don't know what's wrong with "Starman." '

'She likes the TV one better.'

' "TVC 15"? Well, it's a good one, I'll give her that. But not his best.' Harry went over to her stereo to change it back. 'So do they talk to you a bit, Jeanie, the dead?'

'Yep.'

'All of them?'

'Only some.'

That was the thing with the dead; not all wanted to talk or, as Dad said over the years that followed, needed to. Those who didn't, he had decided, given he had no evidence to suggest otherwise, had gotten to say everything before they left, having had the kind of death that meant

26

no unresolved issues remained. Those who chose to speak still had something to say to the world, to those they loved; things they'd never gotten the chance to when they were alive, death taking them quicker than they'd ever imagined possible. Or there were those who liked the idea of an intermediary to finally tell what might have been too hard to say themselves. And then sometimes there were those who simply liked to chat. Were possibly like that in life, so why not in death?

'You know your dad can hear them too?' Harry continued.

I nodded again. I'd watched him plenty of times as they lay in their coffins, as Harry pottered around him. His elbows on his knees, his head bent, looking at the ground, listening. I'd stand by his side and his hand would rise to pat my head or often to hold my hand. Never once shooing me away or telling me these were adult things and little ears shouldn't listen. By allowing me to stay, he taught me that the dead and their needs were ours to bear. They were with us everywhere, in every sentence we spoke, in every dream we dreamed—not to be hidden or shied away from; they were to be embraced and talked about even by a four year old.

'I can't, though,' Harry said, the day she discovered my talent. 'Only some people are that clever.'

I lifted my head to look at her, to watch her

press the button of her stereo to bring it back to Bowie's opening 'Oh, oh, oh' riff and then I listened to Agnes hum along.

'Oh well, this is just great.' That was Mum later that night when Dad brought the news that the daughter she had hoped might follow her into the hairdressing trade, or anything else for that matter, was showing signs otherwise. 'This is you, you know, filling her head with this stuff.'

'I don't, Gráinne, and you know that. I've kept her from it as much as possible, like you asked, but she just won't be contained.'

She said nothing to that. I sat on the top step outside their bedroom door listening long after I should have been asleep. And while now in the retelling of the discussion that ensued that night, I will take liberties by embellishing it with words drawn from the many conversations my parents would repeat over the next twenty-eight years concerning the dead and me, much more than a four year old could comprehend, let alone remember, I still got it, sitting there in my brushed cotton pjs, that this news of my talent was not making Mum happy.

'It's not right, David, this meddling with the dead. Making the child believe she can talk to them. Next thing you know she'll be getting herself in trouble like that Cassidy case.' Mum's voice was straining in its determined whisper, trying not to wake her children.

The case of Danny Cassidy was legendary in our house, not that I knew anything about it then, but I would. In later years, Dad would use it as a prime example of why, at times, it was better to lie about what the dead had said. Mum, on the other hand, considered it evidence enough that talking to them only led to trouble. As he lay in his coffin, Danny told Dad that it was he who—one night, two years prior—had ruined the perfect flowerbedded garden of his next-door neighbour and loyal friend of over thirty years, Catherine Devine, in revenge for her killing his dog. Well, she didn't actually kill his dog and in reality Danny hadn't had a dog either. He'd been hallucinating. He'd gotten a kidney infection and suffered a bout of delirium, believing all sorts of things to be true. Catherine had been heartbroken when she saw the devastation the next morning but never once suspected Danny, with whom she had had the most trusting of relationships. But she never went back to her garden thereafter, had let the grass and weeds grow high, never to recreate its exquisiteness again. He wanted her to know now, Danny had said, that it was him and he was sorry. He wanted her to go back to what she loved. But by this time Catherine had grown deaf, and when Dad sat with her that evening after Danny's admission she took it that *he* was confessing to the crime and not her neighbour at all. Nothing Dad said could convince her otherwise. The following day, when Sergeant Reilly arrived at our house to question Dad further on his very surprising self-confessed crime, Dad explained the mix-up. And though the sergeant accepted his story (he was one of the 'believers' in the town), Catherine Devine refused, saying Danny wasn't capable of such a betrayal, and that this 'talking' to the dead was an excellent foil for any crime when it was nothing short of a mortal sin to tarnish the dead with false allegations. Catherine never used our services when she died a year later, giving written instructions that she should be tended to by the Doyles in Carnegy, the next town over.

'Gráinne, we're not doing this again,' Dad said, as I listened outside their door. 'Cassidy was an unfortunate case. For the most part this job is just talking, helping the dead ease into the next life.'

'The next life? Not all that shit again.'

Perhaps I slapped a hand over my mouth to muffle my snigger at Mum's cursing.

'I'm a funeral director, Gráinne. I believe in God and His plan.'

'I believe we die, we rot, end of.'

'Yes, you've told me often enough. Why did you marry me, Gráinne? Seriously, you knew my job. You knew my beliefs; if it upsets you that much, why decide to spend your life with it?'

'If I'd known back then that you lot were talking to the dead, I might not have.'

'And what if you had?' Dad's voice softened, and I imagine him walking across their squeaking floorboards and his arms curving around her waist. 'Could you really have still resisted me?'

'Oh, would you stop.' A change arrived in Mum's voice too, lifting it, breaking down this wall that would forever stand in their way. The division that they would spend their lives dismantling in times of devotion and building back up in times of war.

Perhaps they kissed or hugged in that moment when no more voices slipped under the door to reach me, when I got up to risk tiptoeing across the landing to press my ear hard against their door.

'I worry about her. What will her life be like now? Always here. Always having to be involved with the dead. I mean, look at all it's brought to your door.'

'I'm OK with that life and you are too, most of the time. We're doing good, you and me, aren't we? And look at Harry, not a bother on her.'

'Harry. Right. I'd hardly call her OK. Nuts, sure.'

'Look, death is as much a part of life as . . . as hairdressing. In fact, it's so much more. It simply takes a tiny mind shift to accept that what's going on here is natural. It's not dangerous or weird—

unusual yes, but that's all. Nothing more harmful than that. And apart from anything else, Gráinne, don't you think we're kind of writing Jeanie's destiny for her? So she can hear them? People are good swimmers but that doesn't mean they all want to be lifeguards. All I'm saying is, she's four. Who knows where she'll be in thirty years' time? She might be a hairdresser after all.'

'You think? I'd like that for her. And not necessarily hairdressing, but anything, something that doesn't mean she has to bear all of this, or the name-calling. The thoughts of what people will say to her. People can be cruel, can't they?'

'This is a big responsibility. But I think that little girl of ours has the power and wit to be anything she wants and get through it all. All she needs is for us to love and support her. OK?'

Did he really say that, or am I simply wishing that at one point in our lives he was willing to let me go?

Chapter 4

'There you are now.' That was Arthur, his back to our kitchen counter, the kettle switched on, the first bite already eaten from the Twix he'd taken from the press as I came through the door later that morning. 'I thought for a minute it was only me in the place.'

I turned to the clock, eleven on the dot. The tradition of Arthur taking his elevenses with us had started long before I can remember. The only times it hadn't happened were due to illness or when the postal service dared to change his route. Each time it was short-lived and soon he would be back to his bike, the town, and having his feet under our table. Arthur wasn't just our postman but Dad's second cousin—or was it a cousin once removed? One of those confusing cousin terms I could never understand. Either way, there was a family tie. When he was around twenty, and his father had died, he came to live with us. Dad and Arthur were inseparable, Arthur becoming Mikey's godfather when he was born.

'Wasn't Mikey out in his shed when you passed?' I asked. My brother wasn't one for going out anywhere so I was confused at the suggestion that no one was around.

'Oh, he was, but he said he's got work to do.

He looked a little stressed. It's like bonfire night out there with all the wood shelving he has. I told him it was a fire hazard.'

'Oh you didn't. He takes everything so literally, Arthur.'

'I know, it was out of my mouth before I could stop myself. I said I was only joking. I'm bringing him out a tea and I'll give him a hand with it for twenty minutes.' He began to fill two teacups with water. 'So,' he said, 'you're looking well.'

I instinctively put my hand to my bush of black curly hair that I'd not two seconds ago gathered into a hasty bobbin. When straightened, my hair reached the middle of my back but when natural, it bunched around my shoulders.

'Any news for me?' he asked.

I rather suspected Arthur knew everything already, my mother and father's retirement announcement and my reaction. Arthur was someone with whom our lives were shared daily, and then more intently when he and Dad had their weekly round-up of Friday night pints in McCaffrey's—when Dad could make it, that was. The undertaking trade was many things, with unpredictability top of the list. Harry used to say she wished banshees really did exist, predicting death as they did, then she could have a proper timetable like every other worker in Ireland.

'Well, Dad made his big retirement announcement last night,' I admitted, a slight catch in my voice, 'but I'd rather not talk about it if that's OK with you.'

'Ah, right. Not another word.' My suspicions confirmed, Arthur put his finger to his lips and clicked his heels, the obedient soldier, and gave a kindly smile. 'Are you having one?' He raised a cup in my direction as I passed him to get a glass of water.

'No, I'm grand, thanks.' I stood at the sink, sipping away, beginning to feel guilty. 'So go on,' I said, relenting to his ready smile. 'Give me the stats for the weekend.'

'Well, now, it's a difficult one. But I'm reckoning three. Molly Greene, Dick Darcy and Tiny Lennon.'

'You said them last weekend and they're still alive.'

'Barely, though. Molly's gone down a lot this week, Kate was just telling me. Met her there on Mary Street before I came in. She was on her way back over to Saint Luke's. Molly'd been there all night, apparently; Kate had only popped home for a shower.'

'Dick and Tiny have been dying, according to you, for two years now.'

'Well, it's not my fault if they keep getting second winds, is it? Tiny hasn't opened the door to me in weeks, though. I've told Sergeant Boyle, but he tells me he's very much alive, just doesn't want to be chatting with me. Don't know what I've ever done to the man—only been polite.'

'Nosey, you mean.'

'Anyway, I've paid my debts,' he said, ignoring my jibe.

For every wager he had lost in his 'dead stats game,' Arthur bought us a Twix. The press was now bulging with them. Every time he won, which was rarer than Westmeath having a fighting chance at The Sam Maguire, we had to return the favour. Of course, instead of buying them, we simply paid him from the stash his losses had accumulated. And even if a bet hadn't been won, he took one for his break-time treat anyway. In truth, Arthur was the only one who ate them.

'I want to be here, you know, when Tiny dies. I want to hear where his gold is buried.'

Arthur was convinced Tiny, Timothy Lennon, two foot at birth and six foot five at eighty-two, was in fact a millionaire, despite living in the smallest of cottages at the edge of town.

'So, who've you got coming in? I see the van is out.'

'Bernadette O'Keefe. Dad and Niall have gone to get her from the hospital mortuary.'

'Flip it! She was on my list last weekend. Do you think she might finally admit who the affair was with?' His eyes now wide in divilment.

'You don't even know who she is,' I laughed.

He sniffed in mock disgust. 'Who is she then?'

'Farmer from out Rathdrum way. Tending a sheep stuck in a fence. Heart attack.'

'Oh, those O'Keefes. Sure she's only what, mid-sixties? You just never know, do you?'

'No. Not in this game.'

'Will I be needed to work this one, do you think?' Arthur helped us out in the evenings and on the weekends when we were busy.

'I'm not sure, I'll get Dad to call you.'

'Right so.'

I turned then to nod in the direction of the two cups. 'That tea's getting cold.'

He picked them up to walk the short distance to where I stood, setting them down again.

'You'll be OK, you know. I'll still be here when the big man finally packs up his fishing rods. I mean, I know there's Niall, and Harry, but we all know I'm the brains of the operation.' He laughed in that soft, gravelly way of his that always made me smile. I patted his chest in gratitude.

'Where's your lucky pen?' I asked, distracted by the forlorn space where it should have sat. For as long as I could remember, Arthur had clipped the silver pen to the breast pocket of whichever jacket or shirt he wore, An Post's aqua green or Masterson's clinical white. Always the same one, left to him in his father's will, although it had originally been his mother's, and refilled every month or so with ink bought in O'Dwyer's Pen and Fishing Tackle Shop on Water Lane.

'I lost it.' Arthur's face instantly drained of its usual happiness. The back of his hand rose to rub at the tip of his nose.

'What? But you never let that thing out of your sight.'

'Sure, don't I know. I had your father searching this place high and low but it's gone.'

'Oh.' I put a hand to his arm. 'But it'll turn up. These things always do.'

'Course it will. You don't be worrying about that now, you've enough to be contending with.'

'Morning all.' Harry came through the kitchen door, distracting me on that mild spring morning, wearing her sunglasses, scarf and leather gloves, the picture of an Arctic explorer, despite only living next door in the apartment over my mother's hairdresser's. She took them off to reveal her smooth oval face and her black-lashed eyes that showed off their blue Masterson centres to a sparkle, an inky blue that would have looked magnificent on a page.

In an instant, Arthur had recovered his cheeriness.

'Harry, light of my life. The woman I want to marry. How are you, beautiful?'

'Think Teresa might have something to say about that, Art, don't you?' She kissed him on the cheek and he instantly took her in his arms and waltzed her around the kitchen. Harry entered the spirit of it all by humming a tune. They twirled and laughed, heads held proudly aloft, delighted at their own talent. When they finished, Harry gave a glorious sigh then came to hug me, still breathless from her endeavours.

'That brother of mine finally told you he's escaping, I hear.'

'So literally everyone knows. When did they tell you?'

'Oh, Jeanie, you know me and your dad. There's not much one is thinking that the other hasn't figured out already.' She considered me for a second. 'You OK about it all?'

'I will be, I'm sure.' I gave a little smile that I hoped convinced her that she needn't worry.

'That's my girl. You'll be great, you and Niall. No better pair.'

They left then, Arthur to bring the tea to Mikey, two Twix bars sticking out of his back pocket, and Harry accompanying him down the corridor, laughing at whatever he was saying.

An hour later Bernadette O'Keefe lay on the embalming table.

'I told you, Jeanie, I'll handle everything today.' Niall stood over her. 'That's why I called Harry in. And your dad's sticking around, he says, so there's three of us, more than enough to do one body.'

'Well, I'm here now so I may as well do it.'

He looked at me and I could see the will in

him to fight. To point out that being a martyr was helping no one, certainly not me, and not him either. But he stepped back from the brink, surmising the battle was already lost.

I watched Harry and Niall work at expert speed and gentleness with Bernadette as I stood to the side, waiting to hear even the tiniest of whimpers. That was the thing about talking to the dead, you only had a certain period of time, a day or so, sometimes two or three; four was really pushing it. For those who had a distance to travel to get to us, it didn't always work. The finite nature was a good thing, really, otherwise I'd never have been able to visit a graveyard for the thousands of voices trying to talk to me at once. It was best therefore to be ready from the get-go, to be around as soon as they were wheeled into the building. Sometimes they chose to talk as the embalming machine was in full swing, which was never ideal, but most decided to wait until they were embalmed, fully clothed and lying in their coffin before they began. Their mouths didn't open or anything. Harry and Niall's handiwork ensured eyes and mouths and other orifices were locked down never to open again.

'I told Helen, Bernadette's niece, not to come over until about two,' Niall said, as they began to wash her. 'She'd have gotten in the van with us if we'd let her. Poor woman, she's distraught, had waited for us all that time with the clothes she wanted Bernadette buried in, chain-smoking outside the morgue. I told her she could've just dropped them here, but I don't think she even heard me. She said you're not to start talking to her until she gets here.'

'I can't stop Bernadette talking if she wants to. They have no schedule.'

Harry glanced up at me, at the slight edge in my voice.

'I know, Jeanie. And I told her that. I'm only passing on what Helen said.'

I nodded, trying hard to find my ease.

'You sure you don't want me to get your dad to do this one?'

'No, I already said,' I sighed, instantly regretting my tone. 'Sorry, ignore me. I'll be fine with Bernadette. It'll all be fine. Like it always is.'

Niall looked as though he didn't believe a word of it, but didn't risk an objection.

Chapter 5

When we were little, before marriage was even a word we knew, Niall and I would play in the park together. Our families didn't know each other intimately or anything. We lived at opposite ends of the town and met only because we happened to be there at the same time most days of the week. My mother worked, of course, so it wasn't always her who brought me for a walk. But between my father, Harry and Mum, and whichever of her apprentices was working that day, I'd be there alongside Niall and his mother Annie. The first day our paths crossed, we toddled toward each other and babbled away. From then on, whenever we were in the park together, the mothers or minders would stop to talk for a minute or two while we stared at each other again.

I remember nothing of it, but Niall says he does. Says we would chase each other or show one another a dandelion or a stone or an interesting stick or, more than likely, a not so interesting stick, but one that was simply magical to us. He fell once, apparently, on the bridge over the pond. Our mums behind us observing our progress, no doubt discussing their toddlers' development as only mothers who are effectively strangers can, diving straight in to poos and sleep patterns and stitches and breast soreness, as if they had known each other all their lives. They were two or three seconds behind us when Niall tripped over. He roared at the red blood that had appeared on his knee and his right hand that had saved him from more serious damage. I watched him sit on his nappy-padded bum for a second before lowering my head to kiss his hand and then his knee, saying 'aw better soon.' By the time his mother arrived, Niall had stopped screaming and was looking at me in wonder. I have his word for all of this. My mother can't remember either. But the day I walked into their house as his girlfriend when I was twenty-three, his mother had turned to her husband and said:

'Didn't I tell you it was meant to be, Simon? This pair. From the minute he fell that day and she bent to him, I knew it was destiny.'

With primary school dividing us, we didn't see each other so much as the years went on. But the odd time when we bumped into each other, our mothers would wave and chat briefly about all that had happened in the time between, while Niall and I would stare at each other once again. I remember pulling my hand away from Mum's and running to the willow, my favourite tree in the park, where he followed me. There we sat picking at the daisies, whispering to each other so we wouldn't startle the birds as they flitted in and out of the branches. I told him my favourite bird was the one with the blue head. A blue tit. If we had known, aged seven, what they were called, we would've laughed into our cupped hands. And I wonder too if someone had whispered in our innocent ears that there, across from the other, was the person we would marry, would we have giggled and widened our eyes at the impossibility of us being forever linked by love?

Niall remembers always wanting to be braver when we met. He wanted to speak up more, he said, to pull something from his shyness that might make me concentrate on him alone. Often, when he knew that they were planning a visit to the park, he'd think of things to say like, 'It's very windy today' Or, 'My brother broke his leg.' Not that Gareth had ever broken his leg, but he thought it might be an interesting conversation starter. But he never worked up the courage. Once, however, he said he offered me a Fruit Pastille from the packet his mum had just bought and that he was supposed to share with Gareth when he got home. While the two women were engrossed, he pulled it from his pocket, opening it carefully and gesturing it toward me. I delighted that the first one was orange. I chewed, or more sucked at my bounty, hoping not to draw too much attention to what was obviously forbidden, and we smiled at our shared deception.

He knew what my family did. Had always

44

known, he told me years later. He couldn't remember when his mother had actually said the word 'undertakers.' He doesn't even know how she might have explained it to him. But he says it was always there whenever we met, his complete amazement that I lived with dead people. He thought that meant I must be really special because being dead was special. It meant you were with God. And God was the most precious thing in the whole world. He wanted to ask me what it was like caring for people everyone loved. His one experience of death was when his 'nandad' Bert, his mother's father, had died. (Niall hadn't been able to pronounce the 'gr' of granddad when he started to speak, so it had come out as 'nandad,' and after that the name stuck.) He'd remembered our funeral home with its dark hallway, the pew along the left wall, the door leading to the coffin display on the right and the reception room next door and the beautiful sunlight falling on Bert as he lay in his coffin for their goodbyes in the wide expanse of the viewing room at the very end. And his mother shaking Dad's hand, telling him he was truly a gifted man, making her father look like a king on his final day. She smiled through her tears, and lifted Niall so he could touch his grandfather's hands and run his own against the silk of the inlay and say, 'Bye-bye, Nandad. Love you.'

Niall said his mother had adored her father, had spent as much time as possible with him when he was alive and then when he died had gone to his grave nearly every day for weeks, bringing Niall with her, filling his head with how very lucky Nandad had been to die in his sleep and now to be with God. 'The dead are special and deserve our love and our flowers and our prayers, never to be forgotten,' she'd said, kissing him on his forehead as she held him close, sitting on the dry summer grass at her father's headstone.

I'm glad he never had to ask me what we Mastersons did. I would automatically have thought he was working up to some kind of cruelty, as seemed to be the wont of the other children in my life. Apart from Peanut, who would get more annoyed than I ever did at the other children's taunts, pushing her red-rimmed glasses further up her nose, her blonde pigtails almost shaking in fury, which made me love her even more, if that were possible.

Peanut, or Sarah Byrne, was my best friend. When we were five year olds and had sat to the pegs and jigsaws laid out on the baby tables on our first day at school, she had raced Aoife Mullally to sit beside me because she knew I was special. She never said those actual words. We didn't have vocabulary like that. But we had feelings. The whole class had laughed when the teacher called her by her nickname, the name her parents had insisted on. She looked around proudly and laughed too. And then she'd leaned over, her hand cupping my ear, her voice and the little bit of spit that came with it tickling my lobe so that I giggled, as she told me her daddy had given her the name Peanut so that the world would always know not to kill his daughter due to her nut allergy.

Turned out Aoife Mullally and I wouldn't have been great friends anyway as two years later she told me I smelled of rotting flesh and that she knew I slept in a coffin and that my dad was crazy. I was in the playground on my own, waiting for Peanut to come back from the loo, when she said it: 'You can't talk to dead people. My mum says he's making it all up.'

'He is not,' I shouted back, horrified that anyone might think Dad anything other than magnificent. We were at that age when children begin to understand how hurtful they can really be.

'He's a liar.'

'No, he's not.' I could feel my eyes fill. Her words an attack on me too, although I'd told no one except Peanut by then that I could talk to the dead.

'Is too.' She circled me, enjoying the power she held.

'Is not.'

'Cry baby.' She shouted on seeing my first tear fall. But with it came a surge of anger that surprised me. It was then I saw Peanut making her way over to me. I wanted her to see that I was worthy of her friendship so I pushed Aoife and she landed on her arse.

'My daddy doesn't lie,' I shouted at her. 'He *can* hear them and so can I.' My first public admission to the world, which meant they never let up again.

I stomped away to meet Peanut halfway, grabbing her arm and turning her so we were walking in the opposite direction of the sharp inhalations of my classmates.

I was hauled into the principal's office later to answer for Aoife's cut hands and sore bum. But I refused to say what she'd said to cause such 'out of character behaviour.' For my silence, I had to apologise, not once looking up at her, keeping my eyes firmly on the grey speckled carpet that covered the office floor.

Dad sat with me that night and told me nice girls don't inflict violence, so something awful had to have happened and he'd really like to know what it was. I couldn't bear to tell him what Aoife had said about him, but in the end the words had come out in fits and starts through tears and wails and rushed intakes of breath. He hugged me then, kissing my curls, telling me I was a great girl but to try never to do that kind of thing again, especially when there was a teacher watching.

That year, Peanut and I sat on the spongy surface of the school playground to 'cross our hearts' promise that when we were bigger we would travel the world together. We were built for air and colour and sky, she told me.

'I'll be an emergency vet, flying across the world to save animals from earthquakes and things and you can be my pilot.'

I nodded in devotion to this girl who felt as delightful as the stick of candyfloss Dad always bought me at the annual Kilcross Agricultural Show. I spat in my hand as she had done, then shook hers and smiled.

I let her down, of course. Never quite living up to my promise to become a pilot and instead staying in Kilcross, a place where the sky sometimes became so dark that its weight and power seemed to curve around everything—the church spire, the houses, the clump of chestnut trees that stood proudly at the highest point of the town on the Dublin Road—a dome reaching to the earth, the sides of which would have been impossible to push through even if I'd tried. I never did travel, other than to Cork and London, and yet by the time we were thirty, I must've had twenty postcards in a box under my bed, from all the places Peanut had visited.

• • •

Niall and I were to meet again in secondary school when we started in the Community College. We'd seen each other on the first day but had averted our eyes almost as quickly as they'd landed. By chance, we had been put in the same class, but we were thirteen and full of that angst at being noticed when all we wanted was to be invisible. It was three days before he bravely stood in front of me, with Ruth, his best friend by his side, and said: 'Remember me?'

Peanut, fearing the worst, had automatically dropped her bag at her locker three rows down and rushed to my side. She was one inch taller than me at that stage, hardly an imposing presence, but enough to make me feel I was protected.

'What does that mean?' Peanut pushed up her now purple glasses.

I should've known that he wasn't like the others from our time together in the park, but I couldn't be sure. What if he'd changed? Children were unpredictable. Turncoats in an instant, liars and bullies in the whip of a magician's cloak.

'It's Niall, Jeanie,' he smiled with those soft brown eyes. Peanut undid her folded arms and relaxed her tensed shoulders. 'Don't you remember? The pastilles? The willow tree?'

Peanut smirked. 'Yeah, Jeanie, the pastilles and the willow tree, that guy.' Peanut had no more of a clue about 'that guy' so I poked her in the arm.

'Oh right,' I nodded, like it was only then the memory of those encounters returned.

'We're in the same class.'

'I'm Ruth.' Ruth, who had been standing right beside Niall, took my hand, then Peanut's and shook both vigorously.

Back then Ruth was about three inches taller than Niall, with a halo of magnificent black curly hair surrounding a near constant smiling face that seemed to give the world the benefit of the doubt.

'I'm in your class too.' She looked straight at me and smiled. 'I like your hair.' I touched what had forever been another source of comedy for the other children in primary. 'Zombie hair,' they called it. Every Sunday I'd beg Mum to plait or straighten it: 'But you are beautiful as you are,' she'd protest. 'And straightening it will only weaken it in the long run.'

'Me and Niall were in Colman's,' Ruth carried on proudly, while Niall continued to look at me.

'Jeanie and me were in Saint Brigid's,' Peanut responded, as I remained quiet.

'I wanted to go there but Mom says it is full of posh idiots. You're not posh, are ye?'

'No, the posh idiots all decided to go to Saint Ciarán's,' Peanut replied.

'That's good then, isn't it, Niall?' Ruth turned

again to see that he was still looking at me. 'Eh, hello?'

'Sorry, what?'

'Never mind.' She considered my hair again. 'I can style that if you want. I can do some really interesting plaits. I could teach you and you can practise on me too.'

'Yeah, OK,' I said, enthralled by this goddess.

'There's this particular braid that I've wanted to try on someone for ages but my brother refuses to let me. It finishes with like a bun on top of your head. Can I?' she asked, giving her books to Niall as she began to examine my hair after I'd nodded my consent. 'Are you free Friday? We'll have to go to your place, my brother is so annoying. We'd have no peace.'

'Maybe we could all go, see how you do it?' Peanut suggested.

'I guess. But your hair is way too thin for me to work with.' Ruth pointed to Peanut's straight blonde hair.

'I don't mind,' Peanut enthused, not wishing to miss out on the fun.

'I have football practice,' Niall happily interjected with what seemed like a genuine excuse.

'That's OK, you can join us later,' Ruth instructed.

'Oh,' he said.

I grinned at him until we found ourselves laughing. Ruth and Peanut joined in, but more in delight at our hilarity than anything else. In that second I felt happy and grateful that Niall had been courageous enough to say hello, increasing my friends from one to three in an instant, something I had never thought possible.

'I live on Church Street,' I said to Ruth, when I'd finally managed to control myself. 'The funeral directors'. You know it?'

'Wait.' She stepped away from me to get a full look at my face, her mouth slightly agape. 'The Mastersons? You like, live with dead people?'

'Yeah, is that OK? You don't have a problem with the dead, do you?' I wondered if this had all been too good to be true and she was going to be a disappointment like everyone else.

'No,' she said. 'So long as I don't have to do their hair.'

Chapter 6

I sat alone beside Bernadette O'Keefe's coffin in the viewing room, waiting for her to speak. I was on my usual chair: a high bar stool but with arms, like the ones you'd see in swanky chrome kitchens. It allowed me to see the dead clearly. While with an ordinary chair I could see their profile, this let me see the whole of them; it felt more personal, that we were closer. I'd bought it especially in Kilmurray's Kitchen Showroom. When I wasn't on duty, it lived in the corner of Dad's office. Sometimes I'd arrive to find Dad's jacket on it, or some post if something personal had come my way, which it often did—a letter from a relative to thank me for my time, my comfort. Or sometimes I'd find a flower, a large daisy picked from the wild patch in the park next door, which would be from Niall. In return, I might've put a bar of Fry's Chocolate Cream in the pocket of the white coat he wore while working, or the Simplex crossword, cut out from Dad's *Irish Times*, which we'd fill in together later over a pint in Casey's.

Bernadette lay quiet in her pale yellow suit and white blouse. Her hair now curled in gentle waves and her makeup, not overdone, was finished to perfection. Lifeless, bloodless skin wasn't much to work with, but by the time Niall and Harry were finished you would think that the dead had simply closed their eyes to breathe in the air, to appreciate the magic of life. My hands lay joined on my knees, as I stared down at the burgundy carpet pile, long compacted from the thousands of shuffling feet over the years—perhaps that might be the first thing I would change—hoping, willing the bell to ring announcing the arrival of Bernadette's niece, Helen. It was easier if the living were there while the dead spoke, so they got to ask everything before their loved one left them once and for all.

'When will they be waking me up, do you think?' Bernadette's words arrived confidently, her voice solid, with not a single hint of the vulnerability that wasn't uncommon.

'Hello, Bernadette,' I said, pulling myself together, ready now for all that was to come. 'I'm Jeanie.'

'When will this anaesthetic or whatever it is wear off?'

Sometimes that happened, they didn't know they'd died. A 'deadly confusion,' Dad had christened it. He thought himself more than a little witty when he'd come up with the term. Throughout the rest of the day of its coining, I'd caught him chuckling to himself on several occasions. I lay a hand to the side of the coffin, taking a moment before I began to explain. But she got in ahead of me.

'I'm in Kilcross Hospital, I take it? Oh God, they didn't bring me to Saint Finbarr's Private, did they? Sure I haven't got the health insurance. I've told Helen that a hundred times.' Her voice strained in panic.

'No, you're not in Saint Finbarr's, Bernadette, I'm afraid you're actually—'

'Oh, thank God for that. Your voice feels strange, dear. Am I awake or asleep? I can't quite . . . Are you the doctor, because this chest of mine is fierce sore and my head . . .'

'Do you remember anything about the sheep, Bernadette?' I tried, attempting to rein the situation in. 'The one caught in the fencing?'

'Of course I do. That was Bruce—always the one to wander. You wouldn't think he was a sheep at all—the most single-minded fecker I've ever had. I once found him all the way over in Mackey's field. Not one of the others had followed him. They're wise to his wanderings. Did I manage to free him in the end? I can't seem to remember.'

'He struggled, Bernadette, put up a good fight—'

'That'd be Bruce. He'll be the death of me one of these days.'

I stayed silent, hoping that the truth of her

56

words might sink in, which it did, but in the wrong way.

'Ah no, he's not . . .' Bernadette stopped, unable to finish the sentence. 'You fool, Bruce, you couldn't stay put, could you? You had to go and kill yourself.'

'I'm sorry, Bernadette, but I think—'

'Don't waste your breath.' Although, it should have been me saying that to her as she was labouring under the weight of talking, her voice weakening, moving in and out like a bad mobile signal, and I knew I wouldn't be able to hold her long. 'It was bound to happen. He was on an IOU for a long time, that one.'

'Bernadette, I'm really sorry about this but I believe Bruce is still very much alive.'

'Well, that's a relief. He's actually worth a bloody fortune. He's always my "best in show." '

I braced myself. 'Bernadette,' I began, 'I'm afraid it was you who had a heart attack trying to free him. I'm Jeanie Masterson. You're in the funeral directors' on Church Street.'

'Oh,' she replied, so sadly that my hand instinctively moved to hers, as they lay crossed over her stomach. She would not even have felt it there. But it's all I had to offer in that moment, my touch a substitute for the loving care of a friend, a mother, a partner. 'You're the one who talks to the . . .' She stopped again, foiled by the word that she could not say. 'Well, may God forgive me, but I should have sold that fecker years ago.'

She grew upset then, but there was no need for tissues to dry those tearless eyes. To the unhearing she was perfectly still and silent. But I heard it, the rage and torment and sorrow. This ripping apart of worlds. This end-of-life horror, realising there was no more tomorrow, no more later. The fact was, there would be no more day and no more night. Everything was gone except for this brief bubble of time in which we could hear each other but that at any second could burst.

'But I don't remember anything,' she said, still trying to come to terms with things.

'The brain doesn't remember everything in times of severe stress, Bernadette.'

'Oh God, but there's nothing done. There isn't even a will. And what about the funeral costs? Sure, Helen doesn't know where anything is in the house. How's she supposed to cope?'

'Tell me, Bernadette. Tell me and I'll make sure she knows.' I kept watching the clock. I knew any minute now the bell would ring and Helen would be there. If I could only hold Bernadette with me so these two women could have one second together then I'd be happy.

'Right, em . . . under my bed, there's a red suitcase. I threw everything that's important in there. The deeds, the bank accounts. Oh Jesus, she'll never manage it all. She's not built for this kind of thing.'

'We'll help her. What I mean is, we'll make sure to get her the support she needs.'

'No, you don't get it. When Frank died, she fell apart. That's my brother Frank, her dad. She was into the drugs and everything. She'll not cope.'

I looked at the clock.

'What would you say to her, if she were here right now, what would you say?'

For a moment she paused and I wondered if that was it, if she had gone.

'I'd tell her,' she began to my relief, 'that she's stronger than she realises. And that she's got a good head on her shoulders, like Frank had, if she'd only just believe in herself.' Her voice was fading now, as though she was walking backwards, further and further away.

The bell rang out loud and clear.

'Bernadette, that's her. Helen's coming. Try to hold on,' I appealed, jumping off my stool to meet the footsteps as they hurried from the hallway. I stretched a hand out to this woman with unkempt hair and frightened eyes.

'Talk to her,' I commanded, as I put Helen's hand on Bernadette's and scurried back to the other side of the coffin so I could see both women clearly.

'Bernie, Auntie Bernie? It's Helen.' She looked over at me with a worried face. 'Can she hear me, or do you have to tell her what I'm saying?'

'She can only hear my voice and only I can hear hers. So I'll talk for both of you, OK?'

She nodded and looked again at her aunt.

'I'm OK, Bernie,' she continued. 'I know you'll be worrying about me but I'm fine. I'll look after everything. Bruce and the rest of them. And the house. And me. Your biggest headache.' She laughed quietly. She looked at her aunt's face, searching it for an answer, and then over at me as I relayed her words. 'I love you, Bernie,' she continued. 'Did she hear that? What's she saying? She's not gone, is she? Tell me she's not gone.'

But she was. There was nothing more for me to hear but the powerful silence she'd left behind. A silence that always reminded me of that split second when you drive under a motorway bridge on a furious rainy day, experiencing the power of its wholly encompassing short-lived quiet. I closed my eyes against the force of my heartbeat, and took a breath to calm me, to remind me not to let the living down.

'Yes, Helen. She's still with us,' I lied. 'She's saying she's very proud of you. And that she's sorry to have left you like this. That she never meant to go so soon.'

'Oh, Bernie, you silly goose, you've nothing to be sorry for. I'm the one who should be sorry. I should've gone down the field with you, not left you to struggle with Bruce all alone. If I had, we mightn't be in this mess.' Her eyes closed and her tears came, flowing freely now as her hand tightened around her aunt's. 'Where would I be without you? And what will I do now?'

Her head lowered to the perfectly pressed shoulder pad of Bernadette's suit.

Other people's tears were like magnets to mine and sure enough, out they came. Never many, one or two, but present nevertheless. I scratched them away, pretending as I always did that I simply had an itch. Dad used to say it was my only weakness—feeling things so deeply. But I knew he felt their sorrow as much as I did; he simply had tougher tear ducts. A clear case of biological difference and nothing else. And besides, I used to argue, how the hell was it a weakness.

'Bernadette says you're stronger than you know, Helen, and that you'll get through this and that she'll be by your side every step of the way. She says when you feel the heat of a sun ray through a window, that will be her, right beside you.' I made things up sometimes. Lots of times, if I'm being honest. To lessen the pain for those left behind, allowing them something to hold on to, something that made this waiting and hanging on to hear what their loved ones had to say worth it.

'She'll be talking about the kitchen window. The sunbeams through there in the morning, when it decides to come out, that is. Bernie, don't you worry, I'll be there, waiting for you.'

'She says you're like Frank.'

'You were forever saying that, weren't you, Bernie?'

'You're brave like him, and kind, she's saying. The most precious thing that's ever happened to her.'

'Oh, Bernie.'

I said nothing for a moment as Helen's hand rose to smooth down Bernadette's hair, which her hug had disturbed.

'She's worried, Helen. That you'll take this hard, like after your dad.'

'No, Bernie. Don't you dare go leaving thinking that. I'll never let you down again like that. I promise you, right here and now, that's all done with.'

She continued to let her hand lightly brush against Bernadette's hair. She began to smile then, as if something lovely had occurred to her. 'You know the way you loved Westlife, Bernie? Well I thought you might like it if we played "You Raise Me Up" at some stage in the funeral.' She turned to me then and asked: 'You don't think the priest will mind, do you?'

'We'll talk to him.'

In fact, our priests did mind that kind of thing. In this era of Pope Francis, it seemed Kilcross had been given the two most conservative priests they could dig out. We were back to long cassocks and only hymns at ceremonies. But I knew if anyone could sort Father Dempsey, it'd be Dad. He had a way with priests that I didn't. Another reason why retirement was a bad idea. I would add it to my growing 'cons' list later—nothing had made it to the 'pros' side as of yet. But we had a fallback: if Dad's charm didn't work, we'd play it here—where we held dominion—before we brought Bernadette across the road to Saint Xavier's.

Helen, Bernadette and I stayed chatting for a few moments more. Me answering as best I could from the little I'd learned before Bernadette had left so quickly, ensuring Helen knew about the red case under the bed, until I deemed it the right time to say:

'She says she's getting tired now, Helen. This is what happens, I'm afraid. She'll begin to drift away.'

'Oh,' she replied, looking like a lost, scared child.

'Sometimes it can be even quicker. These moments are like the last flicker of a candle, not very strong and never very long before it finally dies out. Is there anything else you want to say to her before she can rest?'

'I love you, Bernie,' she called, 'and tell Dad I love him too.' She kissed her cheek and laid her head there for a bit before rising, to touch

Bernadette's hair again, and to give the bravest of smiles.

I felt exhausted. It was always the same—drained from the concentration, the intensity of these few precious moments of ensuring I was doing the best job possible for everyone. Out of the corner of my eye I saw Dad step into the room from the hallway. He moved in closer to get a chair so Helen could sit beside her aunt.

'Stay for as long as you need,' he said, one hand to her shoulder, the other indicating the chair. 'We'll leave you two for a bit. And I'll be back then to go through the arrangements.'

He gave me his crooked arm and we moved to the door, leaving the two O'Keefes, one still chatting, the other long gone.

'Were you there all along listening to that?' I whispered to him. He nodded and squeezed my hand. 'You know she'd gone then, that I couldn't hold her?'

'You were brilliant, Jeanie. If ever I needed proof that your mother and I have made the right choice in leaving you and Niall to this place, it was there right in front of me in those last few minutes.'

Chapter 7

Aoife Mullally from primary school had been right: Dad lied, and so did I. At least some of the time, mainly when the dead had something not so endearing they wanted us to pass on to those they'd left behind.

For example, once I told Carly Kiernan, who'd come all the way from Garna in Donegal, that, yes, her husband who lay in his coffin loved her, when in fact only seconds before he'd admitted it was her sister he'd adored. I never understood why he wanted to tell her that then, when he must've known the damage it would cause. But I took one look at that distraught woman and knew I couldn't tell her. But the thing was, she might've been a horrible wife, beating him, calling him degrading names or worse, and this could've been his one chance to finally feel some power, and I, a young thing—was I even twenty at that point?—faced with this grieving widow, decided to refuse him his moment of glory. And even if she'd been the nicest wife in the world, and him a horror, was it really up to me to save their blushes, and mine? My role was simply to be the conduit, the empty vessel, after all. And yet, I couldn't always do it.

It bothered me, this barefaced lying. After all,

who was I to play God with their lives? But Dad was a firm believer that sometimes there was nothing for it but to lie, to shield the living. And there had been times, particularly in more recent years, when I'd seen the tiredness death had brought to his door, and I'd heard him say to an expectant relative: 'He says he loves you, more than you will ever know, and he is sorry that he had to leave.' A simple and effective message but perhaps not exactly what the dead had wanted him to say.

Sometimes I didn't so much lie as twist the truth a little or file off its hard edges, handing them a half-truth to ease the pain for the living. And sometimes it worked both ways, when I couldn't tell the dead what it was the living wanted them to hear. Once a son stood in front of his dead father and said he hated him. Hated every time he had hit him and kicked his mother, while he lay on the floor begging him to stop. He wanted him to suffer in the afterlife for all he had done to them. This, I was instructed to say to the old shrivelled man who, not moments earlier, had sobbed as he'd begged for forgiveness and asked me would he go to hell?

It was an odd thing this being in a business where faith mattered when I didn't believe. Not that I went around announcing it. I went to Mass up to the age of eighteen with Dad; Mum was the healthiest of nonbelievers. But after that I simply didn't go any more, save for the funeral Masses, feeling my eighteen years and adulthood had earned me the right to stop. I wasn't convinced by the existence of a heaven or hell, and yet to be able to hear those who could no longer breathe was perfectly normal. And isn't that the fascination of being human—not believing one thing that seems curious while another, almost as bizarre, is perfectly acceptable. A simple case of evidence, that's all it came down to for me. Where the dead went to after they spoke, I did not know.

So I sidestepped that frightened man's question, as I often did when it came to matters of faith, instead saying:

'Trevor says you hurt him very much. That it's not something he can forgive that easily.'

'Go on, tell him the rest,' the son had demanded.

I remember thinking then, why weren't we braver, we humans? Why hadn't we the courage to tell it like it was when alive? Why did we let fear haunt us, silence us? And why was I now the one to tell this man his son was glad he was dead. I couldn't, and so Trevor had screamed at his father and pummelled his chest with his fists until Dad and Niall pulled him away. He sat on the chair and sobbed. Me sitting beside him, feeling I had let him down. And I had. His friend arrived and rocked him back and forth until his wails became whimpers and he upped and left, not to attend the ceremony. I'm not sure that bill was ever paid.

Perhaps if there'd been others in this business who could hear the dead too, it might have felt less hard, less burdensome, less lonely. Perhaps if it was simply a normal part of what every funeral director in Ireland offered as a service, like an optional extra for which there was a charge: 'And would you like the "talking to your loved one" package with that?'

'The hourly rate, you ask? Three hundred. But if they speak for less than that we will of course charge pro rata.'

Money was never spoken of so brazenly in this industry. It was a tightly kept secret from one undertaker's to the next. And the discussion of money with the family at a time of grief was barely talked about above a whisper, and sometimes not at all until the bill arrived and then everyone sat up and noticed.

But we Mastersons were alone. What we did was as weird and bizarre to the rest of the world as it was natural to us. We even had our own hashtags, #KilcrossKonartists, #Deadlyliars, and my personal favourite, the more polite #UncouthUndertakers. Of course, there were also others of the opposite hue, #GiftsfromGod, #GenuineJeanie, #BlessedMastersons. There were the believers and nonbelievers. The former flocked to our door while the latter sometimes sprayed nasty messages on it, like 'SALEM,' which Dad found written on our outer gates one morning.

'Kids,' he'd fumed, as he came to retrieve the five-litre bottle of Kleenal from the utility room that we kept for such occasions. But I wasn't so sure the culprits were teenagers, although their ability to be cruel had shown no bounds when I was at school. Adults, I realised, when I became one myself, could be equally disappointing.

At the many industry conferences and gatherings that were held every year in Ireland, I'd mingle with the other funeral directors, smiling. Some smiled back, while others simply nodded and kept their distance. We Mastersons could divide a room in two as neatly and expertly as a heated knife through chocolate cake. Mostly it depressed me, but sometimes I would experiment by joining the conversation of a group of suited attendees, wondering how long it would take them to disperse. Yet even those who made their polite excuses could not help but envy our success. Because the simple fact was the bodies kept coming to our door, often travelling past theirs, across the country. There was enough belief out there in the wider Irish public to make our balance sheet healthier than most. At one stage a guy in Galway had announced he could hear the dead too. But he was rumbled when he mistook Barry, the family cat, for one of the deceased's sons. There was no one else. Just us, the father and daughter who people—by and large—treated with a grudging but often respectful tolerance.

I don't know what it had been like for my dad before I came along. I imagine it felt horribly lonely. The only one with the gift, with a wife who didn't like to talk about it. I suppose there was always Harry to share the burden.

Ted Masterson, my granddad, Dad's dad, had been the first professional funeral director in the family. He'd bought what was a simple grocery shop back in the sixties—a small building on a long strip of land that looked out on Church Street, with a large family home at the rear facing on to Water Lane. Back then the two buildings weren't joined. It was later on that Ted renovated the whole thing and a corridor was built to connect the two.

The original shop had a room on the side where the dead of the town were brought to be laid out by Mrs Simmons, the former owner, and her mother before that. The laying out was more a community service than anything else, a favour to the priest, apparently. There was no embalming then. It was a simple wash and clothe, before Mrs Simmons and the family put the dead in a rudimentary coffin and carried them across the road to Saint Xavier's Church. You couldn't get a more perfect site for an undertaker's: location being everything in this business.

When the funeral directing took off in the seventies and embalming became the very thing, Ted saw pound signs. He grasped hold of it with both hands, going to Dublin to see how it all worked, buying the machinery and giving it a go himself. Back then there were no qualifications as such—not that there's a whole heap now; you could simply do it by having a few training sessions with whoever was willing to share their knowledge. In later years it was Harry who'd taken after him. The gender breakdown in undertaking still weighs heavily toward men, which is odd given women were the carers of family and neighbours, washing and laying them out for centuries, long before science and money and testosterone ever got their hands on it.

Dad, on the other hand, didn't want to be on the embalming side of things, was more into the arranging of the ceremony, the talking to the family, the priests, the grave diggers—the assurer that all would be OK in his careful hands. As the story goes, he began to talk to the dead soon after Ted had bought the place, when the first body was laid out on the table in that small side room.

Their mother Jean, my grandmother, after whom I was named, had a touch of it, Harry told me when I was younger. Harry was the keeper of our Masterson history.

'She'd stop what she was doing, perhaps the washing up at the kitchen sink in our house on Tryell Street, before we had the undertaker's, and she'd say nothing for a moment, her hand held out to stop me and Dave making a racket, like she was listening to something. And then she'd say: "Someone's died." And Dad, your granddad, if he was there, would say, "Well of course someone's died, sure someone dies every second." "No," she'd say, resuming what she was doing, "someone close." And sure enough, within the next hour, the news would've spread through the town, a knock coming to the door, to tell us a neighbour or a cousin had gone. And your granddad Ted would look at her then and smile. I like to think he bought this place for her, because he knew she had some sixth sense. But she died not long after he took out the mortgage on this place in a car accident. The morning it happened, I often wonder if she'd had a premonition of her own death.'

Those moments remain my favourite memories of working in that place: just me and Harry and her stories and the dead. Simple times, when nothing was expected of me: no lying, no burden of the truth, no guilt; when I was free to say what I liked when I liked.

Chapter 8

I sat in the passenger seat of the hearse as Niall drove Bernadette the short distance to the church for the removal that evening. Dressed in our black woollen coats, we followed the fishtails of Dad's suit as they pistoned ahead of us, with Helen and the small community of Rathdrum behind, to the open doors of Saint Xavier's and to Father Dempsey, who stood waiting to welcome her in. We never spoke at these times beyond the instructions of work colleagues, in case the mourners behind thought we were having a chat rather than concentrating on the job in hand. Every move we made, every word uttered in those hours of work was solely about them and their loved ones. We were silent and solemn, focused so hard on them that they would never guess we had private thoughts at all.

Walking slowly to the side of the hearse was Arthur, his post office uniform now changed to his black suit, ready to assist in the placing of the coffin on to its trolley when we arrived.

The journey from Masterson Funeral Directors through the gates of Saint Xavier's Church, up its tarmacadamed driveway to the large wooden front doors, took no more than two minutes at a fast pace, five at the slow march of a cortege. My father loved nothing more than the moment he placed his top hat under his right arm and walked slowly in front of the hearse as it trickled behind him, with the mourners in procession to its rear. This was his defining moment, when he stood at the helm, the thing he loved most in this business, far more than hearing from those who were now quiet.

Bernadette was to repose in the church overnight, awaiting the Mass and burial the next day. After the short ceremony of prayers and blessings and condolences, there was little for us to do except drive the hearse back across the road. As Niall started the engine, Arthur came up alongside to tap Niall's window, indicating the gates that it was his custom to open and close. Niall nodded, then pulled out on to Church Street, ready to reverse. I watched Arthur push back the two solid iron masses and wait as Niall parked in the yard.

'We should employ you,' Niall joked, getting out of the hearse and checking his pockets to make sure he'd left nothing inside. 'Are you coming in, Arthur?'

'No. I'll get home to Teresa.' He'd already begun to leave but I called him back.

'Any sign of that pen?'

'Divil a bit.' He threw his eyes to heaven and

shook his head sadly, a man defeated in his recovery of a thing that defined him as much as his sense of humour, his postal route and his beloved garden.

Mikey worked for us sometimes, but these occasions were rare, and usually a clear indication of our desperation. Like when we realised there weren't any relatives, except Helen, to carry Bernadette's coffin down the aisle at the funeral Mass the next day. She opted instead for the four of us, Harry, Niall, Mikey and me, rather than trying to figure out which neighbours might do it, causing offence if she chose the wrong ones. We four stood each side of Bernadette, with three of us pushing her on the trolley rather than carrying her aloft, given Mikey's refusal to touch anything.

Mikey hated the dead. They were the reason he'd moved out of the house. He said living in a space not connected in any way to them, not by one brick or corridor, would make him happier. The fact that the only space that could accommodate his state-of-the-art shed was within inches of the outer wall of the viewing room seemed to cause no issue: the gap between was all he needed to put his mind at rest.

Mikey was the opposite to me when he was small, wanting nothing to do with the business, avoiding the embalming room totally, refusing to go down the corridor that connected the family side to the funeral home, unless he was carried and even then he would scream.

'Mother of divine,' Mum often said as she tried to control Mikey's flailing arms and kicking legs while en route to talk to Dad about something. I'd look up at my brother in her arms, amazed that he could think anything was yucky beyond those doors. Mum would simply give up and tell me to go get Dad. Whenever Mikey did have to go into the embalming room, he'd find my sleeve, not my arm but the cuff of my sleeve, holding it between his index finger and thumb so that the material stretched. He never let go as he followed his baby sister who constantly told him, 'It'll be OK' and, 'We won't be long,' until at last I'd bring him back to the safety of the kitchen.

The only reason Mikey ever agreed to work with us was so that he had some extra cash for the special offers that fell outside his yearly subscription deal with Osman's military history publisher, which Dad paid for. The fee was quite high, and every year it made Dad huff and puff around the kitchen, as if learning for the first time of their swindle. Mum would tell him to relax, that no price could be put on the happiness it brought their son. Mikey knew the undertaking drill well. He was the perfect, if reluctant, occasional worker, doing it in silence and solemnity, knowing exactly what was needed.

• • •

After Bernadette's burial out in Ballyshane Cemetery, Mikey and I walked to the van. I'd traded places with Harry, asking would she mind going in the hearse with Niall so that I could have a few minutes with my brother. Throughout our lives together there'd been so many moments where I'd have really liked to reach out and touch him; a simple spontaneous tap to his arm, perhaps, or—when smaller—a jovial sibling embrace, maybe, that could morph from hug to neck-hold or severe head-rubbing in an instant. And now that we were older it could've been an arm link, a lean into his shoulder on this quiet pathway to the van, with the mourners gone and no one but us, the gravesides, the birdsong, and the burden of this retirement ahead that would separate us for the first time in thirty-two years. But none of these things was possible with Mikey. If touching were involved then there needed to be a request, followed by a negotiation of exactly where and how much pressure you might wish to apply and for how long. Instead we walked at a safe distance to the van, then pulled out on to the main Kilcross road, long after the crowds had dispersed.

'So this thing about Baltimore, you're happy with moving down there, then?' I asked.

'Oh yes. But it doesn't mean I'm not putting up my new shelves, in case that's what you're thinking, Jeanie.'

'I know. I'm not saying that. No one minds what you build. It's totally your place,' I laughed to ease his anxiety.

'Dad says I can have the games room in the new house for all of my things. Do you remember the games room, Jeanie?'

'Yep. How could I forget the many times I beat you at table tennis,' I teased.

'No. You see, there you go again telling lies, Jeanie. I beat *you*. And I have the medals to prove it.'

On holidays, Mikey and I would have our annual Table Tennis Tournament or 'Triple T' as he called it. The holiday home, soon to be Dad and Mum's new house, had a games room with shelves full of jigsaws and battered boxes of Cluedo and Mouse Trap, with one massive table-tennis table right in the middle. We had no idea of the rules of table tennis but we were big Wimbledon fans at the time so we played according to the male tennis rules, our sporting lives not tolerating any kind of gender discrimination. One match could last the entire week we were down there, with Mikey keeping meticulous score. The winner was given a medal paid for by Dad and a dinner of the vanquisher's choice from the many great restaurants in the village, paid for by Mum. Invariably Mikey won. Mikey chose not to eat in O'Driscoll's where they served the best chips, or The Blue Nile where the burger juices dribbled down on to our clothes causing Mum to have hysterics, or Tanta's, where the pizzas had the perfect, thinnest base. He chose the crêpe stand at the harbour wall. There all four of us sat eating pancakes for dinner, our feet dangling above the water, laughing, totally happy with our lives.

'Are you going to miss me then?' I asked.

Mikey's left hand took hold of his right thumb and there he rubbed at the skin, as he always did when emotions were mentioned.

'Yes,' he answered, turning to look out of his window at three cows whose heads poked out above the hedge of a field near the roundabout. 'And Niall. And Arthur. But we'll be home every now and again. Dad promised.' He nodded to himself and, I suppose, the cows. 'I'm thinking I could separate out my entire collection.' We were now back on the solid ground of warfare, so he looked back to the windscreen and the thumb-rubbing subsided, although he still held on to it in case of another lapse. 'I could have different periods of history for different houses. I could maybe look to some other suppliers to help expand the collection. Beauford's are supposed to be good, too. Colm uses them all of the time. But I'm not sure if I'm quite able for it.'

Colm was Mikey's online buddy, fellow collector of all things military history and player of PS4 games that always involved a medieval thrashing. Colm and Mikey had never actually met and showed no inclination to do so. For Mikey, the online world, devoid of social interaction, was a blessing, and my parents, unlike most, had welcomed its arrival and my brother's joy in its embrace. His world, aged fifteen, had simply changed for the better.

When I was small and became aware that Mikey had no friend who called to him like Peanut did with me, I insisted on playing in his bedroom with my toys as he played with his. We were both happy in our silent and separate companionship. With the arrival of gaming, however, it seemed he didn't need my presence so much, yet for a while I still sat there, eagerly feigning interest in this new world, as he chatted with his invisible friends, eventually giving up and leaving him to it, admitting he was just fine.

'Hmm. Sounds like it could be a hard one, all right? Still, you've plenty of time before you have to decide anything. It'll be at least six months before you're even packing up.'

'Yes. Packing. I'm not looking forward to that, Jeanie. Will Niall help? He's very good with that kind of thing. He's got a very logical mind. You'll ask him, won't you?'

'Of course, but you can ask him too.'

'Yes, but it's best if we both ask him. Then he'll know it's important.'

'OK. No problem. You know we'll do all we

can for you. And we'll make sure the heating is kept on when you aren't around, keeping out any damp, if you do decide to leave some things.'

'I may need to talk to Dad about the possibility of another subscription. I'm not sure how well he'll take it.'

I glanced across to see his hand begin to rub his thumb again.

'Now, Mikey, what have I always told you about these things?' I grinned.

'Ah yes. "If there's money to be spent, never ever go to Dad first, go to Mum instead." ' He gave a little chuckle.

'I'm going to miss you, Mikey. It won't be the same without you. I think it will be very lonely.' I hadn't meant to land him right back in feelings, but it simply came out before I could moderate myself. I didn't need to look to know his poor thumb was probably now bright red.

'I'm sorry, I shouldn't have said that. I mean, after all, it's not going to be that bad. I'll still have Niall, and Harry.'

'And Arthur,' he added.

'Yes,' I said, 'and Arthur.'

By the time we'd got back and Mikey had closed his shed door, there'd been another call. Niall was already out of his suit and back into his civvies, one arm in the sleeve of his jacket and his car keys in his hand when I walked in.

'Who is it?' I asked.

'Timothy Lennon.'

'Tiny? Great. I'll never hear the end of this one.' Niall looked at me quizzically. 'He made it back on to Arthur's list again this weekend.'

'Ah.'

'Do you want me to go with you?'

'No. I'm not going.' Both arms were in his jacket now and he was shaking his left one trying to get his inner sleeve down. 'David's taking this one. Harry and he are fine on their own.'

'So where are you going?'

'I was waiting for you. We're getting out of here.' Niall had given up hoping his sleeve would sort itself. His right hand now searched out the reluctant left garment and with one yank settled the problem.

'We are? Why?'

'We need to get out of here. Talk this retirement situation through.'

There were few times I ever recalled when Niall had a look of such determination, one that was not for turning.

'Right, well, can I change out of these?'

'OK, but don't be long. I'll be in the car.'

Chapter 9

Compared to primary, secondary school seemed a bit easier, there being more power in a gang of four. We were like the insulation on a hot-press boiler, impervious. We protected each other from what the rest had to say about us. It allowed us to grow thicker skins or become deaf to their continued taunts. My peers hadn't changed or matured as quickly as I'd have liked, still as willing to offer their witty opinions on my life as much as ever.

'Here, Morticia, do you do any séances?'

I let their witticisms wash over me, as if they'd never been uttered. Kept walking with the others by my side, not even turning my head. But when they mentioned Mikey: 'That brother of yours is a nut job, d'ya know that?' I'd turn my five-foot-twoness right into their path and tell them to: 'Say it a-fucking-gain.'

But they'd just laugh and walk around me and Peanut and Ruth and Niall, who held me back from getting myself into something I'd not be able to get out of.

For primary, Mikey had attended a special school, but his above-average intelligence meant that my parents were advised to move him to mainstream for secondary. He was two years ahead of me in the Community College by the time I arrived.

Every day I'd find him at lunchtime to see how he was doing. He had a special needs assistant part of the time, but on lunch breaks he was on his own. So we'd spend that time together, me making sure he'd eaten, because sometimes if they'd had a particularly interesting History class, he'd still be reading his book and forget that he was hungry. Or I'd check if he needed help to get his afternoon books ready.

The others knew to find me there. It was Niall who would engage Mikey the most, talking about the latest PlayStation releases. Sometimes, if Niall and I were in different classes before lunch, I'd arrive to find him already there, deep in conversation with my brother, and I would hang back waiting, watching this budding friendship. And I would smile. Niall might notice me then and blush and grin before turning back to whatever it was Mikey was saying, as I carried out my purpose, my checking of Mikey's bag to retrieve his lunch box to put it under his nose.

'Visiting your weirdo brother, Dorothy?' That was Damien Rath, an asshole in our year. In third year he'd started to call me Dorothy from *The Wizard of Oz*. I didn't bother to ask why her and not the Wicked Witch of the West, which I would've thought he'd have considered more appropriate. This day he'd fallen in behind the four of us as the bell rang and I'd waved goodbye to Mikey.

'Shut it, Rath.' I'll never know what it was that made Niall decide to take him on that day. My head swung around to look at him as I wondered why he hadn't just adopted our usual policy of ignoring Damien, when we all knew it was best to let him blab on in the hope he'd run out of steam and walk away.

'It's none of your fucking business, Longley. I was talking to her.'

Niall dropped his head in exasperation and turned into Damien's path.

'It is when you insult a friend of mine.'

'Oooh. Big man, aren't you, Nialler?' A grin spread across Damien's broad cheeks and his eyes widened as he began to point enthusiastically at Niall. 'You fancy the freak's sister, don't you?'

'You're such a dickhead.'

'I'm right, amn't I? It'll make a nice change for her, I suppose, shagging someone who's actually alive.'

Niall raised his fist to punch Damien, but Ruth caught his arm just in time. Damien continued with his pointing and laughing as he moved on past.

'Asshole,' Ruth called after him as he flicked her the finger and she released Niall's arm.

'Thanks,' I said to Niall, who shrugged his

embarrassment away and strode on ahead of me into room C12.

We hung out in my house mostly. With Mikey pretty much permanently in his bedroom, and my folks at work, it was as if I was an only child with a free gaff. In later years we snuck in alcohol or stole it from my father's drinks cabinet but, up to third year, we just lay about in our sitting-room, eating sugary stuff that fourteen year olds really shouldn't be touching and discussing our limited worlds. It was perfect.

Mostly we discussed the people in our class. Or teachers, they were big on the agenda. Each piece of interesting information we possessed, gleaned from earwigging the conversation of others, we tortured and dissected from every angle, until we had squeezed all of its worth, and when that ran out we talked about Peanut's latest animal obsession or Ruth's newest hair-style that I hoped she might demonstrate on me. Of us all, Niall seemed more reticent about sharing his news, which was mostly to do with his Gaelic football and soccer. We very nearly missed that he'd scored the winning goal of the county finals, only I'd seen something in him that Friday evening, a lightness, an easy laughter that made me suspect something had happened. When I eventually found out I drew him the most ridiculous congratulations card with a shamrock and a football. Art was never my strong point.

But Niall was never reluctant when it came to talking about us Mastersons. If it was just the two of us hanging out, he'd ask for a tour of the undertakers'. I'd oblige if there was no one, living or dead, around. I'd walk the viewing room or show him the range of coffins in our display room, or trail my fingers along my father's desk, telling him who we'd prepared that week and what they'd said.

'I don't get it, Niall,' I challenged him one day, as I sat on the chair in the embalming room where the clothes of the dead usually sat awaiting their donning. I think we were fifteen by then. I'd been working part-time with Dad for about a year. An official employee earning an actual wage, no longer just an enthusiastic volunteer. Training me in, he said, for when I could come to work full-time after I'd left school. 'No one who isn't reared in this business is ever *that* interested. I mean, yeah, they all want to hear the creepy stories, but this curiosity is a bit unusual. Maybe I should tell Damien Rath that you're the freak and not me,' I joked.

'I can't explain it really. It just fascinates me. *You* fascinate me.' Niall was looking at the embalming fluid, his back to me, with two hands on the knobs of the open cupboard doors, not yet having realised exactly what he'd said. Until he did, then he closed them quickly and turned. 'I mean, what you do, talking to dead people and all, *that* fascinates me.'

It was the first time I remember feeling it, that little internal leap. We all used the language of 'fancying' people, at least Ruth did quite a bit, but to that point I had never experienced it, or been on the receiving end of it. It felt nice that someone, if my instinct was completely correct here, saw something other than death in me. I smiled at the compliment for a second then pulled my lips in tight between my teeth. Niall and I grew silent, our cheeks ablaze in our shared embarrassment.

'What does it really feel like?' he asked eventually, coming over to lean against the embalming table. 'You know, talking to them.'

And even though we'd had this conversation before, in that moment it felt as different as if it was our first.

'Well, as I've always said, it's not scary. It feels as natural as talking to you now.'

'Except they're dead.'

'Yes. But I like it, most of the time. Sometimes I get it totally wrong, though, what to say to them.'

'What do you mean?'

I shifted in my chair, unsure of talking about this stuff with anyone other than Dad, and yet with Niall, I had to remind myself, it always felt safe.

'Well, like about a month ago, a man called John Kavanagh was here and he asked me to tell his brother Noel that he had willed his part of the farm to their nephew Eamon because he was a far better farmer than Noel would ever be. I don't know what had happened between the pair of them to make him do that or why he chose to tell me, a fifteen-year-old, but I didn't have time to ask and neither would I have, 'cause that's not my job, to solve my own curiosity. It's about them, not me, or even their family, although Dad doesn't agree with me on that, he says it's best to always keep the living happy.'

'You see that there, that's what fascinates me.' Niall was pointing at me now animatedly. 'When you say stuff like that it's flippin amazing. Even when we were little, you were like so . . . I dunno . . . deep. I wish those assholes in school could hear you.'

'Yeah right. They'd think I was an even bigger tit.'

'What did you say to the brother?'

'I shouldn't really be talking to you about this stuff, Dad'd kill me, but you see, I don't like that he says we should sometimes fudge. Not always tell it like it is.'

At the time I was beginning to question the rules, as all fifteen-year-olds should. This 'lying when needed to' policy that Dad had didn't seem fair. All it was doing was protecting us and surely that, I argued over the dinner table for what seemed like every night that year, was not what we were about. Mum refused to get caught up in our debates when I'd looked to her for back-up. 'I'm staying out of it,' she'd say, like a woman who had long since tried and failed to get her point heard.

'Anyway,' I continued with Niall, 'Dad was standing out of earshot so I thought this was my chance to prove to him that lying wasn't the best policy. So I told Noel. Turned to him and said, the farm is going to the nephew. "John says Eamon is a better farmer than you'll ever be," John's exact words.'

'Fuck off?'

'I know, right. My toes were like curling in my shoes and I was shaking, but I was so determined to do it. And Noel, who was like this huge guy with arms and legs as wide as that door, got so red in the face. I was sure he was going to lose it. Dad came running over and stood right in front of me in case he did.'

'Jesus, so what did he do?'

'He cried. Just crumbled to the chair and was inconsolable. I felt so bad, like I was the one who'd said it, which in a way I guess I had. He couldn't speak for ages, just sat there with his massive shovel hands over his eyes. And then he got up and left, didn't look back, didn't go to the funeral the next day even. They found him two days later at the farm. Drunk, threatening to shoot himself.'

'Christ.'

'I was devastated when I heard. I wanted to go over there, to say I was sorry but Dad said no, to leave it. It's like impossible this job. You're fucked if you do and fucked if you don't— someone gets let down either way.'

'Was your dad bulling with you?'

'Well, he was a bit at first. But later on he just said he was long enough in this game to know that the living didn't need to know everything. Although, in this case, he admitted that Noel was going to find out either way, and really that was his point, I hadn't needed to put myself through all of that upset when the solicitor would tell Noel soon enough. He just hugged me and said, I'd find my way with it all, like he had in time.'

My fingers slid in and out of each other as I considered the devastation I had caused. Mum had been upset too. From my bedroom I'd heard my parents' door close at least twice that week, behind which her voice rose and fell in anger and exasperation at my father for exposing me to all of this. I'd even missed a day of school.

'You're like the bravest person I know.'

'Really?' My nose wrinkled at such a big, and I was sure, ridiculous statement.

'Really.' He nodded then looked away again, leaving us back where we'd started—in embarrassment. It felt as though he was toying with something else he wanted to say. I crossed my legs to brace myself for a confession of something deeper and more personal. Only what came wasn't exactly what I'd been expecting.

'Do you think, maybe someday, I could be here when it happens?'

'Be here when what happens?'

'When someone dies and you talk to them.'

'Oh . . . well it's not exactly something you can fit into a calendar. They don't always die when you want them to. And anyway, Dad and Harry are very protective of this space and of the clients. If they knew we were even in here they'd kill me.'

'But what if I want to be an embalmer like Harry. Do you think they'd mind then? Wouldn't it kind of be like training?'

'You want to be an embalmer?' I asked, shocked, instantly becoming like one of those disbelievers who normally turned their opened mouths at me.

'Yeah, why not?'

'Because you will endure a lifetime of slagging at the hands of ignorant people, that's why not. At least I have to do it. You don't. You could be anything you want. Miss McEntee says you're the best in the class at Tech Graphics. "An engineer's brain," she said.'

'Yeah, maybe but . . . I dunno. It's just I like

this place.' He lifted his right hand slightly from his knee, and with an open palm gestured to the room, as he looked at the wall ahead then at the cupboard. 'It makes me feel something.'

If I'd been as brave as he had proposed not two seconds earlier, then perhaps I should have asked: This place or me?

'Do you really mean it?' I said instead. 'This isn't some kind of joke?'

'Don't you know me by now, Jeanie? I'd never mess you about like that, ever.'

'OK. Well, I'll ask so.'

'Thanks. Really, I mean it.' He looked at me sincerely as I knew he would for as long as we both could manage without withering in embarrassment, and there in that pause I began to wonder if the possibility of an 'us' might actually be OK.

Chapter 10

By the time I'd made it back down to Niall waiting in the car after Bernadette's funeral, a half-hour had passed. Irritated at my taking so long, he revved out of the gates, not even bothering to lock them behind us.

'Mikey said he'd do them.' He stared steadily ahead, ignoring my brief look back in question.

As we waited to pull out of Church Street on to the main road, Ciara Considine, the pharmacist, waved, Miles Walker from the garage on the Dublin Bridge beeped his horn, and Ursula Martin tapped on the window to ask us did we know the arrangements for Tiny yet. Sometimes I wished I was unknown in Kilcross, a blow-in. Because unless you raised your head above the parapet for, like, I don't know, winning something that obviously someone local should have, people generally didn't bother with you. You could be a nutter and the full extent of the discussion in SuperValu would have amounted to it being no surprise, given you weren't born and suckled in the place. You had a licence to be different and operate totally under the radar. And to not have to wave at anyone.

Niall drove us deep into the midlands. We

said little and I took the opportunity to close my eyes in rest. Meditating on nothing other than the absence of duty and Niall and me, letting the vestiges of his annoyance at my delay slip away.

An hour later we drove into the car park of the Woodstown Lodge, a wooden, Scandi-style, incredibly expensive hotel on Lough Inver. I looked across at Niall and smiled as we both got out of the car.

'We're booked in for lunch,' he said, 'or at least, we were. They've possibly given the table away by now.'

'How the hell did you manage that? Had you this arranged weeks ago?'

'No,' he said, looking at me over the bonnet. 'I rang them this morning and cried down the phone until they relented.' Although I knew he was being flippant, there was an edge of seriousness to his tone, as though he still wasn't over my dallying earlier, or perhaps this was something more.

'Does that actually work?'

'No,' he relented. 'They had a cancellation.'

I leaned on the roof, my head resting on my folded arms, looking at the hotel and out to the lake, where the water seemed still. But on squinting one eye and concentrating a little harder, I could see it was mildly troubled, its ripples like a twitching nerve on a temple, pulsing away to its own odd, out-of-sync beat.

'Can we just move in here?' I asked, thinking of the luxury bedrooms that I'd never been in but had often drooled over in their brochure.

Niall rounded the car to put his arm around my waist, to encourage me forward. 'Come on,' he said, 'or we'll never get to eat at this rate, let alone move in.'

'I don't deserve you,' I admitted, sitting to the white linen-covered table beside the restaurant window that ran from ceiling to floor, looking out on to the water.

'I know,' he smiled, his first genuine one of the day. The air around us feeling as if it had finally cleared of his earlier annoyance.

The waiter arrived with our menus, and some iced water that we watched him pour. He left, returning almost immediately with a basket of warmed breads and two small dishes of butter that I imagined had been churned that very morning out back.

'It'll be OK, you know, Jeanie, this thing with the retirement,' Niall said, giving me a sympathetic smile as the butter melted into his cut roll.

'Yes, everyone keeps saying.' It came out more sarcastically than I'd meant, causing the air to pollute again, driving us back a step to that place in which he was unsure of me once more. The thing was, we were not strangers to such shaky ground. This shift between consideration of, and frustration with, the other, had arrived and disappeared in a matter of seconds for years now.

'But don't you see, Jeanie,' he said, giving a small laugh of disbelief, 'this is our opportunity to finally have our lives the way we want them. This isn't just about the business, it's about us. A home that's ours alone, not to mention the time and space to feel our way through things without worrying if people are listening at doors. Not that your folks are like that.' His hand shot out to underline he meant no offence. 'It feels like it might be exactly what we need right now. In fact, we couldn't have asked for a better time, don't you think?'

Isn't it amazing how two people can feel so differently about the same thing? Me seeing this impending change as a negative; Niall with his proverbial full glass overflowing.

'I suppose . . .' I managed a small, guilt-ridden smile, and looked down at my hands, which only moments ago had chosen a tomato and fennel roll that I no longer felt any enthusiasm for. 'I hadn't thought of it like that.'

'You need to just have faith, Jeanie, in yourself and in us that we can do this. If we can open up and be honest with each other, this could be our new chapter.'

'You must think I'm the most ungrateful woman to walk this earth. Here we are being handed a house and a business and I'm, like, stamping my feet.'

'You're not stamping your feet.'

'Well I'm not overjoyed.'

'No, but I get it, I know what the place does to you. I know you love it, but it takes its toll. Just because you love a job doesn't mean it isn't a burden either. You think Obama woke up every day thinking, "I'm so glad I'm president of America." '

'I'm hardly the president of America.'

'Well, then, how about this: you love me but it doesn't mean you love me every minute of the day.'

It was a harmless analogy. Nothing suspicious really, on the face of it. And yet there was no cheeky smile accompanying it, only a man unsure of the totality of my love. He sipped at his still water, his eyes flitting to mine for a second before they followed the glass back down to the tablecloth, to watch his hand manoeuvre it until it found the perfect spot. Was that it, I wondered? Was this trip actually about who *we* were and not about the business at all?

The waiter arrived to take our order. We'd hardly looked at the menu but we made our choices nevertheless. We smiled our smiles, answered his questions about how we would like our tuna and steak cooked. On his departure, we were left with a moment's silence in which I wasn't quite sure how to react to what Niall had said, or if it required an answer at all.

'Actually, can I ask you something, Jeanie?' His words pardoned me from my dilemma. I watched his forehead crease in seriousness as he concentrated on his fingers smoothing the tablecloth. 'And please be honest with me. I have to know this before we can move on and plan the road ahead.'

'OK?' I said, slowly, worried now.

'Is it us?'

Something inside me seemed to shift, dislodge. We'd discussed this before; I didn't want to go over it again, not there anyway.

'What do you mean?' I asked quietly.

'Well, we've been struggling lately, haven't we?' I could see the effort this was taking, because he still hadn't looked up; rather he continued to watch his fingers as they moved back and forth. 'And see . . .' He shifted in his seat. 'Well, I'm just wondering if what your dad and mum are doing is finally tipping the balance, making you realise that we are—or rather, *I'm*—not enough.'

He reached again for his glass of water and sipped from it, longer this time, before putting it back exactly as it was.

'But that's ridiculous, Niall,' I protested, as if nothing of the sort had ever crossed my mind.

'Is it?'

'Well, yes. I mean why would you even say that?'

'I dunno, maybe you not wanting children. Never even considering us having our own place. It's like you're keeping yourself stuck in this world you've always had, afraid to step outside of it for some unknown reason that I can only think has to do with me.' He raised a fist to his mouth, as if he might be trying to stop anything else coming out, and looked around at the other guests.

'Ah,' I said. 'The children thing again.'

'No, now don't do that, don't belittle it like it's a disagreement over how to stack a dishwasher. And anyway, there's more to this, Jeanie. I mean, seriously, why are we, four years on, still living in your parents' spare bedroom?'

'But you could fit three families in that place.'

'I get that. But it's hardly the point.'

'Look, I know you've always dreamed of a house by the sea, but I thought that was like years down the road, a holiday home, not for now. I honestly thought you were OK about us living with them. You like my family.'

'No, Jeanie, I *love* your family. And I've gone along with it because they make it easy. But when your dad said they were going and leaving it all to you, I thought, this is it, this is the start of you and me. Finally, at thirty-two, it'll be just us on our own. And no Mikey for you to worry over, either. We might even get to renovate the place the way we'd like. All of this is running through my head and then I look across at you and you looked so scared, Jeanie. Like all the bubble wrap was finally going to be pulled from around you. And I'm thinking, what the hell, is it *me?* Is she afraid of being on her own with me?'

'No, that's not . . .'

Our starters of crab pancake and marinated scallops were laid in front of us, robbing me of what was going to be another lame protestation. I don't think I even managed a smile at the waiter. But I watched him walk away to refill the wine glasses of an elderly couple at the top of the room who looked utterly besotted with each other.

'Should we get a drink?' I asked, wondering if perhaps it might help.

'What? I can't, I'm driving, but you do if you want. Do you?'

'No, not really,' I said sadly, as though here I was disappointing him again. I lifted my fork to push at the crab, then put it down again, feeling sick. Niall hadn't even picked up his cutlery yet.

'I'm getting tired of it, Jeanie. I'm getting tired of living the way you want. Of it always being on your terms.'

'Niall, I—'

'No listen,' he said, sighing now, rubbing at his forehead. 'This is my fault too. I've just accepted it. So how can you know if I haven't had the balls to say it?'

'Please, Niall, can we not—'

'So here it is, exactly what I want: children, a house by the sea—'

'I know this, Niall, I just really don't want to do this here.'

'And,' he continued, ignoring me, his fingers now counting each thing off, 'the biggest smart TV in the whole world, one that stretches the expanse of our sitting-room wall. And a dog. I want a fucking dog.' His head bowed then, in embarrassment, or hurt, I wasn't sure. 'Fuck,' he said, his fingers pinching between his eyes. 'I'm not fucking hungry now. We finally get away to this place and what do we do, argue. This wasn't supposed to go this way.'

I watched as he breathed out heavily, lowered his head. I felt guilt for his exasperation at me, at us.

'I didn't know you liked dogs,' I said quietly.

He had a look of a wasted man.

'How can you not know I like dogs? I practically drool over every one I meet.'

'No, sorry, I mean, I didn't know you wanted one.'

'Well . . . now you do.'

'What kind? If we were to get one, I mean, what kind would it be?'

'A wire-haired dachshund,' he said quietly.

'Wow, you've really thought about this.'

'I have. They're really cute.' He sipped at his water again. 'They remind me of you, small and quiet. Less hair, though.'

'Thanks.' I tried a smile but none was returned. 'We can get one, you know, a dog,' I added, desperately.

'Sure. Great.' His words, devoid of any positivity. Even if I'd produced a dog right there and then, I don't think he would have managed to raise a smile. He looked away.

'And we can do some renovations in the house. A crap consolation compared to a cottage by the sea, I know, but I'm not quite sure how we'd manage that and run a business in the midlands.'

I smiled again, hoping he'd see it, but instead he rubbed at his right eye. And I wanted to tell him to stop, to not damage it. Eyes were too precious to be rubbed with such vigour.

'Look, let's eat,' he said. 'Before you know it, we'll be back in the thick of it wishing we had this time over.' He looked out at the water then.

That might have been the last full voluntary sentence he managed that day. What came out thereafter were one-word—perhaps two-, three- at a push—answers to my attempts at salvaging the day. Conversational smokescreens that veered as far away from 'us' as possible, focusing instead on other people's lives, on the local soccer league, even the weather forecast;

leaving our problems for another day, a day when we might perhaps be more able, more ready with the right answers, more sure of our solidity, a day that, as I scrambled for things to say, I didn't realise would not be that far off.

Chapter 11

In the summer of 2003, aged sixteen, Niall became Harry's weekend assistant. Dad couldn't have been happier. He'd liked Niall from the first minute he'd stepped into our house—a young man who'd shown nothing but respect for our work, a rarity. But it was his care of Mikey that sealed the bond. When Peanut, Ruth and I were in the front room chatting, Niall would often wander off up to Mikey's room to play FIFA, a game Mikey hadn't particularly liked but had gotten anyway because Niall had. There was no greater or kinder person in my mother's eyes than our new assistant embalmer.

We returned to school two weeks later as fifth years. Mikey was now finished with his education, hearing no talk of college, happy to live a protected life at home in his bedroom while Niall and I walked those corridors together as workmates, carers of the dead, with our heads held high. We were still only friends, and although we'd shared more looks across the embalming table, our moment had yet to come. When word got out that Niall was now working for us, he let the slaggings wash over him as if nothing had been uttered at all. Such composure garnered attention. That and the summer's worth of stretching and sculpting he'd undergone. No longer of average height and chubby cheeks, this six-foot man with carved features made heads turn. The whispered words of 'ride' and 'fit' followed him down corridors. Peanut, Ruth and I agreed that Niall was like our good-looking big brother who everyone wanted to be with. I laughed too, but not for as long as they did.

But then there came a new arrival.

'Fionn Cassin, photographer,' his voice said, with all the confidence of an adult, as he stretched his hand out to mine in introduction in the fifth-year locker room one day.

'Oh. Hi,' I replied, pushing the books I was trying to sort back into my locker and shaking his hand. Biology and Geography, my next two classes, no longer my immediate concern. Instead I wondered about the spot on my chin and how my concealer was faring at banishing it from view, and if the collar of my shirt was sitting straight and not, as was the left side's wont, curling under the warmth of my jumper as if suffering from a constant chill. 'I'm Jeanie. Jeanie Masterson.'

He told me weeks later that he'd pushed through the crowd, not caring that everyone looked back at him, this stranger, with disdain, to reach me. I tried to find it in the mirror of my wardrobe, this thing that had drawn him to me. But the girl that stared back, petite, fine-featured, fair-skinned, my mother's summation for our shared 'good looks,' as she put it, was all I could see.

Niall had been standing beside me at the lockers, eyeing Fionn with suspicion.

'Niall Longley,' he said, putting out his hand, breaking up our moment of mutual appreciation.

'Longley? There's a poet by the name of Longley. Any relation?' Fionn's eyes hadn't moved from mine. His Dublin accent, which normally made rural Ireland seethe with bitterness at always having to play second fiddle to the wants and desires of the metropolis, sounded like an addictive, melodic riff that I couldn't get enough of.

'No,' Niall laughed, like this lad was some class of Dublin twat. 'No poets in our lot. We're more into the football than the words.'

'Pity. I rather like poets.' It was only then that Fionn turned to shake Niall's hand.

God, but Fionn was gorgeous, with his wolf eyes, and lopsided smile that showed off his slanting left incisor, his black hair long enough that every now and again he'd blow out the side of his mouth to lift it from his eyes. Not classically handsome but with an edge, more assured than dangerous, and yet I could detect a tiny chink of vulnerability that made my heart fret and want to tell him there was no need to worry, that we would mind him now.

Peanut and Ruth arrived then to observe this unusual specimen. Welcoming him, they asked why the hell he'd ended up in Kilcross of all places.

'Why not?' he laughed in happiness. 'Amn't I glad I did? I mean, what a welcoming committee.' He gestured to us all, his eyes lingering a split second longer on me.

From that day on, Peanut, Ruth and I became Fionn's self-appointed guides to the school, pointing out who he needed to avoid, which teachers he shouldn't mess with and which chippers did the best lunchtime deals. We got to know as much about him as he allowed but, on the issue of leaving Dublin, he was more circumspect than we'd have liked.

I knew Peanut liked Fionn from the off. But I wasn't sure if she was 'into him.' Had she been I would've stepped aside. I owed her that at least for her years of brave protection. I asked her straight out when Fionn wasn't even a week in the school as we walked up the Dublin Road to her house one afternoon.

'Oh no, I like him,' she protested, 'but not that way. That floppy hair reminds me too much of Fred.' Fred was Peanut's older brother, whose actual name was Tom, but her father, true to form, nicknamed him Fred because he reminded him of the overconfident star of *The Flintstones*.

Fred was the lead singer in a band called Damage that was going to be big, apparently, according to Fred. Over the years we sometimes went to their gigs in the back of Fitzer's pub until they broke up over the mic stand that Fred insisted on swinging around the stage when performing, eventually breaking the bass player's arm.

Peanut saw Fionn as a kindred soul, as she'd once considered me—a believer in life beyond Kilcross. Since first year she had been stuck with three people who saw their lives exactly where they'd always been. Fionn was a new ally in her quest for freedom and her determination to convince me that my fate, or indeed my gift, didn't mean I had to stay.

'And he's going to London,' Peanut continued. 'He's got it all mapped out, which college he wants and everything.'

'But that's the bit I still don't get, Pea, why move to Kilcross? London's the total opposite direction.'

'I reckon it was his parents.'

Al and Jess. That's what Fionn called them. Not even 'Ma and Da,' as we always assumed Dublin children did. (Mum grew to hate that he called his parents by their first names—it was so very Dublin, had that *Irish Times* hippy liberalism written all over it.) They'd moved to the country, Drumsnough to be exact, a small rural gathering of houses about five kilometres outside Kilcross, because they needed to feel the air on their skin, Fionn explained. Al was a graphic designer who could work from home and Jess was a community development worker who commuted to the city by train.

'I think I'll go to London too,' Peanut said. 'After I've finished in UCD, that is. They're bound to need a vet like me over there. You should come too. We three could all share a flat together. It'd be great.'

'You should mention that to Fionn tomorrow. He won't think you're mad at all, given we've known him, what, all of five minutes.'

'Yeah, maybe I'll save that wonderful suggestion for another time. Perhaps after you've gotten married.'

'What? I've just met the guy.'

'Oh come on. The way you go all silent around him is a big giveaway.'

'I do not,' I blushed and laughed, clearly confirming that she had indeed found me out.

But Peanut didn't smile as widely as I had thought she might.

'So what about, Niall, Jeanie? I thought you two were, you know, "on the verge." Have you lost interest then?'

Suddenly weighed down by my guilt, I stopped walking and sighed heavily.

'I . . . I dunno, Pea. It's just since Fionn . . . I guess I kind of see now what they mean about "you instantly know." Oh God, I don't know what to do. I mean Fionn mightn't even like me, and meanwhile I'm going to break Niall's heart.'

And it was already starting. Fionn had brought in some of his pictures to show us. One of an old man looking out of a window in a room over a shop, making me feel lonelier than I ever imagined I could over someone I'd never even met. A black-and-white toy abandoned on a park bench, the owner long gone, perhaps crying copious tears somewhere over its loss. And a girl standing, reading at a bus stop, while people swerved around her to avoid a collision. To someone else witnessing that scene that day, perhaps they might only have registered the bustle around her, but not Fionn, he had captured the beauty of her stillness.

'Wow,' I'd said to Niall as we walked to English class after. 'He's like, so talented.'

'I never knew you liked photography, Jeanie.'

'Oh yeah, Dad is a bit of an amateur. You know the pictures in the hallway above the pews—the swan on the canal and the woman and child walking up Mary Street—he took all of them. Lives caught in a quick second. It takes great skill.'

'I've never thought much about it. Maybe I'll look some up.'

I knew he desperately wanted me to look at him, so that I could see him, really see him like

I had before, but I couldn't. Not now that I had met Fionn.

'Sure,' I'd said, avoiding his stare, allowing the distraction of the throng of fifth years trying to push into room A23, against a stream of second years trying to get out, be my excuse for silence.

Peanut bent her head in concentration, searching for some answer in the pavement.

'Well, you can't help what you feel,' she said after a second or two. 'It's not like you can force yourself into liking someone out of guilt,' she consoled, linking my arm then and pulling me on. 'Niall will be OK. Me and Ruth will look out for him. And besides, half the girls want to go out with him now, so it's not like he's going to be lonely. And I wouldn't worry about Fionn, either. Have you seen the way he looks at you? You'd be good together, actually. Both creatives.'

'I'm not creative.'

'I beg to differ. Your shortbread is to die for. And besides, you are gifted beyond the norm so that qualifies.' She paused for a second before continuing, her tone becoming even more serious, 'I still just don't understand why you don't want to get out of here, away from all the shit you deal with. The constant looks and stares day in day out. I worry about you, Jeanie.'

'I'm fine.'

'You don't have to stay to work with your folks. You do know that, don't you?'

I said nothing. My dad simply could not wait for me to work full-time in the business when I left school. I had no one to blame but myself, of course. My years of insatiable enthusiasm for the place had convinced us all that there was no question about what it was I would do with my life. But that was long before I fully understood how hard this work could be.

'A third string to our bow,' Dad'd say. 'No longer two and a bit when you aren't busy with your homework. We've been waiting for you all this time, Jeanie. A true family business.'

'Oh, leave the poor girl alone,' Mum would say, touching my shoulder if I was close by.

Mostly I knew that's what I wanted but sometimes I wondered. How far Dad and I had travelled from that open-minded father who'd once said I could be anything I wanted, and that little girl who only ever desired to be in the embalming room. And since Niall had joined us, Dad couldn't be contained for how perfect our lives would be, thinking himself hilarious at the dinner table when he pronounced what a relief it was that he didn't have to pay a matchmaker when I'd brought the perfect man to our door all by myself. Mum laughed at that, actually, delighted by the thought, given her adoration of Niall, while I raised my eyes to heaven.

'I see how hard it is for you, Jeanie,' Peanut continued, as my step slowed again at her words. 'The responsibility you feel. And it's this town too. It's too small, everyone knowing your business. That would do anyone's head in. I worry sometimes that your gift is more a curse than anything. Like in London you could still work in a funeral director's but you wouldn't have to do what you do here. You could keep it a secret if you wanted.'

'But the dead would know. They'd know if I didn't help them.'

And Mikey, I'd wanted to say, what about him? I wasn't sure he'd cope with that level of upheaval if one of us left. But I kept that to myself, knowing well Peanut would say it was my life not his, and I simply didn't want to hear it. Instead, I looked across the road to the car park of a block of apartments where a girl of about eight got out of the back seat of a car and immediately did a handstand. I instantly envied the freedom of her movement, the absence of any concern for what the world thought of her as she swung her legs upward and wobbled for a second.

'Well, maybe there's something else you want to do with your life? London would be good for you. You could do anything. Imagine, no more pressure.'

I stopped on the pathway, causing a small boy who I recognised as one of the new first years in the college to step into the road to avoid colliding with us. I wondered how much he'd heard as I apologised to him.

'That's OK,' he said, with that kind of awe and delight you felt when a senior spoke to you. I watched him strain forward with the weight of the bag on his back. It threatened to topple his slight form so much that I wondered should I offer to carry it for him. But he'd moved on so fast that the moment was gone.

'I get your concern, Pea.' My attention eventually returned to her. 'I really do. But I'm perfectly fine.'

'I'm sorry, Jeanie. I worry, that's all.' She gently squeezed my shoulder. I nodded and began to walk on again. 'Back to your wedding day then. Blue would suit me best in terms of a bridesmaid's dress.'

I laughed, relieved at my reprieve and delighted by the love I felt for this girl.

'But, you know,' she said, as she linked my arm and we passed the garage, taking a right into her estate, 'you're going to have to tell Fionn well before the wedding what it is you do. And I'd suggest the sooner the better, before he hears it from someone else.'

It must've been the next day, certainly not long after, that Peanut, despite my trepidation, took the matter in hand. Peanut, Fionn and I were sitting on the ground opposite the locker area, with Peanut in the middle, our legs splayed out in front, pulling them in and out like pistons as people passed, discussing why they were still obsessed with Fionn two weeks after his arrival. Fionn had caught Jasmine Daly staring at him, again.

'It'll be a while yet,' Peanut replied, licking her yoghurt spoon then wobbling it in the air authoritatively. 'See, to the Jasmine Dalys of this world, you've got that "bad boy" thing going on.'

'Bad boy? I've never been called that before.'

'You're from Dublin, that qualifies.'

'Ah.'

'If you'd simply been a local and transferred from Saint Ciarán's and were into Chemistry like me, you'd've been yesterday's news by now. You're exotic with your photography, even if you are from Dublin. And those cheekbones.' Her spoon now pointed at his face.

'Oh.' Fionn tentatively touched those very items, checking that he did indeed have the requisite qualifications for such a title. 'Thanks, I think.'

'Oh no, you're not my kind of thing. No. I like a more swotty look, not . . .' she licked the spoon again, allowing her tongue to rest in its hollow for a second as she stared off into space, trying to ascertain just what it was that bothered her about how Fionn looked, '. . . grungy. No offence.'

Fionn laughed a little. 'Wow, you really know how to give a compliment. Actually I'd never have considered myself "grungy." I like to think my look is unique. Not that this gorgeous uniform allows for individual expression.'

'But Jeanie here, now she might feel differently.'

'Is that so?' Fionn leaned forward and looked at me with a smile.

'Don't be minding her,' I replied, totally mortified.

'Listen, pretty boy,' Peanut continued, as if I hadn't just been pinching her left thigh with the nails of my thumb and index finger, 'if I were you, I'd get in there quick. She's a woman of means, you know. She's a funeral director.'

'Ah, yes. Someone mentioned it yesterday when I was leaving.'

I closed my eyes on this news, not wanting to hear what had been said.

'Thought they'd get around to it soon enough, all right.' Peanut eyed the rest of the fifth years suspiciously. 'And what else did they have to say? Any name-calling, any rumours?'

'Nothing really. At least nothing I could make any sense of. And besides, you have me well warned, so I just gave them a polite smile and kept on my way.'

'Very wise. It's best you hear it from us so you get the full picture.'

'Now I *am* intrigued.'

'Right, well, and when I tell you this, if you ever—and I mean *ever*—give her a hard time about it, you'll have me to deal with, OK? I'm going to be a vet, so I know how to inflict damage on creatures.'

'Pea, maybe this isn't the time or place?' I looked around, hoping no one was paying us any attention, checking that Jasmine Daly had definitely left her post.

'She has a gift,' Peanut said ignoring me. 'She can talk to the dead. Just for a little bit, straight after they die. She like sorts out their problems before they pass on. Like lost wedding rings or telling their relatives that they loved them. That kind of thing.' She turned to me for confirmation but I didn't do or say anything. I stared ahead, too afraid to look at Fionn.

'So, wait. You're saying Jeanie can hear the dead?' I could only imagine Fionn's poor bewildered face.

'Pretty much. Her dad has it too. It passed down. Like a "seventh son" thing.'

'A "seventh son"?'

'Oh right, yeah. I forget you have such limited experience of the world being from Dublin.' I imagined her cheeky grin. 'So, round here, the seventh son of a seventh son can heal warts or, you know, other bodily ailments.'

'Right,' he said, sounding even more confused

than before. 'But . . . Jeanie only has one brother, and more importantly she isn't a boy.'

'No, obviously not. I'm just trying to explain that gifts get passed down around here.'

I rubbed my hand up and down the thigh of my polyester trouser leg, wanting nothing more than to run.

'And this is really true, you aren't having a laugh at the expense of the Dub here?'

'All true. Niall works there too. You can ask him.'

The bell rang and I stood up instantly, not looking at either of them. My sole intention being to get as far away as possible, I started to weave my way through the crowd, unaware of where Peanut or Fionn were now, conscious that I had no books for my next class. Toilets, that's what I wanted. To climb to the third floor, the highest point of the building, where there was a small toilet right at the end of the corridor. It was only meant for staff but I didn't care. If I could just get there, close that door, then I'd let myself breathe again.

I moved quickly, my head down, going against the tide on one stairwell, entering the flow of the next until I was there, the toilet door visible at last, a corridor's walk, or run, away. But just as the relief began to settle, a hand caught my arm, pulling me out of the rush of bodies into a small nook that led to an abandoned office.

'Are you OK, Jeanie? It took me forever to catch up with you.'

It was Fionn.

I refused to look at him, just shrugged my shoulders, half-delighted and half-scared at what might follow as I looked through the glass pane of the office door, at the lone chair and desk. A Bic biro sat beside the phone, a new addition since the last time I'd peered inside, someone bringing life to the loneliness.

He released my arm and, in my peripheral vision, I could see him relax back against the opposite wall, his eyes moving from me only briefly as he watched the last of the pupils scurry by. Doors to classrooms closed all around us before he spoke again.

'I knew from the first minute I saw you. I knew there was something about you.' His left thumb hooked on to the opening of his pocket, his fingers free to flex and release as he spoke, emphasising his words. 'You know, you have this look on your face sometimes when the others are talking and it's like, and I'm not explaining this very well, but honestly it's like you're seeing things we can't.'

'I don't see ghosts. It's not like that.' I hugged my arms around my waist as tightly as possible, my eyes dropping to the floor as I realised this boy I was already half in love with might never understand.

'No. No. That's not what I mean. See, how crap I am at this? No, it's like you have this other sense that we don't. Some telepathic, empathic, thing.' When I didn't react, he bent to find my eyes. 'It's amazing. You know that, right, don't you?'

I shrugged my shoulders again, my eyes finding the edges of him.

'Look I'm a guy who relies on senses, instincts, and here you are with this gift I could only dream of.' He shifted slightly so that his foot rose to lie flat against the wall. 'You can trust me, Jeanie. I'm not an asshole. But I am jealous.'

'You wouldn't be if you had "weirdo" painted on your locker.'

I looked down at my feet again, embarrassed at appearing so vulnerable, fearful of risking such honesty.

'That shit happens here too, then. I've had my fair share.'

I hadn't expected that. That this boy, whose confidence could only compare to my timidity by virtue of their being at opposite extremes, would have ever known what it was to be bullied.

'It wasn't just the clear air my folks wanted down here. They wanted me to have a break.' It was his turn to look away and up, considering the low ceiling directly above us, so that I had a chance to look at him, at the sweep of his jawline, at the length of his long neck, blushing at my

121

desire to reach out and touch it. 'I've just always stuck out. A kid with a camera in his hand who's not afraid to say what he thinks attracts a bit of attention. Al and Jess had to replace my camera twice in the last school.'

'Oh,' I said timidly, 'I didn't know.'

'Look, I'm not comparing it to what you've obviously gone through, but I get a bit of it. I understand.'

His smile returned to bewitch me, then he poked his head out into the corridor to check the coast was clear. 'So,' he said, when satisfied it was just us, 'how about we get out of here? Take the day off.'

'Mitch, you mean?' My stomach tumbled at the thrill and fear of breaking the rules.

'Yep. I reckon I've a lot more to hear about Jeanie Masterson.'

I dipped my head for a second, trying to hide the blushes that crept on to my cheek. 'So Peanut was right all along, you are actually a bad boy?'

'Not really. Never mitched before in my life.'

I laughed then, caught on a wave of excitement and risk I'd never felt before, I nodded my agreement. Soon we were tiptoeing down the fire-escape stairwell and out through the school's ground-floor double doors.

Chapter 12

Mitching school in a rural town was a risky business. You were spotted a mile off. At eleven in the morning, the uniform was sure to draw the attention of the many do-gooders who would feel it their duty to ring the school in concern for 'the child most of all' and nothing to do with the sense of power it gave them. Or, if it wasn't them, then it was a teacher nipping to Dunnes on a free class and spotting you, ringing the secretary to report a sighting. Sure enough, Fionn and I were seen by someone, so that later I sat across from the disappointed faces of my parents at the kitchen table, with protests of: 'This isn't like you.' 'What in God's name were you thinking?' And 'Who the hell is this Cassin person?' But I could only stare back blankly, knowing my words could never explain the convoluted depths of what I was feeling, and so I replied with a limp—and barely a note above a whisper—'I don't know.' When what I should have bombarded them with, was: 'It's *love.*'

And then there was the following day to endure, when I was called from class to explain my behaviour to the principal, with Fionn waiting for his turn outside the door, but all of it was worth it for the time I'd had with him.

We'd gone to the cinema, a midday showing of *Lilo & Stitch*. We sat amongst the noisy toddlers and their mammies, watching them tread the well-worn path to and from the toilet, and I don't think I'd ever felt so giddy in my life. Or such abandon. With no care for what anyone said. Write anything you like on my locker or on the backs of the toilet doors, I thought, I finally don't care. We laughed into our popcorn, and threw kernels at each other, swapped drinks, ate each other's sweets. Then afterwards walked our uniformed bodies triumphantly through the town, arriving at the park to stand under my willow tree.

He grew serious then, looking at the ground, the sole of his shoe rubbing at the grassy earth, making me worry that all of this joy might be about to come to an abrupt end.

'Listen,' he started, 'I don't want to tread on any toes here. I mean, I've only just gotten to this town and I don't want to be making any trouble among you and your friends, but . . .' I closed my eyes for a second to brace myself, waiting for an admission of him being into Peanut or Ruth. 'Is there something going on between you and Niall?'

I smiled, and lifted my head to the branches in relief, watching the last of its summer energy beginning to fade as autumn snuck in to take hold.

I'd like if my answer had been 'there is' or 'there might be' or perhaps a risky 'yes.' Something to have marked the truth. Some line notched into the trunk of the tree, recognising that I had not forgotten Niall so quickly. A mark of loyalty to a friend and not, as it seems now, a betrayal.

'Why?' That was my answer. One word that skipped over him, and came accompanied with a smile, the coy side of shy. And yet what else could I have done in the face of how my heart was beating out its desire for this boy whose eyes were gathering in every inch of me.

'Because I was thinking . . .' And there his words petered away as his lips broadened into a smile. With not a hint of hesitation, he took a step forward and placed one hand on the back of my neck and pulled me in. Is there a word for that feeling when lips touch for the first time? If not, there should be. One that captures the joy of handstands in car parks, the exhilaration of belting down hills on your bike, and the deliciousness of that first mouthful of beer on a scorching hot summer's day. It was magnificent, and possibly awkward and lacking in rhythm and flow, but I didn't care and I don't think he did either. We laughed when we pulled away briefly, neither of us wanting to say anything, craving instead the heat and softness of the other again.

'No,' I said finally, 'there's nothing between me and Niall.'

• • •

I had texted Peanut as soon as I'd gotten home. The next morning we walked through the school doors together, Peanut having insisted we meet so I could tell her everything. We navigated our way through the morning traffic; squashing against the walls to avoid students walking backwards relaying some story to their mates, or banging into each other when someone got pushed from the sidelines into the flow. Voices rose higher and higher, wanting to be heard over a mess of words and songs and jokes and shrieks.

I could see Fionn standing at the end of the corridor at our gang's usual meet-up spot, right beside a large window with a sill that could fit three bums at a push. As Peanut and I approached, Fionn caught my eye and grinned slightly, this soft, gentle, barely there movement of lips that drew the same from me. My mouth twisted to the side, trying to resist the urge to laugh. Peanut was saying something that I'd completely missed.

With every step closer, my cheeks burned in delight. I saw Fionn push away from the wall to take hold of my right hand, to twirl me in a graceful spin under his arm so I was tucked against him, his left hand on my waist. The perfect fit. Our eyes locked. Two seconds, no more. Enough for my body to feel as if I'd jumped in Lough Saor on the coldest day in winter— breathless in the hands of something altogether more powerful than me. He then gently pushed me back into the flow of students on the move, but the world felt as though it was at a distance, with only me and him and that moment of pure brilliance in my head.

Ruth and Niall arrived two minutes later. By then Peanut had jumped up on to the windowsill and beckoned Ruth and me to join her, while Fionn stood to my side. Ruth gestured Niall to hers and tried to engage him, but I could see his distraction as he watched me produce my father's old Walkman and a Nick Cave CD that I'd stolen from Harry, offering Fionn one of my earplugs. We replayed 'The Mercy Seat' and nodded at each other in approval of Nick's righteousness and truth.

Pea already had her head stuck in a book about frogs that she'd taken from the library the previous day. Ruth considered her recently-polished nails, having long since given up on talking to Niall, who continued to stare at Fionn and me.

'I like Ansel Adams,' Niall said, out of nowhere, forcing Fionn to take his earplug out. I closed my eyes, realising he'd actually gone off to research photography.

'Adams, really?' Fionn enthused, delighted at any opportunity to talk photography. 'He's a bit commercial for my liking but yeah, I get it. So, what is it about him that gets you?'

'I dunno. He captures something that's hard to put into words.' Niall's eyes flitted in my direction as I looked at him, wishing that he wouldn't do this, try to show me something that might make me turn my eyes away from Fionn. What did he see in my expression? I hope it was kindness and apology, not the shameful pity I felt.

'Try,' Fionn said, relishing this potential debate.

Niall hesitated and I closed my eyes, willing him not to take the bait Fionn had so unwittingly given.

'It's just the light. He's good with the light.'

'Obviously. But, like, how is he better than say what Willy Ronis did in the forties and fifties—how he captured people and what it is to be human. You know Ronis, right?'

Niall's shoulders shrugged, rapidly losing interest, while it was clear Fionn was just getting started.

'Like there is this one image, right, of a naked woman leaning over a sink in this pretty basic room, about to wash herself, and you can only see her from the back. And the room is so bare. There's one chair and little else, and when I look at it I see humanity stripped bare. Wait, I have it here somewhere.' Fionn began to search in his bag as he kept talking. 'I mean, sure, landscapes are beautiful and I get why people like Adams, but what Ronis captures is our vulnerability, which to me is the true expression of beauty. I wish I could just find it, you'd get what I'm talking about.'

'Don't worry yourself,' Niall said, clearly growing uncomfortable with what he'd started.

'Wait, maybe I left it at home.' Fionn looked up from his bag, considering the possibility. 'No, I definitely put it in here.'

As the shuffle of papers and Fionn's sighs continued, I put my hand gently on his shoulder in the hope of stopping him. 'It's grand, Fionn, leave it,' I whispered. He stopped what he was doing then and turned to kiss me. Had it not been in that moment, I would've held him there longer, imparting my desire and true longing for him. But aware of what was going on, I pulled away, unable to look at Niall to see the disappointment I could no longer help.

'Just leave it, Cassin, for fuck's sake.' Niall's outburst halted everything. Every eye in the place turned to him, except for mine. They closed on his hurt and I wished now to be back in the viewing room beside a dead soul comforting them, instead of hearing my friend suffer at my hands.

'Niall,' I managed, flexing my hands as they sat on my thighs. A quiet exclamation in the hopes that it might calm him and bring him back to the placid man we all knew him to be.

'What?' Niall looked at me. 'I told him to fucking leave it and he wouldn't.'

'I just wanted to show you,' Fionn defended, his hand still searching his bag.

And that was when Niall walked right up to him, his face inches away, to grab the bag and throw it hard against the wall.

'What the fuck, man?' Fionn was already turning to rescue his belongings but Niall caught him by the arm so both stared at each other.

'I actually don't give a shit, Cassin. You win, OK. Everything, you win it fucking all.'

And then he released him and turned away to the sharp intakes of breath and staring eyes of all the fifth years, to the rising chant of 'fight, fight, fight,' to the staff room door opening further up the corridor, and to the teachers spilling out ready to break up whatever horror was erupting.

Chapter 13

Our journey home from the Woodstown Lodge had been silent. Whatever conversation Niall and I had managed at lunch had dried up. Nothing I said could draw a thing from him beyond single-syllable answers. After we pulled into the yard he began to check his phone, as if in that fifty minutes he had missed a thousand messages and calls requiring his urgent attention.

Not wanted, it seemed, I went on in to find Arthur already in the kitchen chatting with Dad, as I knew he would be. He would've waited all day to see me and claim his winnings over Tiny Lennon's death.

'Was I right or was I right?' He beamed from across the kitchen.

From my pocket I took out the Twix that I'd stopped to buy on the way home and threw it to him. 'Thought you might be here.'

'Well, would you look at that now. Won fair and square.'

He waggled the Twix that he had caught expertly in one hand, staring at it as if it was a golden cup for which he'd been in training for years.

'I'm sure Tiny will be delighted to know how happy you are that he's finally died.'

'Ah, that was only a bit of banter, Jeanie. Tiny was a good man. I was actually fierce fond of him. And in his own way he was kind to me.'

'What did he have to say, Dad?'

'Tiny? Oh right, yes, I was just on my way down.'

'Ah, Dad, you haven't retired yet, you know. You should've gone down earlier. What if he was waiting for you and is gone now?'

'Well,' Dad began defensively, looking at Arthur then me, as if in one of our faces he might find a perfect alibi. 'Arthur popped in just as I was going down and then we got talking.'

'Ah now, this has nothing to do with me. No need to be pulling an innocent bystander into this.' Poor Arthur, stuck in the middle of us Mastersons as usual.

'I'll go,' I said, with a martyr's huff. And then felt immediately guilty, wondering if my time would be better spent with Niall, trying to rethread the stitches that had unravelled and brought us to this unexpected, frayed silence.

Behind me I heard the outer door close and Niall's slower than normal tread move up the corridor. As he pushed open the kitchen door, he put the car key into his pocket and said, 'I'm going up to the room to watch the match, Jeanie.'

If my father and Arthur hadn't been there, I

might have appealed to him immediately, but feeling constricted by their presence, I said: 'Sure, if that's what you want.'

He moved past me, hunched and sad, to open the fridge.

'How's the lads?' he managed.

'All right, Niall, you?' That was Arthur.

'Was the meal any good down there?' Dad chimed. 'I might bring Gráinne sometime, a celebration of sorts with the upcoming retirements.'

If they had felt embarrassment at our coolness, they hadn't let on.

'Yeah, it was grand.' Niall held up a bottle of beer in offering.

'No, you're fine there, thanks. We're on the hard stuff today.' Arthur lifted his mug of tea in evidence.

Normally Niall would've sat with them for a while. Perhaps he might even have gone for a pint around in McCaffrey's if they were all in the humour. But I watched him take that cold bottle and walk over to the hallway door that led to the rest of the house, his shoulders weighed down with all that was still left unsaid between us. I followed him to stand at the bottom of the stairs, catching him as he was halfway up.

'I might come up after I've talked to Tiny,' I said. 'We might, you know, chat more then.'

'Sure,' he replied, but the word felt limp, as if

I'd finally wrung every ounce of energy he had out of him.

I considered appealing to him but instead listened to his long legs take the stairs two-by-two and imagined him flinging his coat across the floor of our bedroom then lying on our bed, kicking his shoes off as loudly as possible, and clenching his jaw as he watched whoever it was play.

Dad and Arthur exchanged a look when I returned that I gracefully ignored and headed straight for the far door. 'I might go see if Tiny's still around, so,' I said quietly.

'Right you are, love. I'll be down now.' Dad's words managed to slip through the door just as it closed behind me.

Harry was finished tidying up the embalming room. The room was immaculate. Clean to the eye and fresh to the nose, exactly as Harry liked it. Her love of cleanliness and order was not only about the job. Her apartment, which many might have thought would house a collection of cats and dream-catchers and oil burners, was white and chrome and sparse, with flashes of colour brought to it through the royal blue tea towels with the print of a lime right in the middle, or the mossy green cushions on her light grey couch, which were hand woven, no doubt, in a cottage in Donegal, and stuffed with the gathered down of the family goose. She had style, had Harry.

'Hey,' I called, trying to inject as much false happiness as I could muster into my voice. She was standing over Tiny, who was already in his coffin in the viewing room.

'Oh!' She jumped back, her hand at her chest, as she turned to where I stood on the threshold. 'You're back early.'

'Indeed,' I agreed. 'Sorry to frighten you.'

'No, no, you didn't,' she protested, but she was unable to meet my eye. She left Tiny immediately and walked back across the room, patting her black bobbed hair. 'Nice lunch?'

'Gorgeous, yeah.'

'Good.' The word came out long and slowly, flowing with her final step before she reached me. Her sincerity nudged at my already vulnerable tear ducts. 'I hope it helped.'

Ah. I guessed at her discomfort. She, along with everyone else, myself included, was worried about how I was dealing with my parents' news.

'Actually, I wanted to talk to you, Jeanie,' she continued. 'It's about the future. I'm far from retirement so I plan on being around as your right-hand woman for as long as possible. I hope that's OK with you.'

'Of course it's OK with me. This isn't some hostile takeover, Harry,' I laughed. 'I couldn't do it without you.'

'Yes you could,' she said, with such warmth

that I knew if I stayed with her one second longer, I might cry.

'I should really see if this man has anything to say.' I motioned toward Tiny before heading off to Dad's office to retrieve my stool.

'I hope that father of mine at least came down to help you with putting Tiny in the coffin,' I called back to her.

'He did, of course.' Harry always the one to defend Dad.

'You think he'd've just hung on then, in case Tiny had anything to say?'

'He was going to, but Arthur called and he got distracted. Actually, I was just on my way up to get him when you arrived.'

I was back with her now, my stool in front of me.

'It feels like Dad's given up already.' My fingers idled on the white leather of the seat. 'Why do you think he's really retiring, Harry?' And there it was, this suspicion I hadn't realised even existed until it was there, out in the open, awaiting an answer.

'He's just tired. He needs a break.' But her eye didn't fully meet mine.

'Was it a shock when he told you?'

'No, not really. If there'd been a book open on when Dave Masterson might retire, I'd've possibly won a few bob.'

It was then I wondered how it had felt for her

all those years back when her father had decided it would only be his son's name on the deeds. And did she feel she was now being sidelined all over again?

'Ruth popped in a while back.' Harry not so much changed the subject as shimmied slightly left of it. 'She's interested in taking over the salon from your mother, wants the lease.' Turned out Ted had left Harry something in the will, the building next door with its hairdresser's downstairs and apartment above. Harry was my mother's landlady.

'She got you then. I'd told her to call by.' While I'd dilly-dallied getting ready that morning, Ruth'd rung me, unable to contain her excitement at the thought of finally getting her hands on Mum's salon, where she'd been working since she left school. 'We are going to be the bomb, Jeanie. You with the undertaker's, me with the hairdresser's. We could do packages. I'll do the hair of the mourners for half-price and you can do a tarot reading or something for my clients.'

'I'm not actually a fortune-teller, Ruth, and people don't tend to want to get done up like it's New Year's Eve when their husbands have died.' But nothing could contain her. She said all those men in suits would be wanting us at their big enterprise awards ceremonies. 'We'll be entrepreneurs of the year and not just the "special" award for women. We'll win it all.

137

We are going to own this town.' She'd made me laugh, which on that day really did deserve an award.

'So will you give it to her?' I asked Harry.

'Why not? I like Ruth.' She smiled. There was no aging Harry. She seemed to look the same now as when I was five years old.

'We're good, though, aren't we, Harry?' I was suddenly filled with a need for this woman's love and kindness, on this of all days. 'You don't mind that he's handing this place over to me?'

'I gave up on that dream a long time ago, darling. Not that it ever really was one. Your grandfather wasn't exactly ahead of his time. It was always going to be Dave's. And it's only right it goes to you now, you've earned it. We,' she gestured between the two of us, 'are always good, my lovely girl.' She hugged me and I clung to her. 'Right,' she said on letting go, 'as the cavalry has arrived, I shall leave you to it.' She kissed my cheek before putting a hand to her umbrella, despite it being a cloudless sky, and leaving.

I sat beside Tiny. No need for the silk inner sheet to be pulled in too far, there was nothing to hide, no blemishes, no ill-fitting clothes. Sometimes the living gave us outfits that didn't sit so well, especially if the dead had suffered a long illness. Tiny looked perfect.

'Timothy,' I called, 'are you still there?'

There was a moment's silence before his words came cracked and raw, like any voice first thing in the morning attempting to find its level.

'Is that you, David?'

'No it's Jeanie, Timothy. His daughter.'

'But I was waiting for him,' he said, annoyed.

'I can get him if you want?'

'No, no. I . . .' He sighed. 'It's too late now. I suppose I can tell you instead. But call me Tiny. My mother gave me that name the day I was born, when she saw the length of me.'

'I'm sorry. I'm never sure on nicknames.'

'No harm done.' He seemed less vexed now.

'How are you feeling, Tiny? Are you OK?'

'I've been better.' I gave a small grin at that. 'But no, I knew death was on my doorstep for a while now, so it shouldn't have surprised me when it finally came. But still there are no words to explain the awful realisation that you're not coming back. That the cup of tea you've just made yourself is never going to get drunk and that everything you've done in your life is your history now, the definition of who you are, how you'll be remembered. And it's then . . . you bloody wish you'd done things a little different.'

My hand moved to his shoulder.

'Dying is like something beyond fear. Has anyone ever said that to you before?'

'People have said so many things about—'

'It's like God Himself created a whole new emotion just for the very moment when death comes. When I was small a horse reared on me. I was only four maybe, and I could feel my body shake in fright and I had never felt so lost and alone and I thought I was a goner and all I wanted was my mammy but there was no one there. I felt an instant hollow in my heart; no, it was worse, it was a deep wide canyon of loneliness. Dying was like that, only multiplied by a hundred.'

What could I offer this man who had lost all that I still had? The guilt of my very breath caused me to swallow hard. 'I'm so sorry, Tiny.' My words as meek and useless as my extra squeeze to his shoulder.

'Still, I'm here now, this final moment with the living. Not to be wasted.'

'Is there something you stayed for, Tiny? Something you need me to do for you?'

'Yes,' he said, with a determination that, if he'd been alive, I imagine would've been accompanied by a straightening of his tie, stretching his head upward and to the side like men wearing collars sometimes do. 'There is actually. Arthur Aherne.'

Nothing followed. No qualification. His silence awaiting my question.

'Our Arthur, the postman?'

'I have something of his. His pen.'

It took a second for it to register.

'His pen?' I was at once delighted and distrustful. A confusion of d's, not knowing whether to laugh in relief or immediately demand an explanation.

'Aye.'

And then stupidly I began to wonder if perhaps Tiny might be referring to an ordinary pen, a Bic that Arthur had perhaps lent him. Although the ridiculousness of a dead man mustering the energy he needed to be heard so he could return a Bic biro did occur to me, but still I decided it best to clarify the situation.

'So you mean the silver one, the one he always has in his pocket, the one that was his mother's?'

'I know whose it was.' He paused again, as though he might be considering whether to continue. Or indeed whether I was trustworthy enough. But after a moment he relented and began. 'I took it from him, or rather from the pocket of his jacket, which he'd left on the back of the kitchen chair one of the days he called around. He'd gone off to use the toilet and I took it.'

I hadn't been expecting theft. Even before he explained, my mind had gone to Arthur dropping it from his pocket by accident and it rolling under Tiny's kitchen table, or his forgetting to take it with him after he'd used it for some reason, but not robbery.

Behind me I heard soft footsteps, a tread that didn't wish to disturb. I looked around to see Dad come into the viewing room, a finger on his lips, tiptoeing to the nearest chair. It made me happy that he was there, sharing this of all the loads I'd undertaken over the years.

'Can I ask why you took Arthur's pen, Tiny?' My question was deliberate so Dad was up to speed, his eyebrows rising at this bizarre enquiry.

'It was once mine, you see. I had bought it for myself at the age of twenty-four when I'd gotten my first impressive wage working as a travelling salesman. I was leaning up against the counter in Hickey's Hardware when in she walked, Bess Aherne. In passing me she admired it as it sat in my breast pocket. God, but she was stunning.'

Arthur often talked of his mother. She had died when he was five, so he had few memories. Sometimes he said he wasn't sure if he had actually seen her bend to him by their kitchen sink or felt her swing him high in her arms. He wondered if he'd borrowed them from his father's stories of what their little family had once been, making them his own. Arthur carried a picture of her in his breast pocket, beside another of his dad, both together along with the pen.

'I didn't know then that she was married,' Tiny continued. 'She never wore any rings, said the metal irritated her skin, not that it would've stopped me. I'd have loved her anyway—how could I not? She had some power over me that no woman before or after ever had again. I found

142

out her circumstance by accident when I saw her with him—Nathaniel.'

'Arthur's father?' I knew well the story of Nathaniel and his quiet ways. A man devoted to rearing and loving his only child after his wife had died so young. He worked in the post office, getting Arthur a job there when he was fourteen.

'That's the man. She never denied it when I asked her. Just like I could not deny that I loved her. I gave her the pen a month after we were together. A month in which she'd lain in my bed and we had loved each other. Nine months later, Arthur came along. I watched Bess raise him as Nathaniel's. She never told me outright he was mine but I knew he was, as sure as I am that it was me who took that pen three weeks ago. It's the Roman nose, we all had it: my father, his father before him and now my son.'

My head shot back to look at Dad and then shifted left, seeing through walls to the image of Arthur, sitting in the kitchen, eating his Twix, unaware that his life was being rewritten at the hands of a man who'd shut the door on him for weeks. My eyes filled but I put my hands to them, refusing my tears their release.

'The affair continued until one day she stopped coming and I was alone again. I wouldn't have known she'd died, only I read it in *The Kilcross Herald*. I'd have thought she'd just stopped loving me.'

He paused for a second, in which time I looked at his profile, trying to imagine the young man she might have fallen in love with. He was thin, Tiny, and I could see now how sculpted he would have looked. I imagined he had brown eyes, deep soulful ones that suggested secrets, or perhaps wounds that Bess might have wanted to heal.

'I stood at the back of the church on the day of her funeral and watched that man carry Arthur in his arms behind her coffin and I thought, You may as well take me now too, God. I thought my heart would just give up, but He continued to make me pay for my sins. I thought I'd have to take matters into my own hands, if you understand me. But I was so bloody weak and selfish, not thinking of that boy who was mine, so consumed was I by my own broken heart. Seventeen years I was at that, wanting to go but not having the bottle to do it by my own hand. And then one day this young man starts delivering the post and I knew it was him. He must've been in his early twenties by then. As cut off from the world as I was, I opened that door to take my letters from his hand despite having a letterbox. And every day thereafter I'd wait, watching from the window as he approached. I'd pretend I was on my way out, or checking the weather, that's how the friendship started. He'd come in for a cup of tea sometimes; even though I knew he was under pressure, I'd always ask and he never once said no. He talked about his mam and dad, Nathaniel was dead by then. He showed me the pen once, so proud that it had been left to him in the will. For forty years, give or take, I've watched that pen in his pocket, reliving the secret lives his mother and I had together, never letting on what was going on in my head.

'And then I got sick. Two years later, I was dying, with Arthur my only caller. The only one I'd let in apart from the meals-on-wheels. Oh, they tried to get me a carer but I told them to turn around and not come back. He didn't have to call, you know, he had no clue of our connection. He just knew me as the cranky old man who no one in the town particularly liked and yet he knocked on that door to make sure I was OK a couple of times a week. This one day, like I say, he gets up and goes to the toilet and leaves his jacket on the chair and I just leant over like it was the most natural thing to take the pen that she had once held, the pen that drew us together. I didn't want to see him after that. Didn't want to look my son in the eye, knowing I had stolen something precious from him, but neither did I want to give it back.'

He paused then for longer than I'd expected.

'Tiny?' I called in a panicked whisper, hoping he hadn't yet left.

'But I want you to give it back to him now.' From somewhere he had found more energy to power him on. 'And tell him I'm sorry for taking it, for lying to him. It's in my inner pocket. Take it.'

I briefly glanced at Dad again, who watched me unbutton the jacket of Tiny's suit so my left hand could reach in to feel the coldness of the pen. When I drew it out, I looked at it in my outstretched palm, the most delicate of items, closing my eyes trying to hold it together.

'I have it, Tiny.'

'Will you tell him everything?'

I automatically looked around at Dad, the man quite willing to bend the truth.

It all felt too much for me, the weight of this confession, especially that day with Niall now barely talking to me. I didn't want the strain of this truth I was now expected to tell Arthur, a man who brought me Twix bars and made me laugh, who I cared for. I didn't want to see him in pain. And yet how could I not?

'Of course,' I said, my words so quiet and reluctant that I wondered had he heard them at all.

'I've left everything to him, the house, the money. It's all his now. He'll find out eventually when the solicitor gets in touch. But I'd like him to know before he has to hear it that way. Actually, I'd like your father to tell him, that's why I was waiting for him. I know they're close. Arthur talked about him a lot.'

'Dad's here with me now. He's heard it all,' I said, in selfish relief that this burden was being lifted from my shoulders. I looked back at Dad, whose gentle smile seemed lost and bereft.

'Good,' Tiny said, a tremble to his voice, a weakening that signalled his departure. 'I think, I'll go now, if you don't mind.'

I nodded as my tears threatened to fall again. I wiped at them and waited for my breath to steady. 'Rest now, Tiny.' It came out stronger than I expected, caught on the wave of an outbreath. I touched his shoulder again and then looked at Dad.

'You will tell him, won't you?' I asked, when he came to stand beside me and I handed over the pen.

He gave a downcast nod. 'So,' he huffed in disbelief. 'What a turn-up for the books.'

'Did you have any idea about all of that?'

'Me? No.'

'Sorry, I wasn't accusing you or anything, it's just so . . .'

'Sad,' he offered. To which I nodded. It was then my headache started, its pressure thumping at my temple. 'I'm sorry you had to do it all, love, when it should've been me. It wasn't easy for you having to hear all that, especially the bit about the . . .' His hand twirled in the air as he looked at me, unable, I thought, to say the words.

'All of it was awful, really. But I just can't

147

believe Tiny said he was . . .' I broke off. My eyes winced at another stabbing pain. I massaged my head with my fingers as the walls began to close in on all I'd been told, and all that Niall had said and not said earlier. 'I think I need to get some air. But you'll tell Arthur everything like Tiny asked, won't you, Dad?' I was already heading for the double doors to the yard.

'Oh, yes. I'll tell him it was Tiny who had the pen and . . .' And there he paused for a second, as if it was all too heartbreaking to put into words '. . . and the rest,' he concluded, sadly.

I stopped at the already opened door, worrying that Dad was finding this too much and might choose instead, as he had done so many times before, to spare the living.

'Yes, but *everything,* Dad,' I pleaded, desperate for the breeze that I could now feel on my hand. 'No whitewashing. This is Arthur we're talking about, not just another client.'

He looked down at the pen, as if it had only now appeared without his knowledge.

'OK,' he said, quietly, flummoxed and afraid, I thought, for all he'd have to admit to his friend.

I closed the door behind me, smothering his last call, 'But Jeanie . . .' Yet I couldn't go back to the overpowering closeness of that room. I breathed in the air as I rushed away, holding on to my belief that this time, surely, he would tell the whole truth.

Chapter 14

Fionn and I had been going out for nearly a year when Al and Jess planted a willow tree in their garden.

'Just in time,' Jess had called brightly as we arrived one Friday evening. 'Dinner won't be long.'

Fionn had grabbed two slices of bread from the bread-bin anyway, offering one to me that I declined. He began to eat it dry, without a smear of butter, while standing over his mother, approving her landscaping plans and suggesting that if they were going to plant trees then one could be a willow because it was my favourite. Jess bought one for me, or rather for Fionn, the son for whom she would do anything. And while it was a relatively young specimen, there was enough foliage for me and Fionn to sit under its cover when the sun shone drying the earth, to talk and laugh, to listen to music on shared headphones looking back at their house.

Dinner in the Cassins' invariably meant new experiences for me: halloumi or sweet potato relish that felt like silk in my mouth, or talking about the environment or what exhibitions were on at the Royal Hibernian Academy. They liked that I was their blank canvas that they could fill with their colour. They were kind and caring people. People who'd cut down on their plastics by choosing local handmade soaps that smelled of rose gardens, who used refillable laundry liquid and softener containers bought in the health-food store long before anybody else even thought of it. They bought the *Irish Times* and the *Observer* at the weekend and the *The Kilcross Herald* on Tuesdays so they could connect with their new community and understand what made the locals tick. The GAA, Country and Western, and *The Late Late Show*, I told them, which made them laugh.

They took Fionn and me to plays in the Arts Centre, where visiting theatre companies performed works by Oscar Wilde, Frank McGuinness and Edna O'Brien. I'd only ever been there for the Christmas panto, never realising this other world existed. We went to art exhibitions in the county council concourse, and stood in front of paintings that made no sense to me but held Fionn's gaze for minutes at a time. We travelled to Dublin to the photography gallery, to sit in silence looking at the works of Bobbie Hanvey, Colman Doyle, Elizabeth Hawkins-Whitshed— or Greenshed, as I kept calling her, getting it wrong.

'Is this what it's like when you talk to the dead?' Fionn asked me one Saturday, when I'd begged Dad for the day off. We'd gone to Dublin early on the bus to see an exhibition in the Civic Offices of up-and-coming Irish photographers. We were the only ones there at that hour and so we could whisper to each other. 'You know, like just you and them and this . . . connection?' He held a hand to his heart, looking at a black-and-white picture of a boy of about eight, a camera held to his eye looking back at the photographer.

'Yes,' I said, my head nodding enthusiastically, feeling proud that our worlds were linked by the spiritual connection we felt when we worked.

'Not everyone gets it, you know. Not everyone can appreciate its immensity. How much bigger it is than us.'

He continued to look at the picture.

'That's why we're perfect. The two of us.' Without looking at me, he took my hand from my lap and brought it to his lips to kiss. 'We get each other, the need for silence and contemplation and looking into the heart of men's souls.'

How I wished for his ability with words. With him I felt precious and unique, worthy of every moment of longing he ever felt for me. I was so besotted with him: how his fingers flexed before he took hold of his camera or how his eye shifted right when he was trying to explain something, like how to get the correct angle on a shot.

I loved him so intensely right in that moment that I reached to turn his face to me so I could kiss those lips that seemed forever slightly parted as if in awe of life itself.

'I love you,' I said, looking into his eyes; he who knew me better than anyone else, every tiny cell that gave life to who I was.

'I've been waiting for you to say that since I met you.'

I took in his eyes, his smile, the very skin of him; glistening, it felt, with the wonder of me. 'You should have said it first then,' I laughed.

'No, I was willing to wait.'

'Well say it now.' I grabbed at his arm, squeezing it, in desperate need to hear his confession.

'I love you, Jeanie Masterson. Always have. Always will.'

We made love for the first time that evening. We'd gone out to Lough Fen to take advantage of the change in light. He took endless pictures of me. I still have one of them, somewhere. I dug it out not so long ago to see my head tilted toward the sky, my eyes closed as I sat on a rock as cold as ice. At one point, he'd simply stopped, let his camera hang low around his neck, and looked at me. I was about to ask what was wrong when he rose and came to take my hand. He led me far into the woods, beyond the pathway, to kiss me deeply against a tree. There we writhed, not caring, as the sharpness of his underarm sweat reached my nose and my denim jacket grew dark and stained from the wet bark.

With Fionn came my crucial years of learning what relationships were all about, finally turning me away from the 'what might have beens' with Niall. Kissing and fumbling and arguing and making up and making love with ridiculous speed in tight spaces, like downstairs toilets, or sometimes on a single bed when no one else was home. Waiting for texts that never came and phone calls that came too late. Biting nails and thinking of nothing else, not what the teacher was saying and certainly not what the dead were saying, consumed only by the image of his face and the imprint of his hand holding mine as I walked to school. Delicious times. The stuff of badly written poetry and memories that would forever cause an ache even in an eighty-nine-year-old heart.

All that while Niall hung around the edges of the group, never spending as much time with us as he had before, although he and Ruth remained close. By then he was busy with the many girls he chose to date, none ever lasting that long. I had thought he might let the job slide because of what had happened. But his interest in the dead far outweighed all of that. Every Saturday he still worked with Harry, watching and learning how to wash the dead, to brush down the hair and apply the makeup. She claimed he was a natural and would observe his work with a smile and a nod of her head. If there was no client to attend, he'd wash the floors, the towels and sheets, restock the shelves and drink tea with Dad in the kitchen, or play PlayStation with Mikey. But when we had to work together I could feel it, that awkwardness in the air that both of us tried to smile through. Never as close as before, a distance had grown between us, our conversations having receded to those of acquaintances. And even though I missed all that was gone, I felt I had no right to ask anything more of this man I had let down.

By the time the January of our final year in school came round, our individual futures seemed set: Peanut would be heading to Dublin to become a vet, Ruth would be staying in Kilcross to be a beautician or hairdresser, she wasn't quite sure which, and Niall would qualify as an embalmer with us. I'd be staying too, to work full-time at home.

A couple of months earlier, however, Mum had entered a period of panicked frenzy, producing various college prospectuses, circling things like Architecture, Screenwriting, Animation; things I'd never shown the remotest interest in. Although she had caught my eye with Catering. I imagined myself happily making scones with a bright yellow apron in a little café painted sky blue on a street corner in some exotic city.

'I'd be your best customer,' she said, when I stupidly mentioned it.

'Not if it's in Paris you won't. Bit of a commute from Kilcross.'

'Paris. Imagine. Anything is possible, love, you know that. If it's what you want, we'll make it happen.'

'I'm not opening a coffee shop in Paris, Mum. I'm staying here.'

'Are you sure, darling? Maybe another session with Ms Curtis might be a good idea.'

Ms Curtis was my career guidance teacher.

'She's already done every bloody psychometric test there is in the country on me. Something in Social Care, that's what they all said. So I guess here is perfect, looking after people, even if they are dead.'

'I just worry about you, that's all, love.'

'I'll be fine, Mum, honestly.'

And really, in the months that were to follow, with the dreams I began to dream, perhaps I could have counted on her support.

Fionn's plan had never wavered from the moment I had met him: he was still going to London. When he was a boy, he and his parents had gone on a trip there and by chance had come across a photography exhibition showing the work of the students of the London College of Art.

'He was gobsmacked,' Jess told me. 'We had to

coax him with the promise of all sorts of things, one of which was his first camera, before he'd leave. Imagine, he was only nine. We had hoped pizza would do the trick but no, two hundred pounds we spent on that Canon. He hasn't looked back since, sure you haven't, pet?' Her hand stretched across the table to her son, who sat smiling, looking from her to me, two women who knew he would never be for turning.

For his portfolio submission he asked if he could do a project on the undertaker's. As much as my folks had gotten over their initial distrust of this boy who'd led their daughter astray with his mitching ways, they'd never fully been comfortable with him. Mum was suspicious of anyone from Dublin, especially someone with a camera constantly in his hand and quite often pointed at her, causing her to tell me quite early on that if he did that one more time she'd be pointing him toward the door. And Dad, well it was as if he knew from the very start that if anything could upset his future plans for Masterson Funeral Directors and the part I would play in it, it was Fionn Cassin. Though they never said anything, I was well aware of their disappointment that nothing had developed between me and Niall.

'So, I believe you're headed to London, young man,' Dad said from behind his *Sunday Independent* one afternoon in January as we sat waiting

156

for Mum to present her famous Sunday roast.

The first day Fionn had eaten with us was a year prior when he had made a fatal error. Mum had already called us to sit at the table and we were doing so in silence, as was our wont when Mum cooked, for fear a single noise slipped out, adding to her stress, when he'd said, 'Anything I can do, Gráinne? Jess says I'm a natural in the kitchen.' *'No,'* Mum replied, a glaze of sweat on her forehead and a hand reaching to protect her beef as it sat sizzling in its tray, as though he might at any minute try to steal it. 'And my name is Mrs Masterson.'

Mum wasn't the most confident of cooks. Impatient would be more the word. She always marvelled at my ability with the baking. But every Sunday she battled with a roast dinner that she insisted on.

'Yes,' Fionn replied, to my father's statement, enthusiastic as ever to talk about his future in photography. 'The London College of Art, they have an excellent prospectus. I have one here if you want to see it.' He made to stand, to go and rummage in his camera bag, which lay well out of Mum's sight in the sitting-room, but Dad raised a hand, one side of his paper wilting in on itself gracefully.

'No need for that, son.'

'What, Dad?' Mikey asked, lifting his head from his *Campaigns of the Mahdist War*.

'No, not you, son, I meant Fionn here.'

'Oh,' Mikey lowered his head again, delighted at his reprieve, taking a slurp of his MiWadi, his preferred drink on all occasions.

I glared at Dad, wondering why he couldn't have just let Fionn show him. It would've been no skin off his nose, but he refused to shift his gaze even though I knew he knew I was watching him.

'And when will you be going then?'

'End of the summer. That's if I get in, of course. I have to submit my portfolio first. Actually, that was something I wanted to ask you about. Might I do it of you and the business?'

Dad took off his glasses and laid the paper down in his still empty dinner place.

'What do you mean?'

'Well, I was thinking I could take pictures of you and Jeanie and Harry at work. And Niall too, if he's agreeable, to capture the beauty of what you do here.'

'The beauty, huh, there's very few would call it that,' Dad laughed. His elbows by now on the table, crinkling up his newspaper, the end of one arm of his glasses tipping against his lip, growing curious about this boy. To an outsider this proclamation could be seen as a master-stroke by Fionn, but he wasn't manipulative. It would never have occurred to him to play up to a man who considered himself quite handy with a camera. Fionn simply wanted to do the best portfolio he could.

'Feck it anyway.' That was Mum in the background. 'Always bloody lumpy.' I looked around and gave her an encouraging smile, but she didn't catch it as she concentrated on stirring the gravy.

'Well, why not,' Dad stated. 'As long as you don't come in when there's clients.'

'Oh, sure. I mean, obviously. I'll take your lead on what is acceptable.'

'Fine then.'

'Can I start this week? My portfolio needs to be with them at the beginning of March.'

'I don't see why not.'

'Excellent.'

'But tell me this, you're not planning on trying to take that daughter of mine with you when you go, are you?'

Fionn turned to look at me then back at Dad—a case of spectacular stage fright. 'Because if you are then the deal is off.'

I wanted to die there and then. To join Mrs Swarbrigg lying in our viewing room who, not one hour earlier, had told me she wished she'd followed her dream to be a dancer and not stayed in the family outfitter's at the top of Mary Street for fifty-one years.

'No. We hadn't even thought about it,' Fionn protested, perhaps a little harder than was necessary, making me wonder if he, just like me, actually had. I'd dreamed about it. Saw us walking down those London streets, and living in a high-ceiling apartment that looked right over the Thames. And children, we would have children, a boy and girl. I could see them perfectly, their black curly hair with Fionn's spectacular eyes. I loved their heartbeats already. Things that no matter how many times I went to sleep thinking about seemed impossible. My life was here doing what I was born for, and I didn't think I could do it somewhere else without Dad by my side.

'Well, that's all good then.' Dad folded his paper perfectly in four.

'Right, roast beef, everybody.' Mum laid the first plate in front of Dad. 'Papers, books and cameras down. Get it while it's hot,' she said, followed by a quieter and more disappointed, 'and burned.'

The black-and-white photos, in a project Fionn called 'Tending the Dead,' featured Dad talking to Harry in front of an empty coffin in the embalming room; Dad sitting at his desk, his eyes looking to his right out of the office window— very Clark Gable, Mum said; Dad at the opened front door of the undertaker's, looking all serious at the camera; Mum, who insisted on being present that day, with a makeup brush dabbing at some foundation. And me, in a shot taken from below and to the side, shaking out one of the sheets we used to cover the bodies. With the crisp snap of cotton still in my ears, he caught its flight mid-air, ballooning in the centre before its eventual fall to the embalming table. Niall declined to be involved.

They were beautiful and solemn and respectful. Mum and Dad blushed, and I beamed on the day Fionn sat us all down at the kitchen table to show us the prints. Mikey was made to come in as well but once again was too honest to feign interest, and so sat reading an Osman's catalogue.

'These are magnificent, Fionn. Simply magnificent,' Dad said, in patent admiration.

'I'm so glad you like them. I feel I've captured the peacefulness of this place.'

'Well, we try,' Mum chirruped as she looked at the photos over Dad's shoulder, while Harry smirked at her sister-in-law's sudden involvement in a business she normally kept well out of. I could see that Fionn had managed to move himself up a few notches on the 'who Mum likes' barometer, albeit not as far as Niall. Only that day she'd said Niall had the healthiest, thickest hair she'd ever seen, always a winner in Mum's book, not that he needed any more positive attributes.

'Is there any way we could have some copies?' Dad asked. 'We'd pay you, of course. I'm thinking they might be great for the website or a brochure.'

'No need for payment; you were kind enough to let me disturb your work.'

'I insist.' Dad looked at him from above his glasses, ensuring there would be no argument.

'OK, well, if you tell me which ones you want, I'll get them done. All I ask is that you give me the copyright on whatever ones you use.'

Those pictures stayed on our website for a while and continued to have pride of place in frames covering a wall of Dad's office. The one of him sitting at his desk became his Facebook profile picture. But Niall, when he took over running our social media in later years, said they were too dated and instead chose lilies and rippling water to represent us Mastersons.

'You could come,' Fionn said to me later that evening after everyone else had left and we cleared up the fish and chips Dad had bought. 'To London, I mean.'

In the month it had taken him to complete his portfolio, we hadn't talked about it once; both of us too fearful, perhaps, of what the other might say, and yet it sat between us like a pothole we had to keep avoiding.

'Oh,' I'd replied, this moment of my dreams coming true, and yet, my stomach churned in panic.

'Look, Jeanie.' Fionn closed the dishwasher door and took the jar of mayonnaise that I was holding to put on the counter so he could take my hand. 'Peanut and me were talking and we both agree it would be good for you.'

'You were talking?' I asked, surprised, pulling my hand slowly away, hurt that I'd become that troubled friend who needed to be discussed in private.

'I just wanted to suss her out on what she thought you might say if I asked you.'

'*I* could've told you exactly what she'd say. She thinks I need rescuing.' I felt suddenly overwhelmed by sadness, realising that this might be the case for him too, that he saw me as someone trapped, needing him to save me. I sat at the table, my back slumped, my limp hands in my lap. 'Is that what you think too? Is that why you're asking me? Is this the plan you've both hatched to save me from myself?' He came to hunker in front of me, his hands reaching for mine again, looking up at me earnestly. 'Because,' I continued, fighting the desire to cry, 'no one needs to save me from anything. I'm perfectly fine here. I have a job that, really, I quite like. I have a life. I don't need you to pack me into yours like I'm a charity case.'

'No, no, Jeanie . . . look, this is coming out all wrong. You're not my charity case. What you and I have is good. And really, I've been thinking about us and London for a long time, way before your dad even mentioned it.' He hesitated for a second. 'I suppose I just needed a bit of support,

163

guidance maybe, from the person who knows you best.' He smiled, trying to encourage one from me. 'I simply wanted to make sure I didn't mess this up. 'Cause this is big, you know. Please don't punish me for trying to get this right.'

I looked at him, reading his honesty in every crevice of that beautiful face, melting at the appearance of that incisor when he smiled again.

I relented with a nod, pulling my lips in, concentrating on our hands together, still on my knees, but still unable to speak for fear my voice would wobble.

'You know Al and Jess are coming with me, right? We're all moving. And well, I . . . I hope you don't mind, but I asked how they'd feel if you came too, and they said yes.' He leaned in closer. 'I honestly think there's something much bigger out there for you than this town can offer, Jeanie.'

'Like what?' I croaked, frightened because I knew how much my leaving would hurt Dad, and in truth how lost I might feel without him by my side. Perhaps I needed my family and the dead as much as they needed me, I thought.

'I'm talking about London here, Jeanie, with its vibrancy and sense of possibility down every street.'

It was as though he was describing himself. I used to think of him as a light white feather blowing through the grey of Kilcross, refusing to land. Skipping along finding excitement in the tiniest of details: in a weed that grew up through the pavement slabs of Mary Street, in the curve of a passer-by's cheek, in the smile of the undertaker's daughter. It scared me. I realised I never fully felt I could live up to who he thought I was. Something shifted then, dampening down those dreams of a life beyond.

'I can't go, Fionn, even if I wanted to,' I protested. 'There's the business.'

'Right, the business, always the business.'

'They need me. Dad relies on me. He's been waiting so long for me to work with him full-time. And there's the dead, with the two of us we'll be able to cater for so many more. And there's Mikey.'

He nodded, like here it was again, that old chestnut. 'But they can't actually physically hold you here, Jeanie, the living or the dead, not if you don't want it. You have agency over your own life.'

Perhaps I should just have said the words, 'I'm too scared,' and been done with it. And besides, no matter what way I looked at it, no matter how I struggled with the burden of the dead and my family, I knew who I was here and that my gift mattered to me, to the wider community, to the dead. Right here in Kilcross, I was special. But there in London, all of that would fall away and I'd be nothing, nobody, living on the coat-tails of someone else's career. I was too scared to lose that which defined me and yet, and yet this man I loved was asking me to take a chance.

'Can we leave it for now?' I asked. In my head I was running further away from him but unable to let him down, not right then.

'OK, fine,' he sighed, reluctantly giving me a reprieve. 'But just think about it.'

'Like I haven't done that every minute since I met you.' Those whispered words, slipped out as easily as I'd fallen for him.

'Then why not? Why not just do it?' His enthusiasm renewed as he let his knees tip to the floor.

'Because I'm not you,' I exclaimed. 'Everything is not as black and white for me, you know.' It was then I finally burst into tears.

'No, no, no,' he protested, kneeling up to fold me into his arms, to rock me gently. 'This wasn't supposed to go this way. Look I'm sorry. Let's leave it for now, OK? There's plenty of time, yeah?'

I nodded into his chest, my head laid flat against his heart that I loved with every short, gasping breath of my body.

Chapter 15

I never did say no to Fionn. I didn't want to. Couldn't bear to hear the word come out of my mouth. But every couple of weeks after he'd asked me the first time, he'd bring it up again and the answer was always the same: that I was still thinking. And I was. I thought and thought for the month of June, through our exams when a hundred of us sat in rows of ten in the sports hall, heads bent in tense, industrious silence. And for the whole of that sublime July in which we celebrated our freedom swimming in Lough Saor. And for August, as I watched him pack his bags and he considered me through side-glances, wondering if I might say anything at all.

Harry found me one Saturday afternoon sitting alone in the viewing room, where I'd gone to hide. There was no client, just me sitting thinking, trying to figure out what to do.

'You OK, Jeanie?' she asked, as she sat beside me.

'Oh, yeah, sure.' I tried my reassuring smile. 'Did you want me for something?' I was already getting up until her hand stopped me.

'No, I was just concerned about you. Is this something you can talk about, or . . .'

I wondered why I hadn't thought of her long before now, this woman I trusted implicitly.

'It's Fionn,' I admitted, sharing my burden willingly. 'He's asked me to go to London.'

'Oh, I see.' Her eyes widened. 'And . . . What did you say?'

'Nothing.' My forehead crumbled. 'I love him, I really do, but I'm scared.'

'Oh, Jeanie, you poor thing.' She rubbed at my arm. 'Do your mum and dad know?'

'No! And please don't tell them.'

'OK. It's OK.' She patted the air, attempting to calm me down. 'Actually, I was going to go to London at your age, myself.'

'Really?' I asked, totally amazed that this might have happened to her too.

'I never went, though.' I caught the wince before she turned her head away.

'Why not?'

'This place.' She perused the walls of the viewing room, as if they had reached out their stony hands and held her here all those years ago. 'I was in such a quandary about it. I kept expecting I'd wake up one day and I'd know for sure, London or here, here or London. The answer'd just be there, clear as day.'

'That's exactly what it's like for me.' I became so animated, not quite believing I'd found someone who understood. My pitch then dipping as I remembered how my time was running out. 'But I have to tell him soon.'

'Oh, pet.' She gathered me in for a hug when she saw my eyes fill. 'You'll find your way. Something will arrive to point you in the right direction. I promise.'

'Did that happen for you?' I asked, pulling away so I could read her eyes.

'Well, yes, I think it did. The longer I was confused, the more it seemed like going wasn't supposed to be, because I'd have known, wouldn't I, I kept telling myself. So I stayed. I'm glad I did. It's not so bad here.' She blinked slowly, giving the impression that there was so much more she could have said but chose not to. She grabbed for my hand then, in a panic. 'We'd miss you, though, if you went.'

'I know,' I whispered, as I looked into those sad, worried eyes and whatever history it was they held.

Was it the guilt she saw in me that caused her to stand up quickly, shaking off whatever had burdened her?

'Ignore me, Jeanie,' she proclaimed. 'What you need is a pros and cons list. I'm finished for the day, so how about I take you to Kate's Kitchen and we order the most fattening thing on the menu and we do just that.'

'OK,' I smiled, relieved and encouraged again by her kindness.

That list showed me nothing more than I already knew. And even though the answer I was searching for seemed as elusive as before, it did not matter as much, now that I felt less alone.

In the end it was Mikey who unintentionally saved me. A year prior, when Mikey was nineteen, Arthur had gotten him a job. Much to everyone else's delight and Mikey's trepidation, Arthur had put in a word with Brian Fitzgerald, from Fitzer's pub, convincing him he needed a part-time barman who might be best suited to daytime work. As it turned out, Mikey had loved it, especially the taking of deliveries and barrel changing. He enjoyed the order of keeping the cellar clean and neat. For one whole year he wore a pride about him, most noticeable in his step, each foot confidently hitting the pavement as he walked up the road five days a week, his place now firmly in the outside world, a thing he'd never considered possible.

But one year on, at the end of August, things unravelled. Money had gone missing from the till on more than one occasion and, while Arthur had argued that Mikey was no more capable of it than Brian himself, Mikey had been let go. It was a time of great upset in our house, silent dinners and closed shed doors and endless visits from Arthur. But nothing, not Dad's encouraging words, Mum's proclamations of injustice and revenge, or Arthur's less raucous promise to get Brian to see sense, could lessen the wound my brother bore so deeply. I was the only one Mikey'd let in, to sit beside him evening after evening, to watch endless war documentaries, when really my eye was drawn only to him, my heart dipping every time I saw the sadness of his lost purpose. Once he even reached for the cuff of my sleeve, like he had when we were little, and it was all I could do not to cry. I could not leave him. Even if my gift decided to abandon me right then and there and Dad demanded I pack my bags for London, I would not go.

Fionn finally stopped asking. Peanut stopped cajoling, no one ever asking me about leaving Kilcross again. But still, in the furthest corner of my soul, I wondered if I was letting something great pass me by.

At the beginning of September, I held my hoodie tight around my waist as Fionn got into the back seat of his parents' car to drive away permanently. I'd told him that I'd come eventually. But not right then, not when Mikey needed stability. Six months, a year at the most. And besides, he and his folks needed their own space to settle into their new lives in Kennington, I consoled, they didn't need me to worry over. And he'd be back, wouldn't he, for visits? They weren't selling the house, short-term holiday leases, they'd decided, so they'd be home again, surely. And anyway, I'd visit too.

And I did. Many times.

On my first, we walked what seemed like the length of the Thames, along the South Bank, past Shakespeare's Globe, me not caring that my left foot had a blister, holding his hand, him laughing then stopping for no other reason than to kiss me in the middle of the walkway, others having to swerve swiftly around us. And then there was the visit soon after, when we made love on the rug of the sitting-room floor of their Kennington apartment as soon as his parents were out the door. Then three months later, when he brought me to an exhibition in his college at which he had to help. I sat on a stone blob that I presumed was a seat but turned out was part of the exhibition, him passing me by every five minutes or so and winking. I'd stood alone for two hours, leaning against the wall and sipping from a glass of tepid white wine until he took me home, where he fell asleep on his bed fully clothed. And a month after that, when we met up with his new mates, Marko and Ellie and Tyrone, and they drank themselves stupid, I slipped out, leaving them to talk about people I didn't know, to call Peanut, who was by now living on campus in Dublin, happy with her veterinary student life.

'Is it still love?' she asked, the sound of voices fading away as a door closed.

'Of course.'

'Then why are you calling me at ridiculous expense at eleven o'clock on a Saturday night?'

'Cause I miss you?'

'Right yeah, you only saw me last weekend when I was home. Where are you?'

'Some pub called The Dog and . . . something or other, with his college mates.'

'Duck. Bet it's The Dog and Duck. Sounds very English.'

'He's so happy, Pea.'

'That's good, isn't it?'

'But he's happy *here,* in this world, where I'm not.'

'What are his mates like?'

'Really nice.'

'Buuuut?'

'Ugh, it's going to sound stupid, but he hasn't held my hand all night. He always, at some stage, finds my hand under the table, but not tonight.' I felt bad saying it, unfair even to think that his friends had displaced me in his heart, and yet I wanted to admit it to someone, to let it go, and perhaps for her to tell me to cop on.

'Isn't that just young love growing up a bit? It doesn't mean he's stopped loving you.'

'No. I know that. But I feel like I'm not the centre of his world any more. This place is.' That feeling had been niggling for a couple of weeks. I knew it was bound to happen, this distraction from us, even if it was just temporary as he settled in.

'He needs to find his life there, Jeanie, and

it takes work. Besides, love doesn't stay that obsessed for ever; it shifts and changes, but it doesn't mean it's bad.'

'You sound like such a woman of the world, Pea.'

'Well, having a relationship with a narcissist kinda helps.'

'How is Rob?'

'As in love with himself as ever but still I can't resist the man.' Rob was an asshole from Kildare who insisted on a Dublin 4 accent. Pea knew he was an idiot and yet she couldn't seem to dump him, as we often discussed. 'Listen, Jeanie, this arrangement you and Fionn have, it was never going to be easy, was it? Living apart like this. You can't expect that every time you manage to see each other, you'll both be synchronised. That's too much to expect of him *and* you.'

'I know, but I didn't think it would be *this* hard.'

'Oh Jeanie, I wish I could give you a hug. It'll be OK. Just don't think too much about it. Go back in there and have yourself a cocktail or something, and find *his* hand, stop waiting for him to do it. He's a good guy, Jeanie. Just try to relax and go with it. All right?'

'OK. You're right.'

'Good. And next weekend, yeah, if the dead can spare you, come to Dublin?'

'Sure.'

'OK. I suppose I should get back to his lordship. But you're sure you're OK, Jeanie?'

'Absolutely,' I feigned, trying to convince myself as much as her that I really meant it. 'And thanks, Pea. Love to Rob.'

'No, not telling him that, he'll just think you *actually* love him. Go, be happy.'

To my delight, when I went back inside, Fionn looked relieved, as if I'd been missing for hours, and immediately took my hand and kissed my cheek. And yet I knew that this journeying back and forth, this interruption to these lives we'd chosen wasn't going to get easier, and something somewhere would have to give.

A week later, as if he'd read my mind, he rang to say he wouldn't be coming home in three weeks' time as we'd planned. That he'd been thinking about it and it just wasn't fair on either of us, this constant effort, and that perhaps we should just leave it and give ourselves a break and let our lives settle into what it was they were supposed to be. Unless, that was, I'd changed my mind and I might finally move over?

'No, I didn't think so,' he answered to my silent panic, which had returned now, as powerful as ever. 'So, what do you think? Shall we just park this for the minute?'

'Sure,' I'd agreed, thankful that he wasn't standing in front of me so he couldn't see the devastation. 'I understand.'

'So that's it?' he'd said, his assuredness gone as our call drew to a close.

'I guess?' I replied, offering a question mark of my very own.

My family endured weeks of my silence and tears that followed. Dad talked to the dead all on his own, instead of the load being shared; Harry hugged me each time I came in to sit in a lotus position on the clothes chair. Mum even let Ruth off for a couple of hours to do my hair. And Mikey knocked on my bedroom door, an occurrence so rare that I let him in to sit beside me in complete silence as he read one of his latest magazines.

And then there was Niall who, despite the distance that had arisen between us, made me several cups of tea as I sat in my pyjamas at the kitchen table, filling the awful well of my sorrow with stories he'd heard from the other embalming trainees he'd met on his diploma course in Dublin. The mystery of the bottle of whiskey left on a man's grave every year on his birthday that the wife couldn't even fathom but brought home anyway to use in the Christmas cake. And the fifty letters found in the cardigan pockets of the woman who'd written to her dead twin sister every week since she'd died. And the baby who was so tiny they had to have a coffin specially made that the mother insisted should be yellow.

Each endured every moan, every tear, every

scowl, until one Friday evening, a month after Fionn's call, a ring came to the front door. And then there was a rush of feet upstairs, Harry knocking at my bedroom door, telling me to get myself dressed. Down I came to see Fionn standing in our hallway, nervously pacing, until I stopped in front of him, confused, and he took my face in his hands and kissed me so deeply that Harry had to retreat into the kitchen, closing the door. He said nothing, just took my hand and found a taxi to bring me to his house, the house that Al and Jess had never sold and never would, to drop his near empty rucksack on the floor to take me to his bed.

'I don't know what I was thinking,' he said after, as we lay panting. 'It just seemed futile, the whole thing. And I was in such a downer with it all that I thought there was no way out, that we'd have to end. But we can make it, Jeanie, can't we?'

'Yes,' I'd said, holding steady those crystal eyes, believing in this version of our future.

We stayed in each other's arms for the rest of the night and the following day, not admitting that, of course, we were lying to ourselves, that making it work had already proved too difficult and heartbreaking. What we were actually doing in those precious hours was saying our goodbyes, setting ourselves free to live our lives unburdened by this love.

And yet we were true addicts, falling off the wagon intermittently over the following couple of years as we slipped back into the other's arms regardless of who we were with. For him there had been Sophie, or was it Amber? For me there had been Aaron and Paul, who in drunken hazes I had met and liked, and even met again in not-so-drunken hazes—relationships that passed the time but could never match the power and brilliance of what Fionn Cassin and I shared.

Our addiction raged until, one day, when I turned twenty-two, when I came to London to surprise him. I rounded the corner of Methley Street, a bottle of duty-free champagne in my bag, stopping short when I realised he was kissing a woman on his doorstep. She was beautiful. Black and lithe and utterly bewitching. I watched him hold on to her as she tried to turn to leave. His hand gently cupping her neck, pulling her in with that hunger I knew so well, reminding me of our first kiss. And there they stayed in the doorway, so engrossed in the other, until she relented and once again entered, the door closing over. My stomach heaved as my heart dislodged, falling down away to the nethers of me, to hide from the pain at what I instantly recognised as love.

I ran.

Crying loudly, not caring what anyone thought, until I slumped against the outside wall of the Tube station, allowing my body to drop into a hunker, where my blurry eyes made out the stains of old piss and trodden-in pads of chewing gum. I looked up at that crowded city, with its red buses and tower blocks and shouts and beeps and music, and for once I was glad I had never moved there. All I wanted was home: Kilcross and the dead, my only desire.

I was done at last, I thought. Fionn Cassin and I were finally through.

Chapter 16

After Tiny's admission about Arthur, I sped away from the house letting the air course through me, hoping to rid myself of the aching thump in my head. I moved up past SuperValu, with its after-work customers flitting in and out, my head down, trying not to lock eyes with anyone. I passed pubs with music, shops long closed, schools in darkness. I paced over canal bridges. Jaywalked. Skipped around cars parked up on footpaths, and people in the way and bikes locked to lampposts, until I was ahead of them all, striding out on my own.

But no serenity came, only flashes of all the things I couldn't sort, that I had no answers for, rushing in and out of my brain like badly stage-managed actors. The faster I walked, the faster they came. Until I stopped at the low wall of the memorial they had put up three years before, commemorating the 1916 rising. There I stood, heavy-breathed, reading the names on the block of granite: Dan O'Loughlin, Patsy O'Loughlin, Cáit McNamara, Eamonn Kelly; twelve in all who'd marched to Dublin to join the call to arms and died. And who had talked to them, I wondered, when they lay dying on the city streets or behind the barricades in the GPO? Who got to hear what they wanted to say to the people they loved? They had no one and the world didn't cave in. They lived, they died. Not having Jeanie Masterson by their side to hear their final whispers didn't make a whole heap of difference to them the day they bled out on O'Connell Street, did it?

I looked up to watch the starlings bounce from one side of the evening sky to the other, invisible walls propelling them back and forth. I could walk away like Mum and Dad and forget it all. Niall and I could go buy that house by the sea, like he wanted, and have a dog and forget about the dead, and maybe even, yes, maybe even we could think about children.

I rang Peanut who picked up on the second ring.

'I was only thinking about you.'

'Am I disturbing you?'

'No. The kids are down. Anders is asleep on the couch and I'm here beside him trying to remember the name of that guy who used to sit behind us in English. Gingery hair.' After Peanut had qualified, she'd moved to London to work in a veterinary practice owned by a handsome, wealthy Norwegian called Anders. They fell promptly in love, Rob the narcissist at last confined to that bit of the brain where embarrassing memories were locked away. Not long after, at twenty-five, Peanut found out she was pregnant on twins, Oskar and Elsa, and they'd moved to Oslo to raise them there.

'Liam Conway?'

'Yes, the very man. Does he ski?'

'I'm not so sure he does, but I can check with him the next time I see him in Casey's with his beer belly perched on the bar, downing his seventh pint.'

'Ah, he still lives there then. It's just I was watching Anders ski this morning and I swear to God there was this guy there who was the splitting image.'

'Spitting.'

'What?'

'It's spitting not splitting.'

'Oh. Pity it wasn't him, though; it was kind of nice seeing someone I know here, or imagining he was someone I knew.'

'Liam was a dick, Pea. Don't you remember he'd upend our books whenever we walked by him?'

'Oh yeah, that was him. Isn't it funny what the brain chooses to remember? So what news?'

'Oh nothing. Just my world is falling apart. Mum and Dad are leaving. Niall wants a dog as well as children now. And I just don't know why I do this job? It's nothing but hassle.'

Over the next few minutes I brought her up to speed as Anders continued to snore beside her so loudly that she had to move into their bedroom so she could hear me properly.

'Dogs are really good to have around, Jeanie. One might help, actually.'

'Seriously, that's your answer, go buy a dog?'

'Are you really thinking of giving it all up? I mean, after all this time?'

'Sometimes it's so hard and I wonder does it really matter if I hear the dead or not. Does it really matter if someone finds out their father isn't their real father? I mean, what purpose does it serve?'

'I'm not quite sure what you're talking about now, Jeanie, but, yeah, I guess anyone would want to know if their father wasn't their real father. Oh wait, hang on, that could be Oskar— he's not sleeping very well for some reason. He's having these nightmares. Just give me a sec.' I listened to the rustle of movement and then absolute quiet, then rustling again as she returned. 'No, we're good. But Jeanie, I've never heard you say this stuff before.'

'I know, it all feels a bit shaky, Pea. Like I've lost control.'

'I'm worried now. You take so much on, don't you? I mean, remember that little girl, what was her name? Annie or . . .'

I needed no more prompting to remember Anna-Lisa McGarry, twelve years of age, buried in a field not one mile from where I was leant

183

on that cold stubby wall, always so present in my thoughts. I didn't reply but immediately felt the familiar sting in my eyes.

'Oh crap,' Pea said. 'That's definitely Oskar. I'll have to go. I'm sorry, Jeanie.'

'Yeah, sure. Go. Give him a kiss for me.'

'Sorry. I'll ring you back, OK?'

'OK.'

'Bye. Love you.'

I put my hand to my eyes to catch the tears that always came whenever Anna-Lisa caught up on me. Never many, but enough to remind me that for people like her, yes, my presence, what I did, definitely mattered.

Dad had a policy that if ever the guards or anyone else came looking for our services to help find people who'd gone missing, we'd turn them down politely. It wasn't what we were there for. It was tiring enough dealing with the dead in front of us, let alone going hiking down the canal or through forests in the hopes that we might hear them call. And besides, he said, we didn't need any more media attention than we'd already garnered over the years. We'd had our share of local headlines and one or two national ones— mostly good, it has to be said—but still, Dad would've preferred it if everyone just left us to get on with what our job was, and we didn't have to be at the beck and call of others.

But this one evening Keith Hanley called to our house. Keith had been a year below me in school. He was one of the good guys. Mainly because he never slagged me, never called me Morticia. When someone chose not to go along with the crowd, you noticed. You thought, now there is someone decent, someone to whom a favour, if ever it was asked, might one day be owed.

It was three years ago now. Niall and I had gone away for a night for our one-year anniversary and I was still high on that wonderful buzz you get sometimes after being away. We'd gone west to the sea, always Niall's first choice, with its expanse and depths and wildness. He'd stood for minutes longer than my patience would allow, looking out on the horizon. I turned back from further down Kiltern Beach with the intention of calling him to hurry up, but instead I smiled, feeling proud that this solid man with his height and his tight-cut hair and barely there beard was mine.

'Come on,' I'd called, after cradling that feeling for a bit, 'or that promise you're on might run out.'

He'd sprinted after me then. Grabbing me by the waist, and kissing me deeply, then tickling me so much I actually fell over. He pulled me up and in close for one last kiss before he stuck his hand in my back pocket and we walked on.

I'd heard the ring to the front door. Niall was

still a bit reticent about answering it back then. One year on from moving in, he struggled with not overstepping the mark. I never fully appreciated how difficult that transition must've been for him, moving into the home of a family with their ways already set. I'm not sure how long it took him to finally feel that it was OK to open the door before anyone else. He might not know himself. But I bet he'd remember that period when he teetered around the edges of this new life, not fully there yet.

'Jeanie, the very woman.' Keith turned to face me as I opened the door. Keith had joined the guards soon after he'd left school. Since qualifying he'd been stationed in Dublin, but in the last year had gotten a transfer home. He still looked about thirteen in his uniform, despite being twenty-eight, with that smile that would never grow old. 'Could I have a word?'

I brought him into the kitchen where we sat at the table. He refused a cup of tea and the temptation of one of Arthur's Twix bars.

'Look, I know this is out of line, and I wouldn't ask if it wasn't that I have a hunch about something.' He stopped to look at me, perhaps wondering if I might object right away, but when I didn't he continued. 'A girl has gone missing.'

'Ah Keith—'

'No, no wait, Jeanie, hear me out. No one knows I'm here. This isn't an official request. It's just she's only twelve and she's got no one on her side, Jeanie. You should see her. Skin and bone. Goes to school every day because she loves it. But there's been bruises and breakages and all sorts of stuff over the years. And I just, I dunno, Jeanie, I've been watching this bad bastard for a year now and I think he's done something to her.'

'Who?'

'The father. A mouldy drunk of a man. But not so drunk that he doesn't know what he's at. He's a smart one. Knows exactly what to say and who to say it to. Anyway, her aunt Kay, the mother's sister, the dead mother,' his eyes rose to mine to emphasise the tragedy, 'came into the station to say she's missing. There's guards up at the house now questioning the father.'

'Look, Keith, I'd like to help but I—'

'No, see, she runs away from him when he's in one of his "moods," that's what the auntie Kay was telling me. She goes out through a hole in the wall in their back garden and hides in the field until he's calmed down. But the aunt says she's not in the house, not in the field, nowhere. She's been missing a day now and he hasn't reported it. And why would that be, Jeanie?'

I shrugged my shoulders.

'Because *he* feckin' knows where she is.' Keith stabbed his index finger on the kitchen table, watching it for a second, his mouth twitching in frustration. 'All I want you to do is just to go for a walk up there in the estate. You and Niall. I can't. I'm off duty now. And, well, I've been warned to stop putting my nose into this one.'

'Oh?'

'It's just gotten the better of me. They've taken me off the case 'cause I've been "poking around too much" and "too emotionally involved." I don't think you can poke around enough when it comes to a vulnerable kid, but there you go, apparently I'm in the wrong. Look, I'll get you and Niall up there. I'll hang back a bit. Just two people out for a walk, right? They're the last house in the estate, so you go by, then hop the gate into the field, and walk every inch of it. If she's alive you might both hear her, but if she's dead, well . . . then you will.' He looked at me with a tiny hopeful raise of his eyebrows.

'But if the guards are up there already, don't you think they're going to reckon it's a bit suspicious if the undertakers' happen to be in the back field too? We'll end up getting hauled in. It wouldn't be the first misunderstanding we Mastersons have had with the police.'

'Please, Jeanie. I wouldn't ask, but it's like I know she's there. And I know you can only hear dead people for a short space of time, so it has to be now. She's been gone a day. Please, Jeanie, I swear to God, I'll never ask you to do anything like this again.'

I called Niall down, and explained everything in the hallway before he went in to hear it all again from Keith. I held back to stand at the sitting-room door. Dad was with Mum, catching up on their soaps. I wondered if I should knock and tell him. Wondered if he'd break his rule this once and come to try to find her with me. But I didn't. Instead I went into Niall, and looked into his eyes, willing to take his lead.

'If we go up there and the place is swarming with coppers, we aren't doing it, OK?'

'OK, Niall,' Keith agreed. 'They're possibly gone by now anyway. I don't know what this guy has on them but they're just not seeing what I see.'

'Maybe they don't want to see it,' Niall said, then squeezed my hand and off we went.

Keith had been right: the police were gone. There was one single light and a blind pulled down in the upstairs room of the house, but other than that the place was quiet. Keith waited in his car, out of sight, while Niall and I climbed over the gate.

As soon as my foot hit the earth, I heard her.

'Hello,' she called, from the far end of the field. 'I'm here.'

I looked at Niall, but when I realised he'd heard nothing, I knew we were too late.

Her voice, while faint, was determined. From this one pronouncement, I understood that Keith had been right. Here was a girl who despite everything, knew what she wanted, and right now, she wanted to be found.

'Follow the tip of Tullogh Hill. Come that way. As far as you can go.'

In the dusk of the evening we headed to the curve of the hill above the trees until we came to the border. There we walked its length until we found a mound of earth with branches pulled from the ditch to cover it.

'Anna-Lisa,' I called as I knelt down and Niall ran to tell Keith his hunch had been correct, 'are you there?'

'Yes,' she replied.

'They're coming now, Anna-Lisa. Help is coming.'

'No one can help now.' Although her voice held steady, no matter how hard she was trying I could still detect its vulnerability. 'Daddy says he doesn't know his own strength sometimes. He's never hurt me like he did last night, though.' She paused for a second, gathering her resolve. 'He didn't like that the policeman kept coming round to see if I was OK. I told him it wasn't my fault. I hadn't asked him to, but he wouldn't believe me and kept hitting and kicking. I felt it, when my heart stopped.' It was then she let go, her voice breaking under the weight of her own tragedy.

My hands began digging at the earth, dirt

clogging my fingernails as I tried to reach her, to let her know she was not alone. But she was too deep.

'I . . . I knew that he'd done it this time,' she said quietly. 'And I tried to tell him . . . that this one wouldn't mend like the other times. But he couldn't hear me . . . not like you.'

'Why did he hurt you, Anna-Lisa?' I asked, short of breath from my efforts to get to her.

'He said it made the pain go away.'

I lowered my head to the earth, and closed my eyes.

'What pain?' I whispered, trying not to let her hear that I was crying, watching my hands caress the soil as if it was her that they were touching.

'The pain of when Mummy died. Four years and four months and four days ago. He didn't like it when I reminded him like that either. I knew it made him worse. But I'd still say it, like the little bitch he always told me I was.'

I lifted my face to the evening sky, so my tears tracked down my neck. Grey clouds crept across the glow, darkening the land and bringing a sudden coldness.

'Oh, Anna-Lisa, I'm so sorry.' My hand shook as I held it to my mouth, dirt and all, imagining the cruelty this man had laid at her innocent door. 'That's not right that he called you that. And it's not right what he did.'

Behind me, I heard Niall and Keith's feet pound

191

the compacted summer earth as they ran. Their breaths heavy with the effort.

'Up,' Keith called. 'Get up, Jeanie. There'll be evidence. Step away.'

'But we were talking,' I said, turning to him, not willing to be taken from her just yet.

'You have to, Jeanie.' His hand was already on my arm, pulling me up. 'Did he do it, Jeanie, did she say he did it?' Keith of the gentle smile and caring nature squeezed my arm so that my hand raised not so much to get him off but in disbelief that he was capable of inflicting any kind of hurt. His eyes pleaded with me to confirm his suspicions.

'Yes,' I said, and he held the back of his wrists to his eyes saying: 'Fuck, fuck, fuck.'

I looked at Niall, who drew me to him. We watched Keith until he eventually stopped, took out his mobile and turned away to call it in.

'Anna-Lisa?' I stepped toward her again but not too close. 'Keith is here now. The guard who tried to help you. We'll get you out of there soon. And I'll get to mind you for a little bit back at my house.' I couldn't bring myself to say 'the undertaker's.' It wasn't as if she didn't know she was dead, and yet those words seemed too harsh for one so young. 'I'm sorry. I'm so sorry for all that's happened to you.'

She didn't answer. I struggled then, as sometimes I did, with what to say next.

'Is there anything you need me to help you with, Anna-Lisa? Anything you'd like me to say to someone, or something you need me to do?'

'Can you get my pencil case, please?' Such unexpected, innocent words disarmed me so that I found myself kneeling again, forgetting Keith's warning, trying to catch every bit of her instruction. 'Auntie Kay bought me new pens. One of them is purple, and I never got to use it. Maybe where I'm going I could.'

'Of course, Anna-Lisa, of course. I'll ask Keith to find them.'

'And also,' she continued as I waited, willing to do anything for this girl, 'can you ask if Daddy's dead now too?'

'What do you mean, Anna-Lisa?'

'He said that he knew I'd drive him to it eventually.'

'Oh.' I wasn't quite sure what she meant, until I did. 'Oh God,' I said under my breath, before getting up and running to Keith. 'You might need to check the house,' I told him.

In the background the sirens announced the guards' arrival until they were there and Keith was running to them, to stand and point toward us then up to the house window.

'Keith is checking on your dad now, Anna-Lisa, don't worry.' It seemed a ridiculous thing to say, given I didn't know how she felt about this man who had so brutalized her, but it was out of my mouth before I could think.

'OK.' Her voice had weakened by this point, holes arriving in what was once solid.

Two guards ran across the field, calling and beckoning us to move.

'I've got to go, Anna-Lisa. I'm sorry, I wish I could stay longer. But I'll see you later.' But there was no reply as Niall drew me away before they arrived.

I never heard her voice again, not even when her bruised and broken body lay on our embalming table days later. I'd never cried so much over anyone until that day.

After the autopsy was done, after all of the evidence was gathered, Anna-Lisa was eventually buried with her mum. The funeral had to be delayed a bit, though, until the guards were sure they didn't need the pencil case. When Keith brought it, he watched as I put it in under her cold hands, so it was ready for her. Niall had worked another miracle. She looked, if not wholly like the smiling girl in the picture her auntie Kay had given him, at least at rest, with no look of pain or hurt or damage. He had masked it all.

Only Keith and Kay and Niall and I attended the private ceremony of prayers with Father Dempsey before the lid was closed and Anna-Lisa was carried by the four of us up through the chain of honour of her classmates lining her pathway to

Saint Xavier's doors, into the overflowing church where children sang and teachers wept over the little girl they could not save.

Keith looked for another transfer after that. Cork city, I think it was. True to his word, never to ask me again for help.

Chapter 17

The morning after I'd left Dad to talk to Arthur, I woke up with a start, my eyes darting around the darkness of the bedroom, aware that my sleep had been uneasy and that I was alone. Niall's pillow bore no indent. And yet he'd been there asleep when I'd come to bed late the previous night. No chance by then of us talking—much to my relief as I wasn't sure how constructive I would be. But in the early hours he must've gotten up. Perhaps my fitful sleep had disturbed him too.

He wasn't in the kitchen either when I got down but I could see Mikey's shed door was open. The clock told me it was 6.30 a.m. How long had he been up, I wondered? Had he lain awake, unable to sleep, worrying about how to tackle the job of filling his new shelves?

I tapped on the kitchen window until his face popped into view. I raised a mug and pointed at it, but he shook his head and disappeared again. Still feeling muzzy and overloaded from the previous day, I sat to the table wondering should I go back to bed. But instead I decided to make Mikey a coffee anyway.

My offering and I stood halted in his doorway moments later, realising that not only was there no space inside for either of us—every available surface, including his floor, was covered in magazines, but also there was no Niall as I had begun to assume.

'Wow, some major stuff going on here, Mikey.'

'Yes. I decided on expansion *and* reorganisation. Instead of periods of military campaign I began to think "regions." That way I could easily take certain parts of the world with me when we move. Although it got very difficult when it came to Empire invasion—do I categorise that according to the site of the war or the invading army?'

'How long have you been up trying to do this?'

'What time is it now?'

'Six thirty.'

'In the morning?'

I nodded in trepidation of what he was about to say.

'Well then I've been doing this for thirteen hours.'

'Mikey!'

'I got confused. Halfway through I decided it was a bad idea so I started to rearrange it back to the way it was, having it by date, and I've started that over there.'

He pointed to the long pile of magazines on the floor behind his couch, leaning on their sides like fallen dominoes.

'But I'm getting mixed up now going from pile

to pile; it's all too much and I'm beginning to forget which year I'm on.'

'Can I help? What if I tell you what year we are up to, you can then go about your various regional bundles and pick out the ones that come next, and I can keep adding them? Maybe when you've done about ten then you can come over and check that I've gotten them totally right. What do you think?'

I realised this raised the issue of other people touching his magazines. They, or rather we, handled them roughly, apparently. Hence they were only left on surfaces when he was there to protect them. At all other times they were on shelves as far away from the layman as possible.

'I'll be very careful.'

'No fingerprints.'

'Not a one,' I answered, unsure how I might achieve that. 'But how about you drink this first and maybe get something to eat. We can't do this on empty stomachs. Well at least I can't, anyway. Come on. Let's go in.'

I led the way, checking that he was following me in case of a sudden, and not unheard of, change of mind. When we sat to the table we ate two bowls of Crunchy Nut Corn Flakes. When we were little we were only ever allowed sugary treats on a Sunday. All other days Mum insisted on plain Corn Flakes or Ready Brek or porridge, which unfortunately—because she made it—meant lots of rush and sighs and lumps.

'Mikey,' I asked, 'did you see Arthur before he left yesterday?'

'Arthur?' A dribble of milk made its way slowly down the middle of his chin and sat in the groove of his dimple. I wanted to reach over and wipe it away, like Mum had done a thousand times, and that when I was younger I would copy, giving him fair warning of what I was about to do, learning how to mind my older brother.

'I was just wondering if he seemed OK, was he maybe upset?'

'Why?' Mikey rescued the dribble, getting up to pull off a piece of kitchen roll and dabbing at it rather than using the back of his hand.

'Oh nothing, just something Dad was to tell him.'

'Is it about him coming to stay with us when we move?' He sat back to his breakfast. 'Because he told me before that he'll come visit us every month, that he and Teresa really like it down in Baltimore. He says they're going to camp in the garden.'

'Don't be minding him. There's plenty of room in the house. And I can't exactly see Teresa being the camping sort,' I laughed.

'He says they'll set off after his Friday round in the town and they'll be down well in time for a teatime pint in Cotters. And of course we'll be back up. So the way I see it, I don't think I'll have to miss him because he'll be around so much.'

The love I felt for my brother in that moment was strong enough to force itself into an unwanted hug, but I resisted. I wondered how well I'd cope without him right on my doorstep. I thought I might cry at the very idea of his shed empty of his glorious presence. I put down my spoon and looked at the soggy mess in the bowl, not hungry any more for the sugary delight that not two seconds ago had brought a childish grin to my face.

'Do you remember Arthur marching around to Fitzer's to tell Brian it was Ernie who'd stolen the money and not you after all? He said he was tempted to grab the mic out of Danny Tiernan's hand mid-chorus of "Brown Eyed Girl" and announce the truth in front of the customers. I'd love to have seen that.'

'Yes,' Mikey replied. 'He has defended my honour like all loyal comrades.'

We'd found out about the stolen money from Fitzer's when Ernie Grace, who'd worked with Mikey, died from pneumonia two years prior. He'd had dementia and had been in long-term care for a while.

As soon as I'd said hello to Ernie as he lay peacefully in his coffin, he was off, his words exploding out of him, as though he'd a lot to get through.

'I was a compulsive liar from the get-go. First

it was stealing the mother's pink bonbons when I was small. Then it was her cigarettes. Then the money. May God forgive me. I didn't know the truth from a lie by the end.'

'OK, Ernie,' I said, putting a hand on his, hoping to pacify him. 'We can take our time through this.' I wondered if this agitation was part of his dementia. But no, as it turned out, death had cured him and Ernie was now fully compos mentis. This was something totally different.

'I shouldn't have done it. I knew it wasn't fair. Not on a man like that. But it was the gambling, you see. And the Fitzgeralds had enough not to miss the few bob, not in the beginning, anyway.'

I stopped then, the truth of what he meant having slowly edged its way into my understanding. I looked wide-eyed at this sunken-cheeked man. My words taking their time to form coherently as I sat back, then leaned forward again to begin, but he got there before me.

'It was me,' he proclaimed, growing impatient. '*Me* who stole the money all those years back, when I worked with your brother. I saw my chance to pin it on the new guy. Gambling's an awful thing. It'll make you do anything. Hurt anyone. You just don't care. Do you see now?'

'Let me get this straight, Ernie,' I began. 'You're saying you set my brother up?'

'Yes,' he replied urgently.

'My brother, who has never done a thing wrong in his life, who when he was a kid insisted my dad bring him back to Frayne's Newsagent's because they'd given him a penny too much in his change? That guy. That's who you chose to frame?'

'Yes,' he said, timidly, barely above a whisper. 'That'd be the height of it.'

'Oh God.' I replayed those months of my brother's sadness in my mind. Watching his face that could not smile, that battered soul who could not comprehend or ever forgive a world that could be so cruel. 'My brother,' I continued, furiously, 'has refused to hear of any other jobs in the town since he got fired, did you know that? Jobs that he could've managed perfectly, that would've made him happy, that would've meant some kind of normality for him. But he didn't because he was afraid someone would accuse him of something he hadn't done again. He lives in his shed now, do you know that? Comes out only when we make him. He's hidden himself away in there for years.'

'Like me,' Ernie offered meekly into the head-wind of my storm. 'Hiding away behind the anger and confusion of a mind that didn't know who it belonged to any more.'

It's not like I wasn't used to this with the dead—people who weren't so nice in life didn't suddenly become saints because they'd died.

They mainly became maudlin, incredulous that their lives had ended like this. Expecting our sympathy. Like Anna-Lisa's father, who'd cried and cried on our embalming table. Dad and me, standing side by side, listening to him. That man never asked about her once; instead he wept over himself, his death, how there had been no other choice for him.

Dad always said we weren't there to play judge and jury with those who lay before us, but with those two men I found it hard not to. While Ernie had not beaten my brother with his fists, he had condemned a vulnerable man to a life of solitude when Mikey had been capable of so much more than fretting over how to organise his magazines. And neither had I forgotten how that disaster had affected my decision about London.

I would have happily rolled that man across the road and given him to Father Dempsey right there and then.

Realising I wouldn't be able to talk too much longer without my upset showing, I tried to draw the conversation to a close.

'Is that everything, Ernie?' I asked. 'Is there anything else you need to say?'

'No,' he replied quietly, like a scolded child.

It was enough to soften me, to tell my conscience that, after ten years of turmoil, even he deserved my ear until his last words were spoken.

'Well,' I said, more gently, 'I'll be here in case you change your mind.'

'Except of course to tell him I'm sorry, won't you?' Gone now was his panic of earlier, and in its place a soft beseeching. 'Tell your brother it was wrong, what I did. Tell him he was one of the best workers that ever came into that place. A good barman—much better than me, anyway. I never saw a man able to whip a place into shape like him. He likes his order, doesn't he? Always cleaning. And he really tried to talk to people. He wasn't great at it, not exactly the gift of the gab, but he'd try. I used to see him reading the sports results at the counter so he could talk to the punters.'

Mikey reading sports pages to try to connect with people? I never knew any of that. I felt overwhelmed by sadness, realising once again that the effort my brother had made to fit in had all been in vain.

'I regretted it. I often thought about coming clean. In my lucid moments, before this thing rotted my brain completely, I wrote down my instructions, a will of sorts, I suppose, that said they were to take me here when I died so I could tell you. I hoped that I might be well again in death, have all my faculties back, so to speak. But I left instructions with my brother that he was to check with you after the funeral to see if I'd managed to talk to you. He has a letter to explain everything in case I hadn't. There's nothing else I can offer you now, after all this time; only the truth to make it better.'

'Why didn't you just send me the letter back when you'd written it?'

'Because I was a cowardly thief. Afraid that you'd come banging down the door.'

'You were right. I would've.' As would Mum and Dad, not to mention Arthur.

'Will you tell him, your brother?'

'Of course I'll tell him. But, Ernie,' I asked growing distrustful again, 'are you seeking absolution so that your slate is clean in case there is a God?'

'Ha, you've seen through my cunning plan. But does it really matter now if I've told the truth for selfish reasons or not? The fact is you know now and it means Mikey will too.'

He was right in ways, even if he was worried about his tally at the pearly gates: all that mattered was the truth. He didn't stay long after, barely a second or two before I called him one last time and realised his light had finally gone out.

The crowd was small the next day at the funeral. A handful of people. But at the back of the church sat Arthur and Mikey. They didn't go to the grave, but they'd blessed themselves as the carers from the home, along with me and Niall, had wheeled Ernie down the aisle.

Dad had discreetly nodded at Mikey and Arthur as he'd passed.

'Dad told me it was important to forgive,' Mikey said, when I asked him later why he'd been there. 'But I haven't forgiven him. You're not to tell Dad but I only went because Arthur said he'd go too.'

Ernie's brother, a short stocky man in an ill-fitting suit, waylaid me after the burial. He gave me the letter, even though I told him Ernie'd confessed all. I made a passing comment about his settling his account with God and the brother laughed and said he'd never met anyone so unreligious in all his life.

'Ernie only wanted a church funeral because Mam believed so strongly. A making of amends, I suppose, for all he'd put her through.' He sniffed, ashamed at his brother's actions, I suspected, wiping at his rheumy eyes before waddling away, his walk tending to one side, compensating for some enduring pain, as I realised I'd gotten it wrong. Ernie had told the truth for Mikey's sake and not his own at all.

The letter told me nothing more than what Ernie already had, and yet it felt important to hand it to Mikey as evidence of his innocence.

But it changed nothing for him. He continued to sit in his shed, refusing any offer of work, of which there were a few, thanks once again to Arthur. The sorting of letters in the post office, which really was inspired given Mikey's love of categorisation. Or the two-hour goods-in position on a Friday in Billy's Books, even though Billy himself wasn't so sure he needed it. But Mikey said no every time to Arthur's eager and loving encouragement.

We worked hard that morning, Mikey and I, sorting and ensuring those magazines were back in order. I thought nothing of the fact that Niall hadn't appeared yet, assuming he had merely slept in the spare room and was having a bit of a lie-in. But when Dad came looking for him at 8.15, saying he wasn't anywhere about, I went to check and realised the spare bedroom hadn't been slept in, and his running shoes were still in the utility. I rang his phone to hear its normal six rings and then voicemail. I rang it again. This time it only rang twice before the voicemail came on, meaning he must've deliberately rejected my call. I rang one more time to be told the owner had his mobile switched off. Wherever he was, this wasn't good.

'And you're sure he's not answering his phone there, Jeanie?' Dad was beginning to panic now, standing right in the middle of Mikey's shed. Mikey huffed and puffed around him, but Dad was oblivious to the inconvenience of his presence.

'Try him yourself, Dad, if you don't believe me.'

'It's not like him at all, Jeanie. Has something happened between the pair of you?'

'No, Dad, we're grand.' I reached around him to grab the latest pile of magazines that Mikey stretched to me.

'What year are we up to now, Jeanie?'

'Eighteen seventy-four.'

'The Red River War. Now, I'd have put that with North America.'

'Are you sure, Jeanie? After you came home yesterday from your lunch, things didn't seem that great.'

I ignored his concern and redirected us safely away from my marital problems.

'That reminds me, how did Arthur take the news, Dad?' My voice lowered slightly, hoping not to alert Mikey to anything being wrong, not that there was any hope of stopping his sorting frenzy.

'Well, I gave him back the pen but I wasn't able to tell him the . . . what Tiny said.'

'Ah Dad, could you not just tell the truth for once?' I slapped down a magazine in annoyance, causing Mikey's head to rise.

'It's not that I didn't want to, Jeanie, it's that, well . . .' He pulled at the cuff of his shirt, then looked away and sighed. 'It's . . .' he started again then faltered, silenced once more by whatever it was weighing him down. 'We got a call,' he managed finally, 'Andrew's died.' This was enough to stop me in my tracks.

Andrew Devlin was forty-five and suffered from congestive heart failure. He'd been in and out of hospital, having various procedures in the hope of a breakthrough, but with no success for years. He'd spent his final months in Kilcross Hospice. Dad hadn't known the family before they'd rung him six months ago to say that they, along with Andrew, were ready to think about the ceremony. Dad had met and sat with them that first day for two hours, talking about the various options. He'd be laughing one minute, he said, with their banter, and the next, sitting with their silences when serious moments descended. He'd pulled back his hand when Andrew's mother, Sophie, had refused to relinquish the picture for the memorial booklet, everyone watching her as she clasped it to her chest. It was Andrew who had reached for it, taking it gently from her grasp. As he gave it over to my father, he had slipped his other hand into his mother's, into the space his smiling, happy face had left behind.

Dad hadn't pushed them on more decisions that day. He'd told them he would return to look at things again. He went back week after week, when plans had long since been made, to sit with Andrew, to laugh, to bring him the *Irish Times*, his paper of choice, or a book he'd been given that he thought Andrew might like. He went sometimes to watch a match on TV, or simply to sit by his hospice bed when he was sleeping.

Something strong had drawn him to this man, this boy, as he referred to him. Life was good at giving us unexpected favourites. This was the hardest of cases for Dad, a friendship grown when death was standing right outside the door.

'Oh Dad, I'm sorry. I didn't know,' I said, instantly regretting my earlier annoyance.

'I know, love.'

I hugged him, and felt his arms tighten around my waist in appreciation and sorrow.

'I want to go see Sophie and Donal, you know, his parents, for a bit, so I was hoping Niall could pick Andrew up at ten.'

'I can go if needs be,' I said, letting him go. 'And look, if he hasn't arrived by half past, I'll start ringing around.'

'I've got 1875 to 1876 now, Jeanie.' Mikey brought over a pile of magazines, making a big deal of stepping around Dad as he came to stand by me. 'I think it's time for a recheck.'

'OK, Mikey.' I watched him go through those latest additions I'd been working on.

'Can I start to phone anyone, Jeanie? Arthur maybe? He can put the feelers out, get the town on the lookout.' Dad already had his phone out of his pocket.

'OK, but Dad, don't worry, Niall's not "missing" missing. I'm sure he's . . . gone for a walk or something.'

It was then that the gate creaked open. Dad

darted out and Mikey quickly commandeered the space he'd left behind in case of a return. I held my breath as I heard Dad say: 'There you are, Niall. We were getting awfully worried about you. I was about to ring Arthur to see if he'd seen you on the rounds.'

It wasn't until the relief flooded through me that I realised how worried I had been. I moved to the opened shed door and leaned there to watch him head into the house.

'Hi,' I called lightly to him.

He turned back to give me a nod with no smile. He averted his eyes almost immediately as he went on inside with Dad following close behind.

'Right, Jeanie, I think we're ready to go again. So 1877, Russo-Turkish War.'

I found Niall standing in the kitchen ten minutes later, already changed into his suit, adjusting his tie, the car keys on the table in front of him. Dad had left to see Andrew's parents by then. He didn't turn to me when I entered. He knew my footstep, knew my shoes, his eyes didn't need to rise to know his wife had entered the room and the time had come to explain his disappearance.

'Dad was worried.' I stood with my back against the now closed door.

'He said.'

'He told you about Andrew?'

'Yep.' He gave nothing else, which wasn't like him. Niall wasn't heartless.

'What's going on, Niall? One minute you're there asleep and the next you've disappeared. Where did you go?' I ventured further into the room.

'Ruth's.' He still hadn't looked at me.

'Ruth's? You got up in the middle of the night and you went out to Ruth's?' Ruth and Derry lived in a massive house beside Derry's folks at the other end of town. 'What about the kids, you could have woken them.'

'Well, I didn't. And it wasn't the middle of the night, it was one o'clock. Anyway, she'd offered me the spare room yesterday when I texted her. Said I could have it whenever.' He put the car keys in his pocket.

'What do you mean "when you texted her"?'

'She knew we were going for lunch and she was simply enquiring how it had gone and well . . . I just ended up telling her the lot.'

'The lot? And what is the lot?'

He shrugged his shoulders.

'Jesus, Niall, you're not fifteen, you know.' I raised my voice in exasperation. 'I'm your wife, not your mother. Enough with the attitude.'

'So, you finally realise you *are* my wife?'

'What's that supposed to mean?'

'Oh, you know, husbands and wives and how they're supposed to be honest with each other.

It seems you don't always get that. Not when it suits you, anyway. See, Jeanie, I haven't a clue what's going on with you these days. All this shit with your parents and your excuses about having kids when all along I don't think you want them at all. You keep it all in like you always do. And after the lunch and then you not bothering to come up to talk to me like you said you would later, I just thought, no, I'm not taking this any more.'

'But when I suggested we talk more, you didn't seem to care.'

'Sorry for not jumping up and down at the thought of my wife actually giving a shit about me.'

'So you just left?'

'Yep.'

'That's helpful.'

'Well you tell me, Jeanie, how that is different from what you do? You're emotionally absent from me all of the time.'

'Emotionally absent?' I snorted. 'Is that one of Derry's?'

Derry was a new man, very in touch with his inner emotions. Constantly telling Ruth when he felt she was emotionally absent, over which the three of us would normally piss ourselves laughing.

'And anyway, it's not true, Niall.'

'Oh come on, Jeanie, it really bloody is.'

'I'm here talking to you now, aren't I?'

He considered this wife before him with distrustful eyes. As I waited for his verdict, the seconds slipped by as I thought of all the other defences I had, like the dog that we might buy, the house that we might escape to, should I need them.

'You've changed, Jeanie. You weren't always like this, you know. When we got engaged I thought I knew everything that went on in your head. Wholly and totally, and I was like so fucking grateful. How stupid is that? But I was. So grateful that you finally loved me and trusted me, 'cause, dipshit that I am, I'd been so sure you could never see me like you saw Fionn fucking Cassin. But it felt right and good and honest. And now, now I don't know where we stand anymore.'

Every last excuse and justification went out of my head with the mention of that name. The name that rested hidden in the hollows and grooves of my body, that sometimes whispered its presence at the oddest moments, like when opening our front door or lacing up my shoe, or waking on a cold dark winter's morning.

'Oh for Christ's sake, Niall, that was years ago.'

'You forget I watched you after he left. All devastated and not eating. Going to skin and bone.'

'Niall, I was young. This is ridiculous.'

'You know, I kept waiting, waiting for the day

you'd say we were through, but it never came. I don't think I relaxed until we got married. And even then, even then, there's been this tiny little niggle right there in the back of my head saying, nah, you're not home and dry yet, son. You're like this slippery eel I've been trying to hold on to, Jeanie, and all this time I've had a good enough grip but now you're getting the better of me. I mean, I tried. Didn't I try? You can't say I haven't done my best to get you to talk, to open up about our future, but each time you find a way to shut me down, filling the space between us with other shite like fucking dogs.'

'Hold on, you were the one who was talking about a dog, not me.'

'But these past few years it's been building. Ever since we started talking babies—'

'Oh my God, have you like totally lost it? *You* started talking babies.'

'OK, then, all right. Ever since *I* started talking about babies, you stepped one pace back from me and you haven't stopped since. Inching away with every excuse you get. Tell me I'm wrong.'

'I can't take this fucking conversation again.' I threw up my hands in anger and turned to walk away but his words stopped me in my tracks.

'What, will I maybe book it in for five years' time, or ten, or maybe when you're in your menopause? We're thirty-two, we don't exactly have time.'

'You fucker,' I said, turning again, staring him down.

'You know what, Jeanie, forget it. I'm done, you know, done. You want this life with me here and you there, coming together for the odd fuck when it suits you, taking a double dose of the pill in case one of my little men swims to safety. You win. I'm not interested any more.'

'What does that mean?' I panicked at his words, never before so final, so uncaring. It felt like I didn't know who this man was any more.

'Exactly what it says.' He dropped his head, watching his finger begin to tap at the table. 'I think we need to simply take a bit of time here and you need to figure out what you want and I need to figure out what I want. Ruth says I can have the spare room for as long as I need it. So I'm going to move a few bits over today. In fact, I might do it before I go to collect Andrew.'

'What? You can't be serious, Niall.' Had we honestly come to this that he was willing to give up on us? 'Things haven't been that bad. I'm not that horrendous to be with. I mean I'm struggling, yes, with the retirement and everything, but really you're just going to go?'

'I've tried to help. But it's like you've no space for me.'

'But that's not true. Look stay, just stay and we'll work it out, OK?'

'No. I've made up my mind. I need to get some

distance, taking a leaf out of your book. It's all too much here. We can't be free and honest with everyone looking on and listening through walls.'

'But what will I tell them?' I pleaded, unable to bear the thought of each of their faces: Mum, Dad and Mikey. The worry, the heartbreak I'd see there when I told them. Not to mention the questions, the offers of help, mediation even. No, no, this couldn't happen.

'The truth, maybe? Try that for a change. Tell them that we're struggling.'

I had nothing to offer in reply. No words came. All exhausted, muted by what was happening.

He tapped at the table again, glanced briefly in my direction before he walked toward the hallway to take the stairs to our room. I didn't follow. Perhaps I should've protested more, but instead I sat to the table, bewildered and sad, listening to his movements, the opening of drawers, the footsteps back and forth from bathroom to bedroom. And then he came down to stand at the bottom of the stairs, to look in at me sitting forlorn in the kitchen.

'I'm going to walk over with these to Ruth's. I'll be back then to go to the hospice.'

I didn't nod, I couldn't. He watched me for a second or so before going through the front door. I ran to the sitting-room then to watch through the bay window as he slung the bag over his shoulder and crossed over Water Lane, waving back to the driver of the car who'd slowed to let him pass. He walked on in that determined gait that defined him, before finally disappearing as he turned on to Mary Street.

Chapter 18

After my last visit to London, Fionn stopped calling. There were no more desperate flights home to steal me away and proclaim that it would always be me. My instinct had been right, that whoever that woman was who he'd kissed on his doorstep that day, she had broken the spell of me.

I refused to get up, not dressing, not showering, not eating. Dad and Harry and Niall worked longer shifts to cover my absences over the coming weeks. I sat in my room hoping my phone would ring, while willing myself not to call him. I rang Pea instead, sometimes twice a day and cried. Ruth came over at least three times a week with heaps of chocolate and her hairdressing gear. If nothing else, my hair and nails looked beautiful during that awful period.

'You should come out with me and Niall, it'd do you good,' Ruth told me repeatedly.

But I turned her down every time.

Niall texted jokes—though the only one I can remember now is 'Death is always around the coroner'—and pictures of Ruth and him out on the town, their smiles willing me to shake myself from my turmoil and try to live again.

But the only place I was going to back then was Mikey's shed. Our roles had reversed, with me now in need of his care. He was the only one who never suggested I change out of my pyjamas or that I go for a walk or perhaps smile. The only thing he ever wanted of me was that I might occasionally listen to his interesting military facts.

One morning, about four months after the break-up when I'd finally progressed to getting dressed, I sat listening to him tell me about how the Crimean War wasn't considered the first modern conflict simply because of the post-industrial benefits of manufactured weapons. It was also, apparently, because it was the first to be covered by the media.

'But you don't get it, Jeanie,' Mikey said, to my not-so-enthusiastic response. 'What I'm saying is that this reporting in the Crimea was like their Twitter and Facebook. It was mind-blowing.'

Had I not been totally devastated by the loss of Fionn, I might have avoided visits to my brother directly after the quarterly delivery from Osman's. But I liked the distraction, even if I had to endure a two-hour talk on the contents, *plus* what was coming in the next quarter, given Osman's kindly sent a newsletter with each delivery announcing the good news.

'No, I do, I get it.' I tried to sound more convincing.

'And the best bit is—'

'What, that wasn't the best bit?'

He didn't even flinch, or throw a disgusted eye in my direction, he simply took a breath to continue.

'What's that over there?' I asked, my finger barely rising to point in the direction of a red magazine amongst his pile of new arrivals.

'Where?'

'That red magazine. Your ones are usually white, aren't they?'

'Yes, they most certainly are.' Mikey followed my pointing finger to the bottom of his pile of arrivals, eager to root out the imposter. 'That's most irregular. I hadn't even noticed that.' He carefully moved his magazines away from the pretender. 'Oh yes, I remember now. They're diversifying. The publisher. Trying to broaden their base. Going into social history. I had emailed them. Specifically said I didn't want them. Not even their free sample. But here it is nevertheless.' He wagged it at me in disgust.

'G'me a look then?'

'Take it. I don't want it. As you well know, Jeanie, I'm strictly a military man. What were they thinking? Surely my sales history proves that I'm only interested in one thing.'

I started to flick through the pages, not bothering to point out that as Osman's had only ever produced military history to this point, the records of Mikey's sales were hardly going to prove a thing about his other preferences. As he continued to consider their horrific error, wondering out loud if a follow-up email might be the best option to express his disappointment, I delighted in the momentary distraction of people's stories, their images, ghostly in their black-and-white smiles flipping in front of me, until the pages finally fell open to a colour photo of a woman who looked to be in her sixties, opposite an article titled: 'Talking to the Dead: A History of Undertaking in Southern France' by Marielle Vincent. I speed-read it as Mikey wittered on.

When I realised she actually could hear them and this wasn't just some clever headline to encourage readers, I jumped up out of the chair, the first energetic thing I'd done in months, to wave the article in front of him. 'Oh my God, there's someone else, Mikey. Someone else can hear them.'

His eyes squinted as if all the pages had started to spit at him.

'Please don't shout, Jeanie. You know I don't like it when people shout.'

'Yes, yes, OK. Sorry. I just can't believe it. I have to find Dad.'

I skipped through the article again as I headed back inside, making sure I was correct, even though I knew I was, but still, sometimes the mind reads what it wants to instead of what's actually there. But nothing had changed. Marielle Vincent really was one of us.

'Dad,' I called, popping my head in and out of every room until I found him in the kitchen making himself a coffee. 'Dad, you'll never believe this.'

'Jeanie!' he laughed, 'Good to see you looking so happy. I've missed that smile.'

But while Dad was amused about the article, he wasn't flabbergasted. He didn't have to sit to a chair for fear of falling down in disbelief like me. He didn't immediately turn to Google images to see more photos of this miracle woman. He simply leaned over me as I laid it on the kitchen table, chuckled and said:

'Well, would you credit that?'

'She talks to them, like us,' I reiterated, in case he wasn't quite understanding. 'She's been doing it since she was a child too. And this is really the best bit, she was an embalmer but she doesn't do it any more. She refuses. Her husband, Bernard, died three years ago and she just couldn't use the chemicals on him. So now she simply washes and dresses the dead in her home, like you told me Mrs Simmons used to do. After she's talked to them, get this, she buries them in her meadow, her "memorial pasture" she calls it.'

I looked up at him expectantly.

'Well, that is different.'

'But aren't you even a bit curious? About how it started for her and how she deals with it, if the world and his cousin queue up for her services like they do for ours?'

'I'm delighted for you, love, really I am. It'd be nice to get the French perspective on it all. Great philosophers, the French. Very deep.'

'Well, I'm going to email her.'

'Good idea.'

'So, do you have anything you want me to ask her?'

'*Où est la gare*?' He laughed at the only line of French he could remember from his school days. 'No, I'm sure you'll handle it perfectly. Oh no, hang on . . .'

Finally, I thought, some interest. Dad took the magazine from my hand, flipping it back to the front page.

'Is this a new series that Osman lot are bringing out?' He looked at me as though *I* was the child bleeding him dry every three months. 'I hope to God this doesn't mean a new subscription.'

'But all these years, Dad,' I said, still not believing his casual disregard for this phenomenon, 'we've been doing it on our own, and now here's someone else to talk to, to bounce ideas off.'

'Ah now, Jeanie, I've been doing this a long time now. I know what I'm at, I don't need to spend time analysing it with someone else. But you get in touch with her, if you want. I'm happy for you, really.'

He left me in the kitchen then, feeling as if I was wholly inept. The worrier, the one who fretted over what she said to the dead, rather than Mister Cool and Calm, who made up whatever he thought the living might like to hear.

'You OK, Jeanie?' Harry came through the door from the corridor not two seconds later.

'Oh, hey.' I looked down at the article, wondering what it was I would do now. 'Did you ever think you weren't up to your job, Harry? That everyone else around you was super-efficient and together while you were . . . hopeless?'

'Sometimes Niall and his youthful enthusiasm makes me a bit ashamed that I'm not jumping out of the bed every morning delighted with a new day of washing dead people, but I put that down to age.' She sat across from me, awaiting more. 'Why, what's happened?'

My head nodded at the magazine.

She turned it around to read the headlines.

'Is this true?' Her eyes didn't lift from the page as she read on.

'Yep, it really is.'

'Wow.'

'I know, right. I mean, even you get it. But Dad just doesn't seem to care. He's so much better at this than me. Like every time another dead person comes in, I get this fear right in my stomach about what it is they're going to say to me and what it is they're going to need me to do. But not him.'

'Oh, I don't know about that, Jeanie. I think it does affect him but—'

'But what? He's better at not showing it?'

'Maybe.'

'You've no idea how alone I often feel with this, Harry. I know this is going to sound ridiculous, but sometimes it's like it's just me holding everything on my shoulders in this place.'

'Oh, Jeanie, love, you're not. I'm here.'

'But you can't possibly understand how it feels. The worry about getting it wrong. And the lying, Harry, the covering things up and twisting the truth so it's a little nicer for everyone. You could never understand.'

I saw the flinch, the hurt my words had caused.

'No, I guess I don't.' She finally let go of the magazine and let her hands fall to her lap, out of my view. 'You used to talk to me all the time when you were little, especially about them. I liked it. I miss it.' She looked directly at me then. 'You know I'd never think anything you say about this place is stupid or insist you get over it. I know it's hard, I see it in your face every day.'

And I wondered when and how it had happened that I'd stopped talking to this kind woman, who was so much a part of our lives and yet never imposed herself, never raised her voice, never asked more of us than she thought fair.

'I'm sorry, Harry. I shouldn't have said that. It's just I need someone who totally gets it, you know.'

'Of course.' She dismissed my apology with a wave of her hand. 'I understand. I'm glad you've found her. Someone to make you happy again, after all you've been through.' She got up then to boil the kettle for her morning cup of hot water with a twist of lemon.

Marielle Vincent had no online social media presence, and Osman's were not willing to give me any details other than agreeing to forward on a letter—an *actual* letter, not an email.

I waited for a reply. But every day Arthur arrived with nothing. Assuring me that her letter could not possibly have gone astray on the Irish end.

'The very hint is offensive, Jeanie.'

'Really, Arthur, you're telling me An Post have never lost a thing?'

'It'll have been the English. Devious that lot, remember the famine.'

'I'm not even listening now.'

'Or the French? Always on strike. You don't hear of the Irish doing that now, do you?'

Four months later, when I had forgotten I'd ever sent the letter, an email arrived. Marielle started by acknowledging the length of time it had taken her to reply but without apology. Her words were officious and to the point. I couldn't decide if this was her English or if it might be the reply of a person who no doubt had received one or two unkind communications following her article. But she invited more information, about who we Mastersons were and what it was we did. I replied four days later, enough time, I thought, to show due consideration to her message, a maturity that perhaps she would appreciate and might prove that I, of all of her correspondents, meant no harm or wish to ridicule. By her third reply it seemed at last Marielle Vincent believed me.

We wrote every week or so thereafter—long emails detailing what had happened since our last, sometimes punctuated by phone calls, especially if one of us hadn't fully understood the other.

'The dead, they are sometimes cowards using us to do their dirty work,' Marielle wrote to me once on my favourite theme of what it was we Mastersons held back. 'But who can blame them? Would we not perhaps do the same? I do not mind. I tell the family what it is they say. These are the terms on which the bereaved come. "They might say something you do not like," I tell them when they phone. "It is up to you if this is something you want to hear. You can tell me to stop anytime." But I've grown used to it, the tears, the red faces, the anger. I don't have many clients, perhaps that's why. Families choose the local undertaker instead. It is fine, we are all not that brave.'

'I'm not,' I replied.

To which came:

'Because it is the way I choose, does not mean I'm right. Besides, most of the time the dead are kind and say things that give comfort and that is the bit that makes this job. Hold on to that, Jeanie, if nothing else.'

'Nozing ells,' I could almost hear her say the words in my ear. When we spoke, her voice sounded as opulent and soft as a velvet cushion.

For the first time, it truly felt as if we Master-sons weren't alone.

I'd been corresponding with Marielle for a couple of months when Niall found me at Dad's computer reading her latest email. Niall and I had grown close again, the distance between us lessening as soon as Fionn had disappeared from my life, allowing a gentle re-emergence of a friendship that had matured along with our twenty-three years. Ruth and Niall's badgering had finally worked and they'd dragged me out, each of my cells slowly repairing as we ate popcorn in the dingy light of the local cinema and sat on bar stools and at restaurant tables commenting on the world.

'So she really doesn't embalm, then?' Niall asked, coming to sit on the side of the table, to take up a pen and twirl it like a cheerleader's baton in his left hand.

'No, she stopped doing it.'

'So what, she's got twenty-four hours at most before she has to bury them?'

'In or around that, which she says can often be difficult if they live an hour or two away. Sometimes she just says no.'

'Not a slave to the money then?'

'I get the feeling Marielle is a slave to nothing and no one.'

'Can I talk to her sometime about her decision to give up embalming? Maybe send her an email? I'd love to know more.'

'I'll ask her. I don't think she'll mind.'

'I mean, I don't want to ruin what you guys have going on either so don't push it if she's not enthusiastic.'

'No, it's no problem. I owe you that and more for all you've had to put up with what with me and the . . . you know, tears.'

'That? I hadn't even noticed,' he grinned.

'Yeah, right. But seriously, you and Ruth have been really kind taking me out all the time and trying to cheer me up.'

'You're not that bad really. Usually by your

third mojito anyway.' He smiled and added, 'You seem better, Jeanie. It's really nice to see it.' He looked at me in a tiny, weighted pause and said: 'I've missed you.'

And it was then it happened, that little attraction switch flicking itself on inside. The pulse beat under the thinness of the skin on my wrists, in the slope of my neck, in the middle ear of my hearing, letting its presence be audaciously known, demanding that I do something about it, which was, apparently, to burn from my toes right up to my cheek and to push the hair out of my eyes and to look anywhere but at him. But he knew. I saw the blush. Those fruitful years of playing the field had given him an understanding of the vital signs. He smiled then tapped the pen off the table.

'Right,' Dad said, coming in all a-bustle across the embalming room. 'We have a tricky case, guys. It's a young woman, twenty-two. Knocked down by a reversing bread truck over in the Ashdown Industrial Estate. Died instantly. I know the family vaguely, Howard, from that new estate, Greenlands. Alannah Howard.'

'Oh,' I said, 'there was an Alannah Howard the year below us in school, wasn't there, Niall?'

Niall was no longer smiling. Instead a milky-white crept on to his cheek, erasing any blush from earlier. He stared, open-mouthed, at Dad.

'I'm quite willing to call Harry in if this is too

much, Niall,' Dad assured him. 'This won't be easy, not if you both knew her.'

'Are you OK, Niall?' I asked when he still hadn't responded.

'She was out Saturday night.' His words were spoken into that space, that no man's land, between Dad and me.

'What, in McCaffrey's?'

He nodded.

'Oh.'

'I'll call Harry. It's possibly best.' Dad was already taking out his phone. 'Although,' he stopped, 'there's a head injury.'

We both looked at Niall, knowing full well he was the best man for a job like this.

'Niall?' I asked gently, 'Are you up to this?'

He looked at the pen in his hand, then at me, then Dad.

'Yeah,' he said, quietly adding a barely audible, 'Sure,' before getting up and leaving the office to disappear into the yard.

The damage at the back of Alannah's head didn't prohibit an open coffin as the family had requested. Most of it could be hidden with her hair and the strategic placing of a side sheet. And yet I knew that for Niall this would not be good enough. Niall by then had become an expert in reconstruction. He was getting a name for himself, even at twenty-three. He'd taken a couple of additional one-day seminars in Dublin on the subject and watched endless posts on YouTube from the best in the industry giving the latest tips. There'd be days when he'd talk of nothing but fillers and wax and concealers from morning till night. Even Doyle's knew they didn't have the skill and would ask if they could send a body over in need of his expertise. A head wound such as Alannah's would have to be dealt with.

'What if her mother or father leans down to kiss her and they put their hand to her head and feel that hollow, it wouldn't be right,' he declared to my suggestion that perhaps this time he didn't have to do it all if he wasn't up to it. 'I've a duty of care. I'll make her perfect, like she hasn't suffered a scratch.'

And while I had expected his words, I hadn't anticipated the level of upset.

'Are you sure you're OK, Niall?'

He didn't answer immediately but kept looking at her until eventually and very quietly he said:

'She looked at me on Saturday. You know, one of those long stares.'

'Right,' I nodded. And there it was, a tiny pinch of jealousy.

'You and Ruth were chatting away about Derry again.' Derry had by then asked Ruth out at least three times but that night she had finally agreed to a date.

'Has she said anything yet?' Niall asked, as he looked down at Alannah.

'No, she's quiet. Didn't say a thing when she came in, and there's been nothing since.'

He nodded.

'I talked to her. I even got her number. It's in my jacket pocket right now.' We both looked at his navy jacket hanging on the hook over beside the door. 'I just can't believe, she's . . .'

'Oh, Niall.' I reached across to touch his arm. He stared at it so long that I began to wonder if he found it offensive, such a personal display in a place that should be sacred. Or worse, might he see it as some kind of unwanted advance, given all he'd just told me?

He moved away, out of my reach.

'Do you think you could tell her that I need to step away for a minute?'

'Sure, of course, but she's not talking so I don't think—'

'Just tell her,' he commanded.

'OK.' I watched him go, as I put a hand to Alannah's shoulder.

After a while, when he hadn't returned, I followed him into the viewing room where I closed the door gently behind me, trying not to startle him any more than I already had. I spoke quietly into the room.

'I'm sorry, Niall, if that before, my touching

you, was inappropriate. I was just trying to . . .
I didn't mean anything by it.'

He turned to look at me from where he stood a
bit of a ways inside the door.

'It's been a long time since you've touched me.'
His face still wore that slightly stunned expression from earlier.

'I suppose it has.'

'You've been a little preoccupied. A certain
Mr Cassin.' His eyes clung to mine as I imagined
Alannah's had, not five nights prior.

'Ah, him.'

'Yes, him.'

He regarded me for a moment then took a
breath, a big one like you might take before
diving into water, then quickly looked away as
if stopping himself from doing or saying something he might regret; perhaps the embarrassment
of an advance, or the bruise of a rejection?
And I couldn't bear it. Couldn't bear to see this
wonderful man hurt for me, or because of me,
one more moment. So it was me this time who
crossed the divide. Me who, when I reached him,
could feel his quickened breath. Me who looked
into those soft brown eyes whose sadness I
wanted to erase. Me who lifted my finger to touch
his left temple, to lay it gently in its groove.

'I'm sorry,' I whispered, so his forehead ruffled
in surprise.

'For what?'

'For Alannah. And for not seeing you as I should have all these years.'

And then I touched his lips with mine, because I owed him that first kiss. The splinters of my heart receiving a volt of life they had for so long done without. When we parted, he laughed a little, then nodded, looking down to find my hands, to hold them.

'So does this mean,' he looked up with one eye closed, a grin on his beautiful lips, 'that you might actually go out with me?'

'Yes,' I said, happy, genuinely happy. 'If you ask me, I will say yes.'

'Well then I guess I should ask.'

'Perhaps you should.'

'Perhaps I will.'

'Well, I look forward to it.'

'Good,' he said, before pulling me in to kiss me again.

Chapter 19

Over the years I'd heard occasionally about Fionn from Peanut. When she worked in London with Anders she'd met up with him a few times, but they'd drifted apart after she moved to Oslo. I never asked her much, although it took every ounce of energy not to, to know if he was still seeing *her*. And besides, there was Niall and we were doing well.

But then one Thursday I was walking up Mary Street and saw a man with a familiar gait approach. I was twenty-seven; in the five years since we'd seen each other, there'd been nothing, no phone call, no text, no coming home. And yet here he was, his hair shorter, a semblance of a beard, and his camera-bag strap slung over his left shoulder and down across his waist. He looked older, tired. But despite all of that change, that distance between us, in an instant I was back under his spell, suddenly unsure of how the simplest of bodily movements worked, like walking, which foot went first, was it left or right? All the while my heart pounded its excitement furiously in my ear.

'Hey,' he'd said simply, stopping in front of

me, as casual as if we always bumped into each other every Thursday as I made my way to the bank to do a lodgement.

'Hey.' I tried to emulate his nonchalance, and yet every part of me seemed determined to let me down, as my hand scratched at my forehead then attempted to curl some strands of hair behind my ear. 'You're home then?'

'Just for a day or two. Not long. You're looking well.'

'And you.' I looked off to the window of Kate's Kitchen on the opposite side of the street, avoiding that smile and that incisor.

'How are you, Jeanie? It's been a while.' His words were spoken in a considered manner, with the emphasis on the 'you,' like he wanted me to know that my state of mind, my state of heart, really mattered to him.

'I'm good, yeah. You?' Perhaps not the answer worthy of such effort, but I was too nervous to achieve anything deeper.

'Yeah, you know, fine. I'm staying out at our old place. A rare gap in the leasing schedule . . . who knew so many would want to live in Drumsnough,' he laughed. 'I'm here for a rest actually. Jess says it's all the travelling I'm doing. I work a few music festivals in the UK and Europe. It's been full on.'

'Sounds nice. The travel, I mean.'

'Yeah, not as glam as you might think but, you

know, keeps me going. Pays the rent. Let's me photograph what I want in my own time.'

'You're not still in Methley Street then, with Al and Jess?'

'No. I'm all grown up now with a place of my own. I have a two-bed flat in Brixton. A bit further out but I like it.'

'Oh, nice.'

'I used to see Peanut a bit. But now that she's moved to Oslo, not so much. The odd text here and there.'

'Yep, she told me.'

He looked down at my engagement ring, sitting pert and sparkling on my wedding finger, and was taken aback. 'Wow. She told me about you and Niall. But I didn't realise it was *that* serious.'

'Oh that, yeah.' Four months prior, on Christmas Day, when Niall had called around after the dinner, just as we were about to play a game of Cluedo, he'd gotten down on one knee in front of everyone and produced the ring. Before I found my voice to answer I looked around at each of their faces—Dad, Mum, Harry and even Mikey—and saw their wide smiles. Dad had risen to hug Niall before I'd actually said 'yes.' Which I did. And I meant it, even if—as everyone congratulated us—my mind drifted for a second to a street in London. Mum even managed to convince Mikey that he should shake our hands.

I put my hand into my pocket, hiding the sparkle.

'Have you set a date?'

'June, next year.'

'Married at twenty-eight.' There was no amused disbelief in his voice as he said this. If anything, it sounded surprisingly sad.

Helpless at the hurt I saw in that face, I laughed off his statement defensively.

'It's not that young, we're not eighteen or anything.'

'No, I suppose not,' he conceded, his voice quieter now, his eyes moving away to the ground. 'That could've been us, you know, if things had—'

At these words, I thought how right Fionn was: if only I'd had the guts to go to London and if only he hadn't met someone else then that could most definitely have been us. But they were suddenly interrupted.

'Jeanie,' Miles Mercier called out without stopping, raising his hand in greeting.

'Are you well, Miles?' I called back, refusing to dwell any further on the memory of Fionn holding someone else in his arms on his doorstep all that time ago.

'Not a bother now.' Miles twisted his head around so I could hear him as he walked on.

'You're happy then, Jeanie?' By then Fionn had regained his composure.

'Absolutely.' I gave a little laugh as if his question was preposterous.

'Good.' He nodded to the ground again. And smiled a smile that no one would have considered very happy. Resigned, perhaps; yes, more resigned.

'Well, I'd better . . .' I signalled toward the bank, wanting this to end as quickly as possible, not able to take another second of what this man did to me by simply standing on the same street. It was then I first thought of us like Velcro. Able to exist separately, but when together we clung to the other in a desperation and want that bordered on greed, needing to be ripped apart with a ferociousness that was like the ripping of skin.

'Listen, Jeanie . . .' He hesitated for a moment, looking up at the sky for a second. 'Can we, eh, talk? Not here. Maybe later. A drink?'

His invitation churned the fire in my belly but I resisted my want of him. 'I don't know.'

'Look, it's important.' His face was so earnest, defying me to refuse. 'Please, Jeanie. I swear I'll never ask one more thing of you ever again, just this.'

The temptation to drop everything for one second alone with him when anything and everything could happen was so very strong. And yet I knew it was the most dangerous thing I could do. And I wouldn't do that to Niall, not after how far we'd travelled together, the bridges and broken hearts that had been mended, the love that we had managed to find.

'I'm not so sure, Fionn. It's just we're very busy right now.'

And from his worried face he managed a small smile, and it was exquisite and I wanted to kiss that mouth as if I still had the right. It frightened me so much, this utter and absolute power he held over me.

'Sure. I understand. I just wanted to . . .' He sighed then, looking up at the sky again. Then shook his head 'Look, ignore me, I shouldn't have even asked, it's fine.' But there was something more there to be said, I could feel it, something that I would have to sacrifice.

'I'm sorry,' I said.

'No, honestly. I understand.'

'I really should get on.'

'Oh sure, yeah.' He moved so that I could pass, with my racing heart and, I was sure, scarlet cheeks. 'I'm home for a few days, though, if you, you know, are out that way.' The world stopped around me as I fell into the orb of the haunting beauty of those eyes. I could see them plead with me, pulling at my heart to please just do it, to please come just this one last time.

'I . . . I really have to go.' I looked away, casting off his spell, and moved swiftly. My face bent, concentrating on the passing pavement and putting one foot in front of the other and not breathing until I turned out of view into the bank, where I leaned my back against the cold wall just inside the doorway and closed my eyes.

To my shame I had considered lying to Niall, not telling him I'd met Fionn at all. What good would it do, I told myself as I walked back. We didn't need old wounds reopening and spilling out their pus. But by the time I'd gotten home the word had spread. Niall was in the embalming room waiting for me as I walked past to replace the cash bag in Dad's drawer.

'I hear he's back,' he called. 'You were spotted.'

'I see,' I laughed, exaggeratedly. 'Arthur, I suppose.'

'How's he doing?'

'Yeah. He's OK.' I hung back a second or two at Dad's desk before braving it and going to the door. Perhaps I shouldn't have said what came next but I think I wanted Niall to know what he meant to me. 'He wanted to meet up this evening—'

And in that second the temperature rose as I realised that what Fionn and I had been, and what that had done to Niall, still lived on in him like an undesired irregular beat of his heart.

'Are you for real, Jeanie?' he protested before I could qualify it.

'Niall, it's OK. I—'

'Have you seriously forgotten the years of you two back and forth, not caring who the other was with? You think I'm going to be OK with you seeing him tonight?'

'No, let me finish.' I came to take his hand as he stood at the embalming table, but he pulled it out of my way so my fingers only grasped thin air. 'I said no. Look, Niall, that was years ago. Things have moved on since then. I'm with you now. It's not the same. There's nothing to worry about.'

And although Niall's rage dissipated almost as soon as it had arrived, he had more to say.

'Well, I am worried. I spent years watching you two besotted with each other. And now, now when we're finally together, he comes waltzing back and thinks he can just take you from me.'

'That's not what's going on here, Niall. I promise you.' In truth I didn't know what Fionn had intended. Maybe Niall was right. Maybe that's exactly what would have happened, if I'd gone. He'd have reached for me and I would've let him, feeling that power and rush of love stripped bare of loyalty and obligation and gratitude for one more precious moment. 'I'm not meeting him. What Fionn Cassin has to say doesn't matter. He could beg me to run away with him and it wouldn't mean anything because I chose you, didn't I?' I held up the ring that sometimes felt too small as evidence of my promise to this man who'd rescued me and grounded me and made me happy in this place again. 'It's you I love,' I said, meaning every word.

And yet the next day I drove by Fionn's house, let the car idle a while outside the entrance to their driveway. And when the door opened and Fionn stood there looking at me, I held his gaze for a second in which I wanted to get out and run to him, to kiss him intensely as he had done in our hallway all those years ago, but I didn't. Instead, I dipped my head, put the car into gear and drove on.

Later that same year Niall and I tended a man called Maurice Hannigan.

He'd come to us from Meath, the next county over. Requested us not because of our skills but simply because we weren't local. I'd never come across the likes of it before, a man who at eighty-four had taken his own life. I looked at him as he lay out before me on the embalming table and wondered why it was he had ended his days that way in a hotel room.

I wrongly assumed that he would talk so I could pass his message on to his son who'd flown in from the States. But there was only silence.

Niall and I undressed him, folding his suit, his jumper and his shirt and placing them carefully on the chair under the fresh suit his son Kevin had dropped in.

'So, he's saying nothing?' Niall asked.

'No, he's quiet. Not a word.'

Maurice's face bore a look of pure defiance. Like he had never been made to do a single thing he didn't want to in his life. 'Perhaps he's one of the lucky ones and said it all before he left.'

'I'm not sure I'd call suicide lucky.'

'No,' I said, noticing Maurice's wedding finger, and the red shiny mark left from the ring Niall had taken off. 'Of course not.'

We began to wash him in silence. With no hint of what that man's voice sounded like, I had to imagine it from when I met the son the next day, Kevin's voice reminding me of Marielle's comforting timbre. His mouth hung open in the smallest, most vulnerable of gapes, as though he didn't have the energy to close it. He sat by the coffin, rubbing his hands, looking down at the floor then up at his father and down again, repeating this for minutes on end.

When I sat by his side, he looked at me. Was it fear I saw, or grief, or perhaps he was simply unsure of what to say. But before I could take the burden from him, he said: 'I believe you speak to them.'

'Sometimes they speak to me. But he's been quiet, I'm afraid.'

'Yes, he was good at that.' He looked again at his father.

'I wish he had spoken so I could tell you something. That might explain . . .'

'No need. He left a message. He missed my mother. Loneliness. That's the long and short of it.'

'Oh, I'm glad he did. It's hard if there's nothing.'

'If only he'd said something to me long ago, I could've done something. Brought him over to the States, maybe, although he would've hated that too.'

I felt so sorry for this man, dealing with the burden of this guilt all on his own.

'Do you have family around here?' I asked.

'I'm an only child. I've cousins in England. Bristol and Cheltenham. But we wouldn't know each other well. My wife's on the way over with the kids, though. We've two. Boy and a girl.'

'I'm glad they're coming.'

In the background I heard the kitchen door close in the house.

'What do I tell my kids? They're old enough to know things but I don't know what to say.' He hid his face behind his long slender hands, his body beginning to sob quietly. 'He was a grumpy old git most of the time. But he was *my* grumpy old git. And I should have been here more.'

'No, you shouldn't.' And this is the strange thing, I said those words like I had a right, an absolute belief that they were true. I cannot explain to this day where they came from, and why I said them with such authority, as if

Maurice had spoken them himself. 'What I mean is,' I said, trying to clarify my pronouncement without making myself sound even more nuts, 'we have our lives, and we do our best. You, I'm sure, did your best.'

Kevin lowered his hands and turned to smile at me.

'That's exactly what he'd have said. Are you sure he didn't speak to you?' He gave a quiet laugh. 'You'd have liked him. People did. He was such an old codger—a rich one, mind, but there was something that people couldn't get enough of. Wish I had it, whatever it was. He was dyslexic and I never knew. Said he hadn't a clue where I got my writing ability from. But I'd love to have traded his charm for my words for just one day to see what life was like for him.'

He dipped his head, lost in those thoughts of his father.

'What will you tell them, then, do you think, your children?'

'The truth, I suppose. What else do I have? I'll tell them their granddad loved them. And that his heart was simply too sick to carry on.'

I nodded and smiled, impressed by this shattered man.

'Isn't it amazing that we can spend our lives with someone and think we know them? Think we know exactly what they would do in any situation. But never in a thousand years would I have thought this would be my father's ending. And yet now that I'm here, now that I've heard what he had to say, I get it. It's so very him. People are eternal mysteries, aren't they?'

'They sure are.'

'Well, yes, I mean you'd know exactly what I'm talking about. You must get all sorts through the door.' He studied me curiously: 'So how does what you do, this talking to them, even work?'

'They speak if they want to and I hear them. There's nothing terribly complicated.'

'And what do they say?'

'All sorts. Sometimes what they have to say is good and sometimes it's terribly sad.'

'And then you have to tell people like me, who are devastated?'

'Pretty much.'

'Wow. I should do a story about you.'

I gave a quick, embarrassed laugh, not quite knowing what to think. I wasn't sure I was ready for the wider world's attention. And then I remembered Marielle and how life-changing that had been for me.

'Actually, there's a woman in France called Marielle Vincent who is far better at that kind of thing than me, maybe you should talk to her.'

He turned back to consider his father.

'I don't know I'd want it—that burden of truth.'

'It has its moments.'

'And you can't turn it on and off?'

'No. It's there all day every day. If they want to speak then I'll hear them.'

'So until *you* die, that's what you'll hear, even if you try to give it up or retire, they'll keep talking.'

'Yes, I suppose.'

'And who will listen to you when you go? Do you have children you've passed this on to?'

'No.' I smiled almost in apology to this man I didn't know. Niall and I hadn't talked about children by then. I didn't know what it was I thought about that anymore. Once I'd been so sure there would be children in my life but now I was confused. And here was a stranger giving voice to a fear that had quietly niggled at me for years but in that moment appeared loud and clear: that if I passed on my gift, an innocent child would carry the burden of its pressures and expectations, not to mention the weight of public opinion, just as I had. How could that be fair? 'No children,' I concluded, 'So far, I'm the last in the line.'

Chapter 20

For my hen-do, Peanut invited Ruth and me to London to stay in their apartment in St John's Wood. They had kept it after moving so Anders had somewhere to stay when he needed to check on his UK practice. But now they were selling both the business and the apartment. This visit was to be her last in London in their first home.

I hadn't wanted a hen-do actually, but Ruth kept banging on about it and I'd finally caved. Ruth was four months pregnant on Amy and having a tough time of it so Peanut had thought it a nice gesture to cheer her up.

Even though she'd spent the afternoon getting sick in the airport toilets, and on the flight, and when we landed, she couldn't be contained for the happiness of being away from Derry and Tom for two nights.

'I love them, I really do, but Jesus, they won't stop messing up the place. I've only got it tidy but they're there breathing beside me, putting chocolaty hands on my cream couch.'

'Yeah, you should really tell Derry to quit that,' Peanut laughed, as she popped the first bottle of champagne.

'And maybe buy a leather couch.'

'Thanks, Jeanie, but I couldn't stand the squeaking.'

'Oh yeah, actually now that you say it, I wouldn't either.'

The following day we spent the afternoon shopping on Oxford Street, Ruth's choice. When we finally got home to Peanut's, Ruth instantly sought the comfort of her bed and fell asleep, her clothes and shoes still on. Peanut put a blanket over her. From the doorway we watched the beautiful curve of her baby rise and fall.

'So have you told Niall that you're not sure about having kids yet, Jeanie?' I'd spoken to Peanut about my worry of passing on my gift.

'Not yet, no.'

'Don't you think you should before, you know, you commit your lives to each other?'

'I will, it's just I haven't found the right time.'

She nodded, letting me off the hook on this my hen night. She looked at Ruth then and said: 'It's a pity really.'

'What, about me and having kids?'

'No, you big twat, that she's gone asleep. I had the whole night planned out. There's this great sushi bar I want to go to and then I have the perfect jazz club picked out.'

'Jazz? You are fucking kidding me?'

'Yes, I am, my lovely, but it was worth it for that face.' She waggled my cheek and laughed. 'No, it's a normal kind of club. Actually, it's just a late-night bar that Anders and I used to go to, but you can dance if you so wish.'

'Things are good with Anders then?'

'Things are marvellous with that man. He was actually looking forward to having time alone with the twins. As much as I love them, as you have always been so keen to point out, they are exhausting. He's going to take them to the cabin. You should see this thing, it's only a couple of planks of wood short of the hovel my dad used to hide in at the weekends in our back garden when he wanted to listen to a match in peace.'

'So have you talked about marriage lately?'

'No.'

'But you want to?'

'Yeah,' she said as if it was a stupid question. I could see her study me as I knocked back some more champagne. 'You know, if you aren't sure about things with Niall, you can pull out. Nobody would hate you for it.'

'Oh right, except Niall and Dad and Mum and Harry, and definitely Mikey.'

'And what about you, what would you think?'

'I'd hate myself too. And anyway, I love him.'

'Right, but what you haven't done there in that comprehensive answer is shoot me down, been disgusted that I'd even suggest such a thing on the cusp of your big day.'

'Can't we just talk about you and Anders and your beautiful blondie babies and how "stinking rich" you are?' I laughed, trying to distract her.

'Sure. If you insist.' We drank again and looked back at our snoring friend. 'Ruth was so excited though, wasn't she? It was worth it just to see her face as she dragged us into every shop. But how did she manage it in those?'

Peanut indicated Ruth's red high heels with her champagne glass.

'I was even struggling in these and I'm not four months pregnant.' I looked down at my light blue runners with the pink laces. 'Should we take them off her?'

'I guess. Not sure how comfortable a sleep she'll get in them.'

We rounded the bottom of the bed and took one foot each and gently tried to take them off. Her feet, however, seemed determined not to let go. We pushed then pulled, front and back, then side to side. Jiggled until there was nothing to it but to tug hard. We counted down from three then pulled. Propelled back with the force against the wall, we looked at each other in fright of waking her with one red shoe in each hand.

'Thanks, girlies.' Without opening her eyes, Ruth smiled, turned on her side, placing her hands under her right cheek, and snuggled down again with a contented sigh.

We giggled then patted her feet after we'd pulled the duvet over them.

'Actually, do you think Ruth'd mind if we did

go out?' Peanut whispered as we began to leave the room. 'I've something I'd really like to show you.'

'I don't mind if she doesn't.'

Ruth waved Peanut away when she went to hunker beside her to ask if she'd like to come out with us. 'Just for an hour or two?'

'Go away, I'm sleeping.'

'OK but we're going, yeah? You don't mind?'

Ruth just rolled over, ignoring us.

Peanut refused to tell me where we were going. But she insisted I make more of an effort than my pink-laced Pumas. I relented and upgraded to my red knee platform boots, very Harry, that I'd picked up in Oxfam for a fiver, and soon she was fast-walking me to the Jubilee line. She kept checking the time and pulling me forward whenever I stopped to look in restaurant windows.

'Food after, I promise. There might even be nibbles here.'

We crisscrossed roads, skipped under arches, leading to lane-ways and small side streets of white painted buildings with large expansive windows in which sat wall-sized paintings with price tags you might expect to pay on a house in Kilcross. She stopped outside one, where the hum of people inside sounded like the busy beehives that Simon, Niall's father, kept.

'Why are we here?'

I looked at the window in which sat one large photograph. It took me a moment to get what it was, but soon I could see it, the ballooning of a sheet filling the expanse, so that it looked like a wave or a crease in a white rose petal, something gracious and rich and precious.

'Oh, you are kidding me.' My hand shot to my mouth. It was the picture of me flicking out the sheet in our embalming room some ten years prior, only I wasn't there any more. It was just the sheet in flight, the colours and shadows remastered in a kind of sepia.

'I told him I might make it. It's his first really big show in years.'

I kept looking at the picture, not yet able to form the words that would eventually come.

'We're kind of late. I think we might have missed his speech; the English are a bit better at timekeeping than us.'

Peanut turned but I didn't move. I continued to stand and stare. Even when she took my hand and tried to pull me inside, I didn't budge.

'Jeanie? Don't you want to go in?'

'You . . . you should have told me, Peanut.'

'I know, but sometimes friends need to do things like this.'

'Why?' I rounded on her.

'Because, Jeanie, I really want you to be sure about Niall.'

'And you thought bringing me here to see

256

Fionn Cassin of all people was going to do that.'

'Pretty much.'

I moved on past the gallery to find a doorway with a set of steps, where I sat, my hand to my forehead, as Pea came to join me.

'I love Niall, Pea. I've told you.'

'I know you love him. But is it the real deal?'

'Yes, of course it is.'

'OK, look. We don't have to go in. I never told him we were coming. I think he just sent the invitation out of courtesy. I haven't actually seen him in years. I'm just worried about you, Jeanie.'

I looked at this friend who seemed to be in a constant state of anxiety over me and I felt guilty that this was the nature of us, her having to be my defender, my champion, my conscience. My annoyance retreated in an instant.

'I blame the champagne.' I knocked my knee against hers and smiled.

'Yes, let's blame it. Excellent idea.'

I laughed a little. 'Oh look, this is stupid. I'm happy with Niall and there's nothing to fret over. I'll go in there and prove it to you and you won't have to be concerned about me any more. Half-hour round the block. We'll try to find all the pictures of me, 'cause there'll be loads as he was so crazy about me, and then we're out of there, back to Ruth to laugh about this. Deal?'

I held out my hand to shake hers.

'You're sure?'

'Absolutely.' I inched my hand forward again, enticing hers in. And when she took it, she laughed, as did I. We rose then and, arm in arm, walked back toward the gallery and turned in through its doorway.

We couldn't see him. Although he was somewhere. I could feel his presence, smothered amongst the swarm of bodies. Peanut headed straight for the makeshift bar and the smiling waitress. She took two glasses of white, handing one to me while her eyes scanned the canapés the waitress had gestured toward. I no longer felt hungry, my stomach now dining on nerves. Peanut piled three pâté crackers on top of each other and shoved them into her mouth.

'What?' She looked at me in defiance, spitting crumbs on herself and me.

'Should we erm . . . ?' I indicated to the photos on the wall with my glass of wine.

'Yeah, of course. Let me grab a couple more of these boys.' Peanut looked at her wine and—realising the limited amount of canapés she would be able to take should she continue to carry it—knocked it back and put it down, then piled up two more three-tier Peanut specials.

'Don't worry, I'll be back for another glass in a minute,' she told the waitress, who seemed to be growing tired of Peanut's constant return visits, before we began to circle the room. 'I think she likes me. I'd be in there if I were that way inclined,' she laughed.

The almost audible pulse in my veins made me wonder in which corner I would find him or when his voice would finally reach my ear, or if perhaps I'd feel him by my side without need of sight or sound. The very possibility consumed me, making a mockery of my pretend attention to his work, his interpretation of the world. But still I continued, from one picture to the next, nodding at whatever it was Peanut was indicating, making up observations with words stolen from his vocabulary of long ago: aspect, apex, aperture.

I didn't take in the detail of many of those photographs. Not that they weren't any good, or worthy enough of my concentration and praise; nothing could have been further from the truth. Every single one had the capacity to pull me back to him, to churn up every last drop of the unquestionable love and admiration I had felt. Moments of the ordinary, captured in such detail and depth by that mysterious part of him that knew the right moment to press the button, to create such simple beauty, and that made me want to cry.

I closed my eyes on most of them, rushing through the room so that Peanut found it hard to keep up, especially with her constant need to return for more food and wine. It was all I had to fight this urge to find him. But one photo stopped me in my red-booted tracks—a black-and-white close-up of a girl's face. The top left-hand corner, including her eye, in shadow, while a column of light swept across the rest of her, slanting from her right temple to her jaw line, showing up the inky darkness of her right eye, the sharp curve of her cheekbone, the fullness of her lips. Her visible eye drawn up and over to something out of shot. She was beautiful. She was me. I couldn't recall him taking it. Had no recollection of where we were or what it was that had caused that strip of light to illuminate my skin, making my freckles appear loud and lush on my paleness. My breath caught, as Peanut placed a steadying hand on my arm, and said:

'Holy crap.'

We stood in silence, unable to move from this all-consuming face, even when others got in our way, passing by, stopping, none looking back, by the way, making the connection with the girl standing behind them with the black balloon of hair and open mouth. We kept staring ahead until they moved on and she came back into view.

'You found it then?' he said. 'I wasn't sure if you'd make it, Peanut, and I didn't realise you'd be bringing such an important guest.'

'Hey, you.' Peanut turned to kiss him on the cheek. 'Yeah, I wasn't sure either but here we are. We nearly had Ruth too, but she's flaked out in pregnancy heaven back in my place.' She gave a smiley nod then continued. 'So, this is fancy.' She swung around, her new glass of wine spilling with the force as she indicated the room, the people, the photos, and of course the bar. 'Great canapés, by the way.'

'Oh good, glad you like them.'

I hadn't moved a muscle. I realised I was going to have to say something but my brain was having a hard time switching gears to do so.

'So, Jeanie, good to see you. Thanks for coming.'

He looked at me with those wolf eyes.

'Oh, yes, well . . .' I had to swallow before my voice could finally lurch into action. 'I didn't actually know I was coming until I got here.'

'I see.' Fionn smiled at Peanut who raised her eyebrows and gave a 'mea culpa' cheeky grin.

'Sorry, that sounded rude.'

'No, look it's fine. I can imagine it's all a bit of a shock, walking into a gallery in a different country to find your face on the wall.'

I looked at it again, squinting my eyes and trying to recall its moment of capture.

'Where were we when you took it? I can't remember.'

'We were at my house in Drumsnough. In my bedroom.' His eyes dipped away from mine in embarrassment, but the smile lingered.

I remembered then and raised a hand to my mouth. My eyes moistened and I blinked as I realised that had the lens zoomed out, my full body in its complete nakedness would have been in view. His folks were out and we had taken the opportunity to move under his covers until his eyes had widened and he had sighed at the release.

'*La petite mort*,' he'd whispered into my ear as he lay on his back by my side and closed his eyes for a moment.

He'd gotten up then to do something. Grown curious at his rummaging, I'd sat up. It was right then that I'd felt the warmth of the sun on the right-hand side of my face, where the darkness had been cut through by the slight opening of his curtains.

'Stop. Don't move,' he'd called. His left hand out in warning to hold still as he reached for his camera. He took so many shots that I remember growing irritated.

'One more, please. Look over at the wall now, past the curtains. Yep. That's it, perfect.'

'I'm stopping now. Your folks could be home any minute.'

'They won't mind. I've told you, all they say is be responsible and respectful and wear protection.'

He came to kneel in front of me, his camera still in his hand, took one or two more shots then kissed me again. I'd never seen the developed shot until now.

'Jesus,' I said, standing in the gallery.

'I'm sorry. Is this too much? You said I could use any of the shots I'd taken of you. It remains one of my all-time favourites. But I can take it down if you like.'

'No, it's fine.' I breathed in deeply. 'I'd forgotten . . .' I tried again at some coherence but was stopped by the need for air. 'Is there a . . . ?' Seat was the word I was trying for, but instead I circled my hand around behind my arse in the hope that one of them would understand.

'Oh, erm, no I'm afraid—'

'I think I need to get some air.' I pointed to the window, then gave Peanut my long-since emptied glass of wine and left, pushing through the crowds to stand outside, holding on to the railing of the next-door building, grabbing each successive bar as I made my way back to the step on which we'd sat earlier, where I heaved in the air and blew it back out again.

'So that was a wonderfully dramatic exit.' Peanut arrived to sit beside me with a glass of water and one of wine, held not so expertly in one hand so that both were overflowing the edges, and some more canapés in the other. She offered me all of them. I took the water, much to her relief, as she munched and slurped on what was left. 'I felt like I was in a Jane Austen novel, only without the costumes.'

'Yes. I did it totally for you, Pea. I thought it would add to the evening.'

'He's crapping himself in there.'

'What do you mean?'

'He thinks you'll sue him.'

'Why would I sue him?'

'You could make a fortune, say you didn't give him written permission.'

'Seriously, Pea, did you take something today when I wasn't looking?'

'I wish. No, it's the wine. I haven't had so much to drink since before the twins. It's very strong.'

'Or maybe you're drinking it too fast.'

'A possibility. Anyway, he wanted to come out to you but I stopped him. "My friend," I said. "I'll be dealing with her." '

'God, you are so drunk.'

'I know.' She giggled, then finished the last of her wine and snuggled into my shoulder. 'I think I might just lean here for a bit.'

'Wonderful.'

As she sighed her way to an almost instant sleep, I wondered how it was I was here, back in the same hopelessly messed-up place I always found myself when Fionn Cassin was involved.

'All OK now?' Fionn approached me tentatively.

'Oh yeah. Sorry about that.' I smiled as he stepped closer. 'Like you say, it was a bit of a shock.'

'So she really hadn't told you where you were going?'

'No.' I peered down at the top of Peanut's head. 'You got to love her, though.'

'Can I?' Fionn motioned to the wide step.

'Of course. But don't you need to be in there schmoozing and selling?'

'They won't miss me for two minutes.'

He sat and we looked out at the street in this tiny fleeting moment of Saturday night silence, while from far off in much busier thoroughfares we could hear music and the shriek of laughter.

'I'm glad you came, you know.'

'Yeah?'

'Still not married then?'

'Two weeks.'

I caught his eyebrows rise before he looked down at the ground.

'I'd never have put you two together.'

'No. It seems you're not the only one.' I glanced at Peanut again. 'But we're good, you know.'

'It's all worked out perfectly so.'

'Yep. Perfect.'

A moment of embarrassed silence descended.

'So, been talking to any interesting dead people lately?' His words broke our deadlock, pushing us into safe territory.

'Oh yeah,' I laughed, relaxing slightly. 'There's been a few. One of yours recently actually.'

'One of mine?'

'A London Irish.'

'Oh, is that who I am now?'

'Annie Galvin. Eighty-five. She died in a nursing home over here. Had no one left. No one she knew except this woman called Samantha, from the London Irish Centre, who'd visit her every couple of weeks. She told her every time she saw her to make sure she got her back home to Kilcross when she died. All she'd ever wanted was to be buried with her parents. But she hadn't a penny in the bank. So when she was near the end, Samantha took to the airwaves and set up a GoFundMe page, and within two days of Annie dying, she was lying in front of me telling me she wished she'd never left the place. The two of us sat talking about all the things she could remember about the town and I told her all the things that had changed. She was lovely. And when she was ready to go she thanked me like a true lady and said her goodbyes.'

'Wow. See, it's stories like that that help me see why it is you stayed.'

There was a heartbeat of a second before I replied.

'Yep, she was something else all right.' I looked to the end of the street where a taxi pulled up, and I watched a man get out, turn up the collar of his coat and disappear into a building that was in complete darkness. This was Annie's world, a city where mystery and loneliness lived hand in hand.

'Are you glad you moved to London?' I asked, turning back to him, wanting to know it all.

'God, yes. It's been great. The possibilities are endless. I like being the master of my own destiny.'

'Aren't you consumed by money like the rest of them, then?'

'It matters, sure, but I try to keep it in perspective. But I'm lucky, people like my stuff so I can pick and choose. For the moment, that is. Until I am passé.'

'How does that happen then?'

'Complacency. See, the key to it all, Jeanie, is to never think you're done, that you're it and that there's nothing more to learn. Because there always, always is.'

I chuckled at that.

'What's so funny?'

'Oh nothing. It's just you. That right there is what I loved about you. That zest for other things, for exploring, creating, pushing yourself. I was never like you. And could never understand what it was you saw in someone like me.'

I felt embarrassed by the honesty that had slipped out as easily as my unforced smile when sitting in his presence.

'You're still at that, Jeanie? After all these years.'

He seemed almost angry now, like here I was letting him down again.

'Do you ever actually look in the mirror, Jeanie? Do you ever think about what it is you do? I mean, did you hear what you were saying about Annie? You are the most unusual woman I've ever come across. And I've met quite a few who could've given you a run for your money. But no one has come close to what you make me feel. I was so alive with you. The way you'd look at me made me believe I could achieve anything. And it's my greatest disappointment that I could never make you feel the same.'

My breath caught as I looked down at my knees in embarrassment.

'I wanted you to come with me so much, Jeanie, when I left. I thought if I could give you a taste of this world, you'd see how amazing you were, how much you could do. But I think my pushing you was hurting more than helping. So I stopped.'

It was his turn to look away.

'But you have no idea how long it took me to forget you, Jeanie. How hard it was not to text and call and beg you to please get on a fucking plane and just move over. And then I heard you and Niall were together and I thought, yeah, that makes sense. That's safe for her. That won't frighten her. But I hated him. How stupid is that? In fact, when you think of it, I should've rung him up and thanked him for giving you what you thought you needed, that protection.' He gave a small defeated laugh. 'I just wish . . . I wish you'd taken a chance on me, on this, Jeanie, that's all.'

His proclamation over, he put his hand to his mouth, and yet he had more to say.

'I even went back that time to Kilcross to make sure, you know, that you really wanted him. Do you remember standing on Mary Street, and I asked you to come see me but you said no? And then you arrived at my house and for a split second, I thought, OK, this is it, the moment we finally just throw it all up in the air and give it a go. But you drove away,' he laughed. 'And yet here I still am, still hopelessly bound to you.'

Somehow I found a way to hold his eyes without feeling like I might suffocate in fear of who he was and what he was saying. And it was as though we were back in that moment in his bedroom when we could really see the other. He leaned in to kiss me. And it felt right. I closed my eyes on that moment, wanting to hold on to that touch, forever. A memory that could sit outside of time defining the complete vulnerability, stupidity, weakness, strength, and love that was us.

His hand moved to my hair, to dig within its thickness, to hold it in his fist, to pull me closer, so that Peanut dislodged from my shoulder and groaned as she slid down, with me having to pull away from him to save her head from hitting the step, cradling it instead in my lap.

'Fee-on?' From up the street, an Englishman's voice called his name, pronouncing it completely wrongly.

It was enough for his eyes to close in annoyance for a second before reopening and gathering me in his stare again.

'If ever,' he whispered, his forehead touching mine, 'you realise you've made the wrong choice, I'm here, OK, right here waiting. I love you, Jeanie Masterson, and always hopelessly, desperately will.'

Without saying anything else, or waiting for a reply I wasn't sure he was looking to hear, he kissed my forehead then got up and walked away.

I never told anyone what he said that night. Not Peanut, who I had to wake to lead us home. Not Ruth who, when we got there, became incensed that she had missed the reunion and insisted on knowing every word he'd said. Not Niall, who on our return to Dublin picked us up at arrivals, where I wrapped my arms around him and kissed him with a desperate passion that made Ruth wolf-whistle, determined to show him I loved him and to convince myself that I'd made the right choice. No one would ever know, I decided. I would keep Fionn's promise locked inside, nestled beside all the other secrets the dead had told me, in case someday I might need it.

Chapter 21

The first time Niall and I spoke about children was two weeks later on our wedding day when we sat to the top table with sore faces from smiling for the camera.

Niall couldn't take his eyes off Ruth as she wore her growing Amy bump with pride.

'What?' I'd asked, amused by his distraction as he watched her cross the floor in front of the top table where we'd finished the main course and Gareth, Niall's brother, was preparing to get up to start the speeches. Ruth waved to us and blew a kiss, as her other hand held up the hem of her orange dress and her soft curls bounced as she tried to hurry to get back from the loo before the hilarity began.

He laughed at my curiosity and reached for my hand. 'I'm imagining you like that, looking radiant.'

'I don't think she feels radiant. She told me earlier she feels like she has an entire soccer team up there.'

'I can't wait though, when we start all that.'

'What, producing GAA teams?'

'Well, we are twenty-eight so maybe not a full squad. A midfielder, a few defenders would be perfect.'

He looked at me with a quizzical smile when I laughed perhaps louder than I should've.

'But we've time enough yet, Niall? Years before we need to be thinking that way.'

'Sure,' he said, his smile becoming flat-lipped—his 'holding smile,' I used to think, the one that said, 'We'll be revisiting that later'—and turned away from me, my hand still in his as he began to talk to Gareth who'd bent to his ear.

It was then that Peanut, decked out in her self-chosen pale blue bridesmaid dress, leaned over to me and said: 'Do you think I should go rescue Anders?'

We looked over to where he sat, trying to get Elsa to stop putting her jelly in a pool in her lap so that little fishes could swim in it while at the same time attempting to stop Oskar from running up and down the room chasing Tom, Ruth's eldest.

'On second thoughts,' she said, 'he looks fine.'

I'd held Niall off the idea of kids successfully until I was thirty. And then he'd ramped up the pressure, telling me now was the time because we didn't want to have only one, we needed to have two as it was cruel to do that to any child. They'd be bored. Who would they play with?

'And argue with?' I added, as we stood at the kitchen table on one of our rare quiet days, folding the freshly cleaned hair towels and sheets we used on the dead. 'You and your brother, case in point.'

Gareth and Niall couldn't even see eye to eye on how Monopoly got played. Every Christmas it would be the same when we went around to the Longleys.' It would all be OK for the first ten minutes, then the competitiveness set in and one would be telling the other that it was three doubles and not two to get out of jail.

'Arguing is as much a part of bonding as loving someone,' Niall protested. 'And anyway, you can't just have one, because then they'll be alone having to look after us when we get old.'

'Is that why people have children then, so they have someone to mind them when they're ancient?'

'Pretty much. And we need to increase the population so they pay taxes that'll pay for our substantial state pensions.'

'Jeez, it's so very touching. I think you should impregnate me right here.'

'I'd be happy to.' He dropped a towel and made his advance, with me pushing him away, laughing.

'Not everyone has children, Niall. Arthur and Teresa are a case in point.'

'I thought they couldn't.'

'Well, yes, that is true.'

'We don't even know if we can or not at this rate.'

'I'm simply saying there are people who don't and they're perfectly happy,' I sidestepped.

'You want kids, right?' Niall had stopped folding now. 'I mean you're not just saying it 'cause you know that's what I want. That's not what you're doing?'

'No,' I said, as if he was being ridiculous.

I'd stopped working too and was busy winding a loose thread I'd found in one of the sheets around my little finger as tightly as possible.

'So what's the problem?'

'I'm just not ready. It still feels like it's such a big commitment, you know. Everything would change.'

'But you're thirty, Jeanie. Like even if we got pregnant right now that means you'll be giving birth at thirty-one. And then you could be thirty-five by the time the next one comes along.'

'Wow, you've really got this all worked out.' I pulled at the thread, now released from my little finger, harder and harder until it came away.

'You don't want to leave too much of a gap between them.'

'But everyone's having children later these days.'

'Not Ruth and Peanut.'

'No, not them. I mean, other people.'

'Yes, but they are actually having them. We aren't even trying, yet.'

'I know, but look at Ruth and Derry. They're

exhausted all the time. We go out with them and they have to leave at ten.'

'But they cope. They're happy, aren't they? What is it, Jeanie? I don't understand.'

'Well . . .' I began nervously, realising now I was going to have to admit my fears, 'what if, what if he or she has what I have?'

'What do you mean, "has what you have"?'

'You know, the talking to the dead.'

'Oh. Is that something you're afraid of?'

'I guess. I mean, I don't think it's something I want for them. Mum was terrified for me when she found out. She knew what was ahead of me. She'd seen Dad suffer enough with all the dead's burdens, not to mention how the living could be so cruel about us.'

'But they'd be half me, too, remember. So maybe they'll get the "really good with his hands" gene instead.'

'It's not funny, Niall.'

'I didn't say it was. I just didn't realise you felt this way.'

'Well, I do. I don't want them having to put up with all the nasty comments and name-calling. You remember how it was, Niall, you were there. I couldn't do it to them. And it's not just that, this job is hard and it's not like you can walk away from it. It's there every minute of the day, demanding your attention.'

'OK, look,' he relented. 'I hadn't really thought

about it that way before. But I get it. And you never know, it mightn't get passed on. Mikey didn't inherit your dad's gift. And even if they do, they've got us, and your dad. We'd help them through. They wouldn't be alone.'

'But I had Dad and I felt alone.'

'But we'll make sure they don't.'

He gave me an encouraging smile, to which I nodded meekly. He hugged me then, kissed my head, and tucked me in against his chest.

Chapter 22

The day of my father's friend, Andrew Devlin's removal, Niall and I worked alongside each other in relative silence like overly polite strangers. He wouldn't meet my eye, despite my efforts. I grew exhausted, making sure any move I made wouldn't upset him further. But he gave me nothing, no small thread that I could hold on to, no glance in my direction when I had caught him unawares; his displeasure was borne like a true professional.

I'd missed three calls from Ruth by then. The last time she left a message:

'Jeanie, are you not talking to me? I wanted to explain about Niall. I couldn't say no to him about the spare room. Not to him. He's my oldest friend. I hope you understand. I hate this. I don't want to be on anyone's side. I'm here for you too, OK? So you bloody well call me. Call me.'

I sent her a single love heart in a text, an offering of my understanding but unable to give her anything more, not quite yet.

By late afternoon we had finished and, when Andrew lay dressed and ready in his coffin, Niall headed for the corridor, telling me he was going out to get something to eat. Niall always had lunch in the kitchen.

'But, can't you wait until after, maybe an hour or so? Andrew might talk and it'd be nice if you were around, in case I need you to help me.'

'It's never bothered you before to do this stuff on your own.'

'No, but you've always been here. It meant something to know that you were in the kitchen or in the office.'

'So Jeanie Masterson actually needs my support?'

'Is it that hard to believe?'

'Yes, it really is.'

'OK, I know we need to talk about everything going on for us and I want to, I really do. But right now I have to do this. This is Andrew we're talking about and I need you to be here. Can you do that, please?' I felt so weary and strung out by everything.

'Can't you call Harry?'

'No, Niall. I want it to be you. That's how we've always done it.'

For a moment he considered my words. I felt so incredibly sad, begging him for something that had always been a given, our fate having brought us here, to these discordant lives.

'And anyway, shouldn't your dad be doing this one? I thought out of all the dead people we've dealt with, Andrew would be the one he'd want to talk to.'

'It's not easy when you're that close to some-one.'

Niall sighed heavily, rubbing a hand down his face before turning to walk the corridor to the kitchen.

After twenty minutes, Andrew hadn't said a thing. I'd begun to wonder if perhaps Niall had been right, that it should've been Dad sitting here and not me. Maybe I was the reason for Andrew's silence, but then he began and soon he was in the thick of it, telling me everything.

'I hadn't wanted to go, you know, but by the end I held my breath back almost eagerly. My heart's deterioration was too much. And I was ready. *They* were ready: Mum and Dad and the siblings. I could see it in them, their need for this to be over. That grey tiredness, those sad eyes, those worried mouths that had run out of words but still twitched in awkwardness, willing something to come out, something that might ease this horror that had gone on for far too long. After the last surgery hadn't managed to fix me as well as the surgeons would have liked, we were already there, standing at my funeral. I couldn't hold them to this drudgery any longer. So I began to let go, giving them back their lives.'

'Oh Andrew, I'm sure your family didn't see it that way.'

'Now, Jeanie, I'm not here for platitudes. I've had my fill.'

'I didn't mean—'

'Of course, you didn't. But I'm guessing I haven't long so let's use what little time we have on truths.'

'Were you scared?' I didn't always ask such things of the dead, but with Andrew it felt as if I knew him because of Dad, even though it was our first time to meet.

'Petrified. And as for my family, they looked worse than I did most of the time. And I'd tell them, too. It gave us something to laugh about. Levity, always advised when death is in the room.' Andrew had a drollness that I felt could lighten the darkest of moments.

'Yes, we've found that works here too,' I smiled.

'Your father was good to me, Jeanie. I'm not quite sure how it would've been without him.'

'But wasn't it weird having the undertaker visit so often? Were you not thinking every time he walked through the door your number was up?'

'I liked that he was truthful with my family and me about what to expect in death but about life too. Besides, I forgot after a while what he did for a living. I like to think he got as much from our friendship as I did.'

'I think he really did.'

280

'We could confide in each other. Inner thoughts, secrets. I told him I'd fallen in love with one of the nurses. Tanya. She knew how to make me smile. She'd talk to me, like really talk to me, not in that pitying "you're terminally ill" kind of way. We discussed book reviews she'd seen in the papers; new films that were coming out, politics, past loves, favourite food, best holidays, worst dates. We just clicked. I adored every syllable she uttered.'

'Wow.'

'Oh no, don't get your hopes up. I don't think she felt the same. Perhaps she did. But I didn't care. Funny how selfish that sounds, but it's what kept me going those final months. That thrill of her, of all I felt.'

'Did you ever get to tell her?'

'Oh no. I couldn't have risked losing her. What if she'd said she didn't feel the same? She'd have stopped coming or worse, she wouldn't have behaved the same towards me. She'd have brought in a different version of herself, an embarrassed and awkward one. Everything would've been totally gone. No, it was best I kept it to myself. You've got Niall, Jeanie, so you know how precious love is, don't you?'

'Well, yes. Of course.' I tapped my index fingernail gently against the side of his coffin, unable to look at him.

'Ah, now, listen to yourself.' If he'd been

281

able to, I'm sure at that very moment Andrew would've raised his finger and wagged it at me. 'That's what I was afraid of with Tanya, that if I'd told her she'd have given me that noncommittal, in-betweenie, "not floating my boat" type of thing.'

'That's not what I meant. But anyway, would that have been so bad? Is that not love too?'

'Not when you're hoping for the real thing, no, not really.'

'Well, it's not always that straightforward.'

'Isn't it?'

'Well, I think,' I said, trying to put words on what had always lived shamefully within me, 'that there are different kinds of love in the world. Like different-coloured roses, or different kinds of winds or clouds or spiders.'

'Spiders?'

'Varieties of the same thing. Some are passionate, and deep, and make your heart race, and then some are quiet and comfortable; easy, kind of safe.'

'Isn't that friendship, though?'

'No. Well, all right, yes, all love is friendship. But it extends out from that, doesn't it, growing and getting stronger, and yes, deeper. And then the passion comes, in its own time.'

'So you think I should've told her?' Andrew asked, after a spell of silence.

'Maybe. Maybe you should've given her a

chance too. I mean, what if she did love you and now she regrets you going without being able to say it?'

'Hmm. I suppose what better words are there in the English language than "I love you." My parting gift? But I don't know; your easy, comfortable love has yet to convince me.'

'But isn't that why you're here? People usually have things they want me to do, messages to pass on. Isn't this it? Isn't Tanya why you stayed to talk to me?'

'Oh, yes, your father told me all about what it is you do and how you help people like that. Is he around, by the way?'

'No, I'm afraid he's not.' I felt embarrassed for a moment, in case he'd have preferred him.

'Oh no, you misunderstand me, Jeanie. I'm more checking he's not here. I told him not to be. I didn't want that for him. "Leave me with your daughter," I said. 'If I've anything to say, I'll say it to her.'

I smiled. 'You know, years ago, before we funeral directors got our hands on you dead souls, it was family and friends or a neighbour who would wash and dress you. There was no one else.'

'Well, I'm rather glad you lot did then, if that's the case. My family and friends have done enough for me these past few years without me expecting that from them too. Besides, I wanted to meet you. Your father often talked of little else. I knew about the retirement.'

'Ah, that.'

'I'll admit I encouraged him. "Live your life while you can," I said.' Andrew's voice faltered now, a weakness to it which when alive might have elicited a cough.

'Yes, well, I'm finding his bid for freedom a bit hard, to be honest, as you're insisting on the truth.'

'Ah honesty.' His voice was becoming laboured. But through the push and pull of the fight, he said: 'I told him about that too. "Don't leave with things left unsaid. Tell that girl everything." And I really hope he has, Jeanie.'

'What do you mean?' I gave a surprised laugh.

'It's not for me to . . .' Andrew's voice weakened further, losing its power, becoming cracked and tired, moving further from me.

'Stay with me, Andrew, just a little longer. We'll take one breath at a time, the two of us.' And even though I knew he had no working organs, no diaphragm, no lungs and no muscle to push the chest wide, I hoped the sound of my breath might be enough to hold him. With little time left, I knew I'd have to forgo the answer to that quandary he had posed and concentrate on him. 'You should tell me now, Andrew, while you can, tell me what it is you need me to do.'

'Nothing,' he managed. His voice barely

audible. 'I only wanted to be with the living a few minutes more.'

Such a simple request and yet I wondered might there really have been more, something held back. But it was too late, his time was galloping rapidly to a halt and so was he. 'And why not?' I said. 'I'll keep talking so if that's OK?'

'Please do. Let me hear what it is to still be alive.'

He was a long way off now, drifting further.

For ten further minutes I stayed by his side, talking to myself, knowing full well he had left but still not giving up until I was totally sure he couldn't hear the living any more.

I knew Tanya instinctively. In her early forties, I estimated, she seemed oddly familiar, but perhaps it had just been Andrew's words that had drawn her so well, making me think she'd touched my life already. When she stood beside Andrew's coffin, I watched her fingers on his shoulder and I imagined the lift in him as they lingered there, her eyes closing, before she walked on to Sophie and Donal and the siblings. She embraced each of them, her hands pulling them in then spreading wide across their backs, a word spoken in their ears, that I was too far away to hear, Donal almost collapsing into her, this woman who had cared for his son so well.

I watched her take a seat among the crowd, to

lower her head, not lifting it until Dad indicated it was time for the mourners, except the immediate family, to leave. Watching his command of the room, I wondered again at what it was he had told Andrew, the "everything" Andrew had hoped my father would tell me. As I did, I joined Harry and Arthur in ensuring the crowd would line the corridor, the pathway, the street, until it reached the church door as his family had asked. Inside the viewing room, they said their private goodbyes before Dad and Niall replaced the lid. They both then helped his parents and siblings lift Andrew high on their shoulders and walk him through the guard of honour behind Dad. Arthur, Harry, and Niall walked slowly to their rear, should the weight become too much.

I stood just inside the doorway as everyone moved in a silent shuffle behind the coffin as soon as it passed. A line doubling back on itself, a continuous curve of people like a choreographed dance—my job, to wait until everyone was gone to lock up the doors and follow on behind. I was momentarily distracted by the height of the willow tree in the park, its dipping head now visible above the border of our wall. All that talk of love with Andrew made me wonder how many first kisses it had witnessed since mine, so many years ago. So engrossed had I become that I had not realised one of the mourners had stepped out to tap me on the arm.

'Hello,' she said.

'Hello,' I replied, shaking the hand of this woman with the wide smile, and I could see why it was he had loved her.

'You mightn't remember me but I'm Tanya. You tended my mother years ago, Mary Delaney?'

'Oh, yes. I knew I recognised your face. Mary, of course, I remember.' Is it awful to say that I couldn't remember her, not then, not straight away? But I did later. I looked her up and she had been lovely but so incredibly heartbroken to have died, to have left her three daughters and her husband of seventy-five who couldn't even set the table, she'd said. She'd suffered badly as I'd sat by her side listening.

'You were so very kind to the family, not to mention Mam. You told us she was peaceful and hadn't suffered. It made such a difference knowing that. We'd been so worried.' Her fingers, now released from my hand, played with a small gold pendant she wore around her neck as her smile continued to light up her face. 'Did you get to talk to Andrew?'

'Oh, yes, we spoke. We had quite a bit of time together, actually.'

'Good. It's magnificent what you do for us, the bereaved, with this gift you have. His words will be such a comfort to his family. Good people, but my goodness they have suffered.' She looked across the road. The outer line of mourners now nearing its end as the coffin progressed through the church door. 'I will miss him so much, you know. He was like a breath of fresh air in that place. So often people are just in too much pain, but he always had a smile for me.'

'He said much the same about you. You'd become great friends, I believe.'

'Oh we had. We really had. We liked the same things. And he made me laugh.' Her face lit up.

I smiled and swallowed and wondered should I tell her what it was Andrew had confessed about loving her. I closed my eyes, trying to summon him, wondering if it would be a betrayal. Or was it, in fact, my own desperation, and nothing to do with Andrew or poor Tanya at all, a moment where I wanted, no needed, to believe that all love, no matter what the variety, was enough. I chose to put my faith in it, in love.

'He'd fallen for you, you know.' The words flew out of me, scurrying away in case I might catch their tails and pull them back. I stood more erect, trying to appear the picture of confidence. And when I thought about it, it seemed entirely possible, despite his reticence, that this really was the reason he had waited, so I could bring this very message. Despite my new-found conviction, I squeezed my right hand with my left, just like Mikey might have, as I waited for her response, which I was sure would justify this risk. So buoyed was I by my bravery that I even added: 'He said it was love and he could think of no nicer parting gift.'

I was so under the spell of my own delusions that I refused to hear Marielle, a woman I had now come to think of as my conscience, sitting on my shoulder: Why do you meddle, saying things the dead never asked of you?

'Oh.' Tanya's one-word reply was weighed down by such sadness it seemed barely to have the strength to be heard at all. 'I didn't . . . erm. Sorry, I didn't expect that.'

I looked over at my willow tree and felt ashamed. How desperate was I to foist my own troubled heart on this unsuspecting woman.

'No,' I protested, looking at her bent head, 'you've nothing to apologise for.'

'He was lovely, really lovely, and we were great friends. I just—'

'No, look, you don't need to do this.' My hands joined together to plead with her, and then before I knew it they'd taken hold of hers and squeezed them. 'I'm so sorry. I didn't mean to upset you. Maybe I could get you some water?'

'No, no it's fine.'

'Look, Andrew simply wanted you to know you meant that much to him.' Still my hands held hers.

'That was kind.' She thought for a moment, gnawed at her lower lip a little, before looking at me with frightened eyes. 'You know, maybe I could've loved him, pretended even to make his final days better, do you think?'

See, Marielle, would've said, see what you have done now.

'I'm not sure that's what he would've wanted.' My hands squeezed tighter.

'No, I suppose not.' She considered the carpet, as I held her captive.

My head bent too, inspecting my shoes and my own life, hearing Marielle's soft voice in my head: And this is why I don't go where I am not invited.

I finally released her.

'Tanya, this is my fault. I really should have thought it through a bit more, but sometimes I get it wrong. I shouldn't have said a thing.'

She looked up from her worry then, calmer now, and put her hand to my arm—me, who deserved nothing of such kindness.

'But if it's what he said, you couldn't not tell me, you couldn't lie. I understand that, you had no choice.'

And I could feel the tears readying themselves. I looked away and nodded, hoping they would stay put and not pull Tanya into this lair of mine, of us Mastersons, any further. I'd allowed her to think that she was right, that it was simply a case of the pressure of being a messenger and not at all about being a liar or a wife who divided love up into acceptable levels—like spiders, of all things.

'It's been a hard day,' I said, as I wiped at my face where one or two traitors had trickled down. 'More than I realised.'

'It's OK, honestly.' Tanya pulled me into her, just as she had done with Donal. I deserved none of this and yet I let my head fall to her shoulder. 'I can't imagine how hard it must be doing this job.'

I gave a small laugh as I came to my senses and pulled myself away from a grip I didn't want to leave.

'No harder than yours, I think.'

'No, perhaps not.'

We stood for a moment, the two of us smiling, me still wiping at my face, before she finally said:

'Well, perhaps I'd better get on. I'd like to be at the ceremony.' She gave a tight-lipped smile that seemed so full of guilt, of not having loved Andrew, of my imminent abandonment. 'But you're sure you're OK? I can get one of the others to come back to you, if you like.'

'No, honestly.' I wanted to melt in the embarrassment of all I had created. 'You go on. I'm fine. I'll be there now. I just have to lock up here.'

'Right. Well. Lovely to have met you again, Jeanie. And keep going, you know, with the listening. It matters.'

I raised a hand in goodbye to this woman who turned and ran a little to catch up with Andrew, the man who had fallen hopelessly and understandably in love with her.

Chapter 23

'Jeanie?' Mum said in surprise, as she locked up the salon and came to join me. 'Shouldn't you be over at the removal?'

I was still standing at the opened door, shaken by all that I had said to Tanya.

'I'm heading now. I was just . . .' I looked back inside to see what it might be I could fabricate that I was 'just' doing. But it seemed I hadn't the energy to muster a thing so I said no more.

Mum raised her hand to pick a bit of fluff from my jacket.

'You OK, love? You really haven't been right since we told you our plans, have you?'

Mum could never resist touching my hair whenever she came within a foot of me and now was no different. She swept back a straggling curl from my cheek with a gentleness that I appreciated. 'Your mascara is running. Have those dead people been upsetting you again?'

'I'm fine. It's nothing. I'm tired, that's all.'

I watched as the large crowd that had turned out for Andrew slowly filtered into the church.

'Really? Are you sure?'

'Yes,' I said, growing impatient, as only daughters can with mothers. I didn't want to have to admit my stupidity with Tanya.

Dad had by now appeared to talk to those mourners still waiting to get in, directing them to where there was still some seating inside.

'Mum,' I said, recovering a little now as I watched Dad at work. 'Andrew said something weird before he went. He said he hoped Dad would be honest with me about everything. Do you know what he meant?'

'Really?' she laughed, a little too hard. 'What a strange thing to say? I wish you wouldn't put such store by what the dead say.'

'There's something that you aren't telling me, isn't there?'

She ignored my question, choosing instead to watch Dad shake his head apologetically to the remaining mourners, indicating the church was now full and they'd have to stay where they were.

'Is Dad ill, is that what this is? Is that why he and Andrew got on so well, because he could relate to what he was going through? Is Dad dying?'

Mum said nothing to my rising panic, just motioned me back into the hallway, out of earshot of any passer-by, where she took my hands and looked me straight in the eye.

'Jeanie, your father isn't ill. I promise you. Do you think, for one second, I'd be able to keep something like that to myself? I'd be screaming blue murder. Ringing the best specialists in the country—no, Europe, for God's sake.'

I slumped onto one of the hallway pews in relief and exhaustion. I began to cry again. Overcome by everything: the Tanya fiasco, Niall and me, the pressure of the business and, now, relief that at least Dad was well.

'But what did Andrew mean, then?' I managed through my gulping.

She didn't answer immediately but looked at the closed doors of the reception and display rooms, at the viewing room, with its discombobulated seats the crowd had left, and now empty of its dead. She sighed deeply.

'This place has a lot to answer for, you know.'

I lifted my head. 'What do you—' but before I could get the question fully out, she interrupted me.

'Are you and Niall OK, Jeanie? I heard him leave late last night.'

It was enough to start me off again.

'It's all such a mess, Mum,' I heaved.

'Oh, love. This place does strange things to people. The walls are cursed. I firmly believe it. It's all the secrets and the heartache the dead bring with them. I won't miss it, Jeanie, that heaviness.' She put a hand around my shoulder and rubbed at it until I grew a little steadier.

'But it can't have been that bad. You and Dad have always seemed OK?' I wiped the lingering tears away from my cheeks.

'Oh, we've had our moments, believe me. But

you have to remember, Jeanie, I had next door. I could get away. But you're like your Dad, always here, living, eating, breathing this place. It wasn't what I envisaged for you, you know. But you seemed happy with this life from the get-go.'

'Why didn't you just tell me to leave when I had the chance?'

'But don't you remember that I tried to get you to go to university? But you wouldn't hear of it. I'd've been the worst in the world if I'd put my foot down.'

'I know,' I conceded, nodding my head and lowering it in embarrassment at my insistence on staying, when at eighteen the possibility of something 'other' had been in my grasp. I wished then that perhaps I had listened to her a little more, seen her as the ally she truly was.

'Besides, Harry and your dad would never have spoken to me again. You were their gift. Chatting away to the dead like they were your friends or something. It seemed to roll off you with no effort. And you genuinely seemed happy in the job when you took it up full-time. And then, when you and Niall got together and he moved in, it seemed like it had been written in the stars or something, it was that perfect. And not just for you, for us too. I liked that your dad had you both there, halving the load.'

She squeezed my shoulder.

'Honestly, I hadn't a clue that there was a thing

wrong. Although, this past year you've looked tired, love. But I just thought, you know, it was normal relationship stuff. It never even occurred to me it might have been the business. I should've asked you. I'm so sorry, love.'

'No, Mum,' I pleaded. 'This isn't your fault.'

'I don't know, maybe you shouldn't have moved into the house when you got married. Has it been a strain on you both, working and living here, not to mention having to put up with us?'

'No, no, you've been great,' I protested.

'Your dad and I talked about buying you a place at one stage. But, like I say, you both seemed happy. And then we started to think about our retirement and that we'd move out instead. It seemed the perfect solution, really.'

'Look,' I said, trying to smile, to pretend that their plan of escape hadn't been the catalyst for all the upset in the last week. 'It's just I'll miss working with Dad. It means so much, sharing everything with him. It'll be lonely without him.'

'Oh, love.' She rubbed vigorously at my shoulder again and then laid her head gently against mine, the two Masterson women lost in their worries. 'Let me talk to your father. It's not right that you should feel on your own in this. I'll sort this, love. I promise. Leave it with me.'

She stared at the reception-room door as if she was already in there, telling my father he needed to help his daughter. And, despite not quite believing that there was any solution to losing the very person I depended on, her words were a comfort and made me genuinely smile.

'And you know,' she said, pulling her arm away so she could slap her knees as if the perfect solution had just occurred, 'you don't have to take the business on either, Jeanie, if you don't want to. We can sell it. Feeney's in Dublin have been trying to get your dad to sell for years.'

'But what would I do then? I'm not trained in anything else.' What a bundle of contradictions I truly was, panicking at the thought of my safety blanket being pulled away when, apparently, it was the very thing worrying me.

'But I'm sure there's something else you could do, if you really wanted,' she enthused. 'You loved to bake when you were a child, maybe catering. You thought about a coffee shop once, remember.'

'But what would the dead do then with Dad *and* me gone? The Feeneys won't be able to talk to them.'

'The dead are dead, Jeanie. They don't get a choice in your life.'

'Their families then, what about them? Dad's always saying it's really about them.'

'Same goes for them. I'm more worried about this living being right here.' She patted my knee. 'Listen, the first thing you need to do is sort you and Niall. You two need to be united. With the exception of one or two things that I will never agree with your father over, we are at least united on ensuring our love is strong enough to get us through. Solve that and you can solve anything. Meanwhile, let me talk to him. He can sort some of this mess out for you at least.'

I attempted to rise to her enthusiasm, to pretend that such a thing was as easy as it sounded, with a smile and nod of my head. My effort, for all the times when I was young when I'd run to Dad instead of her, and for when, as a teenager, she'd nudge me so I'd hold out my hands and she'd rub them gently with her beloved, and ridiculously expensive, shea butter hand-cream.

'Right, that's better.' She wiped the last of my tears from my cheek. 'Now give me that jacket.'

'What?'

'Give. Come on.' Her fingers beckoned to my black jacket. 'I'll go take your place over there. Lucky I work in a "black clothes only" salon.'

'Your shirt's a bit sparkly, though.'

'Hence the jacket.'

'But you won't know what to do.'

'You don't think I haven't watched you and your father enough all these years to know what's required? You go sort yourself out. And then meet that man of yours after work. Figure out what it is the two of you want. This is your chance.'

'He wants a dog,' I said, taking off the jacket and handing it to her.

'A dog? At least it's not a Ferrari. Less expensive. Smellier, though.'

I watched her adjust the jacket so it sat relatively neatly. She stretched out her arms in front to see what kind of give she had.

'God, being sixty hasn't been kind to me, has it? A little tight perhaps, but it'll do. Lucky you got your slim build from me.'

She kissed me on the forehead then moved toward the door. She stopped there for a second, breathed in deeply, then nodded to herself before striding across the road like a warrior, reminding me I was as much of her as I was of my dad.

Chapter 24

At nine a.m. the following day, an hour before Andrew Devlin's funeral Mass, Niall walked through the door as though he hadn't lived in that house only two nights prior, as though he hadn't been my husband of four years, and as though he hadn't successfully dodged me, much to my mother's disappointment, the night before, not coming back over to the undertaker's after his shift had finished, but slipping away before I could catch him, heading for Ruth's.

I was in the kitchen, having waited since eight that morning. I'd watched from the window as he'd chatted with Mikey, heard him open the outer door, only for him to head southward, away from me, straight to the embalming room. I'd stopped myself from following immediately, refusing to crowd him or to appear too desperate. But perhaps, I thought, confusing myself, that's exactly what he wants to see—my need of him. I couldn't decide what to do.

So I sat to the table again, and to the half-cold cup of tea, to the yet-to-be-toasted bread, to the unspread butter, to the unsmeared jam that Mum had left out for me before she went to work. I wasn't hungry, and even wondered might I ever desire food again. From the utility room, the washing machine spun the towels Harry had loaded earlier that morning. She'd heaved them up from the embalming room, not mentioning that all of that should've been taken care of the previous day and not left to her.

I'd offered her tea, but she'd refused.

'You seen that brother of mine around?' she asked.

'No. Not yet. He's possibly gone already to collect the family.'

'Is he holding up OK, with Andrew?'

'Yeah, I think so.'

But truly I didn't know. He and Mum had stayed on to talk to Andrew's family the previous evening after the removal. Joining them for a quiet drink in the local Carmichael Hotel, Mum had told me earlier that morning. By the time they'd come in the previous night, I was up in my bedroom, refusing to come out. Peanut had called but, like the other five times she'd rung me since two nights prior, I didn't have the stomach to hear my own upset any more.

Harry looked around the kitchen, taking note of the untouched food in front of me.

'It feels sad in here today, Jeanie. You OK?'

I nodded, looking down at my hands lying on the table until she'd left, and I felt guilty withholding anything from her.

The phone rang, startling me. There were many phones dotted around the house, calling us to them should anyone need us at odd hours. Through the opened kitchen door, I looked to the one in the hallway, then to the one that sat on the end of the kitchen counter, and wondered which I could get to quickest or would I bother at all. After three rings it stopped, presumably having been picked up in the office. I would wait, I thought, until this call was done. And then I'd walk the corridor to let it be my excuse to talk to Niall, the wondering who had called, the perfect icebreaker. And so I readied myself, working up my courage as I put the butter, jam and bread away, emptying my mug, wiping down the counters and the table. At the window where I washed and dried my hands, I waved to my brother, who at that moment had looked at me from his shed. I returned the towel to its hook on the press below the sink and moved toward the door, unaware of his sudden presence—Niall, standing perfectly still.

'Oh God, you startled me.' My hand rose to my chest in shock and I surprised myself by laughing.

'Jeanie, there's been a call.' His words were gentle, his face softer than I'd seen it in days, stopping my awkward and misplaced levity.

'Yeah, I heard. I was on my way down to see what it was.' He stepped closer, his face not changing, making me worry. 'What's wrong, Niall? It's not Dad, is it?' Dad's collapsed, I thought, a heart attack, a stroke. Mum had lied, trying to shield me from the truth.

'No, no.' He put his hand out, reassuring me. 'It's not your dad. It's . . .'

I tilted my head and squinted my eyes in curiosity.

'. . . Fionn.'

I stared at him, hoping I was managing to still look composed, belying the burn in my stomach at the mere mention of that name.

'Fionn Cassin, Fionn? What, he called?'

'No, Jeanie. I'm afraid . . . he's dead.'

A second, a small silent second of hesitation when I smiled then stopped.

'Dead? But that's just ridiculous.'

'He died three days ago.'

'But . . .' I tried, then said no more, the sentence slipped away from me as soon as it had begun.

'It was colon cancer, they said. He asked to come back here, apparently, just before he died, he asked they bring him to us.'

I found myself back on the chair I had vacated not moments before. I can't remember crossing the floor from Niall to there. It disappeared from my head, shoved out by panic. But I do remember staring at the crumbs I'd missed earlier. Ridiculous that in that moment of perhaps the greatest loss in my life, my brain concerned itself with whether I should get the dishcloth or sweep them with one hand into the cup of my other or simply let them fall straight on to the floor.

'He's embalmed already. They're putting him on a flight this afternoon, if we agree, that is. I said yes. That's OK, isn't it?'

'Cancer?' His question was now slotted into a queue waiting for my brain to catch up and process everything. 'I don't understand. But he's only thirty-two?' I appealed to Niall, as if he might have the answer.

'I don't know the details.' His shoulders rose then fell, in seeming disappointment at his ignorance. 'It is OK, though, Jeanie, that I told them they could send him?'

I seem to remember a long delay in my nodding, like a drunk unable to coordinate properly. The command finally got through and I managed it, but only once, not taking my eyes from the crumbs. One finger now pushed them into a little pile.

'You don't need to see him, Jeanie, or talk to him if it's too much. Your dad can do it all.'

I shook my head. 'No,' but nothing more, no further words would croak their way out. They were stuck just like me, unable to move, except to lift my head enough to see that Niall understood that no one would keep me from seeing him.

'Listen, Andrew's Mass and burial is about to start.' Niall moved closer, hovered a foot or two away.

'Oh, yes, I forgot.' I attempted to rise, because this wasn't fair, was it, for Niall to see me like this over another man. He came to touch my arm, to lay his wonderful forgiving hand on my back, coaxing me to sit again.

'Stay, Jeanie. You're in no fit state. I've already told Mikey to get his gear on. And Harry's there too, and Arthur has taken a day off the job so we'll be fine. Will you be OK on your own? I could get your mum to pop over or maybe I could call Ruth?'

'No. I'll be fine.' I forced those words out so Niall couldn't see that everything inside of me was splitting, rivers of cracks creeping their way to every cranny they could find. 'It's just a shock, that's all. Go. We can't let Dad down, not today.'

'OK,' he replied, glancing at the door. 'It'll be about two before we're back, you know that?'

'Of course. Don't worry. Go.' I shooed him away, but just as he reached the door he turned back again.

'I'll tell Ruth, but what about Peanut? Will I text her?' There was no trace of the hurt and anger from the previous couple of days. In their place was the kindness I was used to.

'Oh.' I looked down at my hands, sitting limply on my thighs, remembering the last time I'd seen Fionn and Peanut together on that cold step when his lips had reached for mine and he promised his love, and my rescue. I nodded my assent.

As soon as he was gone, I rose quickly, my hand over my mouth, ensuring nothing of my sorrow escaped before its time, to lay my head against the kitchen door, listening. It was only when I heard the outer one close, my brother's protests and the start of the hearse that I let it all go: the whimper that became a scream, the tears that became a flood. The energy that had held me upright giving way so that my back slid the length of the door, leaving me slumped on the kitchen floor, my body heaving, convulsing with the loss of him.

Later, after Andrew was buried in Ballyshane, when Dad and Mum had attended the afters in the Carmichael Hotel and Mikey had long returned to shut his door against the world and I had lain on my bed for hours and hours thinking of no one else but me and Fionn and the lives we'd had and those we'd never lead, Niall and Arthur drove to the airport to bring Fionn home. And after Niall had checked him over, ensuring nothing had gone wrong in the journey and retouching anything that needed it, he moved him to the viewing room, put my stool by his side and came to tell me Fionn was ready. Niall's face was tired and worn, red in spots from the cruelty of the day. And for the first time in a while, I felt the need to touch my husband, to lay my hand on his cheek in gratitude, in love, in apology for bringing all of this to his door. He kissed my palm then let it go before walking away.

I didn't move far into the viewing room, but stopped on its threshold, my hand on the door-frame, watching the oak coffin, its rails cleaned to a shine. The final thing Niall would've done, ensuring not a fingerprint or smudge was left anywhere. And then I moved quickly, closing every door to lock out the world before I approached, my hands squeezing and releasing, my breath blowing out through pursed lips in an effort to ready myself.

And even though Fionn was thinner, his hair, what was left, short and wispy and white, he was still, unquestionably, there, the man I loved. If I hadn't known, I would have sworn in court that it was Niall's hand that had made Fionn seem as if he'd simply dozed and any time now would wake and smile sleepily in my direction.

I shook as my hand touched those worn, veined hands which seemed those of a man of sixty-five and not of thirty-two. I'd seen it so many times before, the wasting, the withering. Hands, they never lie. And yet they were still as precious to me now as the day they'd spun me in C corridor, and had directed me how and where to look when I became his reluctant model. Still and exhausted, they lay across his stomach—no camera to hold, no world to capture in a single second any more.

I took in his face that I had kissed so many times, that nook at his shoulder that was so perfect for my head to rest on when we watched a movie or lay gasping when no parents were home, that chest on which my hand would perch to feel his beating heart, and around which I wound my arms before he turned to leave Kilcross. And those lips that widened in amusement of my tales of the dead or when I simply walked into a room.

And his buttoned suit of marine blue, that showed off the whiteness of his immaculately pressed shirt. A white embroidered insignia on both lapels suggested money spent. No tie. The collar taut and proud. The top button opened in the slightest gape. The dip between the wasted clavicles a mere hint rather than in full view. Those legs that I had to run to keep up with when we walked, two strides to one of his, lying still and strong as if in waiting for the off. Leather boots that looked like they had walked a thousand roads, and climbed a hundred hills, to find the right face or skyline or hands to capture in a photograph for all time. Was it Al or Jess who had chosen them for his last moments on this earth? Perhaps both had knelt in silence to a newspaper-covered kitchen floor. Al with the polish brush, Jess with the shiner, ensuring their son would look his best in his most treasured footwear.

'Jeanie.'

His voice burst forth, hurried and panicked, like a man who'd held his breath for far too long.

'Fionn!'

I was so sure he couldn't have held on all that time, had told myself over and over that afternoon not to expect to hear his voice, yet here he was, with me, beside me, in my ear. Mine, all very mine. 'You waited.'

'I tried so hard to make sure I got here.'

'You came back to me,' I laughed through my tears.

'The girl who never thought she was special and yet,' he paused, in relief at having reached his destination, 'now that I'm dead the only one able to hear me. Do you get it now, Jeanie? To the rest of the world I'm gone, but with you I'm still alive.'

I bent to him again, to touch his cheek, the coldness of it. I pushed its warning away, insisting I remember that no matter how long he stayed and no matter what he said, that he was not here, not really. But I did not pay it any heed. Instead I imagined the blood warm under my touch, the pulse under his skin, and I smiled at this gift of presence, of life, of breath that did not rise.

'Jeanie, how long do I have with you, how long does this last? I don't think I've much left in me.'

I closed my eyes against the words that wished

to rip me from my reverie of us, together forever in the dim light of this room, sheltered from everything.

'Jeanie, are you still there? Can you still hear me?' His voice, fretting in the silence that I had left, leaving him vulnerable, a blind man with no stick, no echo, no dog to guide him through.

'I'm here. I'm here, right beside you. Going nowhere. Always and forever me,' I laughed lightly, trying to hide my desperation.

'Did you know?' I whispered, looking at his lips, as if they might part. 'Did you know when we met at the exhibition, when you told me those things, that you were dying?'

'No. I only found out last year.'

'But . . . why didn't you let me know? I could've . . .'

'What, Jeanie? What would you have done? Left Niall, left this place? Come and nursed me?'

His words hung in the air, shaming and silencing me.

'Look, Jeanie, now is when I need you. More than I've ever needed you before.'

It was enough to bring me back from the brink of despair to listen. 'OK,' I whispered weakly, allowing him permission to begin.

'I've come all this way to make sure you hear this and that you tell her.'

Her? Her. I had not expected a *her*. I did not want a *her*. I wanted only us now. It was him and me, no matter who was in our lives, did he not remember?

'Tia,' he said. 'Tia, my daughter.'

A daughter! A life created with another person, not with me. The child that I had once thought would be our gift alone had turned out to be the fortune of someone else. The bludgeon to my heart was almost too much to bear, but I held on to the side of the coffin, willing myself to fight it, refusing to release one whimper in case it might stop him from carrying on.

'She was only four when I came back that time to Kilcross. I wanted to tell you about her. There was so much I was desperate for you to know on that last hopeless attempt of mine to win you back. But you seemed so happy and determined that your life was with Niall, so . . .' He trailed off.

'And her mother? Are you . . . ?' The question so bravely, yet timidly, asked wasn't one I wanted to know the answer to. And yet to have not known would've hurt as much.

'I'm not with Ife. It was a very short-lived romance, ten years ago, but out of it came someone magnificent.'

And I knew from the minute her name was spoken that it had to have been the woman I saw Fionn kissing on his doorstep. The pain of it still as raw, it seemed, as the day I'd slumped outside the Tube station.

'I think I saw you together once. She was the most beautiful woman I've ever seen. It was my twenty-second birthday and I'd gone to London to surprise you. And there you both were on your doorstep in Kennington.'

We rested in the hollow of the silence for a moment.

'I never knew,' he said, upset again. 'I didn't see you.'

'We weren't together then. We had no claim over each other, so it wasn't like you'd done anything wrong. It was after that I decided to give you up. To stop thinking I'd somehow figure out a way to leave.'

'Oh Jeanie. I'm sorry.'

'And then, well, Niall happened. And here we all are.'

Again the room quietened, emptied of our voices, our possibilities, nothing, only our wasted past, our memory reel moving between us for a moment.

'I talk to Tia about you all the time, you know,' he began again. 'About this amazing woman who talks to dead people. But she doesn't believe me.'

'No,' I agreed with an accepting laugh, 'not everyone does.'

'She's a tough nut, my Tia. Practical, logical, even at nine years of age, she doesn't suffer fools. She refuses to believe I'll still be able to talk to her now that I'm gone. But I said I had proof. I had you. And this is it, Jeanie, this is why I held on for you.'

So not for me after all, I thought; he hadn't come back for me.

'Before I died, I whispered a message that I thought you could repeat to her, and then she'd know that the dead can talk to the living. She'll know to listen for me every day and that I'll be there.'

His voice seemed colourful and melodic now, transformed by his obvious love for her.

'I know it was a risk, I wasn't sure I'd make it back in time to talk to you. I asked Al and Jess to make sure they got me here as soon as they could. And I told Tia how you'd said it didn't always work; that sometimes it was too late. But I told her I was going to try so hard. And that she wasn't to give up on me if this failed, that I'd still be there. Because, I said, at some stage in her life, she'd need me and I'd be waiting.'

It took everything I had to hold my upset inside, to not disturb what he needed to say. 'I'm still listening,' I said, encouraging him on with his message, my words, spoken on an in-held breath, before I let out my sorrow in as silent an exhale as I could manage.

'I want you to tell her that in this life she needs to be brave. That bravery will give her a freedom she has never known.' An unbidden smile rose to my lips at the irony that it would be me, a woman whose bravery Fionn had seen falter many times, who would impart such wisdom. 'Tell her that when she opens her eyes every morning, I'll be there waiting to talk to her, to give her my opinion on whatever it is that's troubling her and to tell her she is amazing. So bloody amazing.' He stopped then, and I didn't need to be inside his head to know that he was holding her, hugging her, loving her. 'And,' he continued, his voice now weakening, the familiar hit and miss of coverage. 'Lemon.'

'Lemon?' I asked anxiously, leaning in closer, making sure I was getting this right, feeling the panicked thump of my heart, imagining that I could still see the rise and fall of him.

'It's her favourite smell. She whispered it to me just before I closed my eyes and left her, so no one else could hear. She said that if you told her that, she'd believe it's possible to hear me.' He was moving further away, his voice leaving me even as he said it.

'Bravery and Lemon,' I repeated, bereft, understanding that his final words would not be for me. I repeated them again, louder this time, forcing myself to look at his beautiful face, where I visualised the broad smile that sat on those lips the day he saw Tia for the first time, and again as he watched her wobble to walking, or bend to pick a daisy or chase a butterfly. 'I'll tell her, Fionn.'

'She was my very world.'

I nodded, and smiled as best I could despite the tears, knowing that here in our final moments, our timings were still all wrong. Our lives forever out of sync, and yet forever joined.

It was a second before I realised that there was nothing more from him. I tapped his shoulder gently, like it might make a difference.

'Fionn,' I whispered. No reply.

'Fionn.' I tried again, my voice giving way.

'Fionn.' One last, desperate time, his name called on my lips, before I lay on his chest, accepting Fionn Cassin was gone. Never again would I be surprised by him at my door, never again would I stop and wonder where he was, and if somehow, he might be thinking of me too.

'I should've just gone,' I said, in my distress and desperation. 'Packed my bags and left this place forever. Been free, just like you and Peanut. You'd have opened that door and there I would've been. And you'd have picked me up and swung me around and kissed me and taken me to your bed.'

I watched him in that darkened room, as still and weighted as a fog-filled evening. Listened, for any sign, any twitch, any sound carried on the breeze of death. Hoped for one last second stolen from the destiny that was now his. But there was nothing, only my breath and my eyes so out of focus with tears. Until I heard it, way off down the end of a barren road.

'We'd have been magnificent, Jeanie,' Fionn's voice still clinging on, nails digging deep into the mountain's crevice, fingers straining to grip, caught on some last flicker of energy, dug deep from within. 'There's an undertaker's under a bridge in Kennington. You'd have worked there. I imagined it a thousand times. You'd have come home every day, telling me the stories of London's dead sons and daughters. They'd have loved you, like I loved you.'

And that was the last time I heard him, his time in this place, by my side, finally over. I cried, into his shoulder, ruffling what had been perfect, soaking what had been dry with the burden of our reality: one of us still alive and one dead, one heart beating, one at permanent rest—the hope, the possibility, the dream finally gone.

Have you ever put your fingers over the plughole of a draining bath and felt the almost magnetic pull? That's how my heart felt in that moment, that it was being sucked out of me, displaced; as though I had finally lost control.

'You weren't supposed to die, Fionn. Our story shouldn't have ended this way,' I whispered, my voice muffled into his neck. 'What am I supposed to do now?'

Chapter 25

It was Niall who came to take me from him. I let him hold me in his arms and kiss my head as I sobbed against his chest. I cried openly, clinging on, in desperate need of his comfort.

When it felt as if I might be able to stand on my own, he closed Fionn's coffin and took me to the pew in the wide hallway where we sat, in silence, looking at the closed doors opposite. His hand reaching for mine every time he heard my breath quicken and I descended once more into my despair.

Perhaps ten minutes, maybe more, maybe less, I can't say how long we sat silent in that space, somewhere between division and togetherness, before Al and Jess arrived. I felt like a little girl again, arms fumbling as I stood to hug them, becoming enveloped by these two people who had once so generously welcomed me into their home and let me love their son.

'Did he talk, Jeanie?' Jess asked, pulling away after a moment, her hands still on my shoulders, her eyes wide in expectation. 'We tried to get here as soon as we could but we got delayed at the airport.'

'He did,' I answered.

'What did he say?'

'It was about Tia, mostly.'

'Of course it was; he loved that girl so much.'

She looked so proud of her son. And I was instantly brought back to how she looked at him the night she agreed to plant the willow tree in their garden, that total joy in making her son happy.

'And you. He told me to tell you and Al, that you were simply amazing. And that it broke his heart to leave you.' Ever my father's daughter, lying once again, but not caring now because it felt right. And besides, I knew even though Fionn had not said those words, I believed if he'd had the time, he would have.

'Oh, my boy.' She pulled me in again. 'It's still there, Jeanie, you know. The willow. The one we planted for you. It's so beautiful, drooping in that way it does. It's like it knows the tragedy of losing him. It was all so quick from the diagnosis to watching him die, not even a year. Did he tell you? And he was so brave.'

Al couldn't speak, distracting himself instead by shaking my father's hand. Dad had arrived quietly and stood waiting at the reception-room door.

'We're thinking we'll move back, Jeanie,' Jess continued. 'We could spread his ashes under that tree. But then there's Tia. It would be so unfair for her not to have her father close by. Oh, we don't know what to do.' She cried loud and long into my shoulder.

'Now, love, come on.' Al stepped in to take her from me and began to try to escort her into the office where Dad had already gone to wait to talk to them about the humanist ceremony and cremation they had requested. 'Let's get through tonight and tomorrow, and we'll worry about that then.'

Niall watched me release her. I stole a glance at him in my embarrassment at what he had just witnessed, but there was no hint of what all of this was doing to him.

'Niall, isn't it?' Jess noticed him then.

'Yes, Mrs Cassin. Mr Cassin.' Niall stepped forward to shake their hands. 'I'm so sorry for your loss. It's hard to believe that Fionn has been taken like this.'

'Thank you, Niall.' Al nodded his head.

'And you got married, the two of you?' Jess took my hand and Niall's and drew us together. 'Isn't that marvellous.' She tightened her grasp, standing between us like a marriage celebrant. 'Marvellous.' I watched as her eyes wandered off a bit, to some other places and times, to things that were and things that might have been.

'Of course, Fionn never did marry. But still we have our wonderful Tia to be thankful for.'

'Jess, love.' Al's hand lightly touched her shoulder.

'And kiddies, do you have any?' she continued, ignoring him.

Niall shook his head with a tight smile. Still her hand gripped ours, beginning to hurt now, and yet I wouldn't pull away from her, never, not if she kept me there all day.

'Come on now, Jess. Let's go talk to Mr Masterson. We need to get some things sorted and let these poor people get some rest.'

Al took her hand, releasing us, and turned to walk her into the room to Dad, his arm around her shoulder as he guided her through. Inside, Dad's comforting voice invited her to sit, as Al popped back out to us.

'Will it be OK if we see Fionn for a moment before we go? Tia and her mother are on their way too. They went to have a little walk in the park there. Apparently Fionn used to talk about it all the time to Tia, about the happy times you lot had there, so she wanted to just go and look.'

'Of course,' Niall said. 'Fionn will be ready for you when you're finished.'

'Thank you.' Al nodded then ducked back in to close the door.

Niall and I stood looking at it, as though at any second it would open again. But when it didn't, we looked awkwardly at the other, as if we were meeting for the first time.

Niall walked back to the pew to sit again, his

arms resting on his knees, one hand rising to slide back and forth across his lips.

'Did he really say all that stuff about his daughter and them?' he asked eventually.

It was my turn to look down, ashamed now that I would have to admit to a lie. I came back to sit at the other end of the pew.

'It was his daughter mainly.'

'And you? What did he say about you?'

'Very little.' I tried to make it sound as neutral as possible, no hurt or pain showing.

'So in his final moments, talking to a woman he'd specifically asked to be brought home to because he was so besotted with her, he doesn't mention you at all?'

'He wanted to get a message to Tia. *That's* why he came home.'

'That can't've been easy, after all these years and all you went through.'

I wasn't worthy of this man's sympathy, and I was about to tell him so when the main door pushed open and a girl stepped in. We stood up immediately. She stopped on seeing us and considered a retreat, looking back for the safety of her mother following behind, the woman I'd seen lured back into Fionn's embrace.

'Hello,' Ife said. 'We're here to see Fionn Cassin.'

'Yes, please do come in.' Niall stepped forward

to shake the hand of the smiling woman and solemn child. 'You must be Tia and . . . ?'

'Ife.'

'I'm Niall and this is Jeanie. We are terribly sorry for your loss.'

'Ah, the famous Jeanie Masterson.' Ife looked at me then back to her daughter. 'Tia's dad talked a lot about Jeanie, didn't he, Tia? About her special gift.'

Tia seemed shy and didn't react too much, other than shaking my hand. I saw a flash of Fionn in the shape and the arc of the eyebrow for just a second before she stared off into the distance.

'We've been taking good care of your dad, Tia,' Niall said.

'We are very glad to hear that, aren't we, precious?'

Tia lifted her eyes to her mother, and squeezed her hand, as if silently reminding her of something.

'Ah yes,' Ife began, 'Tia was wondering if she might be able to see her dad. We said goodbye in London, but she thought if it was OK that she might be able to do it again.'

'Of course,' Niall said. 'If you wait here for just a second, I'll make sure he's looking his best for you.'

When Niall left us we sat to wait on the pews. There we could hear the muffled voices of Dad and Jess and Al.

'Your grandparents are in there with Mr Masterson—that's my dad,' I told Tia. 'They shouldn't be too long.'

'Tia is a lucky girl to have such wonderful grandparents.' Ife kissed her daughter's head.

'Your dad couldn't stop talking about you, Tia,' I said, concentrating on this silent girl who sat two spaces away.

She looked at me out of the corner of her eye.

'Tia doesn't quite believe that her pops will be able to talk to her now he's gone. But I've told her there is no doubt. I haven't stopped talking to my mother in seventeen years. And that woman can talk. I have to tell her to stop in the mornings or we'd never get out the door.' Ife laughed a little.

'Oh, he was definitely talking, Tia. I promise you.'

She didn't look at me this time, but stared ahead unmoving, waiting.

'Right, your dad is ready for you, Tia.' Niall stood at the opened door of the viewing room. Inside, the coffin lid had been removed. Niall beckoned them in while I held back a minute, wondering how I would be able to convince this silent girl of her father's words, given his warning of her reticence, until an idea came to me and I turned back to the display room.

After a few minutes, I arrived to see Tia's graceful hands lightly tip the side of the coffin as she looked in on Fionn, Ife right beside her, her arm around her shoulder in protection.

I stood at the bottom, two strides away from the coffin, giving them space. Tia whispered something to her mother and her mother nodded and then she reached again, this time to touch Fionn's hands.

'You know he asked me to tell you something, Tia.' I approached her a little more.

She didn't look at me, but Ife did and nodded to encourage me on.

'He said you should be brave in this world. That if you are, it will open up so many possibilities. That fear is OK and normal, but you must look it in the eye and say let's work this out because I need to get beyond you. Fear, he said, will mean too many closed doors and he wanted every one to open for you. He was right, you know. And he said you're to listen for him, in the mornings mostly, because he'll be there waiting to talk to you about everything from how you hate school to who you've fallen in love with.'

Her eyes shifted toward me, but still no smile.

'And this.' I stepped in a little closer so I could almost touch the coffin. 'He told me something that he said only you would know. I've written it down so you can always have it and know that he is really there.'

She took the envelope and carefully pulled out the single page that I had taken from the display room moments earlier, on which I'd written the simple word I hoped would have the power to change her mind: Lemon.

And only when she'd read it did her face turn fully toward me for the first time, and she smiled, showing off her wonderful crooked incisor.

Chapter 26

Peanut arrived later that night. She rang the doorbell around ten and it was all I could do not to collapse into her arms. As soon as Niall's text had come through, she'd left the clinic and gone home to pack, in the rush forgetting a funeral outfit, but reasoning, who better than an undertaker to borrow black clothes from, as she ran for her flight southwest out of Gardermoen Airport.

'Oh, Jeanie,' she said, holding on to me, 'I just can't believe he's dead.'

My body felt wasted as I sat limp on the couch in our sitting-room, where once we had laughed and thrown cushions at each other and spilt bowls of popcorn, which I'd have to hoover up before Mum witnessed the damage. I now felt as if I was a hundred, wishing for a long and simple sleep in which I might never wake and feel the pain all over again.

'What we need right now is alcohol.' She got up, wiping at the tears on her cheeks. 'Your dad's drinks press was always the best one of any of our parents'. Is it still in the kitchen?'

I nodded and watched her leave, not as convinced by her plan as she was. I imagined the concerned whispers of my parents next door as they asked Peanut how I was doing. Up until Peanut's arrival, and after Fionn's family had left, they had sat with me at our table. No words passing between us other than theirs: 'My poor pet,' 'Oh, love,' or a combination of the two as I cried relentlessly. Niall had gone by then, back to Ruth's, to stare at the white four walls of the box-room perhaps, or to sit at McCaffrey's bar, to wonder how the hell his life had ended up so badly, having watched his wife cry over the body of another man. Our goodbye at the end of that day had been as sad as our beginning, him clumsily taking my hand after our meeting with Tia, squeezing it, no words, only a sorrowful smile. I'd asked Dad to go look for him after he'd left, the only words I'd managed. He needed someone, I said, but Dad'd refused to leave me and had rung Arthur to track him down.

The first taste of Peanut's incredibly strong G&T didn't so much steady me as make me cough. Pea patted my leg as she drank a healthy mouthful of her own.

'Oh, I needed that.' She looked at her glass and shivered. 'I told your dad to give us doubles.'

'Fionn had a daughter, did you know that?'

She nodded.

'You knew and you didn't tell me?'

'There's a lot I didn't tell you about him. And a lot I didn't tell him about you. Look you were doing OK at the time. You'd both managed to move on with your lives. I honestly thought it was the right thing to do, to let the pair of you breathe without having to know everything that was going on with the other.'

'But the exhibition . . . you brought me right to him?'

'Yeah, I know. You seemed, so . . . I was worried you weren't sure about the wedding and, you know, we'd had a bit to drink and it seemed like a brilliant idea at the time. I'm sorry, Jeanie, I really am. If I could turn back the clock, I'd do it all differently.'

'No,' I sighed, knowing I would never have traded those moments with Fionn, when he told me he still loved me, for anything. 'It's OK, you were only trying to do your best by me, like you always have.' I squeezed her hand. 'Did you ever meet Tia or her mother?'

'No. Honestly, we didn't see each other that much over there.'

'Ife, the mum, is like the most beautiful woman in the whole world. But they weren't together long, apparently. And Tia, the daughter, is lovely. She looks quite like him. She was all he could talk about.'

'Well, I totally get that. I may give out about them, but the twins are my everything. I'd die twice over for them.'

At that moment, I felt as though I'd managed to

lose everything, even the children that I'd never had.

'Oh God, Pea,' I despaired. 'What the fuck has happened to me? Fionn's gone. Niall's gone. My parents can't wait to get out of here.'

'Wait. Niall's gone? When did that happen?'

'Two days ago.'

'Why didn't you tell me?'

'I don't know, it was all too hard.'

'But I kept ringing and you never picked up.'

'I know, I'm sorry.'

'But why did he go?'

'Because he's had enough. All these years, waiting until Fionn and me ran out of whatever it was we had, then picking me up and sorting me out. He deserved more.'

'Oh, Jeanie.'

'And he had to watch me today. Devastated and brokenhearted over someone else.' If in the previous seven years I hadn't felt guilt for all that had lived hidden inside me, I felt it tenfold now.

'So, he's still working here then, even though . . . ?'

I nodded and drank. 'Oh God, I've ruined his life, Pea.'

'You haven't ruined his life. As much as I love Niall, he's a grown-up. He knew what he was getting himself into. He knew you loved Fionn. He decided to take the chance. You didn't make him do it. You didn't lure him in. OK, so right now things aren't great between you, but perhaps it's not the end. Not if you don't want it to be.'

'But that's just it, Pea, I don't know what I want.'

'You really loved Fionn, didn't you?'

'Yes,' I croaked.

Not for the first time that day, I felt the tears begin, and I wondered how my body could still be producing what I was sure had to have run out by now. Perhaps these ones were made of gin.

'I keep thinking I should just have gone to live with him in London.' I wiped my eyes with the by-now-frayed tissue that Mum had given me earlier, then took another sip of my G&T.

'Really?' Peanut asked, swirling her drink. 'But do you ever think that if you *had* done it, like gone and lived there, that it mightn't have worked out?'

'What do you mean?'

'It's just since me and Anders had the kids . . . well, you realise relationships like that, you know, passionate and all consuming, can fizzle out when they're put to the test of grocery shopping and whose turn it is to clean the toilet. See, Jeanie, perhaps you weren't as stupid as you think. Perhaps somewhere in that clever head of yours, which has been bombarded by hundreds of wise dead people since you were a toddler, you knew it wouldn't work, and that staying here in the safety of this place was the best thing for you.'

It was too much for me, trying to comprehend this alternate view that she was offering. I looked into the clearness of my drink and attempted to visualise myself as this all-knowing and confident being she presented me as, but it wasn't working.

'You know all that stuff with the dead, Pea, is just lies. I've told you time and again. I tell lies, to keep the living happy, there's no wisdom there. I was at it today again. My life has been one long lie. Pretending I didn't want to go to London. Pretending I loved Niall enough. Pretending I'm happy in this place, in this town. No, you and Fionn were right all along, I just needed to leave. Live a life. But I was too chicken-shit.'

'Hmmm,' she said, not willing to let go of her theory just yet, 'I dunno. I'm not convinced. See, I wonder now if this love smokescreen you've been keeping up—'

' "Love smokescreen"? I haven't been making it up, Peanut.'

'No, of course you haven't. I'm sorry. That came out wrong.'

'He told me he still loved me back at the exhibition, you know. Said if I ever changed my mind about Niall to find him.'

'What? But you never said a thing.'

'I never told you or anyone, because I just

thought I'd made my choice, when really, if I'm honest now, you were right all along, I wasn't a hundred per cent sure about Niall.'

'Look, Jeanie, none of that matters now. What I'm trying to say, granted ridiculously badly, is that perhaps the real issue here was not who you should have loved more, or who you should have run away with, but simply who it is you are and what it is you really want to do with your life.'

There was a knock to the door and in came Dad.

'Here you go, ladies. I thought another couple of these might be in order.' He placed two more generous G&Ts on the table. 'You need them for the shock. And you needn't be worrying a thing about tomorrow workwise, Jeanie. It's all sorted. We'll all be here, your mother, Harry, Arthur, Mikey, so you indulge as much as you need to.'

'Oh Mikey. What a dote,' Peanut enthused.

'And Niall?' I asked, reaching for my glass.

'Yes, and Niall. He told me he'd be here.' I nodded, feeling once again unworthy of Niall's decency. 'Oh and Gráinne wants me to check again if you'd like some food, Peanut? She can't believe you're not starving. The chipper is only a stone's throw away. To be honest, I think she's going to go anyway, so you may as well choose something you'd actually like rather than take pot luck.'

'She's so good. Sure, why not? A couple of

battered onion rings might be nice. Haven't had one of them in years.'

'Anything for you, Jeanie?'

'No, you're grand, Dad, thanks.'

He left then.

'Did I tell you they're retiring, Pea?'

'You did. I mean, honestly, I leave this town what, only fourteen years ago, and people just go on with their lives with not a care.' She took a sip of her latest gin.

'I should've just listened to you back when we were eighteen and you told me not to stay because of other people. Imagine all those broken hearts I could've saved, not to mention my own, if I'd listened.'

'OK, enough of could've, would've, should've. It helps no one.' We sat with my reprimand, drinking and wincing at the same time at my father's liberal measurement. 'But do you know what could help?'

I looked around, my hand poised, another sip only inches away, waiting for her suggestion.

'Coming to Oslo. You can't solve anything when you're surrounded by all of this. Tomorrow, after the ceremony, come back with me. We'll figure it all out over there.'

'What?'

'Yes, I know, it's a bloody brilliant plan. Tonight we'll pack your bag and we'll explain to everyone that you're coming to Oslo for a while.

It will be great. And we can think and talk—or not talk, maybe just walk—you'll so love the parks. And we'll just breathe and get clear of all of this. Is your passport in date?'

'I think so.'

'Right, where is it? We'd better check before I let myself get excited.' She stood up then she sat down again and reached for my hand, trying to contain herself. 'I'm sorry. My bad again. Excitement isn't the right choice of word, given the circumstance. Ignore me, this isn't about how happy it would make me to have you with me. This is about you, giving yourself time to deal with all of this.'

'But . . .'

'But what, Jeanie? What is it, the dead, your folks, Niall, Mikey? Those who can wait can wait, and those who can't will have to figure it all out on their own. For once, Jeanie Masterson, is it possible for you to put yourself first?'

After the service the following day and the cremation at Saint Jerome's, we'd gone back to Fionn's old house in Drumsnough where caterers had laid on a spread of nibbles in true Al and Jess style: tempura veg with teriyaki sauce, seaweed crackers with chickpea hummus, smoked wild salmon on brown bread, not a sausage roll or chicken wing in sight. I'd caught Mum's 'told you so' look to Dad as she'd put a couple of bits on her plate. In the middle of the room, Tia sat on the couch beside Ife, solemnly shaking the hands of the many strangers who'd come to pay their respects. At one point I caught her eye and I waved and smiled, and she did the same back.

We four—Pea, Ruth, Niall and I—stood at the expanse of their sitting-room window, looking out on the garden, my willow sitting right in the middle.

'Do you remember the night we sat out there around that fire Al built?' Ruth said. 'It was just before they'd planted the trees and Fionn was going on and on about the shadows or something the fire was making and how good a picture it might make, and we all just had enough and piled on top of him, forcing him to shut the fuck up for once.'

'Oh yeah, I'd forgotten about that.' Pea looked at Ruth, a glass of organic white wine in her hand.

'I wish now we hadn't. I wish we'd all just let him talk.'

We looked back out to the trees, which on that day lay silent. No rush of wind to make them heard. They were still, as shocked as us that he was dead.

'Me and him once cycled out to Lough Saor,' Niall said then. 'We went swimming off Corelli Rock. I lent him Gareth's old bike that was way too small for him. He looked like a right eejit on it but he didn't give a crap. I even managed to convince him to leave the camera for once. I'd taken my T-shirt off as we cycled out it'd been so hot. And then that night my back was scorched. I couldn't sleep. I think I got an hour in the end, sleeping on my front.'

'I don't remember that,' I said, looking at him amazed that these two had ever had time like that together and that neither thought to tell me.

'It was just before he left. You were working. Harry'd given me the day off and we'd bumped into each other in town and we just said fuck it. We'd never been the closest, but that day it was like we put it all behind us, like that Christmas truce in 1914, and had a laugh.'

We grew silent again, each with our sad smiles. The skin on my face felt tight and dry from crying.

'Fucking cancer.' Pea rubbed at her cheek then held out her glass to us. 'To Fionn,' she cheered sadly.

'To Fionn,' we replied as we clinked ours with hers then fell once again into our quiet contemplation of who that man had once been.

Later, Niall and I sat outside our house in our car.

'I've decided to take a bit of time, Niall. I'm going away to try to sort out my head.'

Niall tapped his fingertips at the steering wheel. 'Where?'

'Peanut's, for a bit.'

'Right. So it's not a weekend thing then.'

'No, possibly not.'

'Do your folks know?'

'I told them this morning.' Mum and Dad had sat across from me at the kitchen table earlier, their foreheads worn with worry. Are you sure? they'd asked. I am, I'd said. They'd looked at each other then back at me. They smiled those nervous smiles of parents who want to say so much more but are too afraid in case they might tip the balance in the wrong direction.

'And Mikey?' Niall asked.

'Yeah, Mikey, too.' Mikey hadn't wanted me to go. And asked I reconsider because surely there was no need. Such sudden change was not good for anyone. The body wasn't built for such things. And instead I could spend as much time as I liked in his shed and even watch movies that wouldn't be his first choice but that he was willing to consider. And food, we'd get whatever food I liked even if he didn't. Because really, honestly, truthfully, he thought it best I didn't go. But I held my ground this time. Allowing the inevitability of change wash over him as he rubbed his right thumb with his left, and we watched *The Japanese Conquest of Asia* in colour.

'I wish you'd let me help,' Niall said. 'That's all I ever wanted, was for you to let me in.'

'I know.' I looked away when I couldn't offer him anything more.

'How the hell did we get this way, Jeanie? Sometimes I can see exactly why and then others, it's a mystery. Right now, it feels wrong. This isn't supposed to be where we end up.'

'I'm sorry, Niall. I can't seem to separate one thing out from the other here, I'm so confused.' And like Mikey, I began to rub at the skin of my right thumb.

He nodded and tapped the steering wheel again, concentrating on it as the silence grew.

He nodded and tapped again.

'Is this it then?' he asked. 'Is this us through?'

'I don't know.'

'No,' he sighed, 'neither do I.'

Chapter 27

For the first week at Pea's I couldn't sleep, my mind far too consumed with all that had happened. I ate little. The twins sat wide-eyed as I left plates of food, for which they would have been scolded, whereas I received an understanding pardon from their parents.

In the beginning Peanut took some days off from their veterinary practice and, while the children were in school, we sat around her apartment in our pyjamas on opposite couches drinking teas and coffees with Peanut producing endless rounds of toast with jam, which I generally ignored, as she dug down into the depths of me, trying to help. By noon she would convince me that we needed air, and out we would walk, down Oslo streets to parks so vast that my small beloved patch of green back in Kilcross would've fitted into their toilet area. So wide they forced you to fill your lungs with its good clean air. She held on to my arm like she used to as we walked the corridors of the Community College. At times when she strode ahead pointing out yet another naked statue in a corner, I'd wonder at her. Her confidence, her assuredness of who she was, something she'd always known since we were small.

'How did you become so happy?' I asked her one morning when she'd dragged me out of bed at 8.30 a.m., insisting we go eat waffles.

She had the full works of jam and sour cream and the weirdest-looking brown cheese I'd ever seen.

'Try it,' she'd said. But I declined even to sniff it and instead picked at my plain waffles.

'What, you think I'm like this every minute of the day? I'm a mother, for Christ's sake. Children were sent to annoy us, as were husbands. I'm just happy you're here so I can mind you instead.'

'Does Anders mind having to hold the fort at the clinic while you nurse me back to health?'

'Anders is a hero. Norwegians just grin and bear everything. I think they actually like it. Except compliments, they don't do them so well. They're very like the Irish in that way; they can't be dealing with someone saying something nice about them. You know, he actually gets up in the middle of a conversation if I do and will go off and get a glass of water or something. It's like a party trick now that I amuse myself with.'

'You two are good together.'

'Yep, on the whole we are. He's very calm. Says "hmmm" a lot.'

'You do that too.' I laughed.

'Ah, so you *can* laugh. I was beginning to wonder if it was gone for ever.' She smiled as she took another forkful of her waffle.

Anders was indeed a truly good man who clearly adored every bit of Peanut. He was, however, mystified by his wife's best friend, looking at me in the same way an orangutan might view a human when I told him that—amongst the many issues I had brought with me—I wasn't sure I was in the right business.

'So you are going to change from what you have worked at all of your life?' he asked, stopping washing the salad leaves he was preparing for our Friday night meal. It was the end of my first week with them.

'Jeanie,' Peanut said, standing side on, chopping a punnet of tomatoes, 'I should mention, Norwegians tend to do the same thing their entire lives. They don't change careers.'

'But don't you get bored?' I asked of Anders.

'It is what we work at—it isn't who we are. Going skiing, or visiting our cabins or going for saunas, or having time with those we love, that gives us our joy, that is what defines us. Our jobs do not. The question is why you Irish let it?'

'Auntie Jeanie?' I turned to look at Oskar from where he was lying on his stomach drawing in front of the TV. 'Mamma says you talk to dead people.' There was no question. It was a simple statement that Oskar expected me, in that wonderful, confident Scandinavian way, to elaborate on.

Everyone stopped what they were doing.

Anders turned and Elsa appeared from nowhere. I looked to Peanut who nodded, giving her assent for me to tell the truth.

'I do,' I began. 'I've always been able to do it. From when I was even littler than you. I can do it as well as you can draw, it seems. It is my talent, I suppose. They can talk but only for a little while, I don't hear them for very long.'

Elsa came closer, to sit with her legs tucked under her, her hands on the back of the couch watching me. Oskar was now on his back, his elbows supporting him, his picture momentarily abandoned, while Anders crossed his legs and arms, waiting for more, and Peanut gave a little smile.

'Sometimes I can barely hear them and sometimes they only stay for a little while. And they might say: "Tell my wife I love her and I'm sorry." '

'Why "sorry"?' Elsa asked, with the same scrunched-up nose that Peanut had had when she was seven and stood in our empty embalming room one day asking what all the coloured fluid was for.

'Because the man had died, and he knew she'd be sad.'

'What else do they say?' Oskar called from the floor.

'Well, they might say, "Tell my husband I left the money for my funeral in the inner pocket of

my good coat that I only ever wear on Sundays."
Or, "Tell her not to dress me in that horrible navy
suit she said I looked good in. I hate it. It makes
me look fat." '

Elsa and Oskar giggled at that and it made me
happy.

'No honestly, it happened. A man called Joe
Plunkett told me that and I had to tell his wife
who came in later that day with the very suit he
didn't want.' It was nice to remember that sometimes I had been brave enough to tell the truth.

'What happened?' Elsa cocked her head slightly
and laid it on her hands.

'Well, she wasn't happy, but I made her a cup
of tea and we talked about him, and how she was
worried she wouldn't be able for all the jobs he
used to do in the house, like putting out the bins
and bleeding the radiators. She had a good cry.
By the end, she got up and said she was going
home to bring in his favourite leather jacket,
Status Quo T-shirt and blue jeans.'

'So you're like their messenger. Like an angel,'
Oskar stated, in the manner of a man who knew
exactly what he was talking about.

'Well, I don't think I'd go that far.' I looked
away unable, perhaps like his father, to deal with
such a compliment.

'I think you're an angel,' Elsa said, before
standing up and returning to wherever she had
come from.

'Me too.' Oskar rolled back over to continue his drawing.

'Hear, hear,' their mother said, before beginning to chop again.

Anders was still standing observing me with his back to the sink when I looked up, thinking the compliments had stopped.

'And *that* is what you want to give up?' He shook his head. 'Hmmm,' he added, before turning to his salad preparation one more time as Peanut looked at me and smiled.

Peanut did do some shifts with Anders in the clinic when I was there and when he was really stuck. On the mornings when Peanut worked and I was left alone, I'd go for walks or visit the tourist attractions. I'd watch each passer-by, wondering if they could see the loss in my face. How often had I walked down streets in Ireland, sure I could pick out the people who had recently lost someone? I was in mourning for Fionn but also for Niall. All the ifs, buts and ands of us.

After a week, I started to google undertakers and found myself walking down streets with unpronounceable names, to stop outside what looked like any other business with its blinds closed over and a simple plaque beside the door. I'd pass by a couple of times, wondering if the voice of a dead man or woman or child might reach me that far away, saying words that were important but that I could not understand. And sometimes they did, their voices faint and muffled by the bricks and mortar and distance between us. But what could I have done, knocked on the door and insisted that the undertaker listen to this mad woman try to pronounce their words? In the end I simply sat across the street, watching the doors that never opened, growing more upset that the last words of these dead people had gone unheeded, and wondering how, if ever, I might learn to resist their pull.

If Pea had to work in the afternoon, I'd collect Elsa and Oskar from school and we'd go home and I would make them their favourite afternoon snack of pancakes with jam and they'd insist I tell them more stories of the dead. In the evenings, Anders took every emergency call for the entire time, letting his wife stay in with me. Despite having to bear much of the work in the clinic during my stay, his eyes never darted from mine in exasperation when he came through the door to see me still sitting on his couch, perhaps in the exact spot I'd been in when he'd left.

I cornered him the morning I finally left them, three weeks after I'd arrived. It was early and I could hear him moving about as everyone else still slept.

'Anders,' I whispered, into the quiet of the morning kitchen. I found him unperturbed by my arrival, sitting at the kitchen table, drinking his coffee and looking out on to their building's car park. 'I wanted to say thank you for letting me stay here, and for letting me have Peanut so much.'

'Sarah deserves it.' Anders called Peanut Sarah. When first they'd met, she was so taken with him that she thought he'd think her childish if she told him what everyone called her and so had let him use the name he'd read on her CV. Sometimes he'd have to tap her on the shoulder before she realised he was talking to her. But when eventually she admitted the name she preferred to be called, he said he liked that she had thought him that special, so if she did not mind he'd keep Sarah as his pet name for her. 'Being around you makes her happy. It hasn't always been so easy for her here. You know, she gave up so much when we decided to make a life in Oslo, it's the least I can do.' He smiled to himself. 'Besides, I've enjoyed it too. Your stories are truly original. I've been telling everyone in the clinic and of course some don't believe that you can talk to the dead. And yet,' he held up his slice of toast and pointed it at me, 'they all want to meet you.'

I laughed at the idea.

'But don't worry. I've told them they can't have you, that you are my wife's, and Oskar and Elsa's, I think, a little now.'

We smiled at each other.

'You always knew you wanted children, Anders?'

'Yes, of course. You don't?'

'I don't know,' I shrugged. 'But I think if anyone could convince me it would definitely be Elsa and Oskar. I love being around them. They are like adults, only happy.'

He smiled but squinted his eyes in puzzlement.

'You have a hang-up about this happiness business.'

'Doesn't everyone?'

'It is not our default state. Sometimes happiness is like the sun sneaking through the clouds. It's fleeting, that is all. The rest is simply living.' He rubbed his hands together, ridding them of their crumbs. 'So, you are leaving us today?'

'Yep.'

'Was it the cabin? Did it turn you off us Norwegians for life?' he laughed.

According to Peanut, when Anders wasn't taking the children skiing on the weekend, he'd bring them to his parents' cabin, an hour's drive from Oslo into the forest. The previous weekend he'd insisted Peanut and I should go instead.

'It is a waste to come to Norway and not really experience what we're about,' he'd said.

Pea rolled her eyes and laid her head back on the couch. 'But it's so cold and it has no electricity.'

'Yes, my darling, but it is May, and besides you make it warm with the stove and the blankets and you bring lots of soup and you'll be fine.' He came up from behind to lean his head beside hers and to kiss her on her cheek.

'But you're better at that stuff, Anders.' She cradled his head in the crook of her arm so her fingers caressed his ear.

'Go. You'll be fine. You'll have Jeanie.' He kissed her again then stood.

We both laughed at the idea that I might be any kind of survivalist.

'If she can talk to dead people, she can surely build a stove fire.'

'Darling, that's like saying because you are a vet you most definitely can fly a plane.'

'Perhaps I can. All I need to do is try. And besides, I'm fed up listening to you both. Go gossip about Kilcross somewhere else.'

So we left that Friday and found the red cabin with yellow window frames at the end of a track. And there we stayed, with only gas for cooking and oil-lit lamps, chatting under blankets, our feet aimed toward the stove, sleeping in bunk beds and going to the loo outside.

'Actually, it was the double loo that did it for me,' I said to Anders that morning. In their outside toilet there were two holes, complete with seats, one next to the other like two passenger seats on a train.

He laughed. 'It was handy when the children were younger. They didn't care.'

'But no, it wasn't that. It seems I simply miss the dead.'

'Not Niall then?' His eyes flicked toward me and I looked away embarrassed. 'Missing the dead is not something you hear a person say every day. Lily, my nurse, is going to love that one. She says you are like her soap opera. She enjoys it when I come in to tell her your latest tale. She's going to be broken-hearted to hear you are leaving. Her cousin is an undertaker and he wants to meet you too. He thinks you could build a goldmine here between you.'

'Not if I can't understand what the dead Norwegians are saying, we wouldn't.'

'Most Norwegians speak English, you'd be absolutely fine.'

I had loved the cabin actually. It felt so far away from everything. And I could see what Anders meant by it being a return to something, a time of peace and no phones and no TV, and why it was important to him, to them.

'Maybe if me and Niall had a cabin like this we'd have been OK,' I said to Pea when we arrived and I'd walked around all two of its rooms.

'Oh yeah, totally loved up.' Pea came through

the door looking like the Michelin man she had that many layers on, with two armfuls of wood. 'It's so bloody romantic.'

'No, but like the "no coverage" thing. No one ringing. No living in a town where everyone knows your business.'

'So, have you decided yet if it's totally over between you two then?' She dropped the wood with a loud bang on the floor and sighed. It was the first time we'd spoken of Niall in days.

'I don't know, Pea.'

'Have you rung him yet?'

'I've looked at his number at least five times a day, does that count?'

'No.'

'I wouldn't know what to say if I did ring. There's nothing new to report. We'd just sit in silence, too afraid to go over the same old territory.'

'You're going to have to make a decision at some stage, Jeanie. You can't just leave him hanging around over there working for your folks for ever, wondering if you're coming back. That has to be awkward for everyone. And neither is it good for you.' Peanut gave me a tight-lipped smile then bent to open the stove. 'Fucking hate this fucking stove.'

'But it's not easy, Pea. Sometimes I think I'll just get on the plane and rush into his arms and tell him I love him and I'm sorry. But I know within seconds of that it would fade and then I'd be back to what I've always wondered deep down—if I love him enough. And yet I don't know how I'll live without him now.' It was then my phone pinged. 'I thought you said you can't get coverage up here, Pea?'

'Ah yes, a rogue one can get through. It's like the Norwegian sense of humour, playing tricks to make me think I can get online.'

It was a text from Arthur.

'See, this is why Anders needs to come, I can never get this bloody thing to light.'

'Here, give it to me.' I bent to rearrange the wood and lit the match and it took, like I was indeed a miracle firestarter, and then went back to read the text.

'There's a coffee bar in the village. It's the only place you can get actual cover. We can go down tomorrow morning. We can have waffles. You could ring Niall then.'

'Fuck,' I said, sitting back on my hunkers. 'I think I'd better ring Dad first.'

'Oh?'

'He obviously never told Arthur his father wasn't who he thought he was. The flippin' solicitor did.' I felt a rush of shame that I hadn't thought of Arthur once in this whole time.

'What? Postman Arthur? You never told me any of this.'

'No, I suppose I didn't.'

352

'Well, spill,' she said, inviting me to begin the story of Tiny and Arthur as she sat to the chair in all her padding, de-layering about ten minutes later when the cabin had indeed begun to warm.

Chapter 28

The following morning, I had to drag Pea out of the bed to drive me to the village.

'Dad? It's Jeanie.'

As I stood outside the café, through the window I watched Peanut drink her coffee, with her hands around her mug, as if it was the only source of heat on the planet and she was afraid someone might try to steal it.

'Jeanie, love, how are you?'

'I'm OK, Dad.'

'That's good. Things any clearer?'

I'd spoken to my parents a couple of times since I'd arrived, me always reassuring them that I was doing better and, yes, obviously forgetting to check about poor Arthur.

'Look, Dad,' I said, getting to the point, 'I got this text from Arthur last night.' I took in the village with its four multicoloured wooden buildings—yellow, red, blue and green—and wondered why we never made colour compulsory back home. The only colour in Kilcross had been the red windowsills of the SuperValu entrance.

'Ah that.' His voice wavered.

'Dad, you promised me you'd tell him. He's really upset that he had to find out from the solicitor.'

'I know, love. He came around last night.'

'Is he OK?'

'He'll be grand. I'm sorting it.'

'I mean, I know I should have reminded you, Dad, I know, but honestly, I don't get it, of all the people and all the times not to pass on the message.'

'Yes, I know, love, but this is it, you see. I need to explain. With everything going on, you going, Niall quitting—'

He continued to speak but I couldn't move beyond this news of Niall.

'Niall quit?' I repeated, less a question than a way to help comprehend the immensity of his words.

'Didn't he tell you?'

'No.' The word sat reticently on my lips, as if afraid to let go.

'He's gone to work in Sligo for the Molloys,' Dad qualified, meekly.

'Oh.'

'I'm sorry, love. He said he'd let you know.'

I shook my head, as a pressure pushed against the base of my skull. He had done it. Niall had made the decision for us, moving on from our lives. I pressed my hand against my mouth so Dad couldn't detect the whimper that escaped.

'Look, Jeanie, I need to explain to you about Arthur, it might help with everything. I know I should've told him,' Dad continued, as I began to shake and the tears spilled out, and I screwed up my eyes concentrating on not letting him know his daughter was imploding. 'And your mother had me mithered to come clean about this years ago, and she's right, I should've. The thing is, love—'

I took the phone away from my ear, and bent double, trying to breathe and not cry too loudly. My phone lay flat against my knee as I shook and squeezed my eyes shut. I could hear Dad's muffled calling of my name, reminding me of how the dead sounded when they were moving on. I heaved in a big breath, enough to get me through, to get me off the phone.

'Can I call you back, Dad? The reception here is so bad.'

'OK but Jeanie, did you hear what I said? We need to talk. Are you thinking of coming home at all?'

Surely there was nothing now, absolutely nothing to go back to. My life as I had known it for the last nine years was totally and irreparably changed. Whatever it was Dad was trying to tell me didn't seem to matter now. Nothing he had to say could alter that fact. I scanned the rainbow village for the answer to where and what my future might be, and it was then an answer came to me as swiftly as a swallow's dive. 'Marielle's,' I said, desperate to sound confident so I could just get off the phone. 'I'm going to work for Marielle.'

'The woman in France?'

'Yes,' I said curtly, stifling the tears.

'But Jeanie, love—'

'Peanut wants to get back to the cabin now, Dad.' Through the window I could see Peanut, smiling, happy for the first time since we'd left the city as a plate of food was put in front of her.

'What cabin?'

'I've got to go.'

'But Jeanie, we need to talk soon, OK?'

'Yep. Sure. Sorry, Dad.'

As soon as I was off the phone, I texted Niall:

'You've left,' I wrote.

As I waited, I paced, biting the skin around my thumb, putting it away under my arm then biting it again.

'I'm sorry,' the reply came instantly. 'But I needed to let you go.'

I gulped in the air and, with no ounce of grace, lurched to the step and listened to the town move in tiny bursts, the noise of a door opening, the rev of a car, the call of an unseen voice, and it was then I let everything go. My cry rose up above all else in that Norwegian village, so that Peanut came running to throw her arms around the girl that she had rescued.

'You'll come back to us if you need to,' Peanut said a week later, standing at the security gates in Gardermoen Airport, trying to fix my hair, as my mother might have done.

'I will, I promise.'

'It's been so good for me to have you here.' To my surprise, Peanut began to cry. 'I miss home so much.'

'Hey,' I said, hugging her.

'It's funny, isn't it? When we were younger, I was so sure that this was what I wanted—to live somewhere else, anywhere but Kilcross. But as I'm getting older, I miss it more and more. And now look at you, striking out.'

'But Anders and the kids, Pea?' I let her go and looked at her, afraid that my restlessness had started something I hadn't intended.

'You know I love it here, but there are moments when I've wondered if maybe . . .' She sighed and shook her head, banishing her quandary, refusing to fall under its power. 'I was thinking while the kids are still interested, we'll go back for a full month each July, not just a week. Rent a house, you know.' She looked worried then, wiping at her face: 'But you mightn't be there now, though, will you?'

'I'm only at the beginning of whatever this is.' I put a hand to her shoulder.

She nodded her head.

'I guess I simply need to do it for me, like you're doing.' She sniffed then sighed, composing herself. 'So you call me, OK? Tell me you've gotten there safely.'

'Of course.'

'Go on, now. Get going or I'll make you get back in that car with me. And they don't take kindly to kidnapping around here.' She pushed me gently away, denting my heart, which missed her protection and care already— the trepidation of a child forging out on her own.

'Thank you, Pea. I'd never have made it without you.'

I joined the queue, looking back every minute or so to raise my hand, then to blow a kiss, to watch her nod and wave then wipe her cheek again before I stepped behind the screen and she was gone.

Marielle Vincent looked younger than her seventy-five years, with her sallow skin that folded gently at the edges of mouth and eyes. One plane journey, two buses and seventeen hours later, I arrived in the town of Saint-Émile to see her dressed in a mustard jumpsuit, with a tweed grey jacket and a red and amber scarf tied around her elegant neck and with a head of the most luxurious grey hair I'd ever seen, so very silky that I had the urge to touch it. She had no need to search the many passengers who'd gotten off the bus—the pale, freckled, exhausted girl was easy to spot.

'So here you are at last, *ma chère*, Jeanie.' She bent her five-foot-ten inch frame to kiss me on both cheeks. 'It is so good that we finally meet. It makes me so happy.'

Perhaps I should have simply kissed her back, and perhaps it was the exhaustion, the miles, the hours it took me to get to her. But I dropped my cases and, on my tiptoes, put my arms around her neck and hugged her tightly, saying: 'Thank you. Thank you. Thank you.'

I must've looked like a little girl hanging on to her mother, embracing this woman who would teach me how to be brave, to talk in truths and kindness, and to speak better French.

'Oh, how lovely.' She hugged me back and laughed a little. 'All of these years and now here you are.'

'I'm so happy you said yes.'

Six nights prior I had rung to ask if she would mind me coming. My hand had shaken as I held the phone to my ear. 'But of course,' she'd said. 'Nine years I have waited for a visit. You must come, I will not hear of any other plan.' I blushed at the compliment, happy, it seemed, to be returning to the dead. 'Thank you,' I had whispered.

'*Viens*,' she said, that day of my arrival, releasing me, looping my right arm in under her left and taking one of my cases while I took the other. 'I have some food and wine ready. You can eat while I work. Pascal is waiting for me.' Her voice leaned in to me, gentle and soft as a bed of moss.

'We have only a few hours remaining. Pascal was never good at waiting even when alive.'

'*Parfait.*' My French pronunciation was horrendous. What little I could remember of that language from school felt old and rusted on my tongue. Marielle returned my smile generously.

We walked to her blue vintage Citroën van which, when not needed for the dead, I learned later, gave refuge to various bits of furniture from her house. These appeared never to actually go anywhere, except in and out. The eternal victims of Marielle's constant desire to get rid of things and her ache at letting them go. It was Lucien, her neighbour, work colleague and, again, as I was to find out later, boyfriend, who would put them out of their misery, disappearing them to his shed until Marielle forgot about them. He never discarded a thing in case she changed her mind, one of the many quiet expressions of his love that I would witness. That day it was a rose-print chair that had long since seen better days, but that later I commandeered for the room I would sleep in, where the window looked out on to a field of wild flowers in their red and yellow and blue brilliance, pitted with small wooden plaques, some of them in the shape of hearts, bearing a name and date. Four pebbled pathways led from each corner, converging in the middle in a little rise on which a wooden circular bench stood, and from where any visitor could look out at their loved one, no matter where they lay. The outline of the graves, beyond those newly dug, were hard to define in the wilderness. But there was a book in which the names and plots were listed, if someone came looking for a long-lost relative, or a son or daughter who rarely visited stopped by.

Marielle's house was not the old one I had expected—whitewashed with blue shutters. It was a modern two-storey at the edge of a village with more of a bustle to it than she had led me to believe. And the dead, they too died with more regularity than she had suggested in our calls and emails over the years. Her clients came from all over. It seemed there were many who did not wish their loved ones to be filled with chemicals and who most of all wanted to hear the truth of what it was they had to say.

Lucien stood waiting for us as we pulled into her driveway, tipping his cap to me, insisting on taking my bags and running after Marielle to the waiting Pascal and his family. Despite being hungry, I followed to sit to the rear of the room, to watch Marielle's head dip to Pascal then relay words to his waiting widow. There were tears as she lay across her husband, before Lucien and Marielle began to shroud him in a beautiful white cotton sheet edged in blue, hand-sewn cornflowers. They placed him on the stretcher and carried him to the grave.

From the back of the room I'd heard Pascal's words but understood very little, and yet I had closed my eyes and smiled as I lay my tired head against the doorframe. Feeling that in this room, among these people, the living and dead, I had once again found home.

'So, you and Niall are no more?' Marielle asked as we ate the dinner later. I'd already told her most of what had happened on the phone.

'No.' My one-word reply came as my head bent to my plate.

'I liked him.'

Lucien held a piece of soaked bread to his opened mouth, refusing it entry just yet, as his worried eyes rested on her for a second.

'You need not worry, old man. I do not mean it in that way. I liked our embalming debate we had some years back on email, that is all.' She turned back to consider me for a second as she filled her spoon. 'I was thinking it would be good if you stayed until I die.'

'What?' I asked, flummoxed by her unexpected statement. 'Are you ill?'

Lucien put down the bread and stared at her too. She batted away his concern with a wave of her hand.

'No, but I'm bound to go sometime and it would be nice to know that when I do there will be someone to hear what I have to say. I am sure my last words will be magnificent and worth waiting for.' And while she smiled at that final sentence, the rest had been delivered with a determined seriousness.

I was more than relieved. Having, it felt, just found her, I was not willing to lose her yet. 'Well, I was hoping simply to stay for as long as you'll have me.'

'Good.' She turned once again to Lucien. 'Now that I have help you should go see your daughter in Paris before you are too old to travel.' I coughed up the mouthful of stew that nearly escaped my mouth at her brazen instruction. 'I am serious. Look at him. He is nearly bent double. You love that girl, Lucien, and you need to go see her. How often does she beg you to go stay with that little family of hers?'

'I do not like Paris, with its wide streets and its gold buildings. It thinks it is all that.' Lucien was a man of few words, but when they came they were to the point.

'It is not about the place, it is about who is in it.'

Her words stopped me in the same way the lines of a song can suddenly resonate, define your life with such brilliance that you wonder how the singer could ever have known you so well.

'But dig three graves before you go. The muscles on this one are worse than a little girl's.' She looked at me like she might a local politician she didn't particularly rate who was asking for her vote. 'Go the day after tomorrow.'

Three graves in one day, I thought, the poor man will be dead. As if he had read my mind, he looked at me, this woman who had come to upset his happy life with Marielle, whom he obviously adored.

'*Cinq*,' he stated, flashing a proud palm at me. 'Three is nothing. I have dug ten in my day.' Marielle looked at him with admiration. 'Five. I will dig five.' He raised another full meaty spoon to his mouth.

'I didn't know you two had a thing going?' I said as I washed up later. Lucien had left by then and Marielle was still sitting in her chair.

'It is to be expected, an attractive woman like me, a widower like him. Nature, she was bound to take her course.'

'How long?'

'Years, perhaps six, seven.'

'You never mentioned it before.'

'You never mentioned you were thinking of running away either. We all have things that we keep private.'

I dried up the final pots and pans and hung them from the hooks above the cooker.

'Besides, it is perfect. He lives there, I live here. We don't annoy each other that way.' I liked this alternate view of what relationships could be.

She watched me a little longer. Then got up with a moan and a hand to her back. 'An early night, I think. I want to finish my book; the murderer is about to be uncovered and I know for a fact it was the policeman.'

'You've ruined it for me, I won't be able to borrow it now.'

'Don't worry, it's in French,' she smiled. 'I am glad you came, Jeanie. It is nice to have someone around. Especially someone with a set of ears that can hear the dead, even if only in English.'

'Me too. Is Lucien going to go to Paris, then?'

'Oh yes, there is very little he does not do that I command. I know that makes me sound awful. But everything I do, I do because I know it is the right thing for him and he would not go unless I told him to. His daughter loves him so much. She worries I work him too hard. And she is right.'

Chapter 29

There was something very special about working with Marielle. It reminded me so much of when I worked with Niall, the two of us in the embalming room together, working in silence but lifting our heads to laugh at something. I liked the synchronicity. Marielle taught me how to shroud, my hands following hers, echoing everything she did.

Marielle had this way with the dead and their families. When there was something hard to say, I would know, because she would turn from the dead person lying on the long table and take the hands of the loved one, whose forehead might already be creased in worry, looking at them like she held all the answers, which, I suppose, she did.

'*Écoutez*,' she would say and then she would begin. Her head tilting slightly, refusing to drop the eye of those that she must speak to with utter kindness. I watched her tell a wife that her husband had squandered his pension reserve on a vineyard that had yielded nothing only poor soil. The wife had thumped his chest in anger and then she had lain there for the longest time until Marielle's hands pulled her gently away. And to the parents of a four-year-old boy who had run out into the road when his father was not looking, she had said: 'Victor says that he is sorry.' His father and mother insisted that they should be the ones to carry their boy on the stretcher to his grave, but halfway there the father faltered and Marielle stepped in, ensuring Victor did not fall.

Lucien came back from Paris two weeks later. It was as if he understood this rhythm Marielle and I had created and never demanded to return to his former position of shrouding assistant. Instead of being annoyed, he let us be, tending to the outdoor tasks: digging more earth for new arrivals, cutting back branches that might snag a person's clothes, checking on the grave markers to see that none had faded with the sun.

My French was getting better. Even after a month I had attuned. Sometimes, I could grasp a tiny bit of what it was the dead had said, and I might smile quietly when it was something funny, before Marielle even repeated the story to the husband or wife or son or daughter or whoever sat waiting beside her.

It felt as if there was no pressure there in that corner of the world to spare the blushes of the living. All we needed to do was listen and repeat, listen and repeat, until the voice had disappeared and it was time to give them to the ground. And I wondered if I could ever bring myself to do the same, exactly as I had done when I was fifteen and broke Noel Kavanagh's heart, only perhaps with more compassion.

'They can come if they want to,' Marielle said, the day I asked her if she missed being a wealthy undertaker in the town. 'I don't need the income. I do it because I can and I am asked. I will not cry if tomorrow the phone stops ringing. I'd happily potter in my garden, tending my tomatoes all day long if they decide someone else can care for them better. I do it on my terms not theirs. We work for the dead not the living. My only conditions are, no chemicals and no lies.'

And when I discussed again my father's theory on why we might invoke a lie, she said:

'I do not blame you or your father for running your business as you have, Jeanie. I simply do not like lying. Lies do too much damage. But, yes, the truth is hard to take but better out than in, the rottenness soon dies away, like a good fart.'

I nearly choked on my mouthful of tea.

'What, a woman cannot say "fart"?' She grinned at me.

After I'd regained my composure, I challenged her assertion. 'But it's not always better, Marielle. There have been times when I have told the honest truth and it has gone wrong.'

'Ah, but you have not warned the living that the dead are not always loving in their final moments. I do. Why burden myself with the cruelties of others? It is not my responsibility.'

'But aren't we responsible?'

'We are responsible to the dead, no one else.'

'But it's the living who pay the bill.'

'That's why I tell them before they come—"You may not like what you must pay for." It gives them time to change their minds.'

At lunchtimes, on the days when no dead had arrived, the three of us would come together from whichever corners of the house or garden we had lost ourselves in to eat. And then, in the afternoon heat, Marielle and Lucien would drift away to her bedroom to sleep off our feast for an hour, while I'd sit under the east-facing eaves of the house in the welcome shade and try not to think of Niall and how he might be doing.

At first the seat on which I perched was a plank of wood supported by six bricks either end. But one day Lucien produced a rocking chair.

'I have not seen that thing in years,' Marielle said, surprised, as he pushed it in his wheelbarrow across the pathway leading from his house. 'I hated it. It squeaked too much. I thought I had thrown it away.'

Lucien winked at me, then pulled it out to sit it on the dried earth. The three of us stood watching it rock gently back and forth to stillness. I sat in it then, my hands on the armrests, looking up at this wonderful pair, squinting at the force of sun-soaked sky and proclaiming my new-found love.

'Woodworm,' Marielle said. 'Another reason I hated it.'

'Not now,' Lucien replied, taking up the handles of his now empty wheelbarrow and returning to his shed.

'I love it,' I said. 'All it needs is a cushion or two.'

'Go ask Mr Fix-It, he might have some,' Marielle said, only half-jokingly as she nodded in the direction of Lucien's retreat.

'I heard that,' he called, without turning around, wagging his index finger.

'You must have some old cushions, Marielle, that you don't want?'

'My things are not old, Jeanie. They are good quality and can stand the test of time.'

'What, like the clock in the hallway that keeps going slow no matter how many times I change the battery?'

'You might check the garage,' she said ignoring my jibe. 'I think I put something in there perhaps years ago, who knows. Meanwhile, I want to see what else of mine that man is hiding.'

She followed Lucien and left me to root through the garage, full of the jetsam of her life. Under a teetering tower of boxes, I found two flattened cushions in need of plumping and a wash. From there my afternoons would see me rock myself into a doze or read another chapter of one of the twenty Agatha Christie translations I'd found in the library and borrowed every week with Marielle's card. Reading invariably led to the same result, a contented sleep from which I'd wake to the sound of Marielle's voice or the ringing of the phone.

Sometimes I'd take Marielle's old bike, which Lucien had oiled and pumped, despite my protests that I could do it, and cycled into the town to drink coffee in one of the three pâtisseries. After, I'd wander around the market to look at the meat and fish stalls. Red mullet, monkfish and mackerel; pork sausages, pigs ears and trotters; tomatoes the size of apples; olives and anchovies and fresh herbs. Bringing them home to Marielle thinking she might be able to create something wonderful.

'What, you think because I am French it means I am a brilliant chef? Cooking is not my strong point. Ask my husband out there.' She gestured toward the memorial pasture. 'Bernard always complained that I burned his steak. He was the cook in this house.'

Instead I'd google recipes in English and try to create something marvellous. Sometimes it was good, but more often it was mediocre. So we reverted to our soups and fresh salad and boiled eggs and cheese and bread, bought fresh from the bakery every morning. That became another of my jobs I liked to do. Cycling to town at eight o'clock to stand in the queue where Marcel, the rotund bachelor baker, would smile widely and chat with me in broken English, despite the tutting of those waiting behind.

It was on my return one morning, with the baton held in one hand, trying not to squash the life out of its crispness, my other steering the bike, that I saw a familiar figure step out of a taxi at the bottom of Marielle's driveway. It was no surprise that one of them had eventually come. But out of all of them, it hadn't occurred to me that this was who they'd send.

I got off the bike two hundred yards away, to stand watching her take her small case from the boot. The taxi man drove past me on his return and I raised my hand in greeting—I could never quite lose the Irish custom of waving to every car that passed me on those French roads, even though they never once reciprocated, except for Marcel, the baker that was; the man almost climbed out of his driver's window whenever he saw me on the bike.

She disappeared from view as she began to walk up the driveway. I strolled the rest of the way, stopping to stand outside the gate, to pull a chunk off the bread to eat, risking Marielle's annoyance.

'Ah, so you are not dead,' Marielle said, coming out to me as I leaned the bike against my rocking chair. 'I was about to get Lucien to go look for you in the van. You have a visitor.'

'I saw.'

She took the bread, regarding its desecration, then broke what was left in two, giving me back half. 'I'm going to Lucien's to have my breakfast. Your guest might be hungry, go make her some food.' Marielle set off down the pathway through what had apparently started out as a simple hole in a hedge, which Lucien had now expanded enough to fit a certain Citroën van.

'Hello, Harry,' I said.

She was standing waiting for me in the over-crowded kitchen. A cerise T-shirt, with a cerise bandana tied in a knot on top of her black bobbed hair.

'Jeanie.' She stepped forward to hug me. 'You look so beautiful. The colour of you.'

Her arms felt good around my shoulders, making me realise how much I'd missed her.

'I hate my freckles but thank you anyway.'

We let the other go. I drew back to lean against the draining board.

'I think that's the best bit, when the Irish see the sun, their freckles come out, covering every surface like daffodils in March.'

'So, this is a surprise.' I indicated that she might sit. As she did I filled the saucepan to boil the water. I had yet to convince Marielle a kettle was handier. I cut the bread and took out the cheese and tomatoes. And the jam, in case she preferred something sweet. Laying them all on the table in front of her. (Plates and cutlery permanently lived there—what was the point in putting them away Marielle explained, with all that wasted energy going back and forth when they could be within arm's reach.)

'A chance for a bit of sunshine? Are you kidding me, we all wanted to come.' She smiled and I did the same out of politeness.

'Early flight?'

'I got in last night. I stayed in the local hotel. I'm going back tonight.'

'Did Marielle know you were coming?'

'No. I thought it best not to tell her.'

I didn't answer, deciding the reason for such secrecy would eventually come. I looked out of the kitchen window toward Lucien's house, picturing him and Marielle eating their bread.

'You didn't bring any teabags, did you?' I asked, placing her mug in front of her. My stash of Barry's teabags that had travelled to Oslo and now to Saint-Émile was on its last legs.

'As a matter of fact, I did.' She looked over at her suitcase sitting in the corner of the kitchen.

My smile stretched wider in happy relief.

'It's good to see you, Harry. Now eat, or Marielle will think I have no manners.'

Harry took a sip of her black tea.

'You like it here, Jeanie?'

'I love it, Harry.'

I played with a piece of bread before taking a bite and putting it down, no longer hungry like I usually was after cycling all the way back from town.

'How long do you hope to stay?'

The question we both knew she'd ask was out in the open.

'Well, Marielle hasn't asked me to leave yet. And anyway, she said she wants me to be here for when she dies. So I think a little while still,' I answered confidently.

Harry nodded and smiled. Then took a piece of bread too and cut some cheese.

'So you're going to stay here for what, ten, twenty years?'

'Why not?'

'She's paying you a wage, then?' She took a bite of cheese but all the time her eyes watched mine.

'Well no, there isn't a huge amount of money in what she does. And it has to support her and Lucien. But I've got free board.'

She laid down her bread.

'Don't you miss home, Jeanie? A decent wage?'

'I'm happy, Harry. It's hard to explain but I feel at peace. No pressure, no making sure the living are fine with everything so we get paid, so the business thrives. It's just about them, the dead.'

She looked down at her plate. And for the first

time I saw the age in her, the passing of years, the toll this life had taken on her, this quiet, constant presence in our lives.

'So you've come to talk sense into me, is that it, Harry?'

She laughed a little, as her eyes returned to mine. 'No, actually, I've come to explain.'

'Explain?'

'Explain why we've lied to you for thirty-two years.'

Chapter 30

I wished then that I was sitting under the house eaves, sleeping or turning the pages of an Agatha Christie in Lucien's rocking chair. We were having problems in the household assigning possession of said item. Lucien called it mine, I called it Lucien's and Marielle called it hers. Oh, for the sweet simplicity of the mystery Agatha offered rather than this. Because whatever it was that Harry was about to tell me, I knew that it would have the power to upset this escape that I had found.

'You see, Jeanie, for reasons that we thought were good and would protect the business, and well, me, we chose to cover something up.'

'What does that mean?' I laughed.

'Could we walk, Jeanie? I think I need the air.' She made to stand but wobbled, grabbing the back of my chair.

'Would you like some water, maybe?' I was already filling her a glass, taking quick glances as she steadied herself again.

'Yes, perhaps.'

She took the glass willingly and drank the full of it, then exhaled with closed eyes.

'Better?' I placed my hand gently on her shoulder, hoping not to frighten her.

She nodded.

'We can go to the meadow if you like?' I suggested. 'It's the best time to walk actually. It can get very hot later on.'

She inhaled and lay her hand on mine, looking to the back door already. 'I'd like that.'

The gravelled pathway brought us around the meadow then up the gentle rise to its centre via one of the four walkways. Harry seemed hesitant to start what she had come to say, so as we strolled I filled the void, explaining once again what it was Marielle did here and her philosophy. Harry smiled at some of the stories I relayed about what the dead had to say in France. When I told her about the time Marielle had received a call from a neighbour whose dog had died and asked would she bury him in her pasture, she'd agreed, but added she didn't speak canine so not to be expecting a miracle, Harry laughed and said:

'So there are three of us, and all women.'

We'd arrived at the circular bench and the movement and noise of our sitting made me think I must've misheard her.

'Three of us?' I repeated, watching Harry place her hands on her knees.

'That speak to them.'

'You mean the dead? But, Harry, you don't.' I laughed at the ridiculousness of her words.

She took off her sunglasses so I could see her eyes, see that everything she was about to say was wholly and heartbreakingly true.

'Oh but I do, Jeanie. I really do.'

She sighed long and loud out into the memorial pasture, and watched the wild grasses tilt in the brightness, their heads bending, allowing the sun to warm their necks.

'Do you know, Jeanie, all the way over on the plane I wondered where to start with this. I kept changing my mind. Couldn't hear myself saying the words. And here I am, still not able to figure it out.'

She swallowed hard and then began.

'You see, back when we Mastersons were starting out, the industry in Ireland was pretty much male dominated. Not every undertaker's, but most. Your granddad Ted, being old-school, liked it that way. When he realised I could hear the dead, he was happy as it would appeal to "the believers," as he liked to call them, but he thought it would look more acceptable if it was a man who could do the conversing and not a "wailing woman." To have a girl, as I was then, would lessen it—apparently—in the eyes of those who "liked a man in charge." He loved saying that. In his wisdom he decided it would be better if we said it was Dave, and we let him. What did we know? We were young. He was the adult, the one who was supposed to be wise.'

Her head bent at the memory, the fingers of her hands fidgeting with a tissue in her lap that I didn't recall her taking out.

'So I'd listen to them, when the dead chose to speak behind the closed doors of the embalming room, and I'd tell Dave what it was they said. And he would announce it, wheeling them in their coffins into the viewing room, going through the motions as if they were speaking to him there and then. He'd make things up if he had to. Always choosing the easier path of love and missing them and broken hearts. And your granddad would show him off, like a circus master, presenting his phenomenon to the world.'

She gave a sad little chuckle. I watched her in disbelief, listening with no protest, no raise of my hand, no call of 'liar' as she rewrote our history.

'It wasn't nice to be silenced like that. To be overlooked because I was a girl. I wanted to be somewhere else, anywhere where I thought none of that mattered. I dreamed of leaving. Do you remember that time when I told you I'd thought of going to London, too?'

Of course, I remembered, how could I not? And yet I couldn't bring myself to even nod.

'That was why. I was sure I'd find my voice, my bravery, there. Perhaps set up my own practice. But I never went. I wasn't brave enough. Isn't it funny how, years later, when I saw the same desire for escape in your eyes, I prayed and prayed you wouldn't go.'

'But we . . .' Shocked by her words, my voice finally broke out in a breathy protest. 'We made a pros and cons list. You were trying to help me.'

'You're right, Jeanie, I was. I really was. And I'd never have stopped you, if you'd really wanted to go. But neither could I help what I felt. You finally made us legitimate, don't you see? We were at last being truthful with the world.'

In my periphery, I could see her hand wipe at her eyes with the tissue. She cleared her throat then began again.

'After my father died, your dad and me talked about coming clean and telling the world that it was me who could talk to the dead. But it's amazing how when you're told you aren't good enough often enough, you begin to believe it. I wasn't brave, like you. We were scared of what the world would think of us Mastersons. We were years into it by that stage. We'd lied to everyone, there was no going back, we thought. And then you came along. And there was no stopping you. You were a breath of fresh air, showing me all I could've . . . *should've* been.'

'But, Harry . . . you were always the one I looked up to. The one I thought could do anything—be anything—if she wanted. None of this makes sense.'

'We're complicated, aren't we, us humans?

We don't always know what's going on inside another. But watching you helped me become stronger. It was me learning from you, all this time.'

I shook my head in disbelief. 'No, no, this can't be, Harry. All those times when I was little and Dad and me would talk beside a coffin; we both heard them, Harry, I know we did.'

'No, Jeanie, he'd let you tell him what they'd said. I'd watch him at it. He was such a pro. He was an expert at getting you to do the talking without you even realising it. And he was a great man for saying his hearing wasn't so good. It wasn't so hard. And then, as the years went on and Niall came on board, and your father saw how you two were doing so well, a natural partnership, he started to pull away, letting you do more as he put his plan together to finally leave you to it, letting go, at last, of the lies. You were his way out.'

And it made sense, him and Harry a natural pair, then me and Niall. And then Dad growing less interested in that end of the business over the years, me taking more on. But still having Harry to lean on when he was needed. And, if all else failed, his questioning of me, his distraction with some other aspect of the day shaking his concentration so he hadn't quite heard it all, asking could I just clarify one or two issues.

'So,' I said, still piecing things together, 'the

years of feeling like I was carrying everything, I kind of was?'

'In a way, I suppose.'

'But why didn't you tell me? Why didn't you share this with me? Especially when I began to work full-time. We were supposed to be a team.'

'We thought about it, we honestly did. But then there was the threat of London. You were back and forth to Fionn so much we were sure that if you knew what we'd done, the shame would be enough for you to go. We didn't want you to leave. We needed you.'

She turned her upset away from me to consider the tip of Saint-Émile's church spire in the distance. I watched her profile, the face of this woman I had so admired, the confident curve of her chin, still unable to fathom that she had lived this lie.

'And that whole thing with Tiny and Arthur,' I said, finally putting it all together. 'Dad never told him because he didn't actually know what it was Tiny had said. Because he never got the chance to get it out of me fully.'

'Exactly. You know you nearly caught me that day. I was just about to talk to Tiny when you arrived. Two seconds later and you'd have found me out.'

And I remembered now her fright, her rushing away from Tiny.

'Wow,' I said, with a sarcastic smile.

My eyes rested on a bee at the meadow's edge, as he flitted from flower to flower in search of nectar until he found the very one.

'And Mum knows?'

'Yep, always has. She never agreed with what we were doing, though. Thought we should've told you from the start. But she remained loyal to us, as much as it hurt her.'

'Dad must've told Andrew.' My conversation with Mum after Andrew's funeral made sense now. Her reticence to explain what his final words had meant and her insistence that she would talk to Dad and that I didn't have to be alone. Because here was the answer, the person who'd been by my side all along—Harry.

My mind returned to all the times Mum had, in her own way, tried to protect me over the years, tried to encourage me to see a different path. And I felt so sorry for refusing to heed her and all the hurt and worry that must've caused.

'And so what now?' I said, an anger rising in me against the woman who once I had adored. 'Am I supposed to keep this a secret too? Is that what you're here for? Because I won't. I'm not going back to that. I want to stay here.'

Below, I could see Marielle had come out of Lucien's house. Had my voice carried on the wind, alerting her to something? She looked up in my direction, her hand held above her eyes. She appeared old and vulnerable in that moment, and

I felt guilty at what this interruption in her life was doing to her. I stood up to wave, pretending happiness, wanting her to go back inside. She gave a single salute then turned to Lucien who had followed her out, and gently guided him back inside. I stayed there for a second, stuck, it seemed, looking at Lucien's house.

Harry rose to bravely put her hand to my back, encouraging me to sit again.

'I'm sorry, Jeanie. None of this was yours to bear. We didn't mean to hurt you.' I sat forward on the bench, teetering on the edge, not sure what to do.

'So, why are you telling me this now?' I demanded.

'Your father understands if you don't want the business. We all understand. That's not what I'm here for, to try to force you to come home and take it on. Well, at least not in that way.'

I glanced around on hearing those words. 'What do you mean?'

'Well, he's asked me if I'll take it, but that's only if you really don't want it.'

She waited to see if I'd protest. I'll admit I felt the tiniest pang of jealousy. But I said nothing, just looked ahead of me again.

'I've said yes,' she said quietly, tentatively, still gauging my reaction. 'But I'd love you with me. The place doesn't feel the same without you. And I hope, in spite of it all, that you miss it too. You see, I think, if it was us two working together with nothing to hide, it might feel easier for you, Jeanie, as well as me.'

My head turned slightly in her direction, curious now about what she was getting at.

'You see, your going has made me realise how fed up I was of the lies. I don't want to give up what I do, but I want to come clean. Tell the world at last. Give Masterson's a fresh start. With you. Don't you see what we could achieve together? It'd be a bit like what you have here with Marielle. Only admittedly with no sunshine,' she laughed a little, 'or the meadow, and with more embalming fluid. But, actually, the shrouding sounds really beautiful. And times are changing, and people want all sorts of things now and maybe—'

'OK, wait,' I said, interrupting her flow, as I tried to make sense of her proposal. I sat back to concentrate on her fully. 'You telling people that it's you who hears the dead and not dad, is one thing. But what Marielle really does here is more than just shrouding. She tells the whole truth, the God's honest, painful truth. Do you think the Mastersons are up for that, Harry?'

My challenge had indeed dampened her enthusiasm. And I thought this would be it, the fence at which she would fall. She said nothing for a second looking out once more on all Marielle and Lucien had created, looking left then right, finally returning to what lay in front of her. She sighed, closed her eyes for a second and began to speak again.

'How about this, Jeanie: I start with admitting my lie first and see how that goes. We might lose a bit of trade to Doyle's but the fact will still remain that we Mastersons are the only ones in Ireland who can talk to the dead, so that has to count for something. And then well . . .' She faltered but only briefly before turning fully toward me. 'Look, Jeanie, I was never against telling the truth about what the dead said but I understood why sometimes your dad didn't tell it as it was. I think he simply didn't want to hurt anyone. You have to see that, don't you? It was never malicious.'

I considered all of those times I'd witnessed him hold back the truth. Yes, sometimes, as I now knew, because he was making it up, but others, when Harry or I had relayed their parting words, because he thought it was too much for anyone to bear. I'd watched him take the hands of the living in his, in much the same way as Marielle did, and impart his words, lies and truths. But in his eyes there was no doubting the sincerity that simply wanted to lift the burden on those left behind. I *had* seen it. And if I could hear the dead, surely I could see kindness too.

I nodded in agreement.

'But you're still right, Jeanie, we Mastersons

need to be more courageous with the truth. I'm not promising we'll always get it right and there might be times when we soften what the dead say, but I'm certainly willing to try. And with you by my side leading the way, I think we have a chance.'

Relief flooded me at these words. In my heart, I knew I now wanted just that, a willingness to find a way to be honest. And here it was. Finally. I felt my body slacken, my shoulders slumping from their tense perch, the muscles of my back sighing in release, and my eyes filling, for once, in joy. I gave a small, and yes, reluctant, smile, my first since she'd begun. Nothing broad; an almost imperceptible twist to my lips. But she had caught it.

Capitalising on this moment of gentle thaw, Harry took my hands in hers.

'Look, all I'm saying is think about it, Jeanie. You have a life at home, and now you have the opportunity to maybe have one that is a little less stressful and a bit more . . . sincere.'

I looked away again, suddenly struck by all that I had kept hidden from Niall for so long. I was as much a culprit of lying as they had been. And I wasn't sure I had the guts to put all of that right. 'I don't know,' I murmured.

We said nothing further. She let me go and closed her eyes and leaned back, allowing the bench to support her, her body tired, from all she had offloaded, as I kept to the edge of the bench, considering a return to Kilcross and how that might feel with no lies, and . . . no Niall.

As if she had been thinking the same thing she asked: 'And what about Niall, have you spoken to him?'

'No,' I said quietly, shifting my position.

'Is there any chance for you both, do you think?'

'I don't want to talk about it,' I managed, my panic rising, my hands making a steeple to point outwards, to emphasise the drawing of a line.

'I know, Jeanie. I'm sorry. I shouldn't . . .'

I looked back in her direction, to her bowed head, and felt miserable for being so sharp. I wondered how it had felt all of those years when she'd looked at me and wished it had been her.

'I need a drink,' I said, rising quickly, wishing to get clear of this even for a moment, in whatever way possible. The coldness of Lucien's home-made cider that I'd seen him put in Marielle's fridge the previous night seemed like the perfect solution.

Harry followed, trying to keep up with my speed. 'Isn't it a bit early for alcohol?'

'Marielle often has a glass of wine with her toast at breakfast.'

'I like the sound of this woman more and more.' Her breath becoming shorter now as I kept moving determinedly.

'The French have a much healthier relationship with alcohol than we do, they see it simply as another beverage, not a way to pretend they aren't who they are.'

'Are there any clients due today?' Her voice strained so her words might reach me as she lost a little ground.

'Not as far as I know.'

'Good. I'd like to talk to Marielle about things.'

'Harry,' I said, stopping and turning quickly, almost colliding with her, as something occurred to me. 'Did Niall find out about any of this before he left?'

'No.' She shook her head. 'He doesn't know a thing. God only knows what he'd think of us if he did.'

I nodded, relieved. This was something, if I ever got the chance, I'd like to explain myself. 'OK,' I said, quietly.

Harry caught my arm before I turned back to continue on.

'But, you *will* think about my proposal, won't you, about coming home?'

'Yes,' I said, my heartbeat thumping in my ear again. Home, it beat. Take. Me. Home.

Chapter 31

I left Saint-Émile four days later. I took only one bag—enough clothes to last me the week at home that I had agreed to.

'I'm coming back, Marielle,' I told her, standing in her kitchen, attempting to say goodbye. Her eyes darted away from me, refusing to rest on the one who was leaving.

'I know. But what if I need the room for someone else and you have not returned?'

I smiled at her subterfuge. She was hopeless at lying. It was no wonder she refused to do it as a living. 'Why, who's coming?'

'No one. But there might be.'

'I told you I'd be here for when you die, old woman. You aren't getting rid of me that easily. Besides, I'm bringing you back a kettle.'

'I don't want your Irish kettle. I like my saucepan. Plus, I'm not planning on dying in the next week.'

'Death might come quicker than you think if you don't start treating that man better than you do.' Outside I watched Lucien move a wardrobe he'd spent all morning removing from the house. Walking it painfully, inch by inch from the spare room, refusing my assistance, and which he was now trying to get into the van with the help of his heroic wheelbarrow. 'I think he might actually kill you this time.'

'I thought he might find an antique shop on his way to the airport that might wish to buy it.'

'His shed it is, then.'

'What are you talking about? It is a fantastic piece of furniture.'

'It's flat-pack. You didn't inherit it from King Louis.'

'And a good job. My family would have burnt it had it come from that oaf.'

She looked at the case by my side and the coat slung over my arm. 'Will you be needing that?'

'I'm heading to an Irish summer, Marielle. Someday I'm going to bring you with me, and you'll understand our love affair with rain. But until then,' I said, hugging her, 'you stay well and be nice to him.'

I kissed her on the cheek, and she held on to me, much as I had done to her that first day, both of us refusing to say the word goodbye. I arrived in the yard just as Lucien had managed to close the door of the van, leaning against it, panting. I didn't suggest he might like to open it again for my case. Instead I took its bulk to hold on my knee in the passenger seat.

Arthur picked me up from the airport. Insisted, he'd said. Took the day off work to assure me we were still friends despite him having to find out about his family from a solicitor he'd never met before, hadn't even delivered post to him, he was that much of a stranger. He bore no grudge that I had caused an earthquake in my absence, not to mention the broken heart of that lovely Niall who'd gone away to Sligo. Sligo, of all places. The sea, I said, in answer to a question that had not been posed. But sure, wasn't he happy with the lakes all those years? Arthur said, as he threw the money into the M4 toll basket. Isn't there water enough there? I didn't answer but watched each landmark whizz by as Kilcross came into view.

When I arrived in the yard, my brother came out to uncharacteristically hug me.

'It's not right, Jeanie, all this change.' He let me go and stood with his hands in his pockets, blocking my way into the house.

'I know. But look at you. You're surviving, aren't you?'

'I still don't like it.' His sad eyes nearly killed me. I looked across at Arthur who smiled sympathetically.

'Any new journals lately?' I tried.

But he just shrugged his shoulders, refusing to meet my eye, looking off to the side and at the ground.

'Oh Mikey. I know it's hard, but things can't stay the same, as much as you might like them to. It's like your bookshelves. Sometimes you just need expansion to fit everything in. That's what's happened to me. I needed more space, more time to adjust so I could fit in all I was feeling.'

'Don't you need *me,* though?'

'Of course I do. And I've missed you. But I wrote to you. You got my postcards and letters? And the books and DVDs; I know they aren't in English but I thought you'd like them anyway, the pictures especially.'

He didn't answer immediately, withholding his reply in further protestation at my absence.

'Actually, some of the DVDs have subtitles,' he relented. 'And I ordered a Norwegian and French dictionary so I'm working my way through the books.'

'Oh good.'

'But I'm only on page ten of one and fourteen of the other.'

'Ah.'

'Niall's gone too now, Jeanie. Do you know that?'

'I know. I'm sorry. I know that must've been hard for you.' I wasn't sure how much I'd be able to defend myself here, and feared I might crumble and start to cry, and crying really wasn't going to help Mikey, or me.

But Arthur leaned in to assist. 'He's started to teach me how to play the PS. Says I'm a natural, didn't you, buddy?'

'No.' Mikey looked at him in disbelief at what

was obviously a blatant lie. 'You're very slow.'

Arthur smiled. 'The old thumbs aren't what they used to be, I'll give you that, but I'm not the worst. Your father's completely hopeless.'

Mikey gave Arthur the tiniest of smiles and then he looked my way.

'But you're home now for good, aren't you, Jeanie?'

'Well, that's what I'm here to try to figure out.'

'And Niall, will he come back too?'

'You know we're not together any more, Mikey?'

'Oh. I see. But he's still my friend. He texts me all the time. We play online now.'

'Well, good. That's . . . that's really great,' I managed, as Arthur caught my eye and gave another kind smile before stepping in once again to save the day.

'We might let your sister go on in now, Mikey. I'd say she's tired.'

Mikey dutifully stepped out of the way, and I moved past him, wondering how long it would take him to forgive me. But just as I was about to reach the back door to the corridor, he called out:

'I've a new documentary on Field Marshal Sir John French.'

'Who?' I asked, turning around again.

'Well if you're free at eight o'clock tonight you can come and find out. I could make popcorn.'

His face had loosened, some of its sadness

having fallen away, so it felt safe to give him my widest smile.

'I'd really, really like that. Thank you, Mikey.'

'OK,' he nodded. 'But you have to bring the MiWadi.'

Mum and Dad and I sat at the kitchen table. A feast like no other in front of me. Every single thing I'd loved since I was a child offered one after another:

'Madeira cake? Or a Creme Egg? Not so easy to get in the summer, but Arthur managed it,' Mum said.

Arthur beamed in pride, as he stood at the kitchen counter.

'Or perhaps a fry?' Mum persisted.

'Actually, what I think I'd really like is a Twix.'

I watched them all exchange glances, hopeful smiles that I wouldn't make this hard for them.

'We might be out of those,' Arthur said, as he opened the press to its healthy stash, as abundant as ever. He took one out and threw it to me. 'Course you might want to check the date on that.' He left the counter then and came to kiss me on the head and squeezed my shoulders. 'Right, that's me done for the day. I'll leave ye all to it. Teresa wants to go polytunnel shopping.'

'Polytunnels, sure why wouldn't ye?' Dad laughed exaggeratedly.

Arthur was at the door, his hand already raised

in goodbye. 'Mind yourselves,' he called, before pulling it closed.

'We're sorry, Jeanie,' Dad said, as soon as he'd heard the click. 'We never meant for any of this to—'

'Dad, Harry told me everything, we don't need to go through it all again.'

'No, but you have to hear it from me even if it's only the once. You have to know I never meant to hurt you like this. I should never have lied. Your poor mother here was beside herself all these years, wishing to God we'd tell you the truth.'

'I was, love. I wanted you to know.' Mum stretched her hand across the table toward me and I took it gladly.

'We're sorry. *I'm* sorry,' Dad continued. 'Me and Harry, we were just a bit stuck, I think. Your granddad was a hard man. It was his way or nothing. He set the tone for who we became and we didn't know how to manoeuvre ourselves out of the mess we'd created by the time you came along.'

'And we can go through it all again, Dad, just not now. I don't want the strain of it today. Let's just talk business. That I can handle.'

Mum rose to round the table to hug me, to whisper in my ear: 'My gorgeous baby girl.' And Dad came too to envelop me, two outer rose petals protecting the bud.

'So,' Dad said, sniffling, releasing me after a

moment or two, 'Harry's waiting in the sitting-room there.'

'OK so.' I rose and headed for the hallway. 'Let's get this retirement finally started. Lead the way.'

'Actually, love,' Mum said, 'we thought we might go out to eat, the four of us, to talk it over. A late lunch. We've a table booked. If that's OK with you?'

'Sure.'

'We thought we'd go to that place you and Niall liked to go to. That Woodstown Lodge.'

I had to look away as a familiar sting forced my eyes to close.

The deal we struck was this: the business would be Harry's. Mum and Dad would retire, and I would work with her. But if someone came looking for my assistance, the guards, for example, to help with a missing person, then I'd like to do that too. And I'd be going to France for a month or so every year and certainly when Marielle finally said goodbye. And we'd be braver with the truth. We shook on it, the four of us that afternoon. I'd return to Saint-Émile for a week or two, coming home well in time for the big move. They'd survive, they said, with Harry and Dad and the locum-embalmer, until I got back and the new Masterson plan was put in operation.

I also told them that I didn't want the house. It was theirs, and they needed to be able to come back whenever they liked. And besides, I added, it would hurt too much to live there now that Niall and I had split. I'd find a place of my own.

I unpacked my things in the spare room after we returned from the Woodstown Lodge that day, before I sat with my brother for a three-hour session on Sir John French, the British army officer, hero of the second Boer War amongst many other campaigns, and who looked constantly angry. I didn't even open the door of the bedroom I had shared with Niall until the following day, when I sat on the bed that had been ours, and looked at the emptiness of the place, bits of me in every corner but nothing left of him. Nothing to say he was once there and was once mine. It was then I found the bravery to ring him.

Chapter 32

Craven was a small town on the coast of Sligo, where the sea flowed up against a sandy, wind-filled beach. A town that attracted its fair share of visitors and blow-ins who opened upmarket ice-cream stalls and craft shops, and even a French bakery.

The morning I arrived, I found 'Robert's Pâtisserie' on the street that led to the car park, in front of which sat the beach where at eleven a.m. families were already braving the enthusiastic breezes behind windbreakers. Chubby, pale-skinned children seemed not to care about the nip at their skin and ran in races to kick at the frothing hem of the sea, to squat down and scoop up the salty water in their arms and try to hurl it at their siblings in pure delight. I watched them for a while after I'd parked, then walked back the ways to look in the shop windows and discover the bakery, that piece of paradise that made me miss Marielle.

I ordered two coffees and a baton of bread.

'You're French,' I said, when the man had taken my order and busied himself at his coffee machine.

'Your powers of observation are exceptional.' He raised an eyebrow and smiled.

'You don't find many French men in Ireland.'

'You ask only about the men; you don't care about the thousand French women that I've been hiding out the back?'

'French people, then,' I laughed.

'There are a few of us, you'd be surprised.'

'Why though?' It seemed since my escape I'd found it hard to understand that people would come to voluntarily live in Ireland. And yet here I was having already bargained my way back home. 'I mean, why leave France?'

'For love, what better reason?' Spoken like a true Frenchman, like Lucien who suffered the honesty and whims of Marielle Vincent every day and still couldn't resist loving her. And like Niall, perhaps, who had done the same, lived in a place that suffocated us until there was nothing left.

I smiled. Embarrassed now, realising this man was perhaps thinking I was more interested in him than his circumstance.

He handed me the coffees and the baton and, after I paid, I took my feast to the low wall to sit and feel the breeze that seemed miraculously warmer now, to push back my hair as I sipped my coffee and tore chunks off the bread.

'Hello, Jeanie.'

I turned to see his legs stretch over the wall to sit alongside me.

'Hello you.' We watched the waves, and chasing children, allowing the silence to settle.

'Here.' I handed Niall a coffee. And offered the bread that I put between us.

'When you said lunch, I was expecting a table.' Neither humorous nor serious, his words hovered somewhere in between.

'This is just a snack. I only meant to get a coffee but I couldn't resist the bread.'

'Robert does good bread all right.'

'Did you know that he moved here for love?'

'He tells everyone that. But no one's ever met the mysterious love. He lives at the top of the road, alone as far as everyone knows.'

'Oh.' I looked back at the shop front, as if its signage might give me a clue to the puzzle that was the French baker. Perhaps he was running away from love. Perhaps, whoever the loved one was, was actually back home in Paris, living oblivious to this man's heartache. My gaze returned to the bread between us and I wondered how much loneliness had gone into making it taste so perfect.

'We can go somewhere when we've finished these,' I said, observing the half-nibbled baton.

'Sure, whatever, I don't really mind.'

'How long have you got?'

'I'm actually not working today, so whatever.'

I smiled at this gift of time.

'So, you're moving home?' he said.

In our call I'd told him briefly about all that Harry had told me and my plans.

'Yes, it seems I am.'

'Is that what you really want, or have you been browbeaten into it?'

'No, it feels right. I kind of like that it'll be me and Harry. That there'll be someone else with me, you know, to talk things through.'

He gave a small, quiet laugh that stopped almost as soon as it began.

'I always wanted to be that for you. The person who you could talk things through with.'

I paused and took another sip from my cup, giving myself a moment to get this right.

'Look, Niall, it's not that I didn't want that either, it's just different with someone who hears the dead too. I dunno. It's like an astronaut gets exactly what another astronaut is talking about. No one else is going to understand what you feel when you're wandering around up there in space: the wonder, the terror, the excitement. I never meant it to hurt you.'

He looked down the beach, off to the right, as far away from me as he could get.

'It wasn't really the dead I was talking about.' He took a sip of his coffee.

'Ah.' And here it was, our boulder that had stuck between us for all our time together. This silence, this reticence in me to let him in, in case he displaced something precious. 'I'm sorry, Niall, you didn't deserve that.'

I glanced at him again, to see if he might turn

to say—in that quick, fleeting second—that he understood. But his head kept resolutely forward. I breathed in and wondered if there was still time to go home. To stick Dad's car into reverse and get the hell away from this man who deserved— if nothing else—at least honesty and love. Because in that moment, I wasn't sure that I was up to it. I closed my eyes on the wind and let it brush over me, until the words came of their own accord, falling out into the air as if they were always supposed to have been spoken.

'Part of me always thought I was making a mistake getting married. I did love you, but it was like there was this other, wonderful version of me out there that perhaps I was supposed to be living. I was so torn between you and it. And my family, and the job. Always wanting to do right by everyone. And I pulled you into all of that, my desperation to ensure I was being the good daughter, the good sister, the good listener.'

I glanced swiftly at him, skimming by, too afraid to rest to see the hurt there; idling, instead, on the strip of land beyond that hugged the bay.

'With him, you mean?'

'What?' I asked, coming back to his profile.

'This exciting life you talked about was to be with him, that's what you mean, isn't it?'

'Yes.' I bent my head in shame at my whis-pered admission, but forced myself to continue because this was what I was here for, after all, the admitting of the truth. 'I . . . I still loved Fionn but I honestly thought I could move beyond it. When we started up, I wanted to make it work. Believed I really could. But with everything that's happened, Fionn dying, the retirement, I realised he, and the idea that I could leave Kilcross, wasn't out of my system at all. Somewhere, buried deep inside me, I still had this dream that someday Fionn and I would find each other again. Our worlds finally syncing in some brilliant romantic neverland.' As I reached my crescendo, I'd stretched out my hand toward the beach before it slumped down again, slapping against my thigh. 'So, you were right all along, Niall, I was always holding something back.'

'Wow. And there it is, our history in thirty seconds. Niall Longley—second best.' His index finger and thumb swept across the horizon, showing me his headline.

'I'm sorry, Niall. I shouldn't—'

'No, Jeanie, you're right. That's how it was. It's not like I didn't know. But it still hurts to hear it all confirmed like that.'

We sat a little longer in this awful silence, me not knowing how to make it better. When in reality there was no solution. Everything I had to say to this man could never even hope to fit into that category.

'You were right about not having children.

Who'd want a child stuck in the middle of this mess?'

'Niall, I really am sorry.' But he ignored me and my shame and hurtled on.

'And what if it had worked out with you and him in your imaginary reunion?' Niall still faced determinedly toward the sea.

'I don't know,' I admitted. 'We might have been great. Or we might have burned out and I might have ended up back here in the end. Because . . .' And here it was, all that I had gleaned from the wisdom of the dead and Pea and Marielle, finally there in all its brilliance about to be told, '. . . it feels like my destiny—which for so long I thought might be somewhere else—is actually right here with the dead of Kilcross.'

Out beyond us, the sea rushed forward throwing itself against the beach with enthusiasm, sending spray and froth in the air, causing the delighted screams of children. I felt wasted but happy that at last, at thirty-two, I could feel sure of something so important.

'But not with me,' he stated, quietly, reminding me that not everything was so clear. 'Your destiny wasn't with me.' He gave a short, ironic laugh. 'Tell me, Jeanie, did you miss me at all when you were away?' Niall turned slightly but not fully toward me then.

I nodded to my hands and gave a small smile.

'It was more a case of when was I not thinking

of you. But it confused me when I thought about us, so I just tried to concentrate on what it was I wanted. Or at least that's what Peanut kept telling me to do.'

'What did you discover?'

'That . . .' I paused for a second, but then began in earnest, 'that I wanted to stop being afraid. That I wanted to stop lying to myself and others.'

'So, are you saying that if I ask you something that you'll give me an honest answer?'

I nodded, petrified, despite my assertion, of what I knew would come.

'Did you ever love me?'

'Yes,' I said, amazed that he did not know.

'Do you love me now?'

I swallowed, heaved in a breath and began: 'Yes. But not perhaps as much as you deserve.' I wanted to add more words that would make it softer, less harsh, but I stopped myself, because he—more than any living being I knew—deserved the truth of me. I bit my lip, hoping he wouldn't get up and walk away.

He looked at me for a second then his eyes dropped to his hands. 'Right,' he said, nodding, the saddest of smiles coming to his lips. 'I mean, it's not like I didn't know. But still, it's not so easy to hear that someone doesn't love you as much as you'd like them to.' His hand rose to wipe at his cheeks.

'I'm sorry, Niall. I didn't mean for any of this. I tried, I really tried.'

We sat there for a bit with no words uttered, just us and our tears and the breeze and the crashing waves.

'I just don't think I know how to be without you now, though,' I said, my desperate attempt to salvage something of us. 'You've been here all my life and now you're gone, and it hurts.'

He laughed a little. 'Yep, it does, doesn't it?'

He breathed out long and slow, like he'd been holding it in for hours.

'I'm not sure I can be the person you want me to be, Jeanie. I can't just be your friend. I tried that and it was hard. Really, fucking hard.'

I shifted, wanting to run away again from all it was that I'd put this man through.

'I don't know, maybe in time. Maybe. But right now, we've got to go our separate ways. I'm happy here, Jeanie, really, really happy. For the first time in years. I think . . .' He looked at the sea, appreciating its magnificence. 'I think we owe it to ourselves to let each other go now. Friends, lovers, whatever it was we want from the other, it has to end. For good.'

I nodded two or three times at his words, as if the repetition would help me accept that this was how it had to be. The waves kept coming and the children kept screaming, and my tears kept flowing. I was distraught, and not just because of his words, but because of his bravery and kindness that day in agreeing to meet me at all; in letting us at least have this moment of goodbye so I could finally tell him the whole truth.

In my peripheral vision, I could see his head loll, and then he looked up and sighed, and searched the horizon. And when I thought there was nothing further for us to say, that what would happen now was that I'd go get into my father's car and drive away and never see this man again, he said:

'Fuck.' Right out on to the breeze, so it carried on its waves down to the beach and a mother's head turned. He looked at me then, like an idea was forming. 'But, why don't we start that tomorrow? You've come all this way and it's a nice day. And . . .' He didn't finish those words, and instead began to swing his legs over the wall.

'Come on,' he said, as he headed off down the pathway without waiting for a reply. I scurried to catch up, barely hearing what he said next: 'I want you to meet someone.'

His words jolted me for a second. Enough that I wanted to stop moving. But I told myself to keep going forward, that I owed him this; that I would meet anyone, even a woman in a veil waiting for him at an altar, because I owed him that at least. For all the years of never being brave or fair enough, I would meet whomever it was that he wanted. I'd smile and shake her hand, and laugh and discuss the weather and then I'd go home to pack my bag to return to Marielle, to say my goodbyes ready for a life back in Kilcross, in a cottage on the canal that Arthur'd brought me to see that a friend of his wanted to sell privately, that I might buy and paint red and fill with window boxes of yellow and blue and purple and with a garden that I might dig and tend and a polytunnel that I might purchase with Arthur's help to grow tomatoes and cucumbers and salad leaves.

'This,' he said, stopping at our old car, and opening the passenger door, to allow a white dog to bounce in utter joy from its seat, 'is Lex.'

'Oh,' I bent to her, laughing. 'A wire-haired dachshund?' I asked, my head turning up to him, my eyes squinting in the glare.

'Yep.'

I looked at her again and patted her white soft-furred ears. 'Aren't you gorgeous?'

'Yes, I really am,' Niall mimicked. 'We'd like a walk, and we were wondering if you would like to join us?'

'Yes,' I said to Lex, who licked my nose in reply, 'I think that would be really lovely.'

'Lex doesn't so much like the water, so we have to walk the promenade through the dunes.' He bent to click on her lead as I stood up.

'Sure. Great. Whatever.'

'OK then, Lex, let's show the lady the sights.'

And off we went. The three of us, winding our way through the sand dunes, beyond the shops, and out as far as we could go around the pitch-and-putt course, pulling up our hoods and watching families grab everything they could under their arms, including screaming toddlers, when the summer rain decided it was time to fall.

Acknowledgements

I have met many wonderful people in trying to gain a greater understanding of death and how we deal with it. For their time and kindness: David McGowan, Karen Carey, Father Kevin Lyon, Joan and Con Gilsenan. To Michael Clarke, who for three years has so generously given of his time, always positive and supportive, in helping me solve some of the many problems I came up against. Michael, I owe you more than just a pint. Please note any errors or liberties I have taken in this book are my doing and not that of these professional men and women who dedicate their lives to caring for our loved ones.

In researching this book, I also came across many artists who have written plays, short films and indeed a thesis on this area of death and undertaking. Each of these people gave of their precious time, explaining their methods and indeed letting me see and read their material. Their talent astounded me. If ever you get the chance, you must see Keith Singleton and Niamh McGrath in their play 'Looking Deadly' and the magnificent short animated film by Wiggleywoo Productions: 'Tea with the Dead,' so very beautiful. Thank you to Margaret Bonass

Madden for sharing part of her thesis on death in Irish literature.

To those early readers of this book—you have helped move this novel forward with your kind words and your willingness to tell me when things weren't working: Louise Buckley, Mia Gallagher, Conor Bowman, Claire Desserrey, Phil Byrne, Ted Sheehy, David Harland, Una Bartley, Billy Doran, James Lowry and Bríd Ní Ghríofa.

To those who listened to my worries and helped me out with various interesting stories: Adam Lowry, Míde Emans, Ann O'Sullivan, Bernadine Brady, Marése Bell, Mary O'Neill, Charlie Bishop and Séamus Ó Drisceoil.

To two writers who have picked me up when I thought I was getting nowhere: John Boyne and Alison Walsh—your wisdom and encouragement have felt like a lifeline.

To the many people in Sceptre who have guided me through with their skill, and kindness, you have not just been exceptionally skilful but incredibly patient. Emma Herdman, who helped shape this book, who is an expert in the kind word, the gentle push and the beady eye, I miss you. To Lily Cooper and Carole Welch who have taken me on and steered me steadily toward the finish line with their questions and suggestions and ability to see what I have totally missed, a heartfelt thank you. To Penny Isaac and

Barbara Roby for their excellent copy-editing and proofreading skills. To the marketing and publicity teams who have never stopped working on my behalf, Louise Court, Helen Flood, Maria Garbutt-Lucero, Jeannelle Brew and Kate Keehan.

To those at Thomas Dunne books in the US: Stephen Power, Lisa Bonvissuto and Tom Dunne, thank you for your insightful suggestions, I miss you all. To Dori Weintraub whose feedback has been so encouraging.

To those in Hachette Ireland who have tirelessly championed my work: Jim Binchy, Breda Purdue, Ruth Shern and Siobhán Tierney. To Elaine Egan, there is only one word to describe you—amazing.

To the staff of Mullingar Library who so generously gave me a space to work in when I couldn't work at home. Your welcoming smiles and kindness will never be forgotten.

In the very early days of this book I was lucky enough to receive support under the Stinging Fly Mentorship Scheme, and from Westmeath County Council for which I was most grateful. More recently I have been fortunate to receive a bursary from the Arts Council of Ireland enabling me to complete this book.

To my agent Sue Armstrong, who has seen me through a tough year—your belief in me has made me smile on days when I thought it was not possible.

To James and Adam who are still holding my hand, still understanding there are dark days when After Eights and foot rubs are most welcome. I love you both.

Finally, to the readers of my work, what would I do without you? A heartfelt thank you.

Center Point Large Print
600 Brooks Road / PO Box 1
Thorndike, ME 04986-0001 USA

(207) 568-3717

US & Canada:
1 800 929-9108
www.centerpointlargeprint.com